Dark Ararat

Tor Books by Brian Stableford

Inherit the Earth
Architects of Emortality
The Fountains of Youth
The Cassandra Complex
Dark Ararat

Dark
Ararat

BRIAN STABLEFORD

A Tom Doherty Associates Book • New York

DARK ARARAT

Copyright © 2002 by Brian Stableford

Edited by David G. Hartwell

This book is printed on acid-free paper.

A Tor Book
Published by Tom Doherty Associates, LLC
175 Fifth Avenue
New York, NY 10010

www.tor.com

Tor® is a registered trademark of Tom Doherty
Associates, LLC.

ISBN 0-765-30168-7

First Edition: March 2002

Printed in the United States of America

0 9 8 7 6 5 4 3 2 1

For Jane, and all who are able to learn from prophecy

Acknowledgments

Throughout the series, of which this is the fifth-published and penultimate volume, I have made much of the concept of *emortality* without acknowledging my debt to the man who coined the word—Alvin Silverstein, author of *Conquest of Death* (Macmillan, 1979). I should like to make amends for that omission now, with profuse apologies for having left it so long. I should also like to thank Jane Stableford, for proofreading services and helpful commentary; the late Don Wollheim, for encouraging my earlier endeavors in planetary romance and ecological mystery fiction; and David Hartwell, for seeing the series through to its soon-to-be-forthcoming end.

Dark Ararat

PART ONE
Falling into the future

Having just taken a single step that had carried him out of the twenty-first century and into the twenty-ninth, across fifty-eight light-years of the void, Matthew had a million questions to ask. Unfortunately, the doctor—whose name was Nita Brownell—had a million and one, and a selfish tendency to favor her own agenda. Because Matthew felt rather weak and a trifle disoriented she had no difficulty in imposing her will upon the situation.

All that Matthew found out before being beaten down by the hailstorm of Nita Brownell's inquisition was that *Hope* had arrived in the solar system that was its present lodging in 2814, according to the ship's calendar. It was now 2817.

The doctor—who was, of course, a cryonics expert—had been one of the first people to be thawed out, and the three years she had aged in the interim had to be added to the extra aging-time she had lost in the home system. She had been frozen down in 2111, twenty-one years after Matthew. Although Matthew had been born in 2042 and Nita Brownell in 2069 they were now pretty much the same physical age, and the gap in their real ages seemed fairly trivial given that he was now 769 and she was 748.

The doctor didn't mind his taking a few moments out of her schedule to complete these calculations, because his ability to do mental arithmetic was one of the things she was intent on testing. What she was primarily concerned to interrogate, however, was his memory.

That was frustrating, because everything he could remember, apart from his dreams, related to the twenty-first century, to Alice and Michelle, to the ecospasmically afflicted Earth, to the journey to the moon and to the one brief glance of *Hope* that he and his daughters had been permitted before they joined her cargo of corpsicles. All that belonged to the past, and what Matthew was interested in was the present, and the future. He was, after all, a prophet.

One other statistic the doctor soon let slip, more marvelous than the rest in a rather ironic fashion, was that *Hope* had not actually left the solar system—if the Oort Halo were accepted as its outer boundary—until 2178, more than a century after Matthew had been frozen down. By that time, the crew that Shen Chin Che had left in charge of his Ark, when he had joined the corpsicles himself, already knew that Earth's sixth great mass extinction had climaxed in the last plague war of all. Chiasmalytic transformers not unlike the one whose existence had been revealed to Matthew shortly before his entry into SusAn had sterilized the human population between 2095 and 2120. This disaster had helped to avert the greater disasters that prophets like Matthew Fleury and Shen Chin Che had foreseen and feared, and had saved the ecosphere from a devastation so extreme as to make further human existence impossible.

Even though the world had not learned much, if anything, from Matthew's prophecies, its people had not been forced to enact them.

But the Ark had not turned back.

Who could ever have imagined for a moment that it might?

When Matthew was not responding to Nita Brownell's questions he slept. He did not want to sleep, but she had control of some kind of switch that gave him no choice. He was shrouded by machinery, with various leads connected to his anatomy in inconvenient and embarrassing places, and he was drugged up to the eyeballs. The doctor was in no hurry to concede him an adequate measure of self-control; for the time being, he was a piece of meat that required tender defrosting, allowed to think and speak only to confirm that his defrosted body was still inhabited by the same mind that had gone to sleep therein 727 years before.

He did have the opportunity, while answering the doctor's petty questions, to study his surroundings. Alas, the room itself seemed stubbornly uninformative. It had several screens, but none of them was switched on. By far its most interesting fixture, for the time being, was a second bed, which was occupied by a second defrostee.

Matthew was able to elicit the information that the other man's name was Vincent Solari, but it seemed that several hours passed thereafter before he was actually able to talk to his companion and introduce himself.

"Call me Vince," Solari said, when the introduction had finally been accomplished.

Matthew did, but he noticed that Dr. Brownell continued to use "Vincent." She seemed to be slightly uneasy, deliberately keeping a certain distance between herself and her patients.

Matthew didn't invite anyone to call him Matt. He had always thought of Matt as part of the phrase *matte black*, and he was a Fleury, always colorful. He knew from experience, though, that there were plenty of people who didn't feel that they needed an invitation to shorten his name. That was part of the downside of being a TV personality; he was forever meeting people who thought that they knew him, when they didn't really know him at all.

Once the two returnees were allowed to remain awake simultaneously they were able to benefit from the answers to all the questions they had managed to sneak into the interstices of the doctor's methodical interrogation. It was while observing Nita Brownell's responses to Solari's enquiries that Matthew began to understand how uncomfortable she was, and how unreasonably terse most of her answers were.

At first, Matthew told himself that the woman was simply impatient, eager to get through her own program so that she could get on with other new awakeners in other rooms like theirs, but he guessed soon enough that there had to be more to it than that.

The doctor was pressing forward with such iron resolve because she didn't want to submit to the flood of their questions, and the reason she feared their questions so much was that she was intent on hiding certain items of information from them.

But why?

Matthew's newly defrosted imagination was not yet up to speed, and his capacity to feel anxiety was inhibited by the drugs he was being fed, but he struggled nevertheless with the spectrum of possibilities.

Assuming that Nita Brownell was acting under instructions from above, someone in authority over her must have forbidden her to tell them the whole truth about their present situation—or, at the very least, must have persuaded her that it was not in her patients' best interests to be told too much too soon.

It seemed to stand to reason that any news they weren't being told had to be bad. But how bad could it be?

Seven hundred years, Matthew chided himself, and you wake

up paranoid. That's no way to greet a new world, even for a prophet.

Once it had possessed him, though, it wasn't difficult to feel that kind of paranoia even while his brain was soaked with tranks. Was the room he and Solari were in too sparsely furnished? Were the machines gathered around their beds a trifle ramshackle? Was Nita Brownell a woman under undue stress, a custodian of secrets that she found uncomfortable to bear?

Perhaps. Perhaps not.

Perhaps, Matthew decided, it was best to concentrate on happier thoughts. The happiest thought of all, surely—the one item of news that could not possibly be bad—was that after seven hundred years, *Hope* had reached an Earth-clone world. That was an idea to savor: a new Earth; a new home; another Ararat; another chance.

One, at least, of the New Noah's Arks had reached its goal.

Shen had done it. Like Moses, he had brought his Chosen People to the Promised Land.

But the paranoia lingered.

Reading between the lines with a suspicious eye wasn't a kind of game that Matthew relished, but it was one that he could play like a pro. While he did his level best to provide accurate answers to the questions that bombarded him, therefore, he reserved part of his mind to the task of fitting together the bits of information that Nita Brownell did see fit to provide, and supplementing them with whatever he could deduce from an examination of his surroundings.

The basics seemed simple enough. *Hope* had arrived in orbit around a planet orbiting a G-type star a billion years older than Earth's sun. It had an atmosphere and a hydrosphere very similar to Earth's, and an ecosphere with much the same biomass. So far, so good—but he noticed that Nita Brownell was slightly reluctant to use the word *Earth-clone* or to endorse its use. There was some kind of problem there.

There was, apparently, no recent news of the other two Arks that had exited the Oort Halo circa 2180, nor was there any reason to believe that the fourth Ark—the so-called Lost Ark—had eventually contrived to follow in their train. *Faith* and *Courage* were presumably still searching, if they had avoided ecocatastrophes of their own, while *Charity*, for whatever reason, was still locked in a cometary orbit around the sun. No good news there, but nothing especially terrible either.

If the calculations of *Hope*'s patient AIs could be trusted—Dr. Brownell called them sloths, but that was a term with which Matthew was not familiar and whose meaning he had had to ask—then *Hope*'s announcement of its arrival would reach Earth in 2872. If the gleanings of *Hope*'s equally patient homeward-directed eyes could be trusted, there would certainly be people on Earth to hear the glad tidings, and to be glad on *Hope*'s behalf. There would be billions of them—and billions more elsewhere in the system. No bad news there.

Earthly scientific progress had, apparently, faltered slightly in the early twenty-second century, but had picked up pace again soon enough. Biotechnology and nanotechnology had made good on some—perhaps most—of their promises. The people of Earth had discovered the secret of emortality, and had reconfigured their society to accommodate emortality comfortably. All good news there. With what the people of Earth now knew at *Hope*'s disposal—and what was not yet at *Hope*'s disposal would surely be placed there once Earth's reply to *Hope*'s announcement of her discovery arrived, 116 years down the line—the colonists of the New Earth would surely be able to build a New World fit for their own emortal children.

Surely? When presented with that judgment, Nita Brownell's reply was a calculatedly moderate "probably," which seemed so weak as to be little better than a "possibly."

When asked how the doubt arose, Dr. Brownell procrastinated. Matters weren't as simple as they might appear. Things were complicated. There would be time for explanations later.

There were hints to be gleaned, but it was difficult to judge their relevance.

The failure-rate of *Hope*'s SusAn systems—or, more accurately, the deep-frozen bags of flesh, blood, and mind they had contained for so long—had been slightly higher and slightly more complicated than had been hoped. Mortality, if strictly defined, had been less than one percent, but kick-starting brains sometimes failed to recover the whole person. About one in four awakeners exhibited some degree of memory-loss: hence the intensive interrogation to which Matthew and Vince Solari were currently being subjected.

The problem afflicting the majority, Nita Brownell told them in dribs and drabs, was restricted to the process by which short-term memory was converted into long-term. Most sufferers had lost less than a couple of days, only a handful more than a week. Most of the lost time could be deemed "irrelevant," in that it consisted entirely of preparation for freezing down—hours of dull routine spent in the Spartan environment of Lagrange-5 or Mare Moscoviense—or in riding a shuttle to the far side of Earth's orbit, depending on the timing of the person's invitation to join the Chosen People. A minority, on the other hand, had lost more than that. Some of the full-scale amnesiacs had recovered all or part of themselves eventually, but some had not.

Matthew and Vince were apparently among the luckier ones—but when Matthew remembered the long, lucid dream he had had while his IT was preparing to wake him, he could not help but wonder whether it had been a close-run thing.

Mercifully, by the time Matthew had wrinkled and worked all this out, Dr. Brownell had established that if either he or Vince Solari had lost anything, it was a matter of hours—irrelevant hours, if any hours out of a human life could be reckoned irrelevant.

Compared with 700 years of downtime, Matthew thought, a few hours might indeed be reckoned irrelevant. He remembered saying *au revoir* to Alice and Michelle, and that was the important thing. With luck, they would remember saying *au revoir* to him, when their turn came to be reawakened.

Except that Nita Brownell hesitated for just a fraction of a second over the word *when*, and that fleeting moment of evident doubt cast a dark shadow over everything she said thereafter. The problems of awakening from SusAn were not the *real* problems; they were the problems Nita Brownell was using as a screen to hide the problems that would have to be explained at another time, preferably by someone else. She was a doctor, it was not her job, not her place. . . .

It was too easy to be paranoid, Matthew told himself, as sternly as he could while he was still spaced out. He had come from a bad place, and he had had bad dreams, but he was a winner in the game. He had cast his lot with Shen Chin Che, and he had pulled out a major prize.

Earth had not died, but that did not mean that its people had

had an easy ride in the wake of the Plague Wars. Earth, in the twenty-eighth century, had the secret of emortality, which the Earth he had left behind had not, so he might yet be a winner twice over, of a New World *and* a new life. Given that he had awakened from his long sleep with his memories intact, to find *Hope* in orbit around a life-bearing planet with a breathable atmosphere, what could possibly be wrong? What kind of worm could possibly have infected the bud of his future?

Eventually, Nita Brownell's dogged interrogation stuttered to an end, and she left her patients to get acquainted with one another. Matthew knew, however, that she would return soon enough. When she returned, she would be more vulnerable to *his* questions.

"How do you feel?" Vince Solari asked him.

"All things considered, pretty well," Matthew told him. "Tired and tranquilized." Turning to face his companion was extraordinarily difficult, but he figured it was worth the effort, if only to say hello.

"When were you frozen down?" he asked.

"Fourteen," Solari replied, presumably meaning 2114. "I was a late applicant. You were one of the first wave, I guess—the real Chosen People. I was only in my twenties when you went into the freezer, but I guess we're the same age now, give or take a few months."

"We might both get to be a lot older," Matthew observed, remembering that the great pioneers of SusAn technology had encouraged its development in order that they might sleep until their fellows had invented an efficient technology of longevity, rather than for the purpose of traveling to the stars.

"Crazy, isn't it?" Solari said. "You sleep for seven hundred years, you wake up tired. Tireder than when they put me to bed. Good to be back, though, isn't it?"

"Very good," Matthew confirmed. "But I was expecting a warmer welcome. My daughters are still in SusAn, apparently, but it's been three years, and I had a lot of friends—acquaintances, anyway—in the first wave of volunteers. Why aren't they here with flowers and champagne?"

"I expect they're already down on the surface," Solari said. "Apart from people with the doctor's special expertise, there'd be no need for any of the colonists to remain on the ship for very long. The crew don't seem to have done much with the decor while they've been in flight, do they?"

Matthew looked around again. The room that he and Solari were in was as narrow and Spartan as any Lagrange compartment, although there were slots in the wall from which chairs and tables could be folded out. The screens were still blank. There were a couple of VE-hoods mounted over their beds, with extendable keyboards as well as overcomplicated consoles whose layouts seemed disturbingly unfamiliar to Matthew's roaming eye, but they were out of reach as yet. Their beds were surrounded by as much equipment as any man in fear of his life and sanity could ever have desired to see, but Matthew was already enthusiastic for release. He wanted to stand on his own two feet. He wanted to be able to shake Vince Solari by the hand and say: "We made it." He wanted to jump, and walk, and maybe even dance. He wanted to see what was outside the door: what *Hope* had become, after 700 years of crew activity.

He took note of the fact that the ship must be spinning, albeit at a slightly slower velocity than he might have contrived had the choice been his. Everything obviously had weight, but maybe only three times as much weight as it would have had in Mare Moscoviense. It was difficult to be sure while he was still half-cocooned, but half Earth-gravity was the best estimate he could make.

In theory, Matthew knew, his muscles should still be tuned for Earth gravity. The somatic modifications he had undergone, the special IT with which he had been fitted, and the rigorous exercise programs that he had followed since leaving the home-world should have seen to that. He also knew, though, that he and Vince Solari would have to shuttle down to the new world in a matter of days if the low-weight environment wasn't to begin taking a toll. Maybe that was why none of his old acquaintances was here: *Hope* was crew territory, save for specialisms the crew didn't include, like Nita Brownell's. Had the half-gravity always been part of Shen Chin Che's plan? He couldn't remember.

In any case, he and Solari would presumably be turned over to a very different set of machines once they were allowed out of bed, to make sure that their muscles would be able to take the strain.

Within himself, and apart from his paradoxical tiredness,

Matthew felt pretty fit. Seven hundred years in SusAn hadn't left him with any discernible weakness or nagging pain—or if it had, the machine-maintained sleep in which he'd dreamed of Earth's destruction had seen him through it while his IT did its curative work.

His dream of Earth's destruction had, it seemed, been born of needless anxiety—but while Nita Brownell could hesitate over the when of his daughters' reawakening, and could seem so anxious about matters she was not prepared to spell out, there was definitely cause for anxiety of another kind.

TWO

When Dr. Brownell came back the conversational tables were turned. Matthew had a good dozen questions ready. The doctor must have flagged him as the man more likely to ask awkward questions, though, because she went to Solari first and showed blatant prejudice in attending to what he had to say.

It didn't do her much good. Solari had his own questions ready, and they were awkward enough. What fraction of *Hope*'s human cargo had so far been defrosted? Less than a fifth, she admitted. Why so few, in three long years? Because further awakenings were only being initiated, for the time being, on the basis of urgent need.

Curiouser and curiouser, Matthew thought.

"*What* urgent need?" Vince Solari asked, grimly—wanting to know, of course, what urgent need had forced his own emergence.

Perhaps it was the grimness of his tone that made Dr. Brownell repent of her earlier favoritism and turn to Matthew, or perhaps she felt that she had nowhere else to turn.

"Dr. Delgado's death," she said, following her medically sanctioned policy of cutting every answer to the bone.

That, Matthew remembered, was one of the things he had not been able to remember in his dream. The Chosen People had been appointed to the Arks in twos, for safety's sake, and he had not been able to recall the name of his counterpart, his adopted twin.

Bernal Delgado was the name he had not been able to pluck from the vault of memory: Bernal Delgado, expert in ecological genomics; Bernal Delgado, media celebrity and prophet; Bernal Delgado, long-term friend, rival, role model, and companion-in-arms to the slightly younger Matthew Fleury. Not that the mirror image had been perfect; there had also been Bernal Delgado, ladies' man, who fancied himself the twenty-first century's answer to Don Juan. Bernal Delgado was a single man, not a widowed father of two bright and beautiful daughters . . .

Except that it wasn't *was* but *had been*.

Bernal Delgado, it appeared, was dead.

"Bernal's dead!" Matthew exclaimed, a little belatedly. It didn't qualify as a question in Dr. Brownell's opinion, and she was making herself busy in any case with the battery of machines that was still holding him captive, ignoring him as resolutely as she was now ignoring Vince Solari. Matthew had no alternative but to think the matter through himself.

Bernal Delgado had died on the New World, on the peak of the other Ararat, before Matthew had had a chance to join him and shake his hand in joyous congratulation. He had died in sparse company, because new awakenings were only being initiated on the basis of "urgent need." The colonization plan had stalled. Something was wrong with the Earth-clone world. There was a serpent in Eden. Matthew had been revived in order to take Bernal's place. Why, then, had Vince Solari been yanked out of the freezer?

"Are you an ecologist too?" Matthew asked his companion, dazedly.

"No," Solari told him, a trifle abstractedly, having been following his own train of thought. "I'm a policeman."

"A policeman?" Matthew echoed, taken completely by surprise. "Why should Bernal's death create an urgent need for a policeman?" He had addressed the question to Nita Brownell, but she wasn't in any hurry to answer it.

"It wouldn't," Solari pointed out, having evidently given the question some consideration already. "Unless, of course, he was murdered. *Was* he murdered, Dr. Brownell?"

"Yes," she said, brusquely. "The captain will brief you, just as soon as . . ."

She left the sentence dangling, trailing the implication that she had work to do, and that they would get their answers sooner if they let her do it. Her concern was their bodily welfare, not the reasons for their reawakening—but when she eventually left the room again it seemed to Matthew that she was running away, with her work not quite done.

"Whatever the story is," Matthew observed, "she's embarrassed to tell us. She thinks we're going to disapprove. However they've screwed up, they're obviously self-conscious about it."

"The machines must have reassured her that we're doing okay physically," Solari said. "She already checked our memories.

Maybe now she'll let someone come in to tell us what's gone
wrong. Apart from Delgado being murdered, that is. Somehow, I
get the feeling that that's just the tip of the iceberg—if they have
icebergs on. Did she mention the world's name?"

"No," Matthew said. "She didn't."

The door opened again. This time, it was a young man who
stepped through.

There had been nothing conspicuously out of the ordinary
about Nita Brownell. She hadn't looked a day over thirty, according to the "natural" standard that had already become obsoles-
cent when the construction of *Hope* began, although she was
actually in her mid-forties in terms of actively experienced time.
Her appearance and her mannerisms had seemed *familiar*; the
moment Matthew had set eyes on her he had made the assumption—without even bothering to think twice about it, that she
was a well-educated, well-groomed twenty-first century utilitarian, crisis-modified version. Like Matthew, Nita Brownell had
been playing Sleeping Beauty for centuries, for exactly the same
reasons. She was an Earthwoman in strange surroundings, not an
alien.

The newcomer was different.

The moment the newcomer met his eye, Matthew knew that
the young man was space-born and ship-nurtured.

The Ark could, in theory, have been navigated by its cleverest
AIs, but Shen Chin Che and his fellow protégés of the New Noah
would never have entertained the notion of putting *Hope*'s cargo
in the care of Artificial Intelligences. *Hope* had always been
intended to cross the gulf between the stars under the guidance
and governance of a human crew: a crew whose members had
had a life-expectancy of 120 years when Matthew had been
frozen down. Perhaps they still had the same life-expectancy, but
it was at least possible that they had been able to benefit from the
great leap forward that Earth–based-longevity technologies had
made after *Hope* had left the system. This youth—if the appearance that he was little more than a boy could be trusted—might
be eighth- or tenth-generation crew, or maybe only third- or
fourth-. He was thin and spare. His blue-gray uniform was a
smart one-piece without much slack, but its lack of fashion-con-
scious shape contrived to make it look almost monastic. He
moved like a creature long-used to low gravity, with a mannered

grace that put Matthew in mind of a nimble but easygoing lemur, too laid back to have evolved into a fully-fledged monkey. His skin was papery pale, but not Caucasian off-white; it had a tint to it that was more green than brown or yellow. His eyes were green too, but far more vivid.

The whole ensemble was unsettlingly *un*familiar, almost to the point of being alien, even though the only thing about him that looked wholly exotic was his feet.

Matthew thought at first that the young man was barefoot, although he realized almost immediately that the smart clothing must extend over the youth's feet, as it did over his hands and face, in a fashion so discreet that it had become a near-invisible second skin. The feet were decidedly odd; the toes were elongated, like fingers. Although the youth was standing quite still, the manner in which they were set upon the floor gave the impression that they were trained to grip, and perhaps to grapple.

"Hi," the newcomer said. "I'm Frans Leitz, crew medical orderly. I'm Dr. Brownell's assistant. The captain has asked me to send you his compliments and welcome you back to consciousness. He's anxious to see you as soon as you're free of all this paraphernalia, and to tell you everything you need to know about the situation, but he's asked me to answer any preliminary questions you might have. You're Professor Fleury, I suppose? And you're Detective Solari?"

"I'm an inspector, not a detective," Solari said. Matthew decided that it wasn't worth the bother of trying to explain that he wasn't, strictly speaking, a professor. Niceties of rank were Old World matters—except, perhaps, where the crew was concerned. The boy's uniform bore no obvious insignia, but Matthew was certain that a medical orderly didn't qualify as an officer. Had the captain really sent a glorified cabin boy to "answer any preliminary questions he and Solari might have," Matthew wondered. If so, what did that say about the captain's opinion of them, and of the *urgent need* that had occasioned their awakening? And what did it say about the captain's attitude to Nita Brownell, who seemingly couldn't be trusted to answer their questions herself? What had happened to drive a wedge between the crew and the reawakened Chosen People?

"What's the new world called?" Matthew asked, softly.

"Well," said the boy, amiably, "there's a certain amount of disagreement about that, so it's still under negotiation. Some members of the first landing party wanted to call it Hope, after the ship, but the crew mostly want to call it Ararat, in keeping with the Ark myth. Several other alternatives have been suggested by way of compromise—some favor New Earth, some Murex, some Tyre—but that's only served to complicate the situation. Mostly, we call it *the world*, or *the surface*."

"Why Murex?" Solari wanted to know.

"Because the vegetation is mostly purple," Leitz replied. "All the grass and trees, almost all the animals . . . except that the trees aren't really trees, and the animals aren't really animals, and the giant grass is made of glass. You'll be briefed on all of that by our senior genomicist, of course, Professor Fleury. It'll be a lot to take in, and it all sounds pretty weird to me, but you're a biologist, so you'll get the hang of it soon enough."

"Start off," Matthew said. "If you're the doctor's assistant, you must know *some* biology."

The boy blushed slightly, although the color of his skin made the blush seem more gray than pink. It took him a couple of seconds to decide that he couldn't play *too* dumb.

"The panspermists and the chemical convergence theorists were wrong, it seems," he said. "Evolution here and on the orphan followed distinct and different paths. DNA isn't universal. Nor is chlorophyll, obviously, or the world wouldn't be purple. The surface looks pretty enough in pictures, but the people on the ground say that it's rather disturbing up close."

"What orphan?" Solari put in, while Matthew was still working out how to phrase a more pertinent question.

"A sunless but life-bearing world we bypassed in interstellar space. It was long before my time, but it's all on record, including the genomic analyses. It was a sludgeworld—nothing bigger than a bacterium. There are others, apparently, able to support life because their internal heat and thick atmospheres keep the surfaces warm and wet. Lots of probes came this way after us, all traveling faster—it's easier to accelerate when you're small—and we've harvested a lot of information from them. There's nothing else like this world, though—not yet. It's the one-and-only Earth-clone, for the time being. It's not just *your* world. So far as everyone here is concerned, it really is *the* world."

"Long before your time," Matthew echoed, anxious to stake a

conversational claim before Solari asked another question. "I presume that means you're as young as you look. Dr. Brownell said that the people back on Earth are emortal now—does that apply to the crew too? Do you have the means to modify *us*?"

"It's not as simple as that," Leitz countered. "Yes, I'm as young as I look—nineteen. No, I'm not emortal, and never will be. True emortality has to be built in from scratch by genetic engineering of a fertilized egg-cell. Our rejuve technologies have improved a little since we left Earth, but we haven't been able to develop our nanotech nearly as rapidly as the folks back home. I can't tell you how long you or I will live, barring accidents, because I don't know how much we'll benefit from further progress, but two hundred years is generally reckoned to be a fair guess. By Earthly standards, we're primitives. On Earth, survivors of the Old Human Race are freaks."

"What happened to Bernal Delgado?" Solari asked, presumably feeling that theoretical issues could safely be left to one side until more practical issues had been addressed. "Who killed him?"

The youth's eyes swiveled away from Matthew to meet the detective's. Matthew was slightly surprised to find himself relieved: the green gaze had been slightly disconcerting, although it had seemed guileless enough.

"We're hoping that you can find that out," Leitz told Solari. "It *looks* as if he was killed by aborigines—"

"The world's *inhabited*?" Matthew interrupted—but Leitz continued looking at Solari.

"But it can't be the way it looks, because all the evidence says that the aborigines are extinct. Which probably means that it was set up to look like Delgado was killed by aborigines, maybe just to deflect attention away from whoever did kill him, but maybe to persuade people that the aborigines aren't extinct at all. That would change things, you see, and it might not take more than a few votes swung from one side to the other to create a new majority among the groundlings. If they were all to get behind a formal request for a withdrawal, that could cause *real* problems for the captain . . . and for everyone else."

Matthew could see that Vince Solari was just as astonished by this puzzling flood of information as he was. The detective had no immediate follow-up ready, so Matthew was able to step into the breach again. "Are you telling us," he said, slowly, "that after seven hundred years, we've arrived at the only Earth-clone world that any of Earth's probes has so far managed to locate, but that the colonists you've so far managed to land are split right down the middle as to whether or not they want to *pull out*?"

Frans Leitz shrugged his bony shoulders. "It seems crazy to nearly everyone up here," he admitted. "But yes, there are a lot of people on the ground who want out, for one reason or another. Mostly, they don't think the world is anywhere near Earthlike *enough*. Some are scared because the local humanoids have become extinct—others are worried that if the aborigines aren't *quite* extinct, our arrival will tip them over the edge. The bioscientists can't seem to agree about what will happen to the local ecosphere if we establish a colony here . . . or, for that matter, to the ecosystems we introduce. This may not be a sludgeworld, some say, but it's a real can of worms. It's not easy for me to judge, being ship-born and ship-committed. I'm crew—my future's here no matter what"

"And what about Shen Chin Che?" Matthew wanted to know. "What does *he* think?"

The boy's face had been quite relaxed before, but it became suddenly taut now, and there was a flash of wildness in those eerie eyes. "I don't know," he said, guardedly. "He's not involved in the discussion."

"Is that because you haven't woken him up?" Matthew was quick to ask.

"No," the boy said. "It's a bit more complicated than that."

Matthew had already opened his mouth to ask another question before he realized—belatedly, it seemed—that he might already have asked at least one too many. Frans Leitz might be just a glorified cabin boy, and Nita Brownell a bona fide doctor with a businesslike bedside manner, but that didn't mean that every word that he and Vincent Solari spoke wasn't being overheard elsewhere in the ship, and very carefully studied. Matthew had no idea what side he was likely to be on in the ongoing dispute, because he had only just realized that there *were* any sides, but now he knew that there were, he wondered whether he ought to be careful. Newly hatched into a situation that obviously wasn't as simple as it ought to be, he might need to get his bearings before showing his hand to interested parties.

He had been awakened, it seemed, to replace the other member of his pair, *who had been murdered.* However the land lay down on "the surface," this was a matter of life and death. It had always been a matter of life and death, from the very first moment he had exchanged polite bows with Shen Chin Che, but Matthew knew that he must not lose sight now of the fact that within the larger matters of life and death—upon which hung the fate of worlds—there were tangled threads upon which his own life dangled. It was not impossible that whoever had wanted Bernal dead might want him dead too—and until he knew *why* Bernal had been killed, it might be as well to be careful.

"I think we need to see the captain as soon as possible," Matthew said to Frans Leitz. "In fact, I can't help wondering why he sent you to talk to us, instead of coming himself."

"The captain is just as anxious to see you as you are to see him, professor," the young man replied, blithely ignoring the second part of the statement. "He'll send for you as soon as Dr. Brownell has made perfectly certain that you're fit and well. Now, can I get you anything before I go?"

"You could turn the TV on," Matthew said. "I'd like to catch the next news bulletin."

"We don't have broadcast TV," the youth informed him. "The captain broadcasts occasionally, but we don't need routine news bulletins. Everybody knows everybody. All we have to do is talk to one another."

"What about the people on the ground?" Matthew asked.

"They make their reports, of course. They all have belt-phones, just like on Earth. We've established a chain of comsats. But Base One doesn't have broadcast TV either. There's no need. We have VE-hoods for entertainment. I'm sorry—I hear that you used to be on TV a lot, on Earth."

The youth said it as if he were trying to frame a compliment, but Matthew couldn't hear it as one. He might have been slightly flattered to think that his reputation had preceded him, even at this distance from Earth and the twenty-first century, but his mind was elsewhere. To him, not having broadcast TV—not even having *news*—seemed a far more significant symptom of a breakdown in communication than the fact that the doctor was reluctant to talk to him and that a cabin boy had been sent to answer his immediate questions.

"Things have gone wrong, haven't they," he murmured. "Badly wrong."

Frans Leitz blushed again, but the blush seemed as odd and unhealthy as its predecessor. "No," he said. "Not really. Not yet. But they might, if the people on the surface can't see sense. Everything depends on them—on their willingness to do what they came to do."

"After seven hundred years of SusAn, they're not sure whether they're willing to do what they risked *everything* to do? Surely you mean their *ability* to do it?"

"Well, that's what they say, of course," the young crewman replied, ingenuously. "But it's only a matter of determination. It *is* an Earth-clone world, even though it's a little peculiar. Maybe you'll be able to make them see that, Professor Fleury. We certainly have an urgent need for somebody who can."

THREE

atthew was enthusiastic to try out his legs, but Nita Brownell seemed to be in no hurry to complete the disconnection process and let him get out of bed. Frans Leitz helped her, with an easy alacrity. The fact that the young man had obviously been trained to operate as a medical orderly made Matthew feel slightly guilty about continuing to think of him as a "cabin boy" but it didn't stop him doing it.

The moment he was released from the machines Matthew tried to spring into action, but immediately realized that his mental tiredness was a symptom of a general physical weakness. It was astonishingly difficult to sit up, let alone to step down to the floor.

When Matthew expressed surprise at his weakness, Nita Brownell—who was perfectly willing to be loquacious about purely medical matters—explained that the vitrifying agent that had protected his cells from damage while he was frozen down had only been able to preserve the basic structures. Many of the proteins involved in routine cell metabolism had suffered degradation, and had therefore required replacement. Unfortunately, the messenger-RNA system for transcribing exons from nuclear DNA and establishing templates in the cytoplasm had also been partly disabled, and was not yet fully restored.

"You must have been warned before going into SusAn that we couldn't just defrost you," she told him sternly, as if it were his fault that he had not remembered that particular item of information. "We had to give your cells time to get their internal acts together, and then restore function to your tissues. Even with IT support, it's been a slow process. The machines kept you asleep as long as possible, but the final phases of the tune-up have to be completed while you're alert and active. You'll feel a lot better in a few hours, and you'll probably be able to leave the room this time tomorrow. You'll be shuttling down as soon as possible—within fifty hours, if all goes well."

"Fifty hours!" Matthew exclaimed.

"Sorry," the doctor said. "That's ship hours. Five days, in the old reckoning."

Five days still sounded a trifle hurried to Matthew, although he knew that if he'd been kept aboard ship for an extended period he would soon have become impatient. It was difficult to believe the reassurance that he'd be back to his old self within five days when the effort of standing up seemed so extreme, and the prospect of taking a step almost impossible, but once he'd actually contrived a step and had found it merely uncomfortable, he buckled down to the serious business of reminding his body what human existence was like.

For the first couple of hours of relative freedom, Matthew and Vince Solari were too wrapped up in what was happening to them to pester their helpers with awkward questions about the situation aboard ship, but the easing of their concerted interrogative pressure didn't seem to lighten the minds of their coy informants; everything either of them said or did seemed to touch slightly raw nerves.

Given that the ship's spin was only simulating half Earth's gravity, Matthew was not surprised to find that once his muscles had got the hang of working again they soon began to feel quite powerful. Unfortunately, learning to move about efficiently and economically in the unfamiliar gravity-regime was frustratingly difficult. His memories seemed to be virtually unaffected by their long storage, so the exercises and tricks he had learned as he passed from Earth to the moon, and then to remoter parts of the system, were still fresh in his mind. Unfortunately, his body had spent forty years adapting to Earth and a mere matter of months in variable low-gee. All the old expectations were still built in.

"Don't worry about it," Nita Brownell advised him, while she studied the manner of his blundering with a connoisseur's eye. "It doesn't matter if you're awkward and clumsy up here—in fact, it's better that you don't have time to begin getting settled. The real task ahead of you is adaptation to the surface. That's oh point ninety-two Earth-gravity, but you'll find that oh point oh-eight makes more difference than you'd imagine."

"If it's oh point ninety-two Earth-normal down on the surface," Matthew growled, "wouldn't it make more sense to simulate oh point ninety-two up here?"

"Well, yes it would," said Nita Brownell, cautiously—but she was immediately interrupted by Frans Leitz.

"This is crew territory," Leitz said, brusquely. "It's adapted to our requirements. It's always been this way, and there's no reason to change."

"*Your* requirements," Matthew repeated. "*Yours,* as opposed to *ours.* Since when did *you* and *we* become opposed sides, with contrasted interests?"

He realized as he framed the words that it was a stupid question. Since when? Since the twenty-first century, obviously. The corpsicles' yesterday, the crew's ancient history. A lot could happen in 700 years, even in a mini-ecosphere set to maintain itself far more rigidly than Mama Gaea. The crew had obviously developed ideas of their own as to what their purpose and destiny ought to be. But how, exactly, had they brought them into conflict with the colonists whose needs they had been put aboard to serve? From what he had been told so far, it was the colonists, not the crew, who were having doubts about their role.

Nita Brownell had already reverted to what she obviously considered safer ground. "As soon as you go on to autopilot on the surface," she was saying, "the old reflexes will come into play, and you'll find that you're just that little bit out of step. You'll need to take the adaptation process seriously. Do your exercises. Play some ball games, if you can, and don't get too frustrated by your initial inability to judge a catch or a throw. It'll take weeks, at least, maybe months. Longer than you think, at any rate. The lingering impression of being in the wrong place will sink to a subliminal level, but someone of your age could easily be troubled for *years.* We think that's one of the major reasons for . . ."

She paused, the momentum of her discourse having carried her away from the safe ground to which she had resolved to stick.

"For what?" Solari prompted.

She took up the sentence readily enough, if a trifle guardedly. "For the sense of unease and disorientation that seems to have taken near-permanent hold of many of the surface-dwellers," she said.

"Near-permanent?" Matthew queried.

"We believe that it will wear off eventually," she insisted, before hurling herself back into her work with a concentration that excluded further inquiry. Matthew wondered whether she really counted herself part of that particular *we*.

Dr. Brownell had seemed relentless in her pursuit of possible gaps in their memories and possible failings of intellectual ability, but that had not been her primary field of expertise. Now that she was checking on the efficiency of their organs and metabolic pathways she had stepped up another gear. She had been bare-headed before but she was wearing a tiara now with side-lenses placed at the edges of her peripheral vision, and her eyes were constantly flicking back and forth as they read the data transmitted to the tiny screens. Some of it was reportage of tests carried out elsewhere, on samples extracted from the newly defrosted bodies, but most was the result of "live" transmission from the cleverer elements of their Internal Technology as they put the various parts of their bodies through a battery of tests.

"There's a certain amount of peripheral cell-failure in most of your tissues," she told them both, when they collapsed back on to their beds, their tiredness transformed to utter exhaustion, "but you've both been lucky. Because the vitrification and cooling processes proceeded unevenly, and there was a similar unevenness in their undoing, there's always a slight problem at every tissue-boundary, especially where the cells are unalike, but neither of you has suffered unusually heavy losses anywhere. Vincent's worst problems are in the dermal layers, while Matthew's are the shrouds of the long bones, but both deficits should be fully remedied in a matter of days.

"Your alimentary canals and kidneys will take longer to make up the shortfall and flush out the debris, so you might both have some slight trouble with your digestive systems. I won't program your IT to blot out the discomfort because I may need all the warning signs I can get. Don't get paranoid about slight belly-aches, but if there's any sign of allergic reactions of any kind let me know *immediately*. The tailors are already at work on your surface suits. We won't be fitting them today but they'll have to be well grown-in before you're ready to shuttle down. This part of the ship is supposedly an ultrasafe environment, so we won't be issuing you with specialized ship suits at all—but when I say *supposedly* I mean that we can't be absolutely certain, so it might not be wise to go wandering around, and certainly not without a guide."

"What's wrong with the other parts of the ship?" Solari wanted to know.

Again, it was Leitz who answered what appeared to be a ticklish question. "We've suffered some systems failures," he said. "Their effects are variable, but we've been forced to close some sections temporarily. Even the sections over which we have full control can be hazardous to non-crew members, though. The ship isn't a homogenous environment, of course, even within the inner shell. When you came aboard it was probably no more than a glorified steel box, but once we'd hitched a ride in the comet core the hybrid began to evolve, and it's been evolving ever since. Seven hundred years is a long time in the history of a world as small as this one, and we've been making progress all the while. It's not just a matter of needing suits to go out into the ice—there are a dozen intermediary regions, and only a couple are exclusively AI territory. You'll find the surface very strange, Inspector Solari, but don't make the mistake of thinking that *Hope* is a little slice of home. In its own fashion, it's a good deal stranger. If the people below understood that better, none of them would be laboring under the delusion that they'd be better off aborting the colony."

"Okay," Matthew said, blandly, when it became obvious that the sermon was over. "Message understood. We won't take any long walks without a guide. These surface suits you mentioned, Dr. Brownell. How thickly do we need to be insulated down there?"

"They're not much bulkier than ordinary clothing," she assured him. The air filters are unobtrusive, although you'll be aware of them in the sinuses and throat until they settle in, and they'll modify your voice slightly. It hasn't been necessary to take them all the way down into the lungs, although the whole of your gut will have to be resurfaced. You won't be consciously aware of the gutskin at all, although its extension is the most difficult part of the fitting. We're operating on a precautionary principle, of course—everything's assumed to be biohazardous until it's proved otherwise.

"Once you've been briefed by the crew's genomicists you'll probably be better able to assess the risk factors than I am, but so far as we can tell the local bacs aren't at all enthusiastic to set up home in Earthly flesh, and mammalian immune systems are perfectly capable of forming antibodies against native proteins. They're so competent, in fact, that the main difficulty is over-response. Animals exposed to the whole chemical symphony of the surface environment tend to go into reaction-overdrive; those that don't collapse with anaphylactic shock develop high fevers and lapse into comas when their blood is glutted with defensive factors. More gradual exposure allows them to adapt, but it's a slow process. It could take generations to produce Earthly domestic animals that can operate naked on the surface and feed themselves adequately on local produce. It's the same for people—except, of course, that human generation times are a lot longer. The colonists and their crop-plants will be living in bubbles for a long time yet—but they will make progress. Slowly but surely, they'll make themselves at home." She said it stoutly, but she didn't sound entirely convinced of the last assertion.

"But *they* don't think so, do they?" Solari said. "They don't think this is an Earth-clone world at all. They think they're in greater danger here than they were on Earth. They think they've jumped out of the frying pan into the fire."

"No," said Leitz, firmly. "They don't. All those who aren't cowards know full well that they can live here, if they're prepared to make the effort. The greater part of the surface community is in full agreement with the crew that the colony *has* to go ahead."

"And how big is the majority?" the policeman countered, scornfully. "Not so big, apparently, that a few votes couldn't swing a demand for withdrawal."

"Votes don't matter, inspector," the boy said, rattled to the point of recklessness. "The people on the surface aren't in a position to make demands. The only way they'll get back up here is if we take them in—and we won't. The colony has to stay, and it has to succeed. We wouldn't have woken the two of you up if we didn't think that you would both work toward that end."

"Was Bernal Delgado working toward that end?" Matthew asked, keeping his own voice scrupulously level.

"Yes, he was," Leitz replied, flatly—but Vince Solari was on to that inconsistency as fast as he'd taken hold of the other.

"And *maybe* that's why he was killed," the policeman said. "Or maybe not. Maybe he was killed because he was about to switch to the other side."

"What end is Shen Chin Che working toward?" Matthew

asked—but that was one question the boy wasn't about to answer. Had Matthew and Solari still been hooked up to all the life-support apparatus, Nita Brownell would probably have sent them off to sleep again, but she couldn't. All she and Leitz could do was beat a retreat, and they didn't manage that until Solari had lodged an insistent request for a suit of clothes, of whatever kind might be available, and the personal possessions—including his notepad and beltphone—that had been put into store for him.

Nita Brownell promised to see what she could do, but Matthew got the impression that she might not be able to do very much.

When they'd gone, Solari said: "This isn't quite the awakening I envisaged. The party atmosphere isn't up to much, is it?"

"It was always a danger," Matthew reminded him, soberly. "There was no shortage of prophets to tell the people of my generation that we couldn't escape Earth's problems by running away, because we'd only freeze them down along with us: all the festering conflicts; all the innate self-destructive tendencies. Those who fail to learn from prophecies are doomed to enact them. I can understand the differences of opinion—what I can't understand is how they've become so bitter. We were all supposed to be on the same side—that was the heart and soul of the whole enterprise. How can it have soured so badly? What are they still not telling us?"

"The crew have had seven hundred years to develop their own ideas and their own internal conflicts," Solari said, pensively. "It's not just their feet that they've modified. The ship is *their* territory, the kid said. They have plans of their own—perhaps more than one, maybe with a few undecided votes holding the balance up here too. One of the things they're not telling us is what's happened to Shen Chin Che. Did you know him personally?"

"Yes, I did," Matthew said, wondering how much the people who must be presumed to be listening in on the conversation knew about his relationship with the Ark's owner, "and I'd certainly like to know where he is."

"Jail, maybe?"

"Maybe. But holding out on us isn't the right way to win us to their side, is it? Quite the reverse, in fact." He was speaking as much to the hypothetical eavesdroppers as to Solari, and the policeman understood that.

"Right," Solari confirmed. "If I were the captain, I'd be down here right now, laying everything on the line. I can't understand why he isn't."

"Me neither," Matthew lied. He presumed that the reason the captain wasn't laying his cards on the table was that the captain wanted to know exactly where his new guests stood before doing so. The captain wanted to know which way they were likely to jump, once they understood what was at stake and how many different sides there were in the conflict. But to what lengths might he be willing to go, if he decided that they were likely to take a side of which he didn't approve?

"Well," Solari said, "it could have been worse. We might never have come out of the freezer at all. We might have come out without our most cherished memories. The mere fact that we're here makes us winners—and if nobody else is prepared to celebrate, let's raise a salute to one another."

Matthew raised his arm willingly enough, and met Vince Solari's desperately tired gaze as frankly and as forthrightly as he could.

"Congratulations, Vince," he said. "A tiny step in humankind's conquest of the galaxy, but a great leap forward for you and me."

"Congratulations, Matt," Solari replied. "Wherever we are, we sure as hell made it. Whatever we're mixed up in, we're already way ahead of the game. Amen."

"Amen," Matthew echoed, and meant it.

FOUR

The smartsuits Matthew and Solari were given to wear while their surface suits were being tailored were very similar to the ones they'd worn in the months before being frozen down, and not much different from the ones Matthew had worn on Earth—he'd never been a follower of fashion or a devotee of exotic display. They were, however, conspicuously unlike the white exterior presented by Nita Brownell or the pale blue-gray one manifested by Frans Leitz, which were presumably the "specialized ship suits" they weren't being given. The main color of the smartsuits was modifiable, but only from dark blue to black and back again, and such style as they possessed was similarly restricted. Matthew guessed that if he and Solari were to go a-wandering they would stick out like sore thumbs in any line of sight they happened to cross.

The doctor told them that they'd get their personal possessions back "in due course."

By the time that he and Solari finally got to eat an authentic meal, in the middle of the second day of their new life, Matthew was expecting a veritable orgy of sensual delights. He was disappointed; the flavors were too bland for his taste, the textures too meltingly soft and the net effect slightly nauseating. The doctor and her assistant had left them to it, so they had no one to complain to but one another.

"It is the food, or us?" Solari asked.

"Mainly us, I think," Matthew told him. "Our expectations were probably too high. Until our stomachs are back to normal they'll be sending out queasiness signals. On the other hand, the crew have had seven hundred years of cultural isolation, so their tastes have probably changed quite markedly."

"Have to wait till we get to the surface, then," Solari said, philosophically. "At least they'll have had three years practice growing Earthly crops."

"I don't suppose it'll be a great deal better," Matthew said, "given that their staples will be whole-diet wheat- and rice-mannas. If we're lucky, though, these gutskins they're going to extend from our lips to our arseholes via our intestinal labyrinths will enhance taste sensations rather than muffling them, and nausea will be out of the question."

"I'm beginning to get a sense of how long I've been away," Solari mused. "The fitter I get, the more obvious the differences become. Bound to happen, of course."

"It was always going to be a wrench," Matthew agreed. "But things are definitely more awkward than we could have wished. I suppose we have to be patient, with ourselves as well as our careful hosts. We'll rediscover all the pleasures, given time—and we'll probably find that the keyboards attached to those hoods and display screens are a lot more user-friendly than they seem at first glance. Seven hundred years of progress can't have obliterated the underlying logic. Once we get used to them, we'll presumably have access to the ship's data banks—and then we can catch up with *all* the news, good and bad alike."

Solari looked over his shoulder at the consoles behind his bedhead, then up at the hoods and dangling keyboards. He pulled down a hood and fitted it over his head and eyes, but had to lift it up again to reach for a keyboard.

Now that the two of them were free to sit up in their beds, or even reconfigure the beds as chairs, it was easy enough to bring down the hoods over their heads or activate wraparound screens, and use any of half a dozen touchpads. Unfortunately, no one had taken the trouble as yet to brief them on the use of the controls. In theory, everything they might want to know was probably at their fingertips, but *Hope*'s crew seemed to be in no hurry to educate their fingertips in their art of searching.

"We could probably figure them out, given time," Solari said, as he pushed the hood back up again. "But will we have the time? They seem keen to send us down to the surface *before* we can figure out exactly what's going on up here. There's a hell of a lot to be learned and we've been thrown in at the deep end. The colony's first bases are already in place, if not exactly up and running—although the endeavor's obviously made enough progress to produce its first major crime."

"Its first *unsolved* major crime," Matthew said. "The first, at any rate, that has proved so awkwardly problematic as to provoke demands for an investigation by fresh and practiced eyes—

and a replacement for the victim. *Thrown in at the deep end* is probably an understatement."

Solari had decided that he had had enough to eat some time before Matthew finally decided to give up. The detective had pushed his plate away in order to begin playing with the overhead apparatus, but he gave up on that now in favor of more adventurous action. He took one last swig of water before swinging his legs over the side of the bed and dropping lightly to the floor. Once he had tested the strength of his limbs he went to the door of the room and pressed the release-pad.

The door slid open immediately, affording Matthew some slight reassurance, although he knew that it wasn't actually necessary to lock a door in order to secure a prison.

When Solari stepped out into the corridor the door slid shut behind him, cutting off the sound of his voice as soon as he had begun to speak.

Matthew shoved his own food away and took a last sip of water before stepping down from his own bed. He looked speculatively at the door, but there was a certain luxury in being alone for the first time since his emergence from SusAn, so he took time out to dispose of the degradable plates and utensils they had employed.

By the time he had finished clearing up the door had opened again and Solari was coming back into the room.

The policeman came to stand very close to him and spoke in a confidential whisper, although he must have known that lowering his voice was unlikely to be enough to prevent his being overheard.

"There's a man standing guard outside," he said. "He says his name's Riddell. Same uniform as the boy—except for the sidearm. Same feet too. He says he'll be only too glad to take one or both of us anywhere we might want to go, *when we're well enough.*"

"What kind of sidearm?" Matthew wanted to know.

"Looks like a darter. Probably non-lethal, but that's not the point."

It certainly wasn't, Matthew thought. No matter how quick the man outside their door had been to reassure Solari that he wasn't there to keep them prisoner, his armed presence spoke volumes. What it said, first and foremost, was that there were people on the ship who might want to talk to the newly awakened, and might have to be actively deterred from so doing. Who? And why were the captain's men determined to stop them? Matthew looked at the hoods and keyboards, then at the wallscreens. Even if there was no broadcast TV on *Hope*, there had to be a telephone facility. Either no one had attempted to call them, or their calls had not been put through. Was that why their personal belongings, including their beltphones, had not yet been returned to them?

"Seven hundred years of progress," Matthew said, keeping his own voice low even though he knew as well as well as Solari did how futile the gesture was, "and even *Hope* is home to armed men. For all we know, there's a full-scale civil war in progress. If Shen Chin Che were dead, he'd be spinning in his grave. If he's not . . ."

He wanted to follow that train of thought further, but Solari was keeping a tighter focus on the matter in hand. "Whoever killed Delgado on the surface may have friends up here," the policeman observed. "Mr. Riddell might be there to protect us." He didn't sound as if he believed it.

"We were all supposed to be on the same side," Matthew went on, angling the trajectory of his conversation very slightly to take aboard Solari's comment. "Crew and human cargo, scientists and colonists, all working together in the same great scheme. The whole point of building the Ark was to leave behind the divisions and the stresses that were standing in the way of saving Earth. We were all supposed to be united in a common cause, having put the past behind us. How could that go badly wrong in three short years?"

"And seven hundred long ones," Solari reminded him.

"Are we being too paranoid, do you think?" Matthew asked.

Solari didn't have time to answer that one before Frans Leitz came back in. "The captain will see you both at eight-zero," the boy said. "He apologizes for not having been there to greet you when Dr. Brownell brought you out of the induced coma for the last time, but he's very busy."

Matthew realized that he had no idea what the present time was, and couldn't be sure what eight-zero might signify. There was no clock on the wall of the room, and he remembered now that Nita Brownell had said something odd about fifty hours being the equivalent of five days of "old time."

When he asked for an explanation, Leitz explained to him that the ship operated on metric time, using an Earth-day as a base because it suited the Circadian rhythms built into crew physiology. Each day was divided up into ten hours of a hundred minutes, which were further subdivided into a hundred seconds. Surface time had kept the same basic structure, but had adopted the local day as a base, thus resulting in a desynchronization of ship and surface time. The local day, determined by the planet's rotation, was 0.89 of a ship day.

"We think that's another of the reasons for the groundlings' continuing unease," Leitz told them. "It's proved to be surprisingly difficult to modify the physiology of Circadian rhythms, but we're sure that they'll solve the problem soon. If only they could be patient . . . anyhow, the planet's year is one point twenty-eight Earth-standard, but its axial tilt is very slight, so its temperate-zone seasons aren't nearly as extreme. That's not problematic, although Professor Lityansky thinks it has something to do with the strange pattern of local evolution. He'll explain it when he briefs you tomorrow, Professor Fleury. That's at three-zero, provided that you're up to it. How do you feel now?"

"Better," Matthew assured him, drily. "Professor Lityansky's busy too, I dare say."

"Extremely busy," the boy replied. "He's working flat-out trying to figure out exactly what we need to do to make the colony work. He's under a great deal of pressure, because the groundlings hold him primarily responsible for the decision that the world is sufficiently Earthlike to qualify as a clone. The decision to go ahead with the colonization wasn't entirely his, of course, but his genomic analyses provided the relevant data and his judgment of their significance was crucial. He feels badly let down by some of the people on the surface."

"How come their judgment is so different?" Matthew asked.

Leitz hesitated, but eventually decided to answer the question. He was becoming more relaxed now, and a certain boyish enthusiasm was beginning to show through. "Our data was limited, of course," the youth conceded. "Our nanotech is way behind Earth's, and we haven't been able to improve our probes to anything like the same degree while we've been in transit. Apart from evidence gathered at long-range by our instruments, we had a very limited range of surface-gathered samples to work from. They were adequate for genomic analysis, but most of what we had on which to base our decision was fundamental biochemical data. The photographs taken by our flying eyes showed us what the local plant life looked like, but we didn't have any real notion of the ecology of the world, or even of its diversity, let alone its evolutionary history. Once the first landing was complete, the biologists on the ground began to fill in the other parts of the picture—and they began to get alarmed.

"Some of the groundlings began to argue that Professor Lityansky had made a bad mistake, because he hadn't been able to think through the consequences of his genomic analyses. The extreme view is that the colonization should have been put on hold as soon as it was realized that the local ecosphere wasn't DNA-based—but that's absurd, isn't it, Professor Fleury?"

Matthew could see what the young man was getting at. When *Hope* had set out from the solar system its scientists had not the slightest idea exactly how alien any alien life they discovered might turn out to be. Having only had a single ecosphere on which to base their expectations, they had no way to arbitrate between hypotheses that held that life throughout the universe was likely to be DNA-based, or that DNA would turn out to be a strictly local phenomenon unrepeated anywhere else.

Matthew had always had more sympathy for the former opinion, not because he lent any credence to the panspermist myth—which held that life had originated elsewhere and arrived on Earth while being dispersed throughout the expanding cosmos—but because it seemed to him that natural selection operating in the struggle for existence in the primordial sludge would probably have found the same optimum solution to the business of genetic coding that would materialize elsewhere. In the absence of any comparative cases, however, the matter had been pure guesswork—until Frans Leitz's forbears had found the "sludge-world" whose bacteria employed a different molecule.

Armed with that foreknowledge, Lityansky and his fellows would have been less surprised than their newly defrosted colleagues to find that the new world's ecosphere also had a different coding-molecule. Indeed, Professor Lityansky might well have taken that as good evidence that DNA *was* a purely local phenomenon, unlikely to be repeated anywhere in the universe—given which, any would-be colonists of new worlds would simply have to take it as given that they could not expect to find conditions entirely to their liking.

"I wouldn't call it absurd," was what Matthew was prepared to say to Leitz at this stage. "People had argued about what might or might not qualify as an Earth-clone world long before *Hope* was a gleam in Shen Chin Che's eye. It wouldn't have been regarded as an extreme view to say that an ecosphere had to be DNA-based to qualify as a clone. On the other hand, we didn't set out with the proviso that we had to find DNA in order to found a colony. We set out with the intention of making the best of whatever we could find."

"Exactly," said Leitz. "And that's what we have to do. The fact that Earth came through its own ecocatastrophe doesn't make any difference to our quest; there was never any question of going *back*. And the fact that the other probes sent out in this general direction haven't located any other world that's even remotely Earth-like means that we simply *can't* pass up this chance. Isn't that so?"

"I can't answer that until I have more facts at my disposal," Matthew said, "But aren't you avoiding the most important issue of all? If this world is inhabited . . ."

"It isn't," Leitz was quick to say. "It was, but it's not now. The colony had been active for more than a year before the so-called city was found. It was overgrown to such an extent that it was virtually invisible from the air. Nothing else has shown up, in spite of increased probe activity. The people at Base Three found not the slightest evidence of recent habitation, until . . ." He stopped.

"Until Bernal was murdered," Matthew finished for him.

"By one of his colleagues," Leitz said, stubbornly. "The killer may have used a weapon tricked up to look like a local product, but it *must* have been a human hand that wielded it. The people at Base Three seem to be determined not to carry out a full and proper investigation of their own, so we had no choice but to wake Inspector Solari."

Matthew was still puzzled. "Are you implying that the people Bernal was working with are running some kind of scam?" he asked. "You think they're *pretending* that he was killed by aliens? Why?"

Leitz's discomfort deepened yet again. "I don't know," he said, defensively. "But there are certainly people at Base One who've added the possible continued existence of the aborigines—however unlikely the possibility may be—to the list of reasons why Professor Lityansky should never have initiated the landings. The people who want to withdraw from the planet are desperate for any justification they can find."

"So why not let the ones who want out withdraw? Wouldn't it be better to have a colony of committed volunteers than one whose members are fighting among themselves?" Matthew thought that he already knew the answer to that one, but he wanted to see Leitz's response.

It was, as he'd anticipated, almost explosive. "But that's the one thing we *can't* do!" the youth exclaimed. "If the colony is to be viable, it will eventually need the full repertoire of the skills possessed by the cargo—and even if one member of each notional pair decided to stay, that would still leave the colony with a dangerously depleted gene pool. It's absolutely vital that they *all* accept the necessity of making the colony work. You must see that, Professor Fleury. You *must.*"

Must I? Matthew thought.

Vince Solari's interest in genomics was limited, and he obviously wanted to get back to more immediate concerns. Matthew's reluctance to endorse Leitz's categorical imperative gave him the opportunity to butt in. "Why is the guard in the corridor wearing a gun, Mr. Leitz?" he asked, bluntly. "In fact, why should *anyone* aboard the ship be wearing a gun?"

Frans Leitz colored, but the greenish tint in his skin lent the blush a peculiar dullness. "It's purely a precaution," he said.

"I figured that," Solari came back. "What I want to know is: against *what?*"

"There have been . . . policy disagreements concerning the administration of the ship and the control of its resources," the boy admitted. "I'm really not competent to explain the details—I'm just a medical orderly, and a trainee at that. The captain will tell you everything. But it really is a precaution. No one on the ship has been injured, let alone killed, as a result of the . . . problem."

"But who, exactly, is the precaution intended to deter?" Mathew said, modifying Solari's question slightly without softening the insistence of the demand. "Are we talking about mutineers, or what?"

"I suppose so," the boy replied, steadfastly refusing to elaborate—but he must have read in Vince Solari's eyes that he wouldn't be let off so easily. "The captain will tell you all that. He can explain it far better."

"I'm sure he can," Matthew said, drily, "but . . ."

Frans Leitz had had enough. "Eight-zero," the boy said, as he turned to flee from the uncomfortable field of discussion.

"Before you go," Solari was quick to say, "can you give us a quick introduction to the equipment by our beds. There's so much we need to know that the sooner we can make a start ourselves the better equipped we'll be to ask questions of the captain."

Leitz hesitated, but he had no grounds for refusal—and he knew that if he were busy lecturing the two of them on basic equipment skills he could probably override more awkward questions with ease.

"Sure," he said, only a little less warmly than Matthew could have wished.

FIVE

When the first picture of the new world came up on the wallscreen Matthew caught his breath. He had thought himself more than ready for it, but the reality still took him by surprise.

The image reminded him, as he had expected, of the classic twentieth-century images of the Earth as seen from the moon, but the differences leapt out at him much more assertively than he had imagined. The new world's two moons were much smaller and closer than Earth's, and they were both in the picture, which had obviously been synthesized from photographs taken from *Hope* while she was much further away than her present orbit.

The second thing Matthew noticed, after absorbing the shock of the two moons, was the similarity of the clouds. It was as if his mind were making a grab for something reassuring, and that it was able to take some comfort from the notion that the old Earth and the new were clad in identical tattered white shirts.

But everything else was different.

The land masses were, of course, completely different in shape, but that was a trivial matter. The *striking* difference was a matter of color. Matthew, having been forewarned, was expecting to see purple, but he had somehow taken it for granted that it would be the land rather than the sea that would be imperial purple, and it took him a moment or two to reverse his first impression.

Even at its most intense, the purple of this world's land-based vegetation was paler than he had expected. It seemed somehow insulting to think in terms of *mauve* or *lilac*, although those shades were certainly the most common. So vague and careless had Matthew's anticipations been that he had not factored in the oceans in at all, and would not have been at all surprised to find them as blue as Earth's. They were not; they were gloriously and triumphantly purple, more richly and stridently purple than the land.

Matthew remembered that the first aniline dye to be synthesized from coal tar in Earth's nineteenth century had been dubbed Tyrian purple. That, presumably, was why Tyre had been added to the list of potential names for "the world." The murex, he supposed, must have been the source of the imperial purple of Rome, and there were probably mollusk-like creatures of a similar sort in the purple oceans of the new world, but Murex did not sound quite right to Matthew as the name of a world. Tyre and Ararat seemed somehow far more *fitting*.

Matthew might have paused for a while to wonder whether the oceans were so richly purple because they were abundantly populated by photosynthetic microorganisms and algae, or because of some unexpected trick of atmospheric refraction, but his companion had the keyboard and Solari was already racing ahead in search of more various, more intimate, and more detailed views, while Frans Leitz looked on approvingly. The former hypothesis, Matthew decided en passant, seemed more likely as well as more attractive—but so had the hypothesis that DNA would always be selected out by the struggle to produce true life from mere organic mire.

"Can you find a commentary?" Matthew asked.

Solari shook his head. "None available. I guess they haven't had time to add the voiceovers yet." He glanced at Leitz as he spoke.

"We didn't think a commentary was required," the crewman said.

Other surprises followed as the mute viewpoint moved a little closer to the surface. Matthew had not been expecting the desert areas to be so silvery, or the ice caps so neatly star-shaped. He saw both ice caps as the synthesized image rotated about two axes, always presenting a full disk to the AI-eye.

"The symmetry of the continents is a little weird," Leitz put in, obviously feeling some slight obligation to substitute for the missing commentary. "The polar island-continents are so similar in size and shape that some of the first observers thought that the planet had been landscaped by continental engineers. The star is nearly a billion years older than the sun, so evolution has had a lot longer to work here than it had on Earth, but Professor Lityansky reckons that the relative lack of axial tilt and tidal drag haven't added sufficient agitation to the surface conditions to move evolution along at a similar pace. He reckons that Earth was unusually lucky in that respect, and that's why we seem to be the first starfaring intelligences in this part of the galaxy. The surface isn't very active, volcanically speaking, and the climatic regimes are stable. The weather's fairly predictable in all latitudes, although it varies quite sharply from one part of the pattern to another."

The viewpoint was zooming in now, as if free-falling from orbit, then curving gracefully into a horizontal course a thousand meters or so above the surface.

The sky was bluish, but it had a distinct violet tinge, like an eerie echo of the vegetation.

At first, Matthew thought that the grassy plain over which the AI-eye was soaring wasn't so very different from an Earthly prairie. The lack of any comparative yardstick made it difficult to adjust the supposition, but when Leitz told him that the stalks bearing the complex crowns were between ten and twenty meters tall he tried to get things into a clearer perspective.

"The rigid parts of the plants aren't like wood at all," Leitz said. "More like glass. Professor Lityansky will explain the biochemistry."

There were very few tree-like forms on the plain, but when the point of view soared higher in order to pass over a mountain range, Matthew saw whole forests of structures that seemed to have as much in common with corals as with oaks or pines. They seemed to him to be the kind of trees that a nineteenth-century engineer—a steam-and-steel man—might have devised to suit a landscape whose primary features were mills and railroads: trees compounded out of pipes and wire, scaffolding and stamped plate. Given what Leitz had said about the structures being vitreous rather than metallic, the impression had to be reckoned illusory, but it still made the forests and "grasslands" seem radically un-Earthlike. If this world really could be counted as an Earth-clone, Matthew thought, it was a twin whose circumstances and experience had made a vast difference to its natural heritage.

When the low-flying camera eye finally reached the shore of a sea Matthew saw that its surface layer was indeed covered with a richer floating ecosystem than he had ever seen on any of Earth's waters. The inshore waters were dappled with huge rafts of loosely tangled weed, and the seemingly calm deeper waters were mottled with vast gellike masses. Matthew did not suppose for an instant that they really were amoebas five or fifty miles across, but that was the first impression they made on his mind. He tried to think in terms of leviathan jellyfish, gargantuan slime-molds, oceanic lava lamps or unusually glutinous oil slicks, but it didn't help. There was nothing in his catalog of Earthly appearances that could give him a better imaginative grip on what he was looking at.

It was difficult to make out much detail from the present height of the viewpoint, but that disadvantage was compensated by the sheer amount of territory that was covered. Matthew was able to see the black canyons splitting the polar ice caps, and the shifting dunes of the silvery deserts. He saw islands rising out of the sea like purple pincushions and he saw mountains rising out of the land like folds in a crumpled duvet.

The mountains had no craters; they did not seem to be the relics of volcanoes. Perhaps, Matthew mused, the continents of the New World had been as richly dotted with extinct and active volcanoes as the continents of Earth a billion years ago, but a billion years was a long time, even in the lifetime of a world. Perhaps, on the other hand, the New World had been just as different then, or even more different. If it qualified as an Earth-clone at all, it was because its atmosphere had much the same precious mix of gases as Earth's, calculated to sustain a similar carbon-hydrogen-nitrogen biochemistry, not because it was actually Gaea's twin sister. Perhaps *Earth-clone* was entirely the wrong word, applied too hastily and too ambitiously because truer clones had proved so very hard to find—but Matthew reminded himself of what he had told Leitz. He would be better able to make up his mind when he knew all the facts.

The viewpoint became even more intimate, picking out a strange collection of objects that looked like a huge, white diamond solitaire set amid a surrounding encrustation of tinier gems. The whole ensemble was situated on a low-lying island some twenty or twenty-five kilometers from one of the major continental masses.

"Base One," Leitz told them. "The soil inside the big dome was sterilized to a depth of six meters and reseeded with Earthly life, but there are dozens of experimental plots mixing the produce of the two ecospheres in the satellite domes."

"Is that where Delgado was killed?" Solari wanted to know.

"Oh, no—he was at Base Three, in the mountains of the broadleaf spur of Continent B."

"Continent B?" Matthew echoed. "You can't agree on a name for the world, you're numbering your bases and you're calling its continents after letters of the alphabet? No wonder you don't feel at home here."

Leitz didn't react verbally to his use of the word *you*, but the gaze of his green eyes seemed to withdraw slightly as he retorted: "It's not the crew's place to name the world or any of its features, and it's not the crew's fault that the colonists are so reluctant."

But it was the crew who selected and surveyed this world, and decided to call it an Earth-clone, Matthew said to himself. If the colonists have discovered that they've bitten off more than they can chew, why shouldn't they blame the people who woke them up with reckless promises? But why would the crew jump the gun? Why would they decide that the world was ripe for colonization if it wasn't? He didn't voice the questions, because maturing suspicions had made him wary and because an appointment had now been set for him to see the captain—the man with all the answers. He would be in a better position to listen and understand when his body had caught up with his brain and he was a little less tired.

"How big is Base Three, compared with Base One?" Solari asked, still clinging to his own tight focus on practical matters.

"Tiny," Leitz told him. "Only a couple of satellite domes. It wasn't part of the original plan—Base Two is in the mountain-spine of Continent A, only a few hundred kilometers from Base One, and there was no plan to establish a third base so far away from the first—but when the surveyor's eyes spotted the ruins the groundlings had to improvise. They're establishing supply dumps and airstrips in order to create a proper link, but it was very difficult to transport the first party, and we had to top up the personnel with a new drop."

"Why did it take so long to find the ruins?" Matthew asked.

"The overgrowing vegetation obscured what's left of the dwellings and broke up the lines of the fortifications. We had trouble surveying Continent B because it's very difficult to get signals back from ground level. Flying eyes are too small to carry powerful transmitters, and the crowns of the giant grasses and trees block them out. Standard beltphones aren't much better, so anyone calling from Base Three or its surrounds has to be sure to stand in the open."

"Can we get a picture of Base Three?" Solari interrupted.

Leitz played with the keyboard for a few moments, and the viewpoint shifted to a more intimate and slow-moving aerial view of hilly terrain.

To Matthew, who had seen the Andes and the Himalayas at close range, this seemed a fairly poor example of a mountain range, not so much because of its lack of elevation as the relatively gentle contours of its individual elements. There was a big river meandering through the lowlands, which the viewpoint followed from the edge of the grassy plain towards its distant source.

A couple of minutes went by before they saw the bubble-domes comprising the Base. It wasn't too hard to understand why the nearby ruins hadn't been easy to pick out from directly above, given that the treelike forms had taken it over so completely. Now that there were extensive patches of cleared ground and paths running between them it was easy to see the stark outlines of artificial structures, but it was impossible to tell how extensive the ruins were.

"You can just about see the outlines of the fortifications in the undulations of the overgrowth," Leitz said, pointing.

At first, because they followed the contours of the hillsides and because there were so many of them, Matthew thought that the "fortifications" to which Leitz was referring must really be terraces from which some or all of the enclosed soil had been leached by centuries of rainfall. But when he was able to compare cleared sections of the walls with the buildings at the core of the vast complex, the proportions suggested that they really *might* have been fortifications. Against what adversaries, he wondered, could a maze like that have been erected? What kind of enemy could have made such lunatic industry conceivable, let alone necessary?

Close-ups showed various sections of wall in much greater detail, including two into which pictures had been carved. The pictures were primitive and cartoonish, but Matthew drew in his breath sharply as he realized that the bipedal stick figures could have passed for a child's representation of human beings. Apart from the humanoid figures the sketches also showed arrays of bulbous entities, vaguely reminiscent of obese corncobs, and much bigger structures, triangular in silhouette, that might have been conical or pyramidal.

"They're *people!*" Solari exclaimed.

"They appear to have been humanoid," Leitz admitted.

"So what killed them off?" the policeman wanted to know.

"That's one of the things the people at Base Three are trying to find out," Leitz said. "It isn't easy, because their specialisms are only peripherally related to the job. The Chosen People didn't include any archaeologists—the nearest thing we could find when we thawed out personnel to make up the second half of the team was an anthropologist."

"Why are you so sure they're extinct?" Matthew asked. "If your flying eyes can't get information back from ground level, the whole continent must qualify as terra incognita. The fact that the city-dwellers abandoned the site doesn't mean that their cousins aren't still around."

"We've done what we can to find them," the young man assured him. "Agricultural activity should be easy enough to detect, even at a far more restricted level, and even hunter-gatherers need fires. If anyone had lit a single cooking fire in the last three years, anywhere on the world's surface, we'd have been able to home in on it. If they were alive somewhere out in the long grass, invisible from the air, they'd have to have gone back to the very beginning, eating what they hunt and gather in its raw state. That seems unlikely. Incredible, even. The people on the ground who believe that the aliens are still around have their own reasons for wanting to believe it."

"The human race had some pretty narrow squeaks," Matthew said, pensively. "There used to be more genetic variation in a single chimpanzee troop than in the entire human race, before chimps became extinct. Mitochondrial Eve had lived not much more than a hundred and forty thousand years before *Hope*'s odyssey began. Animals as big as humans are more vulnerable to catastrophes of all kinds than their smaller and humbler cousins. If these guys had never domesticated fire, they'd be even more vulnerable than our ancestors. Still . . ."

"Which side was Delgado on?" Solari asked Frans Leitz. "On the extinction question, I mean."

"I don't know—but he was enthusiastic about building the boat."

"What boat?" Solari asked.

"I think it was Dr. Gherardesca's idea. She's the anthropologist. She figured that if it wasn't possible to recover data about ground-level activity in the grasslands from flying eyes, the best way to do it would be to take a boat downriver. It was just about ready when Professor Delgado was killed, although they'd asked for one last consignment of equipment—we're holding that so that we can send you down with it."

"How many other people were working at Base Three along with Delgado?" Solari persisted.

"Seven."

"Seven!" Matthew could hardly believe it. "You found a ruined city made by intelligent humanoids, and you sent *seven* people to investigate it! The biggest news story in history, and *seven* people is all you can spare to follow it up."

"There *were* eight," Leitz pointed out, blushing grayly yet again as his discomfort increased by an order of magnitude. "And will be again, once you're there." He was already turning away to resume his interrupted retreat. "I really must go now. You'll soon get the hang of the keypads if you keep playing with them. There's plenty more library material. Someone will pick you up when it's time for you to see Captain Milyukov."

SIX

V ince Solari waited until the young man had left the room before saying: "Milyukov? Wasn't the original captain called Ying?"

"That was seven hundred years ago," Matthew pointed out. "*Captain* isn't a hereditary title. A ship's crew has to be run on strictly meritocratic principles—supposedly."

"Why supposedly?" Solari had relaxed, allowing the keyboard to hang loosely from his tired hand. The image on the screen had frozen while displaying the internally lit bubble-domes of Base Three, strangely forlorn in a gathering evening that was turning everything purple to matt black.

"Seven hundred years is a long time," Matthew said, "and the ship was always capable of running itself between big decisions. Five or six lifetimes, maybe as many as twenty generations, can produce considerable social and political changes, and meritocracies always have a habit of backsliding."

Solari nodded, slowly. "I see," he said. "There's another factor that needs consideration too. Most of the Chosen—including you, I guess—were frozen down before the new generation of plagues had begun to do their worst. Interplanetary distances weren't quarantine enough to keep the chiasmalytic transformers and their vicious kin on Earth. At least some of the crew must have been sterilized before *Hope* left the system. They must have been forced to adopt whatever countermeasures allowed the reconstruction of Earthly society."

"How bad did things get before you left?" Matthew asked, quietly.

"I was frozen down twenty-four years after you," Solari reminded him. "The chiasmalytic transformers were running riot. Nobody had given up hope of finding a cure, but they were stripping the eggs out of the ovaries of aborted fetuses and little girls, and splitting viable embryos so that they could keep the clones as spares . . . all kinds of weird stuff. And every week seemed to bring news of some new breakthrough in longevity technology that *might* beat the Miller Effect, and *might* put us all on the escalator to emortality, and *might* make it possible for civilization to go on forever even if no one ever had another baby for as long as the ecosphere lasted. Not that it made a jot of difference to the doomsayers and the defeatists, the neohysterics or the hyperhedonists. You missed some crazy times, Matt. Times that only a prophet could have relished. I remember seeing you on TV, you know, when I was a kid. Couldn't really miss you, until you dropped out of sight."

"If you hadn't been a kid," Matthew told him, leaning back against his bed so as to take some of the weight off his aching feet, "you'd have understood that I was never the kind of prophet who could take delight in saying *I told you so*. I knew what the chiasmalytic transformers might do—what they were *made* to do—but I never relished the thought."

"Made to do? I remember you as a bit of a ranter, but I didn't have you pegged as a conspiracy theorist. The official line always said that the seetees were Mother Nature's ultimate backlash—Gaea's last line of self-defense. The idea that they were a final solution cooked up in a lab was supposed to be a neohysteric fantasy."

Matthew winced slightly at the casual suggestion that he had been *a bit of a ranter*, although people had called him a lot worse things. "It matters not whence Nemesis comes," he said, recalling another of his not-so-classic sound bites as if it had only been yesterday when he had last deployed it. "It only matters where she goes."

"They might have found a cure after I was frozen down, I guess," Solari said, pensively. "We ought to look that up, oughtn't we? We've got a lot of history to catch up on."

"And not enough time," Matthew said. "Not until we're down on the surface, at any rate, and probably not then. Still, it looks as if your job won't be as hard as it might have been, so you might be able to get back to your homework fairly soon."

"Seven suspects," Solari mused, lifting the keypad up to his face and studying the layout of the keys with minute care. "Eight if you count the hypothetical alien. It doesn't sound too difficult—but I'll be way too late to get much from the crime scene. Until I have the facts . . ."

"If the murderer *is* an alien," Matthew observed, "I don't suppose we'll attempt to bring him to trial. The discovery would be far more momentous than any mere murder. The greatest discovery ever—and they seem almost determined not to make it. Maybe the crew don't quite understand, but the people fresh from the freezer . . . I can't understand *their* attitude at all."

Solari obviously didn't share Matthew's wonderment. "Do you want to go on playing tourist flyby," he asked, "or shall I try to find something more interesting?"

"Try to find something more interesting," was Matthew's vote. He had seen enough purple vegetation for the time being.

As yet, though, Solari wasn't sufficiently familiar with the equipment to be able to exit from the image-catalog, and he stopped trying when the sequence moved on to animal life.

In the absence of any oral explanation it was difficult to determine the principles according to which the images had been filed and organized, but the first impression formulated in Matthew's mind was that the new world was improbably rich in soft-bodied invertebrates. He couldn't remember exactly what a murex looked like, but there was such a wealth of sluglike, clamlike and snaillike creatures among the images on the screen that he figured that there had to be a murex-analogue in there somewhere.

The worms were even more multitudinous, but worms were fundamentally boring, and Solari kept his thumb on the button that fast-forwarded through that section of the array before slowing down to take a closer look at various entities that seemed more interestingly chimerical.

"What's *that?*" Solari demanded, finally making use of his discovery of a pause function. He obviously thought that Matthew, being a biologist of sorts, ought to have been able to master the fundamental taxonomy of the local ecosphere by courtesy of the hectic sequence of glances he had laid on.

"I've no idea," Matthew confessed. The creature in question looked like a cross between a giant liver fluke and a sea anemone, but he was biologist enough not to want to issue a description of that crude kind. The image was a film clip, which showed the creature gliding along like a snail, but the tentacles sprouting from its humped back remained limp and it wasn't possible for Matthew to come to a firm decision as to their function. "It's not very big," he pointed out. "The scale on the baseline puts it at twenty or thirty centimeters from end to end."

More film clips followed, slowly working up to images of more complex creatures. Eventually, Matthew supposed, they would reach fishy things, amphibians and other vertebrate-analogues, but he was not sure how many orders of invertebrates they might have missed. Were there really so few arthropod-analogues?

"How about *that* one?" Solari followed up, this time pointing at something that looked rather like a translucent horseshoe crab. Matthew wondered whether the impression that the creatures he was seeing were soft-bodied might be an illusion born of their mauve coloration, but when this one began to move—more rapidly than he had expected—he judged that the outer tegument was too flexible to qualify as a "shell."

Solari had to scroll through many more quasi-molluscan and vermiform organisms of widely varying dimensions before the tape reached creatures that had any sort of backbone, but he got there in the end. The analogies between these creatures and their Earthly equivalents were so obvious that Matthew's faith in convergent evolution was soon restored. Although the new world's Gaea-clone hadn't been able to select out DNA as champion coding-molecule, she obviously knew lots of ways to design a perfectly adequate fish. There were things like mudskippers and land-going tadpoles, polished snakes and glassy froglike forms.

Even after an hour's trawling, though, Matthew hadn't seen much that could pass for fur and feathers. Even the local rat-analogues seemed to be naked. Unless they had contrived to miss out on the relevant folder, bird- and mammal-analogues were rare. And yet, there had been enough lemuroids around to produce humanoids, and enough humanoids to produce a race of city-builders that might have been alive and active when Mitochondrial Eve was mothering the entire human race.

One thing that Matthew didn't see while the parade continued was any immature organisms: no nests, no eggs, no infants. Even when there were shots of entire herds of grazers, there was no sign of any young. Nor, for that matter, could he see any sign of secondary sexual characteristics on the adult organisms. In the absence of a commentary, however, he was reluctant to take these apparent absences at face value.

"There must be *some* real animals," Solari complained, meaning that there ought to be more mammal-equivalents.

"There ought to be some quasi-arthropodans too," Matthew said. "Even if this world's tacit planner didn't have the same fondness for beetles as ours, there'd be no sense in missing out on a whole range of viable adaptive forms. Insects are among the most efficient products of Earthly evolution. If the rats had crashed out with the humans, the cockroaches would have inherited the Earth."

"I can do without spiders, myself," Solari told him. Matthew didn't want to insult him with the pedantic insistence that arachnids weren't insects, so he let the comment pass.

It eventually turned out, though, that there were a few monkey analogues and even a few flying creatures, although they were more like furless bats and flying squirrels than birds. Natural selection on Ararat-Tyre didn't seem to have come up with hair or feathers, although it had just about mastered scales.

Solari breathed a deep sigh of satisfaction when he found the monkey-analogues, as if they had always been the only worthy objects of his search. They were pale purple, just like everything else, but they didn't seem as conspicuously alien as the vegetation that surrounded them. Indeed, they seemed quaintly familiar, save only for the fact that they had no young, nor any sign of the kinds of fleshly apparatus employed by Earthly mammals to produce and nurture young.

Matthew noted that the bat-analogues were all tiny, though not as tiny as insects. Some of the monkey-analogues grew quite tall—though none were human-sized—but they were very lean and lithe, and somehow rather *mercurial*. There was nothing reminiscent of a cow or a hippopotamus, still less of a large dinosaur. The top predators seemed to be stealth-hunters. There were shots of creatures resembling glorified weasels pouncing on their prey and stunning them with the aid of stings mounted in their tongues like hypodermic syringes.

Matthew found the lemuroids strangely unsettling, because rather than in spite of the fact that they were uncannily similar in most respects to the extinct Earthly lemurs he had seen on film. It wasn't so much that they had the same huge forward-looking eyes and the same gripping hands. It was the strangely elastic way they moved—slowly when contented, rapidly when panicked by the advent of a weasel-analogue—and their perpetual nervous alertness. There was obviously something strange about the way their limbs were articulated, but that was only part of it. Although he knew that he had to be even more careful of the dangers of anthropomorphic thinking here than he had on Earth, the lemuroids seemed to Matthew to be perfect incarnations of an anxiety so deep as to be blatant paranoia. Their feet were mostly equipped with elongated toes that reminded Matthew of the feet of the crewpeople, modified for a way of life that humans had never been able to follow in Earth's gravity-well.

On Earth, Matthew knew, the genus *Homo* had descended from a long line of tough and sturdy apes: apes that had learned to swagger like baboons; stand-up-and-fight apes; playground-bully apes. Their near cousins the gorillas—yet another species Matthew had only seen on film—had taken the gentle giant route, while the hominids had clung most steadfastly to the mad psycho alternative, but the whole family had been unmistakably *butch*. There were no butch lemuroids in the movies taken by *Hope*'s flying eyes—so what kind of ancestry had the humanoids had? Had they been the last of a line to go down to inglorious extinction? If so, why had the entire batch of strategies failed? If not, how had the ancestors of the seemingly timorous extant lemuroids contrived to produce something as amazing as a city-builder?

If adaptive radiation had ever been as prolific here as it had been on Earth, Matthew thought, an extremely high fraction of its inventions must have been consigned to the dustbin of paleontology. Perhaps it hadn't been. Perhaps, if this had *always* been a much quieter world, nature had never had to be so recklessly ingenious in making up for mass extinctions. Perhaps this ambiguous home-from-home had not required nearly so many trials and errors before discovering the phylum and the family that human vanity had always placed at the pinnacle of creation.

"What do you think?" Solari asked, as the sequence finally cut out of its own accord, having presumably run to one of its potential termini.

"Maybe we came in late and missed the arthropods," Matthew mused. "If not, there's a conspicuous shortage of exoskeletons. Maybe the local coding systems can't make chitin. On the other hand, the whole animal kingdom seems a trifle anemic, except for slugs and squishy worms, so maybe it's not much good at bone either. On the whole, there seems to be a noticeable lack of tough stuff, of no-nonsense leverage and substantial solidity."

"How odd would that be?" Solari asked, although he wore the expression of a man who didn't expect to be able to understand the answer.

"It's hard to say, when we have only one other case for comparison," Matthew admitted. "An adult insect is only a maggot's way of making more maggots, of course, but if the gimmick worked so well on Earth, why not here, where there certainly doesn't seem to be any shortage of maggoty things? The lack of birds and mammals might not be surprising if the mammals that do exist hadn't contrived to evolve a humanoid—albeit one that may no longer exist."

"Maybe Earth was the beetle planet, and this one's the slug and snail capital of the universe," Solari suggested. "It *could* have been worse." Matthew guessed that he was probably thinking about spiders again.

Matthew nodded sympathetically. "It certainly looks like it," he agreed. "Unless we only got half the story. It's difficult to believe that nothing flies down there but a few itty-bitty bats and the time."

The door of their room opened, making them both start slightly. Time had indeed flown while they were engrossed. Eight-zero had apparently arrived, and the someone Leitz had promised had arrived to lead them to the captain. The way Solari nodded to the newcomer told Matthew that it must be Riddell, the man who had been standing guard outside their door.

Matthew inspected the holstered sidearm, and decided that it was indeed a darter. The armed man's suitskin was the same color as Frans Leitz's, but its present shape had been organized to give the impression of sharper edges and physical efficiency. On the whole, though, he looked like a soft person pretending to be solid, not a natural tough guy. As such, he seemed to fit the general situation surprisingly well.

It was not until Matthew raised himself up, putting all his weight back on his feet, that he realized how soft he too seemed to have become. He cursed himself for not taking the opportunity to lie down and get some proper rest, but he knew that he still had an enormous amount to learn, and not much time to learn it, if he were to be able to take a significant hand in the unfolding history of the new world.

"Okay," he said to their appointed protector. "Take us to your leader." It wasn't until he saw the blank look on Riddell's face, signaling a complete failure to recognize and appreciate the cliché, that Matthew finally began to feel the width and depth of the cultural gulf that separated the two of them.

SEVEN

The corridors through which Matthew and Vince Solari were conducted were narrow and mazy, with no ninety-degree turns. They reminded Matthew of the subsurface lunar habitat in which he'd stayed before joining the frozen Chosen, but that wasn't surprising. That too had been a mini-ecosphere located within a much larger, essentially inhospitable, mass. He guessed that the principal differences between the two habitats would only be obvious on a much larger scale—a scale that was difficult to appreciate from within.

The Mare Moscoviense maze had been a cone whose sharp end pointed toward the moon's center of gravity; life on the kind of space-habitat that *Hope* now was had to be organized in cylindrical layers, in which "down" was also "out" because gravity was simulated by spin. Knowing this, Matthew found nothing surprising in the fact that the spaces inhabited by *Hope*'s mini-Gaea were curved and intricately curled. Nor was there anything particularly startling about the fact that so many of the side passages were dark; many parts of Mare Moscoviense had been fitted with human-responsive switches that provided light where and when it was needed and allowed darkness to fall when there were no human eyes.

What did surprise him, a little, was the dust. Mare Moscoviense had not been an unduly tidy environment, and its walls had accumulated a rich heritage of ingeniously stubborn graffiti, but it had been relentlessly swept clean by resident nanobots programmed to collect flakes of human skin and other associated organic debris for recycling. *Hope* must have started out on its long journey equipped with similar nanobots, but they seemed to have fallen into disrepair. Dust had been allowed to accumulate on surfaces and in countless nooks and crannies, to the extent that it supported its own ecosystems of mites and predatory arachnids. Cobwebs could been seen dangling from ceilings and masking high-set corners.

Matthew was reluctant to take it for granted that *Hope*'s dust was a symptom of decay or slovenliness, but when he added the observation to other evidence of unrepaired malfunctions—wall-panels moved to expose bundles of cables; makeshift handles glued to doors that should have been automatic; cracked keypads and taped-over screens—the general picture did seem to be one of lost or forsaken control.

It was only to be expected, Matthew knew, that an ecosphere and mechanisphere as small as *Hope* would suffer a continuous erosion of organization. The comet core into which the original metal ship had been inserted had been intended to serve as a source of organic materials as well as providing invaluable momentum for the initial phase of the journey, but Shen would have been extremely fortunate to find an entire wish list of elements in its stonier and ferrous components. On the other hand, *Hope* had been in the new system for three years, and if the system contained an Earthlike planet it must also be rich in other supernoval debris. *Hope*'s drones should have been able to scavenge an abundance of new resources from the outer system while the decelerating ship plotted a course toward its present orbit. The ship's environments should have undergone a spectacular renaissance by now, unless the deterioration of its machines had become chronic, or its manpower seriously depleted.

It was, eventually, impossible to resist the conclusion that something was seriously rotten in the state of *Hope*, and in its mission to found a new world. The people on the surface were at odds with the crew, and seemingly with one another, and the crew seemed far from contented in their own little empire.

But what can you expect in a world without TV, Matthew thought. If the only person who ever broadcasts to the whole population is the captain, it's no wonder that there's no social adhesive to hold things together, no force of consensus.

It was wishful thinking, of course, but he couldn't help dallying with the notion that there was nothing amiss here that couldn't be corrected by the voice of a professional prophet: a man trained not merely to see the bigger picture but to provide it with an appropriate soundtrack.

Seen from another viewpoint, Matthew decided, there was something rather homely about the sight of dust-filmed shelves and broken latches. They could be taken as reminders of Earth's surface, of the world in which Matthew had grown from infancy to adulthood. Nothing here seemed to be *alien* to him, except perhaps the purple face of the planet they were circling—and he did not find it at all difficult, as yet, to think of that as an authentic Earth-clone nurtured and educated in a slightly different fashion.

The crewman leading him through *Hope*'s corridors, by contrast, had presumably never known any environment but the ship; to Riddell and all his fellows, *Hope* and *Hope* alone was home, refuge, and prison.

With what uneasy eyes must the crewpeople regard the kinds of images that Matthew and Vince Solari had been studying? To them, Matthew decided, the new world must be exactly as exotic, and as utterly alien, as Earth.

They passed other crewpeople in the corridors, often having to swing their shoulders in order to pass by without making contact, but the crewpeople did not seem to regard them with any conspicuous curiosity. At first, Matthew put this down to the fact that any novelty value that the reawakened had possessed three years ago must be long gone now. There was, however, something odd in the character of their disinterest, as if it were contrived or pretended. They put him in mind of extras on a TV set, whose function was to fade into the background—but he was too curious about them to accept that kind of bid for invisibility.

The crewpeople varied as much as might be expected of people whose ancestors had been plucked from half a hundred different Earthly nations, but they were all lean of limb, they all moved with a graceful athleticism, and they all had somatically modified feet. They all went seemingly barefoot, the smartsuit overlays on their long-toed feet as transparent as those on their hands, and their gait was peculiar. Living in half-gravity, they had not the same need as Earthpeople for stout, supportive legs. They were still walkers, clinging to a pedestrian way of life in their curving corridors, but many of them would have to spend at least part of their lives closer to *Hope*'s central axis, where they weighed much less—and even those who did not *have* to do so had the option. At the heart of the planetoid legs would be virtually useless—but an extra pair of gripping limbs would not.

Matthew could not help comparing *Hope*'s "native population" to the lean and lithe mammal-analogues of the as-yet-nameless Ararat at which the ship had recently arrived. Matthew wondered whether his own thick thighs seemed ugly as well as clumsy to the crewpeople, and whether his lightly shod and stub-toed feet seemed lumpen and deformed. The somatic modifications adopted by the crew—and there must be others, he realized, in addition to the long toes—were essentially discreet, but their subtlety did not make them any less unsettling. The surface gravity of the new world was 0.92 of Earth's, he had been told—but he had also been told that the remaining 8 percent made more difference than one might imagine. In much the same way, the slight alterations to human form that the crew had adopted made more difference than Matthew could have imagined on the basis of his acquaintance with Earthly "cosmetic engineering." The same principle must apply in reverse; his stouter legs, stubby toes, and sturdier frame must seem alien as well as ugly to the crew.

Solari and I must be stronger by far than they are, Matthew said to himself. We're still adapted to Earthly gravity, whereas they're born and bred for half-weight. They may be the gymnasts and long-jumpers of the interplanetary Olympics, but we're the weightlifters and shot-putters.

Within a moment of framing the thought he pulled back from it, regretting the competitive impulse that had framed it, and wondering whether that same instinct might be partly responsible for the tensions that existed between crew and "cargo."

He would have followed the line of thought further had he not been interrupted by the sudden clamor of someone shouting his surname. At first, because of the curvature of the corridor, he could not tell from what direction the shout came, but as he looked around he realized that it must have come from a side-branch which he, Riddell, and Solari had just passed. Already, however, the extras on the set had ceased to be mere background and had made a busy crowd of themselves. The space behind him was filled in with remarkable rapidity by passers-by intent on forming a queue—and when he tried to turn around, the queue would not even stop, let alone open its ranks to let him retrace his steps. The crewmen were light, and far from powerful, but they could occupy space as insistently as anyone, and Matthew could not thrust a way through without resorting to actual violence.

"We're nearly there, Professor Fleury," Riddell called back to him—but Matthew suspected that the loudness of the call was intended as much to drown out the continued appeals of whoever had tried to speak to him as to give him information.

Matthew overcame his automatic hesitation quickly enough, and tried to thrust a way through the suddenly gathered crowd. Mere rudeness made no impact, and he actually had to throw his weight at the people blocking his way. Had it been a straightforward barging contest he would have won with ease, but they were far too clever for that. They moved so that his arms met empty air—but his clumsy feet had nowhere to go.

In effect, they meekly allowed him to trip over their clever feet—but they were far from careless of the damage he might do to their toes. Even as he stumbled they began a litany of complaint that really did drown out the voice of whoever had called out.

Matthew could not see what was going on in the side-corridor because he could not force a way back to it, but the person who had tried to attract his attention had obviously made as little headway as he.

When Riddell helped him back to his feet, Matthew had to admire the slickness with which the operation had been accomplished. No one else in the corridor was carrying a sidearm, and no one else was an obvious member of an escort party, but everyone there had been ready to act in concert as soon as anyone unauthorized to do so attempted to make contact with the two defrosters.

"What's going on?" Solari demanded of Riddell, his detective instincts immediately coming into play. "Who was the man who called out? Why was he not allowed to talk to Dr. Fleury?"

"I'm very sorry, professor," Riddell said, ignoring Solari and addressing himself solely to Matthew. "These corridors are always busy, and we've had to cultivate skills and etiquette for coping with that. You're not used to it, so you can't help being clumsy. These people really should have got used to giving colonists more leeway."

There was an immediate clamor of apology as the people who had tripped him up assured him that it was entirely their fault—

but the wall of flesh remained quite impregnable. No one moved a centimeter to make way for him. There was no way for him to go but forward.

"It's okay," Matthew said to Solari. "An accident." But while he said it he was looking into the green eyes of their guide, observing the reflexive hostility of the adamantine stare that met his own half-contemptuous glare. He really does think he's at war, Matthew thought. However this conflict first arose, it's infected each and every one of them.

"No harm done," Riddell said, tugging gently on Matthew's arm to urge him forward again.

"None at all," Matthew assured him, deciding that from now on, he had to exercise all possible caution in his dealings with the crew. He allowed himself to be urged into action again, and only glanced back once to marvel at the way in which the sudden queue had melted away.

As they resumed their progress through the curved corridors, Matthew followed the train of thought. These people presumably no longer had the commitment to the mission that had carried their forefathers out of the solar system. It had only required five lifetimes of isolation, and maybe twice as many generations, to turn them into a new species with their own ideas and objectives. Whatever else they wanted, they probably wanted rid of every sleeper in their vaults. They wanted rid of the past, of the pressure of inherited obligations. They wanted their freedom. But how far were they prepared to go to get it? And how fast would their remaining inhibitions decay if the awakened sleepers remained obdurate in their insistence that *Hope* belonged to *them* and had no reason for being except to serve *their* purposes and answer *their* demands?

That, Matthew realized, must be the true cause of the rebellious attitude simmering on the planet's surface. There was a matter of principle at stake. The would-be colonists were trying to recover and assert the authority that was, in their eyes, their *right*. But where was Shen Chin Che, the owner of the Ark and guarantor of that right?

"This is worse than I thought," Solari whispered in his ear.

"Whispering is probably futile," Matthew whispered back. "They can hear everything, if they want to—and they're probably interested enough to listen hard."

Their guide paused before a door that seemed no grander than the rest. It opened when he brushed the keypad with his fingers, but he did not follow them through. Presumably, he remained on guard just as he had while they were in their temporary quarters.

EIGHT

The room to which they had been brought was luxurious, after a fashion, and reassuringly personalized in its decoration. Captain Milyukov was a family man, and his walls proudly proclaimed the fact. He appeared to have at least four children, and perhaps as many as six, although three of the faces smiling from the photographic ensembles were so physically distinct from him and from one another that they seemed highly unlikely to be biologically related. It did not seem inconceivable to Matthew, however, that Milyukov might have been biologically related to his ultimate predecessor as captain. Although the cast of his features was not as flamboyantly Oriental as Shen Chin Che's, and the color of his skin was the same verdigrised parchment hue as Frans Leitz's, he looked more typical of *Hope*'s first cadre of masters than his name had suggested.

For some reason, Matthew took heart from that—but he was still anxious to know exactly what had become of Shen Chin Che, and glad that he now had an opportunity to find out.

"My name is Konstantin Milyukov," the captain told them, as he stood up to greet them. "You are Professor Fleury, of course, and you are Inspector Solari." He ushered them to high-backed armchairs clad in some kind of cultured leather. Milyukov's gestures seemed strangely grandiose to Matthew's Earth-educated eyes—more so than Frans Leitz's, even though the medical orderly had also been adapted by long habit to the low gravity. The captain took a third chair, which had been positioned to form an isosceles triangle with those set for his visitors, with Milyukov at the peak. He didn't offer them food or drink.

"I wish that I could welcome you both to better circumstances," the captain went on, "but you will already have gathered that this is something of an emergency. I wish that it had not been necessary to awaken you until the colony was on a much firmer footing, but our plans have been overtaken by events. We all need to know exactly how Bernal Delgado died, and why the people at Base Three are refusing to reveal the identity of his murderer."

"Refusing?" Solari echoed. "Are you sure they're refusing? Perhaps they don't know who killed him, or why."

"One or two of them may not know," Milyukov admitted. "Perhaps as many as four—but if those innocent of any involvement had mounted their own investigation in a methodical manner, they would have been able to find out easily enough what happened. Perhaps negligence held them back, or perhaps they were unprepared to face up to what they might find. In any case, the situation requires a newcomer with a proper sense of duty. To tell you the truth, Inspector Solari, I do not expect this to be a particularly challenging case, even if you arrive at Base Three to find a solid conspiracy of liars—but we do need you to ensure that charges are brought and that the truth of this sad charade becomes clear."

"Who's *we*?" Solari wanted to know.

"Everybody," Milyukov replied, without hesitation. "You will have gathered, of course, that there are disagreements aboard *Hope* as well as conflicts on the surface, but it is in everybody's interests to know why Professor Delgado was killed, in order that the rumors that have begun to circulate can be quashed. It is in everyone's interests to know the truth."

"Except the murderer," Solari observed, "and anyone shielding the murderer. If, as you seem to think, there are at least seven people shielding the murderer, I'm inclined to wonder why they're so conspicuously uninterested in the truth."

"Sometimes," Milyukov said, "people intent on attaining a certain end become rather short-sighted. They sacrifice honesty to the cause of winning the argument—but in the long run, an argument won by dishonesty always leads to disaster."

"Can we cut the crap?" Solari said. "So far as I can tell, you want the colony to stay here, and you want all the people who were frozen down before the ship left the solar system down on the surface. You presumably have the power to attain that result regardless of what anyone else wants, simply by waking up the sleepers a few at a time and shuttling them down whether they like it or not, but I guess you haven't yet resorted to that kind of solution because you still want to win the argument and you still think it's winnable. You want me to find out who killed Delgado because you think it will help you win the argument. How?"

Milyukov didn't seem to be at all disturbed by the full-frontal assault. "It is in everyone's best interests that the colony succeed," he said, mildly. "If it were to fail, that would be a catastrophe from everyone's point of view. There is a faction on the surface that claims that it is impossible for humans to remain on the surface without precipitating an ecocatastrophe more devastating than the one that was threatening Earth when you and your companions decided to leave it behind—and that the possibility that the planet is inhabited by intelligent humanoids makes that doubly unacceptable. It is my belief that Bernal Delgado was killed because he believed that he had discovered something vital to the settlement of this debate. I believe the crude pretense that he was killed by an alien was intended to favor the cause of those who want to abandon the colony—a cause that he did not support."

"Are you certain of that?" Solari asked.

"I have no reason to think otherwise," Milyukov said, blithely ignoring the fact that it was not at all the same thing. "Delgado certainly intended to travel downriver, but he never gave any vocal support to those of his colleagues who looked on the expedition as a straightforward attempt to prove the continued existence of the humanoids. If they do exist, of course, I want to find them as badly as anyone—but I want the matter settled. I need you to put a stop to this ridiculous pretense that Delgado might have been killed by an alien, inspector."

"And why, exactly," Matthew put in, "do you need me?"

Milyukov's eyes were not quite as green as Leitz's or Riddell's, but their relative dullness did not make their gaze seem less penetrative.

"For exactly the same reason, professor," the captain said. "To discover the truth—if you can. I've studied your background, just as I've studied the inspector's, but I don't hold your reputation against you. I've seen tapes of your TV performances, but I know that you began your career as an entirely reputable scientist."

Matthew had been damned with faint praise before, but this seemed a trifle unwarranted. He had always been an entirely reputable scientist, and his TV presence had never compromised his scientific integrity.

"Bernal Delgado was my friend," Matthew observed. "I'll do my very best to take up where he left off."

"And you will also want to see justice done in the matter of your friend's murder," Milyukov said. There was no overt trace of sarcasm in the captain's voice, but Matthew was reasonably sure that the man was completely insincere. Matthew could not believe that he had been brought back from frozen sleep because the captain believed that he was a potential ally. His acquaintance with Shen Chin Che was probably sufficient to make him a potential enemy, in the captain's eyes. There was a diplomatic game in progress, and his awakening must surely have been a concession to the people on the ground who had demanded that Bernal must be replaced, in order that his work might continue.

Matthew decided that it was time to follow Solari's example and try to cut through the crap. "Where's Shen Chin Che?" he asked.

Milyukov was ready for him; the glaucous gaze did not waver. "Somewhere on the microworld," he said, calmly. "I don't know where, exactly. It *is* a microworld now, of course, although the recently awakened habitually refer to it as a ship. If *Hope* really were a mere ship, a man could hardly contrive to hide for long, but her inner structure now has the floor space of a sizable Earthly town."

"Shen's in *hiding*?" Matthew said, incredulously. "Why?" He already knew why, of course. Shen had built the Ark. Shen had *owned* the Ark. Shen must have come out of SusAn believing that he still owned the Ark, and that he had the final voice in any adventure undertaken by the Ark. The crew had obviously taken a different view—but they had been unable to persuade Shen to align his view with theirs, and they had been unable to hold on to him when he had decided to go his own way.

"Because he laid claim to an authority that was no longer his," was Milyukov's version, "and because he resorted to violence in a hopeless attempt to reclaim it. He, more than anyone else, is responsible for the deterioration of the relationship between crew and colonists, and for the factional divisions that have subsequently arisen."

"He was one of the prime movers in the construction of the four Arks," Matthew pointed out. "Second in importance only to Narcisse himself. *Hope* was his personal contribution to the great quest. You can hardly blame him for harboring proprietorial sentiments."

"Shen Chin Che did not build the original *Hope*," Milyukov retorted, flatly. "He did not shape a single hull-plate, nor did he drive home a single rivet. He merely directed the flow of finance, and the money that he regarded as his was, in fact, the product of long-term dishonest manipulation of markets and financial institutions. Perhaps, within the corrupt economic and political system that then embraced Earth and the extraplanetary extensions of Earthly society, that was sufficient to establish ownership to the original vessel, but even if that claim were justified, *Hope* is a very different structure now. We—the crew—were the builders of the new *Hope*, in a perfectly literal sense. We planned the reconstruction, and we carried it out. *Hope* is ours now, and always will be."

"Are you telling me there's been a mutiny?" Matthew said, knowing well enough what Milyukov's counterclaim would be but wanting to hear it formally stated.

"What I'm telling you, Professor Fleury," the captain retorted, coldly, "is that there has been a *revolution*. *Hope*'s crew and cargo have been liberated from the crude restraints imposed by the obsolete political and economic system that was temporarily in force when the original *Hope* was constructed."

Matthew did not want to reply too swiftly to this news. He knew perfectly well that 700 years was a long time in the evolution of a human society, even one that was probably no more than a few hundred strong. It was not difficult to imagine that successive generations of crewmen could have come to a notion of their role in the scheme of things quite different from that imagined by their original employers. It might have been stranger had they contrived to avoid coming to the conclusion, by slow degrees, that the ship they were reshaping again and again was *theirs* and ought to remain *theirs*.

Solari was not as shy as Matthew. "A *revolution*," he repeated, guardedly. "A *socialist* revolution, you mean?"

"It's not a word we use," the captain informed him, "but labels are unimportant. What matters is that we, the makers and inhabitants of the new *Hope*, have set aside all the claims made by the original *Hope*'s so-called owners, on the grounds that they have no proper moral foundation."

"But what kind of new society are we talking about?" Solari demanded. "A democracy, or an autocracy? Are you telling us that *you* run everything now, or do we still get a vote?"

"It's not as simple as that," Milyukov said, as Matthew had expected him to.

"You must always have known that the Chosen wouldn't play ball," Solari went on, recklessly. "So you decided to get rid of them at the earliest opportunity. They were promised an Earth-clone, and they don't think this world qualifies—but you don't care. You want to maroon them here, whether they have a real chance of survival or not. You've turned pirate."

"Absolutely not," was Milyukov's unsurprising judgment of that allegation. "It is, in fact, the crew who are, and always have been, intent on fulfilling their manifest destiny: the role in human affairs that they, and perhaps they alone at present, are capable of fulfilling. Everything we have done in reshaping *Hope* has been devoted to that end. They only pirates aboard *Hope* are Shen Chin Che and his gang of saboteurs."

Solari had been slightly wrong-footed by the reference to "manifest destiny" but Matthew knew what it must mean.

"The crew have decided that this is the first in a potentially infinite series of seedings," he told Solari. "They do want to set up a successful colony here, and they're probably becoming desperate in their attempt to believe that it's an attainable goal, but their long-term goal is to repeat the exercise again and again. Some of the would-be colonists are realistic enough to settle for delaying *Hope*'s departure for as long as possible, but the rest are holding out for a better Earth-clone. The captain is obviously a reasonable man, so he's willing to come to an agreement with the former group, but he wants Shen Chin Che out of his hair and down on the surface. He's trying to persuade us that we should see things his way, by necessity if not by choice."

"So where does Delgado's murder fit into the argument?" Solari asked, pointedly addressing the question to Matthew rather than to their host.

"He doesn't know," Matthew guessed. "But he daren't neglect the possibility that if he can't find a way to use it, someone else will. Bernal's testimony as to the long-term prospects of the colony might well have been vital to whichever cause he decided to support, not just because he was a leading expert in ecological genomics back on Earth but because of the reputation he brought with him as a prophet and a persuader."

"I must repeat," Milyukov said, finally letting his irritation show, "that the situation is more complicated than you can possibly guess. You bring to it an understanding that is seven hundred years out of date. Earth has changed out of all recognition since you went into SusAn, just as *Hope* has, and all the assumptions you brought with you are quite obsolete now."

Matthew had to restrain himself from expressing aloud the opinion that this was nonsense. The political and economic systems now in place within Earth's solar system were of no particular relevance to *Hope*'s situation, but the ideologies and ambitions that the would-be colonists had brought into SusAn were very relevant indeed. Whether or not there were still Hardinists on Earth, there was an abundance of them among Shen Chin Che's Chosen People, and not one of them was likely to accept that his or her politics were now "obsolete" simply because the crew had decided to stage a takeover bid. Earth—a planet apparently still occupied by billions, even after a near-terminal ecocatastrophe—had surely had time for a dozen revolutions, counterrevolutions, and counter-counterrevolutions of its own, and its inhabitants would doubtless react to news of *Hope*'s discovery as they saw fit, but how could that make an iota of difference to the reactions of the awakened colonists? Perhaps the machines ruled Earth now, as some of his rival prophets had warned, operating the Ultimate Autocracy, or perhaps the anarchists had finally contrived a rule of law without corruptible leaders, but here in the new world's system, all the popular shades of twenty-first century Hardinism, all the nuances of Green Conservatism and all the factions of Gray Libertarianism were alive. Some of them might still be frozen down, but those that were not would be kicking.

Shen Chin Che, whom many had considered to be the boldest of all the pharaohs of Earthly Capitalism, had awakened to find himself a stranger in a society that had reshaped itself in his absence, but it was absurd to imagine that he could ever have accepted a new status quo meekly. Shen had gone to his long sleep not merely a builder and an owner but a hero and a messiah. If he had woken up to find himself an overthrown dictator, fit only for ritual humiliation as the representative of an obsolete order, he would instantly have transformed himself into a revolutionary: a zealot bent on the restitution of the old order. How could Milyukov's people have failed to anticipate that? By the same token, Matthew thought, how could Shen not have anticipated the possibility of exactly such a revolution as Milyukov's ancestors had carried out? He must have. Might he actually have expected it to happen? Perhaps. And if he had, might he not have made provisions?

That, Matthew guessed—in spite of Konstantin Milyukov's assurance that guesswork would not be enough—was why everybody kept telling him that things were not as simple as he had been ready to assume, and why an armed guard had been stationed outside his room, and why the people in the corridor had acted so quickly to ensure that no one could pollute his mind before the captain had briefed him. Perhaps it also accounted for the fact that the ship seemed to be in such a poor state of repair. Shen and his "gang of saboteurs" were not merely in hiding. They were in active opposition. If the shooting had not already started, it soon would—unless a compromise could be attained, and a treaty made.

Matthew felt a sudden wave of despair sweep through his weakened body. *Hope* had been intended to escape all of the curses that had brought Earth to the brink of destruction, not to reproduce them with further savage twists. What hope could there possibly be for the future of humankind, if *Hope* itself were now embroiled by an orgy of internal strife that could very easily lead to the mutual destruction of all involved? Even Gaea had proved so fragile as to have avoided destruction by a fluke; the ecosphere-in-miniature that was her pale shadow here could not tolerate a similar strain.

Vince Solari must have been mulling over the same awkward possibilities and dire anxieties, but his approach was as practical as ever. "So who, exactly, am I supposed to be working for now?" the policeman demanded. "You?" His voice was not disdainful, but it was certainly skeptical.

"For the human race," Captain Milyukov told him, without a trace of irony. "For the truth. For justice. For all the future generations whose fate will depend on what *we* can accomplish in the years to come."

"In other words, for *you*," Solari repeated, making no attempt to keep his own voice free of sarcasm.

"No," Milyukov said, making the contradiction seem effortless although his manner was still aggressively insistent. "I am the captain of *Hope*. My responsibility begins and ends in the microworld. *Your* future will be spent on the surface, within whatever society is eventually established there. If your people want to make Shen Chin Che—or anyone else—the owner of the planet, or the emperor of its human colony, that is entirely their affair. If your people want to design and implement their own political system, they are entirely free to do so. But they must realize and accept that we have the same right, and that we will exercise it. *Hope* does not belong to the colonists, and they have no power of command over her.

"It would obviously be best for everyone if your people and mine could work together, in full agreement as to our goals, our methods and our timetable—but if we cannot agree by mutual consent, agreement will certainly not be coerced by Shen Chin Che or anyone else. If we cannot agree, then we shall have to be content to disagree. When I say that you are working for the human race, for truth, for justice and for future generations, I mean exactly what I say. Perhaps such formulations seem vague or pompous to you—I cannot pretend to understand how the men of the distant past reacted to ideas and situations—but they are taken very seriously aboard *Hope*."

Vince Solari looked sideways at Matthew. The policeman did not know how to react to this strangely strident declaration, and Matthew could not blame him.

"When *Hope* was under construction," Matthew said, treading very carefully, "the assumption was that all of its resources would be devoted to the support of any colony it succeeded in establishing. Although it could never land, the intention was that it would remain in orbit around the colony world, an integral part of of the endeavor."

"We shall, of course, provide the colony with the support it needs to become self-sufficient," Milyukov said. "But our ultimate purpose and manifest destiny is to go on toward the center of the galaxy, spreading the seed of humanity as widely as we can."

"But you're only carrying so much human cargo," Matthew pointed out. "The embryos in the gene banks could be split repeatedly, I suppose, cloning entire new sets, with only a small percentage loss at each stage, but you can't replace the people in SusAn: the primary colonists."

"Of course we can," Milyukov retorted. He didn't elaborate, electing instead merely to stare at Matthew. The stare implied that a man of Matthew's intelligence ought to have no difficulty following the thread of his argument.

What Captain Milyukov was thinking, Matthew had to suppose, was that the living colonists could indeed be replaced. Their genetic resources could be duplicated by nuclear transfer cloning, and the resultant children could be educated aboard *Hope* to something like the same level of attainment as the donors. When their education was deemed to be complete they could be replaced in the empty SusAn chambers, ready for decanting all over again. There would be an attrition rate, of course—but even the amnesiacs whose minds had not survived the 700 years of stasis could still be counted a genetic resource, replaceable as biological individuals. Assuming that *Hope* was still in contact with probes sent out from Earth—and with Earth itself, although a 58-year transmission time would make meaningful dialogue enormously difficult—the gradual loss of inbuilt knowledge and expertise could probably be compensated by imported wisdom.

There was nothing intrinsically impossible about the crew's new plan. *Hope* might indeed seed a dozen worlds rather than one, if her indefatigable crew could find a dozen that were sufficiently hospitable—but any estimate of her chances of success would have to take into account her experience in attempting to seed *this* one. If this colony succeeded, others would probably succeed too, but if it failed, the crew's "ultimate purpose" and "manifest destiny" might begin to seem horribly impractical. This was the critical point, at which the whole scheme might be most easily aborted. Milyukov knew and understood that. He knew that the future he and his people had planned for themselves depended very heavily on what happened here and now. If the colony succeeded, in spite of the fact that the world was a marginal candidate for acceptance as an Earth-clone, the prospects of further success would seem very rosy, but if this attempt ended in disaster the crew would have to reassess the fruits of their revolution.

"Now I understand why you need me," Matthew said, mildly.

"It will need an ecologist of genius to figure out whether a colony deposited on the surface and abandoned by *Hope* could ever be viable, and a televangelist of genius to sell the idea."

The dull green gaze fixed itself upon him. "Nobody expects miracles from you, Professor Fleury," Milyukov assured him, unable now to suppress a note of sarcasm. "You have been fully awake for less than twenty hours, and cannot hope to catch up with everything that has been learned during these last three years—but your opinion will doubtless be weighed for what it is worth. No one, incidentally, has proposed that the colony be *abandoned*. Everyone recognizes that there will come a time when the colony no longer needs pseudo-parental supervision—when it too, can declare its independence, its freedom, its ability to decide and define its own destiny. What we all need from the scientists on the surface is a carefully measured and meticulously reasoned account of the best strategy that will lead us to that goal. If you are to make any contribution to that mission you will need to do a great deal of work. Andrei Lityansky is ready to begin your education at a moment's notice. He'll give you as much help as he can while your surface-suits are made ready."

Matthew was careful to remain impassive, although it required an effort. "You're absolutely right, captain," he said, calmly. "I really should get on with that as soon as possible." He stood up immediately and moved toward the door. When Solari put his hands on the arms of his own chair, as if to lever himself up, Matthew added: "That's okay, Vince. I dare say the captain wants to give you such details of the crime as he's managed to collect. I'm sure our friend with the gun can take me where I need to go. I'll see you back in the sick bay."

He opened the door and stepped out, without bothering to look back at Konstantin Milyukov.

nine

The man with the sidearm was still waiting patiently outside, as Matthew had expected. He seemed slightly surprised to see Matthew emerge unaccompanied, but he nodded readily enough when Matthew asked to be taken to see Andrei Lityansky. He took a phone from his belt and thumbed the buttons. He didn't put it to his ear: the text-display obviously told him what he wanted to know.

"He's not in the lab just now," Riddell reported, "but I've paged him. He'll meet us there as soon as he can. This way."

Once they'd rounded a couple of bends and taken a branching corridor Matthew could no longer tell whether they were heading in the same direction as the one from which they had come or a completely different one, but he took note of the fact that there were not nearly as many people about now that he had been fed the captain's point of view.

He glanced behind several times, catching glimpses of another man who was obviously heading for the same destination but seemed to prefer that the curves of the corridors obscured him from sight. The follower did not seem to be carrying a gun.

Having no idea how long the journey would be, Matthew felt constrained to act quickly. He waited until they came abreast of one of the blacked-out corridors, and then turned on Riddell without warning, grabbing him by the throat and attempting to slam the man's head against the corridor wall. Had he been fully fit the power of his muscles would have been easily adequate to the task, but his coordination was awry. Riddell sustained a nasty bump but he ducked far enough forward to make sure that he was not knocked out.

Knowing that reinforcements would arrive within seconds rather than minutes, Matthew brought his knee up into the other man's groin, then threw his whole body sideways in order to slam his victim into the wall for a second time.

It was ugly and untidy, but it worked. Riddell went limp.

Matthew grabbed at the gun, but he was far too clumsy to be

able to snatch it out of the holster. Indeed, he was so far off balance in the unfamiliar gravity regime that he slammed into the wall himself, bruising his arm. He had no time to nurse the bruise—he had to regain his footing immediately in order to respond to the follower's rapid approach. Knowing that brute force was his only option, he lashed out with his uninjured arm. The attacker tried to duck, but he had been in too much of a hurry. The punch caught him under the nose, and snapped his head back with a horrible *click*.

Matthew cursed volubly, fearing that he had broken at least one of his knucklebones, but he still had the presence of mind to hurl himself into the dark corridor and run as fast as he could along it.

No lights came on as he passed through the corridor; it was presumably dark because the lighting had failed. That was his first stroke of luck. His second was that he did not cannon into anything solid before stabilizing his lurching run and sticking out a hand so that he could trail the fingers along the wall, tracking its contours.

Running blind was more difficult than he had anticipated, but he slowed to a walk quickly enough. He took a left turn, then a right, then backtracked to avoid light up ahead. He was already completely lost, in an environment whose layout and dimensions were utterly unknown to him, but knew that if he failed in what he was trying to do he could always surrender to the crew.

In the meantime, he just kept moving, clinging to the darkness.

The darkness, he now assumed, must be a result of Shen Chin Che's "sabotage." The darkness was where the territory that Shen had reclaimed from Milyukov had to be. There might, however, be an awful lot of darkness. If *Hope* had the floor space of a sizable Earthly town, there might be a lot of empty space to which no one had bothered to lay claim. To judge by the photographs in Milyukov's office the crew had recently been busy increasing their numbers, but they had started from a tiny base; they had hardly begun to implement their "manifest destiny."

He was beginning to wonder whether he might have made a horrible mistake when he saw an anomalous light in the distance: a green light. One of the dead wallscreens had come to life. He hurried forward, and was relieved to find that the green glow was shaped like an arrow. A single word was etched in black on the shaft of the arrow: *Follow*.

He followed the arrow. The corridors' overhead lighting remained inactive, but screens continued to light up as he came to junctions and corners. The next few arrows were mute, but the sixth had the word *Hurry* incorporated into its shaft.

Matthew tried to accelerate his pace, but he was too clumsy. By the time he had rounded half a dozen gentle corners he had lurched into the wall twice, cursing the fact that his mass remained the same no matter how light his weight might be. He ignored the pain and tried to concentrate on following the course at a steady pace. Running was out of the question anyway; he was out of condition and already out of breath. He was unable to take long strides because he was so utterly unused to the conditions and so incompetent in the management of his momentum. He had plenty of time thereafter to be astonished by the length and intricacy of the route he was following.

When Milyukov had said that *Hope* had the floor space of a town, Matthew had automatically pictured the area in question as a circular arena crisscrossed by thousands of mazy walls, but *Hope*'s metallic kernel was more ameboid than spherical and there was also a third dimension to be taken into account. There were no flights of steps and not very many doors and airlocks to negotiate, but Matthew soon became aware of subtle variations in his weight as he was guided closer to the ship's inner core, then away again, then back and forth for a second time. His newly light head began to spin, and he could not quell the rising tide of dizziness even with the aid of his IT.

He tried hard not to fall, palming himself off the wall as he stumbled, but he paused too late. His inner ear gave up the unequal fight and he collapsed, flattening himself against the floor as if it were a vertical surface from which he might begin to slide at any moment. Not until he had remained perfectly still for more than three minutes—*his* minutes, not ship-minutes—did he recover possession of himself.

The darkness and the dereliction seemed to be weighing down on him, mocking him. He had already worked out, on a purely intellectual level, the magnitude of the trouble that *Hope* was in, but now he *felt* the cold antipathy of circumstance. He had not noticed the cold so much while he was walking, but now he was lying down it was seeping from the floor into his bones. He was acutely aware of his own tininess by comparison with the artifact in which he was contained—but he was aware too, of the tininess of the artifact itself. Sheathed in cometary ice as it was, it must be gleaming in the skies of the world it was orbiting, but it was no more than a spark in the void: a spark whose name had taken on a cruelly ironic gloss now that its internal community was riven with such awkward disagreements.

Whether the new colony was fundamentally viable or not, Matthew realized, it could not succeed without far better support than Konstantin Milyukov was presently minded to deliver. The crew knew that, and the colonists knew it, but three years of strife had made them stubborn—stubborn enough for their own internal divisions to be widening into cracks, slowly but inexorably. Everyone had someone else to blame for the mission's predicament. He, newly arrived without the stain of any original sin, could blame *everybody*, and he did.

Except, of course, that he was no longer *quite* without sin. He had attacked Riddell, and hurt the other man set to watch him. He was involved now; he had planted his own flag, and stood ready to defend it as stubbornly as anyone.

But the real enemy, he knew, was the darkness and emptiness of the void. Although *Hope* had arrived in a new solar system, the void was still here, still everywhere.

He sat up, peering into the darkness of the inclined corridor.

At first, he could see nothing through the gloom but an arrow of light, but after a few minutes the arrow changed into a text message.

Not Much Further, it said.

Matthew groaned, and hauled himself back to his feet. The arrow was restored, and Matthew followed it.

He was passing through doorways more frequently now, but the winding corridors were so extensive and so utterly deserted that *Hope* was beginning to seem a ghost ship: a starfaring *Mary Celeste*. There was living space here for tens of thousands, Matthew realized, perhaps hundreds of thousands. The crew must have been working on the inner architecture of *Hope* ever since she had left the system, but their robots had been put away for the time being and they had yet to move on to the next stage in the process of evolution: the one that would make the ship into an authentic microworld, with a microworld's population. Had they begun to fill these spaces with their own descendants immediately after their departure from the solar system, the reawakened parent-colonists would have found themselves a very tiny minority indeed, but the revolution must have happened in the later phases of the voyage. That part of the revolutionaries' scheme was still in its early stages—and what disaster might Shen Chin Che's counterrevolution have precipitated if these spaces had not been empty? Perhaps they would not have been filled in any case, given that space would have had to be reserved for the colonists' future clone-children, whose generative nuclei had not been removable until they were unfrozen.

Matthew was expecting a return to the light and a genuine rendezvous, but he was disappointed. Instead of a room as homely as Milyukov's, all he found at the end of his rat-run was one more wallscreen at a darkened corner, displaying a half-familiar face.

There was a camera eye positioned above the screen, but Matthew did not suppose that the glimmer of reflected light could do justice to his features. That, he thought, was a pity. He realized that he had not seen his own face since he came out of SusAn, but he was sure that it could not possibly have changed as much as the face that was peering at him from the wall.

"Shen," he said, to acknowledge that he could see the face. For the moment, he couldn't say anything more.

"I'm sorry, Matthew," the face said. "I can't take the risk of bringing you in."

This wasn't the kind of welcome Matthew had been expecting. It wasn't the kind of greeting he felt they were both entitled to, after the kind of epic journey they had made.

Had Shen actually been present, Matthew could have bowed first, then thrown his arms around the smaller man . . . but as things were, he could only stare at the unexpected image on the screen.

Shen Chin Che looked a good deal older than he had been in 2090, when Matthew had last seen him. Matthew realized, belatedly, that what had been a matter of days for him must have been a matter of years, or decades, for the other man.

"We made it, Shen," he said, defiantly. "No matter how badly the hired help has contrived to fuck it up, *we made it!* Fifty-eight light-years. Seven hundred years."

Shen Chin Che blinked in surprise, as if he too had forgotten to factor the difference in their ages into the equation. "It *has* been a long time, Matthew," he conceded.

Matthew remembered what Nita Brownell had told him about the vulnerability of memory, and wondered how well Shen's memories of him compared to his memories of Shen. He also remembered that the first great prophet to lead his people to a Promised Land, across a wilderness that must have seemed just as intimidating as the desert of the void had seemed to the men of the twenty-first century, had not lived to join his people in that land, seeing it only from a distance. Shen's age, Matthew realized, might be the greatest advantage Konstantin Milyukov had in the struggle for possession of *Hope*.

The Chosen People had been subject to an age restriction; the idea had been that the parental generation must be old enough to have proved their wisdom, but young enough to have more than half a century of life before them. Shen had obviously made an exception of himself. Shen had remained awake to supervise the building and equipping of his Ark—perhaps a little too long.

"When were you frozen down?" Matthew asked, soberly.

"Not till 2139," Shen told him.

Matthew made the calculation easily enough, although he couldn't be sure of the exact fraction of the three years since *Hope* had arrived in orbit that Shen had lived through.

Shen Chin Che was about fifty years older than he had been when Matthew saw him last, when he had already been the older man by more than a decade. He was now more than a hundred years old—and it was probably safe to assume that he would not easily get the benefit of any advances in longevity technology to which the crew had gained access en route.

"Why are we meeting like this?" Matthew asked him, trying not to seem too aggrieved.

"There's a possibility that Milyukov woke you up in order that you might serve as a Judas goat," Shen told him. "Even if that wasn't his sole intention, he's bound to have sowed your suit-skin with the cleverest bugs his people can devise. They have some new tricks, thanks to their exchanges of information with the probes that overtook them—if they hadn't, I'd have won by now."

"Well," Matthew said, philosophically, "it's good to see you anyway."

"It's good to see you too, Matthew," the old man assured him. "Your memory's good, I hope—you must remember our last meeting a great deal better than I do."

"I remember it very well," Matthew said. "I won't say that you don't look a day older, but you always wore well."

It was true. Shen Chin Che was not a tall man, nor had he entirely resisted a certain inherited tendency to rotundity, but on and off Earth he had been a man of iron discipline as well as a man possessed of state-of-the-art IT and smart clothing. He always had *worn well*. His light brown skin still seemed to have the same near-golden glow that Matthew remembered, undulled by age or by recent years spent beneath the meager glare of the ship's artificial lighting, but it was wrinkled now.

"We may not have much time," Shen said. "Some day, I'll fill you in on the history of my last half century, but that will have to wait. We have to do the important stuff first, in case we never get a chance to do the rest." His voice was harrowingly bleak.

"I understand," Matthew said, although he wasn't entirely sure that he did. "So tell me the important stuff."

TEN

I don't have time to fight a long, drawn-out war of attrition," Shen Chin Che admitted. "Which is a pity, given that it's the kind of war I've been landed with. I can't win it, so someone else will have to." He didn't name any names.

"How many men have you got?" Matthew asked.

"Let's not bother with matters of trivial detail," the face on the screen replied, politely reminding Matthew that even if their conversation were not being monitored it was almost certainly being recorded. "It's not the number of men that counts. The real battles were fought by AIs. The crew thought they'd disabled all my Trojan horses before they brought me back, but they hadn't. Unfortunately, they *had* contrived to equip some of their own systems with better defenses than I'd anticipated. This siege seems likely to continue for a *lot* longer than ten years, whether I survive to lead it or not."

Matthew realized that Shen Chin Che was talking through him as well as to him. Among other things, their conversation was the latest move in a long-running war of words.

"You knew I'd try to make a break when I realized that I was a prisoner, didn't you?" Matthew said. "That's what the commotion in the corridor was for—to drive home the point in case I hadn't noticed. You needn't have worried. Milyukov was just as keen to annoy me as you were to have me annoyed. He knew that I'd make a break too. Maybe he *wanted* me to run to you, so that he could tell the people on the surface that they wouldn't be getting a replacement ecologist after all, due to circumstances beyond his control."

"He's not that devious, Matthew," Shen replied, earnestly. "He's a man completely out of his depth, and I think he's beginning to realize the fact. You and I know more about politics and public relations than he'll ever be able to learn. If he were cleverer, he'd be easier to deal with. He thinks he can't lose this contest in the long run because he has more guns, more people, and more time, but he doesn't understand that it's not the kind of war that can be won by force. If force wins, we all lose. The only way to win is to work together—*all of us.*"

"It's not going to be easy to forge a consensus," Matthew observed. "I've only been awake two days, but I've heard enough to know how bad things are."

"We need something new," Shen told him. "We need an issue that will allow us to put aside our differences and look to the future. We need a common cause, like the one that brought us all together in the first place."

"What brought us all together in the first place was the urgent threat of an all-encompassing disaster," Matthew reminded him. "I remember it as if it were the day before yesterday."

"Of course you do," Shen Chin Che retorted, venturing a wry smile. "You were there. You weren't responsible for the disaster, but you did lend a helping hand to the urgency. I knew its value, even if others didn't. You were as important to the Ark project as I was, in your own way. I had the money, but I didn't have the hearts and minds. You were my prophet, my messiah. Cometh the hour, cometh the man. The hour has come around again, Matthew—and so have you. It's the first stroke of luck I've had."

"I'm a little late," Matthew felt obliged to point out, even though the flattery was music to his ears. "I don't have the authority of celebrity any more, even among the Chosen. I was frozen down while most of them were children. The crew don't even have TV—just VE tapes and mute pictures relayed by flying eyes."

"I know," Shen said. "But you can change things. It's what you do."

"Two days, Shen," Matthew murmured. "If you send me back, they'll put me down on the surface within another three—four at the most. It won't be easy to catch up. Impossible, even."

"It won't stop you, if you're determined enough," Shen told him. That, at least, was what his lips said. What his eyes were saying—in a manner that was surely invisible to any bugs Milyukov had planted, no matter how clever they might be—was something else entirely.

What Shen Chin Che's eyes were saying, loud and clear, was: *You're the only hope I've got left. I'm finished. If you can't pull the irons out of the fire, no one can.*

As "important stuff" went, there wasn't much to it—but Matthew had to admit that it was something he needed to know.

"I'm not in a good position, Shen," he said. "Worse now than before. I showed my hand when I hit Riddell. Milyukov won't give me any kind of platform."

"Milyukov's authority over his own people is slipping," Shen told him. "Not quickly enough, I admit—but all it will take is one good push to set him sliding. The people on the surface will be ready to listen to you. More than willing. They have no leader, Matthew. They have no direction. They're losing heart, and they need to get it back. If you can't find a way to give it to them, no one can."

Matthew couldn't help shivering. The cold that had entered into his flesh while he lay on the floor was still there. He knew how desperate Shen must be, to seize such a feeble straw in this fashion. What a foul reward for all that he had done in the home system! He had anticipated—even expected—that the descendants of the crew might have developed their own agenda, but he had underestimated the extent and effectiveness of their treason. Seven centuries had been too long an interval—but the fact that it had taken seven centuries to find a world that even the hopeful pilgrims of *Hope* thought unsatisfactory was eloquent testimony to the difficulty and necessity of their mission.

"The crew think I'm doing all this out of spite, because I won't play the game unless I'm running the show," Shen went on, "but you know me better than that, Matthew. You may not understand the situation as yet, but you do trust me. *You* know that I'm not just an old-fashioned capitalist clinging to his property like grim death because I can't bear to let go. I'm a Hardinist through and through. A *real* Hardinist. The years haven't changed me." He seemed slightly anxious, as if he were not at all convinced that Matthew would still recognize and trust him. He did not carry the burden of his extra years lightly.

"I know who you are," Matthew assured him. "I do understand—better than Milyukov can, I think. All he's ever known is *Hope*. He can't really understand what was happening to Earth in the 2080s, or what it meant to people who loved their world enough to leave it. When the IT was pulling me gently out of SusAn, I dreamed I saw the Earth die. It was a vivid dream, even when it became lucid. It could have happened. Milyukov knows that it didn't, but that knowledge prevents him from obtaining any real understanding of the wellsprings of our motivation."

"Those who fail to learn from prophesies are condemned to fulfil them," Shen quoted, with the ghost of a smile. "The stupidest thing about this whole farce is that on the most essential point of all, Konstantin Milyukov and I are in complete agreement. His most fervent desire, and mine, is that the colony should succeed, and succeed gloriously. It would be a terrible irony of fate if our difference of opinion as to who should control *Hope* and its resources were to cause it to fail. I don't know nearly enough about what's going on down there, or why the people at the bases have been so badly spooked, but I do know that it would be a dreadful waste of an opportunity that might never come again if they were to throw in the towel and demand to be taken up again. I'm very grateful that you came to talk to me, Matthew—and if Milyukov has any sense he'll be grateful too. I need you, Matthew. The colony needs you. We need your scientific expertise, and we need your rhetorical skills. They do remember you, Matthew—even the ones who never knew you know who and what you were. They need you."

"They had Bernal," Matthew pointed out, uneasily. He was uneasy because he knew that few other people on *Hope* remembered him as fondly as Shen. Shen had been impressed by Matthew Fleury because Matthew Fleury was a kindred spirit: another lonely voice crying the same warnings in the same dread wilderness—but Shen had not spent much time on Earth during the 2070s, and none at all in the 2080s. He had come to see things from an extraterrestrial perspective, and a prejudiced one. Matthew, like the proverbial prophets of old, had been a man not much honored in his own country—and he had always thought of the whole world as his own country, his potential constituency.

"They didn't see Bernal as a potential leader," Shen said, "and rightly so. He was a pleasure seeker at heart, too preoccupied with his prick."

"They won't see me as a potential leader either," Matthew said, soberly. "Not for the same reasons, maybe—but it takes more than a lack of romantic ambition to establish a man as a serious individual. To many of them, I'm more TV personality than scientist, and on Earth in the old days nothing trivialized a man like TV. There's only one man in this solar system who could assert any kind of real authority over the people on the surface, and that's you. Milyukov may have misjudged your capacity to

hurt him, but so far as the people on the ground are concerned
he's managed to marginalize and neutralize you, Believe me,
Shen, I'm no ready-made substitute. Milyukov must know that."

"He can't," Shen said, stubbornly. "He doesn't know you. You
can make a difference, Matthew. I know you can."

"Almost everyone down there has had three years' head
start," Matthew countered. "Every single one of them will take it
for granted that they understand the world far better than I do—
and they'll be right."

"You have the advantage of a fresh eye," Shen pointed out.

"That's true," Matthew conceded, perversely glad that he had
found a point to concede. "I don't suppose, by any chance, that
you have any idea why Bernal was killed, or by whom?"

"None," the old man confirmed. "I am, as you must have sur-
mised, somewhat out of touch." He went straight back to what he
thought was the *important stuff.* "I chose you for a reason,
Matthew. Because you were an ecologist, able to see woods where
others were only capable of seeing trees, but also because you
were a hero. Bernal was as good an ecologist as you were, but he
wasn't as good a hero."

You heard my voice from far, Matthew thought, and recognized it as an echo of your own. But it wasn't. It was always mine.
The flattery was beginning to wear thin; he had already over-
dosed on it.

"I can't win here, Matthew," Shen went on, his voice little
more than a whisper. "I can hold Milyukov at bay, but I can't win.
Perhaps I and my successors can make certain that *Hope* remains
in this system for a very long time, but that would be self-defeat-
ing if we prevent her from offering wholehearted support to the
colony in the meantime. We all need a new way to look at things,
Matthew, a new way to look forward. Nobody else seems to be
capable of providing that. Not even Bernal, although I don't
doubt that he was working on it."

"I'm heartened by your confidence," Matthew said, wishing
that it might be truer than it was. "But it won't be easy."

Shen turned his head, presumably to listen to someone out of
shot. Matthew couldn't hear what was being said, but he studied
the nodding of Shen's head as the old man responded. The
motion seemed almost robotic. Shen was still the man that
Matthew had known, albeit briefly, in the late 2080s, but his

mannerisms had become more distinct. Matthew wondered how much mental flexibility he had lost, how much capacity for self-reinvention. He must be living a hand-to-mouth existence, unless he had sufficient control over a large enough fraction of the ship's resources to maintain his internal technology and support his most cherished habits. Either way, Shen was an old man by the standards of the world he had left; his IT might be able to sustain his body and mind for another twenty years, but it could not maintain their agility.

Matthew took advantage of the pause to wonder whether he might have made matters worse than they had been before by running away to meet Shen, given that he had not actually learned anything much to his advantage. If he'd inflicted more damage on Riddell or his friend than he'd intended, he might be facing criminal charges himself, without ever getting a chance to find out who had killed Bernal and why. If he had ever had a chance of persuading Konstantin Milyukov that he might be recruited to the crew's cause, it had gone now. But he had needed to see Shen, if only to reassure myself that he really was alive and well.

It occurred to him then that he could not be *entirely* reassured on that point. All he could see was an image, of a kind which even a stupid AI could maintain and animate.

"Thanks for this, Matthew," Shen said, returning his attention to the camera's eye. "I wouldn't have expected any less of you, and it would be a pity if Captain Milyukov were to hold it against you. *Be careful*, Matthew. Whatever the new world is, it's certainly no Eden—but that doesn't mean we can't make our peace with it. Earth was never an Eden either, no matter what the Gaean mythologists may say. We have to make the most of our experience, and we have to make a stand somewhere, or we'll be on the run forever." It had the ring of a farewell, and a dismissal—and also, perhaps, the suggestion of an olive branch extended in Konstantin Milyukov's direction.

Matthew nodded, but realized that the light was too poor to allow the gesture's meaning to be clear. "I'll do my best," he promised. "Not just for your sake, but for the sake of the children." Shen would know that he meant all the children, not just Alice and Michelle.

"Good-bye, Matthew," Shen said. He didn't add: *This will be the last time you ever see me*, but it was understood between them.

The screen blanked out before he had time to reply.

Matthew decided that he had been right to make his break from Milyukov's custody, no matter what effect it would have on the captain's attitude and conduct. He had needed to see Shen. He had needed to see and know that the past wasn't dead: that it had leapt the gulf of 700 years to extend itself rudely and proudly into the present. He had needed to get a grip on the fact that the mission was still in progress, and that the torch sustaining it had not begun to dim.

Matthew had never been a Hardinist, nor any other kind of confirmed Capitalist, but he understood—as Konstantin Milyukov probably could not—exactly why Shen Chin Che was the hardest of Hardinists. He understood too exactly why Shen considered that no matter who, if anyone, eventually came to own the vast territories of the new world, he and his allies had an unassailable right to own the new *Hope*, just as they had owned the old.

ELEVEN

Shen Chin Che posted more green arrows to guide Matthew back through *Hope*'s inner maze, and Matthew followed them, confident that he would arrive soon enough at a place where Milyukov's people could welcome him back. While he walked, less hurriedly than before, he tried to make sense of what he had discovered.

Shen's references to a "war" between his AIs and Milyukov's had to be largely metaphorical. No armies of superviruses were hurling themselves upon one another in the dark wilderness of the ship's software space. There were a few systems that were under Shen's control and a lot that were under Milyukov's control—but wherever those systems interfaced or performed actions that had consequences within the other there was no control at all, and hence no function. The "war" was a stalemate: a software gridlock whose ramifications were stifling 80 or 90 percent of the activity that should have been going on aboard the ship if it had been offering full support to its own inhabitants, let alone to the bases on the surfaces.

It was no wonder that the people up here were as jittery as those on the ground—and no wonder that *everyone* had begun to doubt that the colony could ever become viable. But a stalemate was a kind of situation that could change *very* rapidly once it was broken, no matter how long it had endured. And once the situation became fluid, it became manipulable. The breaking of a stalemate was the ideal opportunity for a fresh voice to be heard—for a fresh *message* to be heard. It might not matter much if the voice were a voice from the past, even if it were a voice whose knowledge of the present left much to be desired; what mattered was that it could offer a new and brighter future.

He knew that Shen had appealed to him out of sheer desperation, but that didn't mean that Shen wasn't right. There were moments in time made for prophets, and perhaps this was one of them. Perhaps Bernal Delgado had understood that. Perhaps whoever had killed him had understood it too. If Bernal *had* understood it, and had set out to prepare a way, there was a possibility that by stepping into Bernal's shoes, Matthew might be able to carry his scheme through to completion rather than having to devise one of his own. And perhaps Bernal's killer understood *that* too . . . or was he being too paranoid? The only danger facing him at present was that there were so many empty corridors around him, all cold and all dark. If the arrows were to vanish . . .

He passed numerous intersections at which unlit corridors led away into the darkness. Now that he was not hurrying he had the opportunity to notice that most of them slanted "upward," toward the zero-gee core: alien territory, for which even the crewmen were ill-adapted.

The emptiness became increasingly disturbing. The darkness seemed so ominous now that he was no longer playing the buccaneer, that he was astonished by his earlier temerity in launching himself into it. As he walked on, Matthew began to feel unnaturally light, as if his imagination were finally coming to terms with the sensations associated with the low gravity. At the same time, though, he felt bone-weary, as if he had over-taxed himself to the point where he needed to lie down and sleep for hours. It was a curious, almost paradoxical, alloy of sensations, like nothing he had ever experienced before.

On Earth, where he had spent all but a tiny fraction of his not-quite-fifty active years, exhaustion had always been echoed in heavy-seeming limbs, and alertness in a subliminal awareness of physical power. The present dislocation was presumably mild when compared to what long-term moon-dwellers must feel, but the moon had seemed such a radically alien place that every move he made there had been tentative. *Hope* was not quite alien enough, at least in this sector, to overturn his ingrained expectations—whose failure had, in consequence, come to seem like a kind of betrayal.

On the surface, Matthew recalled, his weight would be 0.92 Earth-normal rather than 0.5. In theory, that ought to be a great deal more comfortable, posing problems of adaptation that were objectively trivial. But would that objective triviality be faithfully replicated in his subjective sensations? Might it not be the case that the narrowness of the difference between the new world's surface on Earth would enhance the sensation of betrayal? And

might not that too, add to the jitters that the people on the surface were feeling?

He would find out soon enough.

When two of the crew members finally did contrive to locate
him, coming at him at a trot, he took due note of the fact that
their first impulse, upon catching sight of him, was to reach for
their guns. Only one of the two—a small, slender, short-haired
woman who looked no older than eighteen or nineteen Earth-
years—actually drew her weapon, but the difference was too
small to be reassuring. Her companion, also a woman but considerably taller and a trifle more mature, had rested her fingers speculatively on the butt of her own weapon before deciding to leave
it where it was. They both seemed very anxious, as if they
expected him to charge them with waving fists.

Matthew put his hands in the air, making the gesture as theatrical as he could.

"Hey," he said. "I'm just lost, that's all. I'm not some alien
marauder intent on taking the control room by storm." He knew
that *Hope* did not have a "control room" as such, or even a
"bridge," but he felt entitled to a modest theatrical license.

The woman who had drawn her gun did not return the
weapon to its holster. She didn't say anything; she was still looking at him as if he were a mad dog, utterly unpredictable as well
as dangerous. The taller woman had pulled out her phone instead
of her gun, but she had turned away in order to speak into it, so
that Matthew could not make out what she was saying.

"Have you ever actually fired that thing?" he asked the
younger one, letting his annoyance show. "If not, I'd rather you
didn't point it my way."

"It's non-lethal," she retorted. Matthew took that as a *no*. He
also took the whole charade as an indicator of the fact that Konstantin Milyukov really did have it in mind to take his renegade
systems back by brutal force of arms if there seemed to be no
other way. Matthew didn't dare to assume that it couldn't be
done. The crew had been building the ship for hundreds of
years—the transition from Earth's solar system to interstellar
space had been only a minor punctuation mark in the long text of
that endeavor—and they must know its present physical layout
far better than Shen's people, no matter how cleverly Shen had
concealed his software shock troops.

The taller woman still had her phone in her hand, and the line was presumably still open, but she had turned to face Matthew again and seemed to be waiting for him to say something more.

"I had an appointment with Professor Lityansky," Matthew told his captors, "but I fear that I'm a little late. I'm sure he's as anxious to get on with it as I am, but I'm rather tired. Perhaps we could postpone it until tomorrow, when I'll be more able to give my full attention to what he has to say. Can you take me back to my room?"

"Did you hear that?" the older woman said, into the mouthpiece of her phone. The answer was presumably affirmative, but Matthew couldn't hear any of the reply.

"You shouldn't have done that," the taller woman told him, when she finally replaced the phone in her belt. "Riddell's not badly hurt, but you broke Lamartine's jawbone."

"I'm sorry about that," Matthew said, sincerely. "But it *will* mend. Fists are supposed to be non-lethal too, if you use them sensibly. Am I under arrest?"

"You'll be down on the surface soon enough," was the only answer he received. "We'll take you back to your room." She gestured to her companion, who only hesitated for a couple of seconds before returning her weapon to its holster. Both women still seemed very nervous, unwilling to get too close to him. When they led him away they stayed ahead of him, and they didn't look round.

Seven hundred and twenty-seven years before 2090, Matthew calculated, would have been late medieval times in Europe. The Black Death would have come and gone, and populations would have been exploding again in a period of relative climatic generosity. Had a man of that era stepped out of a time warp to confront the people of Earth he would have seemed uncouth in the extreme, and his hosts would have taken it for granted, rightly or not, that his inevitable paranoia might explode into violence at any moment. These people had far more in common with him than the men of the twenty-first century would have had in common with a visitor from 1363—most importantly, a common language—but a tiny, self-enclosed society like that of the crew, afloat on a mote in the hostile void, had to look back on the history of Earth with a certain horror.

The twenty-first century had only been the second most violent in human history, but one of the consequences of the spread of IT and the increasing capability of medical science had been the encouragement of widespread interest in extreme sports, including hobbyist combat of all kinds. Even as a boy, Matthew had never gone in for the kind of fighting that would put his IT to the test, but he belonged to a generation in which even the pettiest disputes had routinely escalated into brawls and knife fights. It had been easy enough to do what he had had to do in order to slip the leash of his subtle captivity, almost unthinkingly. It wasn't too difficult now, though, to place himself imaginatively in the shoes of the two women from a very different place and time, in order to envisage what he had done as the act of a barbarian, or a dangerous psychopath.

Was that, he wondered, how Milyukov's people saw *all* the Chosen People?

It certainly seemed so when he got back to the room he shared with Vince Solari and found himself confronted with an exceedingly angry Nita Brownell.

"Are you *mad*?" she demanded. "Do you have any idea what you've *done*?"

"I had to try to see Shen," he replied, in a mild tone that was neither feigned nor disingenuous. "It was the only way to get a proper understanding of the situation."

"You haven't even begun to understand the situation," she told him, conveniently forgetting that one of the reasons why he didn't understand the situation was that she had gone to such perverse lengths to avoid explaining it to him. "Captain Milyukov's got trouble enough trying to keep the more extreme factions in check, without you adding fuel to the flames. You'll be down on the surface in two days' time, but some of us have to live and work *up here*. What do you think your antics have done to *my* position?"

"What *extreme factions*?" Matthew wanted to know. He couldn't drum up much sympathy for the doctor's personal troubles.

"The faction that wants him to dump all the cryonic travelers, pull out and start over," she replied, unsurprisingly. "The faction that argues that the revolution didn't go far enough, and has yet to be brought to its proper culmination. The faction that thinks the people of Earth were so criminally negligent in the management of their own world that they oughtn't to be trusted with another. The faction that thinks that you and I and your children, and everyone else's children, ought to be regarded simply as genetic raw material, because our minds are so corrupt as to constitute cultural poison."

"That's a lot of factions in a population of a few hundred," Matthew pointed out, mildly.

"Far too many," the doctor agreed. "Which makes it all the more remarkable that the captain's on *our* side, you poor fool. He's the one who wants to let us fulfil the quest for which we undertook to be frozen down. He's the one who wants to *help* us. It's bad enough that Shen Chin Che is rolling round *Hope*'s decks like a loose cannon, without *you* blasting off as well."

While this tirade was in progress Vince Solari had hauled himself off his bed and had come to stand with them, ready to play the peace officer by imposing his body between theirs should it prove necessary. All Matthew said was: "Is it really *that* bad? Are the crew so bitterly divided among themselves?"

"Captain Milyukov doesn't seem to think so," Solari put in. "The doctor may be a little overanxious. She's in an awkward position."

"What do *you* know about it?" Nita Brownell retorted.

"Only what the captain told me," Solari said, soothingly. "Are you all right, Matt?"

"I might have broken a knuckle," Matthew admitted. "Otherwise, it's just bruises. My IT has blanked the pain, but I'm a little spaced out and *very* tired."

Nita Brownell picked up his right hand and felt the knuckle, without any conspicuous tenderness or concern. "It's not broken," she concluded, giving the distinct impression that she would have been happier if it had been. "Unlike the jaw of the man you hit."

"He was about to hit me," Matthew pointed out.

"I think we both need sleep," Solari said. "Perhaps we should postpone further recriminations until morning."

Nita Brownell was ready enough to agree with that, although she insisted on giving Matthew a further examination once he was horizontal on the bed. Matthew was past caring whether her real concern was for his health or to recover some of the bugs that had recorded his conversation with Shen Chin Che.

When the door closed behind her, Solari said: "Anything I should know?"

"Not urgently," Matthew assured him. "It was a personal thing. I know Shen. I owed it to him to pay my respects, whatever the effort required. The crew don't understand how much they owe him."

"That's the way it is with children of a revolution," Solari observed. "They tear up the past, demonize the ancestors they used to worship. But when they've tried out the extremes for size, they usually swing back. The wheel tends to come full circle—that's why they call them revolutions."

Matthew wasn't sure that was true, but he hadn't the energy to argue, or even to reply. As soon as silence fell, he was asleep.

TWELVE

Andrei Lityansky was as tall and slim as the majority of the crew, but his skin was too dark to manifest the curious greenish tint that many of his fellows displayed. The cast of his features was slightly Semitic—a point of Earthly reference that Matthew found oddly reassuring—and his hair was jet black. He wore a neat triangular beard, the first one Matthew had seen on *Hope*.

Matthew had hardly had time to finish his unappetizing breakfast before Riddell had turned up to guide him to his appointed rendezvous, but Lityansky didn't look like a man who had recently woken from refreshing sleep. He seemed a trifle fractious, like a man who did not appreciate the disturbance of his expectations by the kind of unexpected delay that Matthew had imported into his schedule. He was nursing a cup of what looked like coffee, but he didn't offer any to Matthew.

"How is Shen Chin Che?" the crewman asked, with ostentatious irony. "We haven't seen much of him lately."

"As well as can be expected," Matthew replied. "How are Captain Milyukov and the man I hit?"

"The captain's untroubled. He had no intention of keeping any secrets from you. There was no need for you to seek out the renegades—as you must have discovered. Lamartine's broken jaw will heal, but the other damage might be more serious." Matthew took the second remark to imply that Lityansky had heard the tape of his conversation with Shen. The last sentence was more worrying, but he didn't want to discuss the crew's ambivalent attitudes to their passengers. He wanted to hear what Lityansky had to say about the ecosphere of the new world; and its underlying genomics.

Lityansky understood that, but he had his own order of priorities. He insisted on "putting the information in context," perhaps because he thought it necessary and perhaps because he wanted to inflict a little subtle punishment on Matthew for screwing up his schedule.

"You might have heard mention of a life-bearing orphan

planet that we passed close by two hundred years ago," the biologist said. "We've had reports from Earth's robot probes of two others, and of half a dozen life-bearing planets in solar systems closer to Earth than this one. That knowledge had already informed our grandfathers, long before we arrived here, that the panspermists and the more extreme convergence theorists were wrong. DNA isn't the only basis of life to be found in the galaxy, and doesn't appear to be common. Perhaps one coding molecule will eventually win the cosmic struggle for existence by out-competing all its rivals, but that certainly won't happen soon—and by *soon* I mean any time in the next few billion years. Everything we have so far discovered suggests that we live in a galaxy in which life is very various."

"But most of the rivals to DNA you've so far discovered," Matthew put in, "aren't capable of producing anything but bacterial sludge."

"We don't know that," Lityansky said. "DNA probably couldn't produce anything but bacterial sludge in the context of an orphan planet, and we've no reason to think that any of the alternative coding molecules present on such worlds would be incapable of producing complex life if they had the resources of a sunlit planet like Earth or Ararat to work with. It might, of course, be unreasonably arrogant of us to think of such worlds as the primary abodes of life or as the highest achievements of evolution. It is at least conceivable that one of the many kinds of bacterial sludge that exist in less balmy conditions will ultimately out-compete everything else, proving that metazoan creatures—including sentient humanoids—are merely temporary follies of creation."

"Fair enough," Matthew said. "So tell me about temporary folly number two."

"I think you'll find it intriguing," Lityansky told him, teasingly. "Until we arrived here, everything we had learned from our own orphan and the data harvested from Earth's probes suggested that there was one candidate rule of comparative evolution that seemed to have held firm. In all the other cases known to us, each ecosphere had only one fundamental reproductive molecule—DNA and RNA aren't sufficiently different, of course, to be reckoned fundamentally different. The coding molecules were all different, but each ecosphere was derived from a single biochemical ancestor. Earth is now a partial exception to the rule—the news from home says that Earthly biotech has been enhanced by a whole new range of artificial genomic systems based on a molecule whose primary version was dubbed para-DNA—but that was the result of clever artifice. Ararat is a genuine exception: a *natural* exception.

"The inference we had taken from the fact that each new ecosphere had only one fundamental coder-replicator was that in any limited arena, one reproductive molecule would be bound to win out over all others in a primordial competition—a biochemical variant of that discredited pillar of primal ecology, Gause's axiom. That axiom can now be discounted at the biochemical level as well as the specific level. Here on Ararat there are two fundamental reproductive molecules, whose competition has been resolved in a rather peculiar way."

"Go on," Matthew prompted, when Lityansky paused—but he had paused for a reason, to use a keypad to summon a set of formulas and molecular models to the wallscreen behind him.

"As you can see," he went on, "one of the molecules is a double helix that codes for proteins in a fashion roughly similar to that of DNA, although it's a little more versatile. We call it meta-DNA, but that's just for temporary convenience. There are too many viable molecules in what we now recognize as the DNA-para-DNA-meta-DNA family to be discriminated by the customary tags—doubtless we'll eventually work out a whole new terminology, and maybe a whole new branch of science.

"The second molecule, *here*, is the oddity: a freak whose like hasn't yet been encountered anywhere else. All the coder-replicators in the DNA family are basically two-dimensional structures, even though they're twisted repeatedly in order to wind them up into compact structures like plasmids and chromosomes. As you can see"—here Lityansky animated the image on the screen so that the second molecular model began to rotate—"Ararat's second coder-replicator is three-dimensional even at the most basic level of structure. We thought at first that it was tubular, like the more complicated buckyball derivatives, but those are just carbon complexes with occasional add-ons, and this has other components that are far more complex. The amplifications are mostly nitrogen, hydrogen, and oxygen, as you'd expect, and you won't be unduly surprised by the phosphate residues—but look at the silicon and the lanthanides! You've never seen anything remotely like *them.*

"The silicon was an almost-expectable shock, I suppose, because we've always preset our probes to search high and low for traces of silicon or silicone-based life, both in and outside the home system. We never found any, but we kept hoping. Even running across silicone-like formations working in collaboration with rare earths as well as carbon didn't seem so very surprising in retrospect, in view of the way that nanotech development has proceeded on Earth since we've been away. There's been a dramatic convergence of the organic and the inorganic at what more recent jargon calls the picotechnological level, and the inorganic materials involved in the convergence are the descendants of the old silicon chips and modular doping arrays—but that's artifice too. *This* is natural, although I ought to admit that there are some mavericks on the surface who aren't entirely convinced."

"Why not?" Matthew asked, wondering whether the "mavericks" in question included Bernal Delgado.

"Because they're excessively impressed by the fact that this world is a billion years older than Earth. They're not convinced that evolution happened here at a much slower rate. They wonder whether there might have been an advanced civilization here at one time: one as advanced as Earth's. If so, they argue, it too might have developed artificial coding systems for biotechnological and nanotechnological purposes. Personally, I find it impossible to believe that any such civilization wouldn't have left more obvious relics."

"After a billion years?" Matthew countered.

"A sophisticated inorganic technology ought to have left *some* identifiable traces," Lityansky insisted. "There's no evidence of any such traces on the surface. Anyhow, the situation *now* is that Ararat's second coding molecule is associated with a whole new sideline of organic chemistry, which collaborates with the one that's a close analogue of Earthly organic chemistry. Given that fundamental collaboration, maybe it isn't so surprising that we also find biochemical collaborations of a much more adventurous kind.

"With the aid of hindsight, perhaps it isn't so unusual that all the metazoan cells in the Ararat ecosphere have two differently based genomes. After all, you and I and all our animal cousins have two genomes too, although the nuclear genome and the mitochondrial genome are both DNA-based. Collaboration between genomes is obviously possible, given the Earthly example, so it's not such a huge stretch of the imagination to wonder whether it might somehow be necessary, or at least very advantageous, to the production of authentically complex organisms. It's hard to believe that it's mere coincidence that the only other place in the galaxy where we've found evidence of humanoid organisms—albeit, perhaps, unsuccessful humanoid organisms— built them on a double-genome basis."

Matthew had been studying the molecular models carefully, hoping for some insight into their potential, but it was no more possible to deduce the organisms he'd studied with Vince Solari from the formulas on the screen than it was to deduce a housefly and a human being from the formula of DNA. It took him a few seconds to realize that the bearded man had paused again, this time in order to invite a response.

"*Collaboration* was an emotionally loaded word where I come from," Matthew observed, cautiously. "It didn't sit too well within the theory of evolution by natural selection. It's not a word that Bernal Delgado was wary of using, but he wasn't the hardest-centered Darwinian in the selection box."

"Were you?" Lityansky asked. The way his lips had pursed when Matthew mentioned Bernal Delgado's name told Matthew that Bernal was indeed one of the disapproved mavericks— almost certainly their loudest spokesman.

"No," Matthew admitted, "but whenever Bernal and I got together, I was prepared to play devil's advocate."

"You can call it assimilation if you'd prefer that way of looking at it," Lityansky offered, as if he were making a generous concession. "Lichens are the only obvious Earthly example of that kind of cross-category fusion, but there are a lot more here. On Ararat, the distinction between plants and animals is unclear. Lots of animals, of many different families, possess chloroplast-analogues."

"One could argue that *all* Earthly plants and *all* Earthly animals are the products of cross-category fusions," Matthew pointed out. "Chloroplasts and mitochondria probably started out as independent organisms that became resident in other kinds of cells."

"However the association between nuclear and mitochrondrial DNA arose," Lityansky said, doggedly, "it's there and it's productive. It produced a selective advantage that enabled organisms with it to out-compete organisms without it. Something similar must have happened here. The metazoans with two genomes won out over any metazoans that tried to get by with one, whether the one was two-dimensional or three-dimensional."

Lityansky dismissed the various images of the new world's coding molecules from the screen, and brought up a new set of images. At first, Matthew couldn't make head nor tail of them, but then he realized that they were electron microscope images of cell-clusters, including some cells that were in the process of division and some clusters where neighboring cells appeared to be undergoing some kind of fusion or exchange of nuclear material.

"Can you see what's happening here?" Lityansky asked.

Matthew couldn't, but he wasn't prepared to look stupid. He felt obliged to make a tentative guess.

"Reproduction," he said. "Shuffling the genetic pack. The local equivalent of meiosis. But there's a twist. There's something odd about reproductive processes on this world. I never saw any young in the archive photographs, nor any obvious secondary sexual characteristics."

It was close enough to wring a grudging flicker of respect from Lityansky. "That's the heart of the matter," he conceded. "I believe that biotechnologists had already begun to explore techniques of artificial chimerization by the time you left Earth?"

"Mosaic organisms had been produced by embryo fusion long before then," Matthew said. "It was never more than a gimmick in my day, used to produce experimental interspecies hybrids and children for same-sex couples. But it's different here, right? Chimerization is routine—and the mavericks who reckon that the genomic duplex might be a relic of ancient biotech also wonder whether the local chimeras might be echoes of a glorious past. On the other hand, patterns of chimerization must have been built into metazoan evolution when the first local slime-molds started experimenting with communal living and cellular division of labor. From there, they were handed down to the entire range of metazoans, conserved in every new burst of adaptive radiation." His guesses were growing more elaborate now, as he picked up cues from Lityansky's body language that told him that he was on the right track. "At any rate," he concluded, "that's why the big animals don't seem to go in for sex, even though convergent evolution has made them in the same image as their Earthly counterparts in other respects. So how *does* reproduction work here?"

Lityansky frowned, partly because his prepared script had been subverted and partly because he was now aware that he had underestimated his pupil. Like Milyukov, the genomicist had seen tapes of Matthew's TV performances, and like Milyukov, he had formed an unjustly modest estimate of Matthew's intelligence.

"As you can see," he said, although he probably knew well enough how opaque the electron micrographs were to anyone unfamiliar with their context, "the local organisms do manifest a physiological process analogous to sexual reproduction. Individual cells do exchange genetic information—but it's not meiosis because it doesn't produce gametes. The exchanges are between different somatic components of chimerical mosaics."

It took Matthew a few seconds to get his head around that. Put very crudely, what Lityansky was saying was that different bits of local organisms had sex with other bits of the same organism, which had a different genetic makeup, but that whole organisms didn't have sex with one another. Sex on Ararat/Tyre wasn't a matter of individuals at all; it was strictly a cell-on-cell business within chimerical individuals.

If he'd been talking to a man like Bernal Delgado, Matthew would have called it mind-boggling, but Andrei Lityansky didn't seem to be the kind of man whose mind went in for that kind of thing.

"We've observed this in a wide range of primitive plants and animals," Lityansky added, while Matthew was catching up. "We assume the same thing goes on in higher plants and animals, but that's only speculation at present."

"Why?" Matthew asked, genuinely surprised.

"Why *what*?" Lityansky retorted.

"Why is it only speculation? Why haven't you found out?"

"The live specimens brought up into orbit had to be accommodated to the constraints of our biocontainment facilities," Lityansky told him.

In other words, Matthew thought, Lityansky had never seen an alien creature he couldn't fit on to a microscope slide.

"The work we've done on *Hope*," Lityansky continued, "has consisted of fundamental biochemical, genomic, and proteonomic analyses. The biologists at Base One have had more opportunity to observe more complex organisms in the wild, but their lab work has had to be devoted almost entirely to the practical problems of adapting Earthly crops and animals to live in native environments."

"That's ridiculous!" Matthew said. "Are you telling me that you've been confronted for *three years* with a world whose higher plants and animals don't appear to have any sex organs or to produce any young, but that you haven't made any significant attempt to find out how they *do* reproduce?"

"What I'm telling you," Lityansky said, frostily, "is that we've had too few people working on far too many problems to have made as much progress as we would have liked, or as much progress as we *need*. We had no idea, when we began, how strange the physiology of the most primitive organisms would turn out to be, but we have taken the view that if we can unravel the mysteries of the simpler entities first, we will then stand a far better chance of understanding the mysteries of the more complex."

"So how do the simple entities reproduce themselves?" Matthew wanted to know.

"Some by simple fragmentation, others by sporulation."

"Just like a lot of simple entities on Earth," Matthew pointed out. "Not much help there in figuring out how the monkeys and the weasels do it. What's the favorite hypothesis?"

"I don't have a *favorite hypothesis*," the bearded man told him. "That's not the way I work."

"So what's the favorite hypothesis of the people who *do* have favorite hypotheses? What was Bernal Delgado's favorite hypothesis?"

Lityansky pursed his lips. "Professor Delgado had become fond of speculating about *gradual chimerical renewal*," he admitted. He seemed reluctant to dignify the phrase with elaboration, let alone explanation, but it only took Matthew a moment to connect the term to its most celebrated referent.

"Gradual chimerical renewal is a fancy name for the Miller Effect," he said. "That's not reproduction. That's a kind of emortality."

"Gradual chimerical renewal is a general concept, one of whose specific instances is the so-called Miller Effect," Lityansky said, using pedantry to avoid simple agreement.

"I get it," Matthew said. "It doesn't remove the need for an account of reproduction, but it *might* explain why rates of reproduction are so slow that it's almost impossible to observe immature individuals."

"It's pure speculation," Lityansky pointed out, "and it's *very* difficult to put any such hypothesis to the test. There's no way to establish how long any individual is potentially capable of living if you can only observe it for a limited period of time. May I return to matters of which I *do* have some reliable knowledge?"

"I'm sorry I interrupted," Matthew said, hoping that he didn't sound too insincere.

"We *have* been able to study the various ways in which the simpler chimeras are compounded," Lityansky went on, "and the ways in which certain individuals seem to hybridize types that would have been considered on Earth to be different species. Earth wasn't entirely devoid of natural chimeras, of course. Mules and zeehorses, tigons and ligers were the most obvious—all compounds of closely related species, and they were unable to reproduce themselves because they were almost invariably sterile. There were, however, others far less obvious. In species where multiple embryos were simultaneously implanted, producing litters of fraternal twins, two embryos would occasionally fuse into a single individual. If the result was a *fetus in fetu* it usually aborted spontaneously, but in rare instances it resulted in a mosaic individual: a single-species chimera not unlike one of those produced by artifice for same-sex couples. The phenomenon was not unknown even in humans, although very rare.

"After it became possible in the late twentieth century to identify such same-sex chimeras by DNA analysis, some studies did suggest that animals of that kind could manifest a kind of hybrid vigor, because the fact that their individual tissues included two complete sets of chromosomes instead of one made them less vulnerable to genetic deficiency diseases. That was irrelevant from the viewpoint of natural selection, because each individual sperm or egg produced by a mosaic individual could only be a product of one set of genes . . ."

"But if the mosaic identity had been heritable," Matthew put in, "then Earthly mosaics might have had sufficient selective advantages over single-genome individuals to have become the norm!"

Lityansky had grown used to Matthew's interruptions by now, and accepted this one with better grace. "Perhaps. Here, where sexual exchanges occur between the cells of chimerical individuals rather than between the whole individuals, and where primitive reproduction is a matter of fragmentation and sporulation, the fundamental situation is very different. We can only speculate as to what happened in the earliest phases of evolution on Ararat, but the situation *now* is that sexual exchanges between chimerically associated genomes produce new types of somatic cells, some of which are then shed, or encapsulated as spores, which may then meet and fuse with the similar products of other individuals, eventually growing into new chimerical wholes. The vast majority of those we've so far catalogued are equivalent to Earthly same-species chimeras, but some are more ambitious combinations, of a kind manifest on Earth only in the lichens—"

"Hold on," Matthew said, as he was struck by a sudden inspiration. "I'm not sure that's true."

"*What's* not true?" Lityansky snapped back.

"That the only ambitious chimeras on Earth are lichens. What about insects?"

Lityansky was mystified. "What about insects?" he countered.

"Well, what's an insect but a serial chimera? The imago is only a maggot's way of making more maggots, so they're exactly like lichens in being strapped into a specific straitjacket by the limitations of sexual reproduction, but what an insect has, in essence, is a genome that codes for two quite different physical forms."

"I don't think it helps to introduce the notion of *serial chimeras*," Lityansky complained. "The whole point about the situation here is that the vast majority of organisms on Ararat are made up of *simultaneous* chimerical combinations of cell types."

Matthew didn't want to be slapped down so easily. "When Solari and I were trawling through the data banks yesterday," he said, "arthropod analogues seemed conspicuous by their absence. Assuming that the insects and their kin didn't just slip into the cracks of our admittedly slapdash search, mightn't that have something to do with the prevalence of un-serial chimeras?"

Lityansky wasn't impressed. "It's true that Ararat's ecosphere has a dramatic dearth of exoskeletal organisms," he admitted. "We think it's because the local DNA-analogue has a blind spot where chitin and its structural analogues are concerned. We think that the principal reason for the apparent depletion of the vertebrate-analogues by comparison with Earth is due to the same blind spot. The local organisms aren't good at producing hard bone. Their endoskeletons are more like cartilage, which means that the bigger animals need more complicated articulations to produce similar leverage. The organisms you saw in those photographs aren't as similar to their Earthly analogues as they appear at first glance. Each individual might almost be regarded as a fusion of several disparate individuals, routinely combining as many as eight different genomic cell types. In some cases, only half of those cell types are sufficiently similar that they'd be reckoned as same-species in Earthly terms. We've hardly begun to extrapolate the possibilities opened up by that fundamental difference."

Or to investigate it, Matthew added, silently.

"So the ultimate question—the one that dominates all our minds—is admittedly less simple than it seemed to be three years ago, but also more intriguing," Lityansky added. His rhetorical manner suggested that his discourse was nearing some kind of climax.

Matthew knew that the question Lityansky must have in mind was whether or not it would be possible to establish a viable colony on the surface of the new world. "Go on," he prompted.

"We had assumed, before arriving here," Lityansky said, "that the question of whether we could introduce DNA-based ecosystems into an ecosphere that had its own distinct DNA-analogue was relatively straightforward. There was a possibility that DNA organisms might not be able to hold their own in the resultant competition, or that the local organisms might be at a disadvantage, either case presenting a conservation problem. With respect to Ararat, however, we have to ask the question of whether the second genomic system might be integrated into DNA-based organisms, to work in association with them in much the same way that it works in association with the local DNA-analogue. We also have to ask whether we can turn the chimerical constitution of the local organisms to our own technological advantage. In both cases, I believe, the answer is yes. Given what the biotechnologists of Earth have accomplished by taking over the innate natural technology of Earthly organisms, there is good reason to believe that they might accomplish just as much—if not more—by taking control of the natural technology available here, whose potential we have only just begun to glimpse.

"In brief, Professor Fleury, there is abundant potential here for a biotechnological bonanza that will have Earth's megacorporations racing one another to establish a presence here and reap its benefits."

Matthew could easily see how attractive that possibility might be to the crew of *Hope*. If the new world could attract enthusiastic support from Earth, it wouldn't need the kind of support from *Hope* that had been built into Shen Chin Che's original plan—not, at any rate, for very long.

But there was another side to the coin.

"By the same token," Matthew said, reflexively taking on the role of devil's advocate, "there might also be potential here for an ecocatastrophe of an entirely new and previously unenvisaged kind—an ecocatastrophe that could devastate the colony. That's why the people on the ground are so nervous, isn't it? That's why so many of them are ready to give up on the dream that brought them across fifty-eight light-years of void and seven hundred years of history.

"If the three-dimensional genome is capable of producing infectious agents, its biochemistry is so radically different that all the painstaking technological defenses we've built against bacteria and viruses will be useless against them. If the processes by which local organisms can produce exotic chimeras can be extended to embrace Earth-originated cells, we might encounter whole new modes of infection.

"In either case, this world could be a potential death trap!"

THIRTEEN

W hen Matthew returned to the room in which he had awakened, the complex possibilities that Andrei Lityansky had laid out for him were still causing him considerable distress. He threw himself down on his bed as soon as he was inside—not, this time, because he was exhausted but because he needed to think.

Lityansky had, of course, done everything within his power to soothe Matthew's suddenly inflamed anxiety. He had assured Matthew that there was not the slightest evidence that local pathogens could infect DNA-based organisms or that local organisms could form chimeras in association with them. Although the people on the surface had sustained all manner of cuts, bites, and stings, there had not yet been a single case of alien infection. Nor, the crewman had insisted, was there any reason to suppose that Earthly medical scientists could not devise defenses against such an infection, if one ever did arise, with exactly the same alacrity they had demonstrated in the Earthly plague wars, when they had been required to respond to some extremely ingenious and exotic threats.

The last point would have been more convincing had Matthew not heard news of the havoc wreaked by the ingenious and exotic chiasmalytic transformers, but Lityansky had refused to concede the point. The people of Earth had survived the last plague war just as they had survived the others, and had gone on to achieve true emortality. In the meantime, they had harnessed the new technology of para-DNA to many different purposes, revolutionizing the construction biotech pioneered by Leon Gantz.

Ararat, Lityansky had continued to insist, was a potential biotechnological Klondyke, for whose right of exploitation the colonists should be exceedingly grateful.

Matthew attempted to explain all this to Vince Solari, who had come over to stand by the bedside, looking down at him. Although the policeman couldn't follow the technical aspects of the discourse, he was perfectly capable of reacting to phrases like "potential death trap" and "biotech bonanza."

"I take it that you don't think Lityansky's trustworthy," Solari said.

"Oh, he told me the truth as he sees it," Matthew admitted. "But his viewpoint is way too narrow. The pattern of discovery here is the reverse of the one that steered the history of Earthly biology, and he hasn't seen the implications of that."

"I don't even know what it means," Solari said, a trifle resentfully.

"On Earth," Matthew told him, "scientists had an enormous amount of information about plant and animal species before they began to get to grips with the mysteries of organic chemistry. By the time biochemistry got going there was a rich context in place, provided by centuries of painstaking work in taxonomy, anatomy, and physiology. Lityansky and his colleagues have started at the other end, doing the genomic and biochemical analyses first. They haven't a clue, as yet, how that biochemistry relates to the anatomy, reproduction, and ecology of actual organisms—and they don't seem to be in any particular hurry to find out. They're being very methodical, starting with the fundamentals and working their way slowly forward, but they haven't the slightest idea what the big picture might look like when all the pieces of the jigsaw are fitted together. They think people who try to make guesses—people like Bernal Delgado—are getting way ahead of themselves, but that's stupid. We have to try to come at the puzzle from every direction if we want to solve it any time soon."

"So what about these mavericks?" Solari asked. "Could they be right about the planet's biosphere being the wreckage of some long-past ecocatastrophe? I mean, if things had gone differently on Earth, and the human race really had gone belly-up there, we'd have left an awful lot of biotech debris. When I used to see you on TV, you were fond of saying that there was a possibility that the ecosphere might be cut back all the way to the bacterial level, and that the only footprint we'd leave in the sands of time would be a few hundred long-term survivors out of hundreds of thousands of new bacterial species that had originated as technological products. Might that have happened here, hundreds of millions of years ago?"

"If we really had contrived an ecospasm as extreme as that on Earth," Matthew said, pensively, "I suppose there might not be much material evidence of it after a hundred thousand years of lousy weather, let alone continental drift and supervolcanic basalt flows. Given that the biotech products that were already at large in my day had been built to last, though, some of them would have held their own in the ensuing struggle for existence and joined in a new tidal wave of adaptive radiation. If I knew more about this stuff that Lityansky calls para-DNA, I might be able to make a start on figuring out the likelihood of something like that getting so thoroughly mixed up with the bacterial residue of an ecospheric meltdown that a new metazoan adaptive radiation would have taken it aboard . . . but I'm not sure how relevant it would be. This planet is much quieter than Earth, and I'm not sure that all material evidence of a technically sophisticated civilization could have been so thoroughly obliterated *here*."

"But the planet might have been a lot more active in the distant past," Solari pointed out. "Even if it wasn't, the evidence would be buried pretty deep by now. To say that the people on the ground haven't even begun scratching the surface would be an understatement. But what really matters, I suppose, is whether you're right or wrong about the world being a death trap *now*."

"Unfortunately," Matthew said, "the answer to that one depends on the answers to all the other questions—including the ones Lityansky didn't want to address, like the possible relevance of serial chimeras. Maybe the relative dearth of chitin and hard bone *isn't* the product of a blind spot in the protein-coding mechanism. Maybe there's another factor militating against rigidity."

"Serial chimeras?," Solari echoed. "Like werewolves, you mean."

"Not exactly—but I'll have to devote some time to figuring out what I *might* mean. What have you been doing while I've been taking lessons in xenobiology?"

"Checking the list of murder suspects."

"Really?" The news was sufficiently interesting to make Matthew lift his head a little higher and turn to lie sideways, supporting himself on his elbow.

Solari had obviously been practicing his keyboard skills, because it required no more than a casual sweep of his fingers to replace the single image on the wallscreen with a mosaic consisting of seven faces arranged in two ranks, four on the upper and three on the lower. Matthew took due note of the symbolism of the empty square at the right-hand end of the bottom rank: the blank where a photograph of one of the alien humanoids might be, if the alien humanoids still existed. Even at a relatively oblique angle, Matthew had no difficulty identifying two of the faces.

"The second from the left on the top row's Ikram Mohammed," he said. "A first-rate experimental genomicist. Did some remarkable work on intron architecture and functional gene-nesting. I met him a dozen times at conferences. Bernal would have known him fairly well too—whatever Bernal was working on or thinking about, he'd have shared it with Ike. More of an acquaintance than a friend, but I feel confident saying that he's not a likely murderer."

"I've looked at his CV," Solari said, noncommittally. "Do you know any of the others?"

"Lynn Gwyer, directly below him. Genetic engineer specializing in agricultural pharmaceutical production. Did a lot of work on bananas. Regarded by some—but certainly not by me—as a plague-war draft dodger, mainly because she dedicated her efforts to attempts to protect Third World innocents rather than First World software engineers. Bernal probably knew her better than I did, maybe better than he knew Ike Mohammed. Again, an acquaintance rather than a friend, but also not a likely murderer, in my opinion. In fact, a highly unlikely murderer."

"None of them is a *likely* murderer," Solari said, a trifle impatiently. "Few murderers are, alas—especially when it comes to domestics. This has to be reckoned a domestic of sorts. They'd all been living together for months. One big happy—or not-so happy—family."

"Why *not so happy*?"

"There's always friction in living space that small. There were disagreements. Personal as well as theoretical." He didn't elaborate, presumably because it was gossip rather than real evidence.

"Who are the others?" Matthew asked.

Solari started at the top left-hand corner, with a man who might have passed for Shen Chin Che's son in a dim light. "Tang Dinh Quan," he reported. "Analytical biochemist. Very accom-

plished, apparently. Two daughters still in SusAn, but no partner—just like you. Reported to be showing signs of strain and
acute anxiety in the last few months, becoming increasing vocal
in his support for the Base One party advocating withdrawal
from the world."

"Reported by whom?" Matthew inquired.

"The resident doctor, Godert Kriefmann," Solari said, passing on to the image on the other side of Ikram Mohammed's face,
of a solidly built, square-jawed man whose head had been comprehensively depilated. "He's a medical researcher too, of course,
but the doctors on the surface have had more work to do than
they expected. The smartsuits designed for surface use are reasonably strong, and they seem to work very well inside the body,
protecting the lungs and the gut from orthodox invasion, but
some of the local wildlife is pretty dangerous. Some wormlike
things have nasty stings and surprisingly powerful jaws, and
some of the mammal-equivalents have tongues like harpoons. To
make a smartsuit capable of resisting all the local armaments
would inhibit movement considerably. Fortunately, the toxins are
more painful than life-threatening, and Kriefmann's working to
develop antisera with Maryanne Hyder, toxicologist." Solari's finger dropped to the image beneath Kriefmann's. It was a study in
contrasts: Maryanne Hyder's face was slender, almost elfin, and
she had an abundance of carefully coiffed blond hair.

"She seems to be the one that Bernal was playing happy families with at the time of his death," Solari reported. "Very cut up
by his loss, apparently. Quiet and methodical beforehand, now
more hysterical than Tang. On the surface, the least likely of all
the suspects—but if it is a domestic, she's the closest thing we
have to a spouse, which might put her under the microscope
ahead of all the rest if this weren't such a bizarre crime. In my
experience, domestic murders don't often involve alien artifacts,
real or faked, and they almost always take place inside the home,
not in a field two miles away."

The policeman's finger moved on to the only remaining
woman, whose picture was at the far end of the top row. She was
darker than any of the others, and her face was extensively scarred,
as if by smallpox or some other supposedly extinct disease.

"Dulcie Gherardesca, anthropologist," Solari reported. "The
most recent arrival at the base, sent to study the ruins of the city

in the hope of building a fuller picture of the technological resources and folkways of the humanoids. Spent less time safely enclosed in the bubbles than most of the others, although Hyder and Mohammed both picked up more injuries. Probably better equipped to fake alien artifacts than any of the others, and with more opportunity to do it, but everything else in her background makes her just as unlikely a murderer as the others. A victim of plague war in infancy, very nearly died—said to be fiercely dedicated to her work."

The last remaining picture showed a blond man wearing a hat and a wide smile. He was carrying a rifle.

"Rand Blackstone," Solari reported. "Specialist in survival skills. Professional soldier, served with UN forces in half a dozen shooting wars—all spinoff from the plague wars. Argumentative type, but most of his arguments seem to have been with Tang, not Delgado. No doubt at all that he's capable of killing, but he was there to protect the people at Base Three, and losing one of them is a blot on his reputation. If Milyukov's right about there being a conspiracy to protect the murderer, it's difficult to believe that he'd be in on it. Insofar as there's been an investigation, he's done it—but he's no detective. He seems to have made up his mind very quickly that it wasn't any of the people stationed at the base, and must therefore have been an alien, even though he hasn't seen the slightest sign of a humanoid since he was commissioned to help set up the operation—he was part of the original group sent over from Base One, along with Mohammed, Gwyer, and Delgado. The others shuttled down a couple of weeks later."

"Does anyone except Tang have family still in SusAn?" Matthew asked, curiously.

"No, but Kriefmann has a wife, also a doctor, at Base One. Gwyer's ovaries were stripped and the eggs placed in storage in the gene banks, so I suppose she could be said to have potential children up here—but then, all the males have made sperm donations. Gherardesca's the odd one out on that score. She was sterilized by a plague-war agent that nearly killed her. Nothing as refined as a chiasmalytic disruptor—an artificial variant of systemic lupus erythromatosus, whatever that is."

"A very nasty virus," Matthew told him. "That would explain the scars—although she could have had them removed by elementary somatic engineering."

"Making a political point, apparently," Solari told him. "Thought the effects of plague war on the disadvantaged ought to be made manifest. Made herself into a kind of walking ad. Your friend Gwyer would presumably have sympathized."

"There's no need to sound contemptuous," Matthew objected. "*I* sympathize."

"You would," Solari observed. "As an adman yourself, I mean."

"I wasn't an adman," Matthew told him. "If I was a trifle over-theatrical it was because I was trying to ram home an unwelcome message. As William Randolph Hearst himself was fond of saying, the news is what somebody wants to stop you spreading—it's the rest that's the ads. I was spreading the news. So was Lynn Gwyer. So, apparently, was Dulcie Gherardesca. We had to work hard at it because it was news that a lot of people seemed determined not to hear. We had to make them pay attention. Apparently, we succeeded. If we hadn't, Earth *could* have been devastated all the way down to the bacterial level."

"Okay," Solari conceded. "I'm not trying to pick a fight. Well-intentioned or not, Gherardesca's an oddball. She was frozen down not long after you—part of the same intake as Delgado. Lucky to be here, I guess. She might have been eliminated from consideration if Shen and his collaborators hadn't been so idiosyncratic, although I suppose she's as clonable as the next person. Why do you think that someone having family in SusAn might have a bearing on Delgado's murder?"

"I don't. I was wondering whether it might have had an effect on Tang's state of mind and his conversion to the party demanding withdrawal. As you pointed out, I have two daughters in SusAn myself. If I became convinced that the surface was direly unsuitable for colonization, I might not be prepared to expose them to risks I'd gladly face myself."

"Is it *direly unsuitable*?" Solari wanted to know. "Can we establish a colony here or not?"

"I don't know," Matthew told him. "But I can understand why the people on the surface don't want to wait around for Andrei Lityansky and the one-step-at-a-time brigade to come to a firm conclusion."

"Maybe we could do something about it even if there turned out to be awkward problems," Solari said.

"Maybe," Matthew agreed. "In theory we could probably dose the entire world with weed killer, a few hectares at a time, and replace the alien ecosphere with a duplicate of our own, converting it into an authentic replica of Earth. It might be the case that releasing Earthly organisms into the planetary ecosphere will eventually have that effect anyway, because it would begin a competition of replicator molecules that would eventually be settled by the absolute victory of DNA over its alien rivals. Unfortunately, you don't have to be a radical Gaean to think that murdering an entire ecosphere, or standing back and letting DNA do the dirty work for us, would be an unforgivable crime.

"What we actually *want* is to be able to set up a situation that would allow DNA's rival replicators to continue to flourish, and also allow us to benefit from the bounty of their natural technology. How easy that might be to achieve I can't even begin to guess—and given the unanticipated complexity and flexibility of the local ecosphere, it might be exceedingly difficult to come up with a confident answer in the space of a single lifetime. The seven hundred years it took to get here might be needed to be doubled before we can be certain that any colony we found is genuinely secure. The worst-case scenario is that this isn't our Ararat at all, but our Roanoke."

Solari nodded to indicate that he understood the reference to the most famous of America's lost colonies. "Yeah," he said. "Well, we'll have to find out the hard way—on the surface. I'm not going to solve this case by looking at pictures and CVs. The sooner we can get down there the better, from my point of view. I'm not looking forward to this suit-fitting business, but the quicker we get kitted out the sooner we can get stuck in."

He blanked the screen and hopped up onto his own bed, stretching himself out in much the same pose as Matthew's. Matthew let himself relax onto his back again, but he didn't close his eyes. He knew that he, like Solari, wouldn't even be able to begin to fit the pieces of his puzzle together until he was actually on the surface, able to gather evidence at first hand, but he still had a lot of preparatory thinking to do. When the opportunity arrived to see the wood in spite of the trees, he had to be as ready as he possibly could.

FOURTEEN

In theory, the suit fitting should not have been an unduly unpleasant experience. It wasn't unduly uncomfortable, in purely physical terms, and probably wouldn't have been alarmingly painful even if Matthew's IT had not been ready to muffle anything worse than the mildest discomfort, because the human body had few pain receptors ready to react to the kind of invasion that the suit mounted. The fact that the problem was psychological rather than physical didn't make it any less troublesome, though.

Matthew belonged to a generation that had grown used to the idea of smart clothing. Even as a baby he had been swathed in living fibers charged with taking care of the various wastes that his body produced, but he had also been used to smartsuits as things a man could put on and take off at will. He had never worn "dead clothes" but he had nevertheless thought of his smartsuits as clothing to be changed at regular intervals, or whenever the whim took him, rather than as symbiotic companions more intimate than any lover.

The various kinds of physiological assistance his previous smartsuits rendered had always seemed valuable but peripheral, essentially subsidiary to matters of display and appearance, fashion and style. The smartsuits he had worn on the moon and in L-5 had been "heavy duty" suits that might have become vital to his survival had there ever been a serious mishap, but he had not lingered long in either location, and had never fallen victim to a life-threatening accident. There was nothing in his experience that had even begun to bring about a fundamental change of attitude. He was, therefore, quite unprepared for the kind of suit he would need to wear on the surface of the new world.

As a biologist, Matthew had always known that everyday notions of what was "inside" and "outside" his body were not very precise, and that there was a significant sense in which the long and tangled tube constituting his gut was "outside" rather than "inside." His new smartsuit, unlike the ones he had worn at home, really would have to cover and protect his entire body, which meant that it would have to line his gut from mouth to anus, forming an extra layer over every nook and cranny of his intestines. Strictly speaking, he would not be able to "feel" the growth-process that would extend the new layer of surface once he had swallowed the initial bolus, but he was conscious of its progress nevertheless, and his imagination readily supplied the slight unease that his stomach and bowel refused to generate.

It would have been even worse, he thought, as he lay on his bed while the application was completed, if the new membrane had had to descend all the way into his lungs, to coat every single alveolus, but the air filter did not need to be quite as sensitive or capable as the food filter, and the crucial barrier was established in his bronchii. Nita Brownell assured him that he had no need to be anxious that it might leave him short of breath in crisis—quite the reverse, given that it maintained an emergency supply of oxygen—but his imagination was not yet ready to take that on trust. He was able to see, quite literally, that the extra layer added to his conjunctiva did not threaten his eyesight in the least, but he was unable to extend the analogy as easily as the doctor could have wished. She too was an ex-corpsicle, but she had been awake for three long years and had spent far longer in various low-gee environments before being frozen down.

"Just take it easy for a few hours," Dr. Brownell instructed him, severely. "If you can lie still, the process will proceed with maximum efficiency." She was still annoyed with him for the shame that he had allegedly brought on the entire population of sleepers by virtue of his vicious attack on Riddell and Lamartine.

"How useful is the suit, really?" Matthew wanted to know. "According to Vince, the stings and fangs with which most of the local wildlife seem to be equipped go through it almost as easily as they'd go through bare skin. Even if Lityansky's right about the unlikelihood of any biological infection, anything that gets injected that way is likely to be toxic."

"Very few of the organisms you'll meet on a day-to-day basis have stings or fangs," the doctor assured him, "and they seem to be as reluctant to use them as Earthly organisms. They're last-resort defenses, not means of aggression. Even the most poisonous ones haven't killed anyone yet. Not that we're complacent—we're working flat-out to produce more effective defenses, but we're only partway there. The main problem is the sheer profusion of likely reactions. So, no matter how good your IT is it'll hurt like hell if you get stung by anything bigger than my thumb, and it might take as much as a week to clear all the poisonous debris out of the affected tissues.

"The suits are far from perfect, as yet—but they're no less vital for that. If you didn't have an artificial gut lining and air filter you'd be in deep trouble the moment you stepped down on to the surface. If he stayed inside the big bubble at Base One, drinking sterilized water and irradiated food, a man without a suit would probably get by, but you're going to Base Three and you'll be spending a lot of time outside. You'll probably need all the protection the suit can provide, even if you don't get bitten or stung."

When she had turned away Matthew lifted his arm so that he could inspect the fabric of the suit. Once the molecular layers were properly set he would be able to reprogram the outer layer for color and certain modifications of shape, but for the time being the syntheflesh covering the hand was transparent and the "sleeve" beginning above the wrist was matt black. When he flexed his fingers he could hardly feel the extra epidermal layers, but the back of his hand looked odd because the suit had dissolved the hairs that normally grew there. He lifted his hand to touch the top of his head, and was relieved to discover that the hair growing there had been allowed to grow through. His sideburns were neatly excised at the point he had selected twenty years ago.

He opened and closed his mouth experimentally, running his tongue around his teeth. They did feel slightly strange, but he couldn't tell whether it was the extra layer of tissue on the tongue or the extra layer on the teeth that was responsible for the difference. There was a peculiar taste in his mouth, like slightly moldy dough. His breathing seemed slightly labored, but he didn't feel that he was in any danger of choking. He wondered whether the filters in his bronchii could keep water out of his lungs if he were ever in danger of drowning, and whether the artificial tissue could extract enough oxygen from water to let him continue breathing if he were immersed.

Although Nita Brownell had told him to lie still he decided, in the end, that stillness was exaggerating his psychosomatic symptoms, and that it would be better to put himself through the program of exercises that the doctor had designed to test and develop his inner resources. At first he stayed on the bed, but when stretching his arms and legs rhythmically back and forth began to relieve his feelings of queasiness he leapt down to the floor to practice push-ups and sit-ups.

Solari made no attempt to copy him. "I'm glad this is an Earthlike planet," the policeman commented, as he inspected his own forearms minutely. "Imagine what we'd be wearing if it weren't."

"It's because it's Earthlike that the problems are so awkward," Matthew told him, as he counted sit-ups. "It's not just food allergies we have to worry about. We may not seem very appetizing to the local worms, and we're probably not nearly as nutritious as their natural hosts, but an amino acid is an amino acid and sugars are always sweet. Just because there've been no recorded cases of infection or parasitism so far doesn't mean that we'll be safe indefinitely. Everything local that we come into contact with, deliberately or accidentally, is likely to retaliate by trying to eat us. We have all the technological advantages, but the locals are fighting on their own turf, and they have a few tricks that we've never encountered before."

"You're still worried about the insect thing, aren't you? Not to mention the werewolves."

"Werewolves are a red herring," Matthew told him. "There's a difference between serial chimeras and shapeshifting. The absence of insects may be less significant than I first thought, given the absence of flowering plants."

"Do the plants really have glass thorns?" Solari asked. "That's what Delgado was killed with, you know—a glass dagger. Or maybe a glass spearhead."

"It's not as simple as that," Matthew told him. "But in crude terms, yes. Plants and animals alike seem to use vitrification processes to produce their strongest structural tissues. Most of the products are more like sugar crystals than window glass, but some of the upland plants that grow around the ruins have rigid tissues that can be splintered like glass to make sharp edges, and filed like glass to make sharp points. Photographs taken from above the canopy of the so-called grasslands show multitudinous globular structures like goldfish bowls that *might* be reproductive structures of some kind. I'd like to have a closer look at those."

"I can't make head nor tail of it myself," Solari admitted. "I suppose I'll have to try, though, if I'm going to spend the rest of my life down there."

"It might be as well," Matthew agreed.

"So tell me the difference between serial chimeras and were-wolves—in terms I can understand."

"Caterpillars become butterflies. Tadpoles become frogs. It's a gradual progressive metamorphosis, not a matter of switching back and forth every full moon."

"So you think the reason we didn't see any young animals is that the animals we did see might really be different forms of the same animal?"

"Different *forms*," Matthew echoed. "That might be the essence of it. On a world of chimeras, it might not make sense to think of different *kinds* of plants and animals—only of different forms. Everything related to everything else. Creatures that don't just use gradual chimerical renewal as a means of achieving emortality, but as a means of achieving continual evolution."

Solari sat up and began stroking his limbs experimentally, as if savoring the sensations of his new skin. Matthew still felt the need of distraction, so he continued his callisthenics.

"So the city-builders might not have died out," Solari said. "They might just have changed into something else. They tried humanity and didn't like it, so they moved on."

"It sounds unlikely," Matthew said, "but everything's conceivable, given that nobody seems to have taken the trouble to find out where the limits of the chimerization processes actually lie. No—that's unfair. I mean, nobody's been able to figure out a way of finding out where the limits lie. If the natural metamorphoses are slow and gradual it might need more than a human lifetime just to observe them."

As Nita Brownell had promised, Matthew felt a lot better now than he had the previous day. His body, assisted by his dutiful IT, had been working overtime to make good the deficits incurred by his organs during their suspended animation. The acceleration of his cellular-repair processes was probably going to knock a year or two off his potential lifespan, but he figured that if he could hang around until the crew obtained more information about contemporary longevity technology from Earth he would surely get some compensatory benefit from that. True emortality was apparently out of reach, but seven centuries of progress must have produced much better ways of keeping unengineered individuals healthier for longer.

"So, all in all," Solari said, "you don't think Delgado could have been murdered by a humanoid who shifted out of some other form and then shifted back?"

"I don't know enough yet to rule it out completely," Matthew said, cautiously, figuring that it would be unwise to say that *anything* was impossible until he had a much firmer grasp of the facts. "I'd have to say, though, that it seems extremely unlikely by comparison with the hypothesis that one of your seven suspects stabbed him for reasons we haven't yet determined. Or, for that matter, with the hypothesis that someone sneaked over from Base One in a microlite aircraft."

"It's a hell of a long way," Solari said. "The people at Base One have started establishing fuel dumps and supply caches to make long-distance travel feasible, but it would be extremely difficult for anyone to make an intercontinental flight without making elaborate preparations. To do it without anyone else knowing about it would be extremely difficult, especially with comsat eyes in the sky. My money has to be on one of the seven. But which one?"

"The real question," Matthew observed, "is *why*? I can't believe that any of them would have gone so far as to kill a man in order to prevent him revealing some discovery he'd made. Not so much because all of them except Blackstone are scientists— although that would surely be reason enough—but because they're all Shen's Chosen People. No one would have signed up for this crazy expedition unless he or she had a very powerful commitment to the notion of starting over with a clean sheet, trying to avoid *all* the mistakes that cursed the development of human history on Earth. They must all have arrived here with a strong determination to keep murder out of the picture for as long as humanly possible. If one of the seven did do it, I can't imagine the kind of shame he—or she—must be feeling, knowing that his—or her—name will go down in history as this world's Cain."

"Maybe that's why they're not keen to own up," the police-man said, drily. "You do have a point, though, about the kind of baggage we brought with us. I dare say you took the same kind of flak I did when you told your friends you were shipping out— probably a lot more, given your celebrity. I didn't mind being called a coward, but being called a fool stung a little harder. I don't know how many times I was told that we couldn't possibly solve Earth's problems by setting out to spoil another world. I wish I'd had a better answer to give all the people who just assumed that we'd simply repeat all the same mistakes we'd made on Earth, individually and collectively."

"I was the man who kept reciting the formula that people who fail to learn from prophecies are condemned to enact them," Matthew reminded him. "If I hadn't thought that we were capa-ble of learning, I wouldn't have bothered, but if I hadn't thought that it was extremely difficult, I wouldn't have had to."

"You did take a lot of stick, didn't you," Solari remembered, frowning as he tried to think back more than twenty subjective years, to his childhood. "You had the newsvids on your back as well as your friends. The price of fame."

"I had two daughters to use as an excuse," Matthew told him. "The newsvids always liked family values."

"How many of us would have been murderers if we'd have stayed on Earth?" Solari wondered aloud, his voice becoming gradually more somber. "And how many of us would have been murder victims? According to Milyukov, Earth's in good shape now, but it had to go through hell in order to get there. I never killed anyone, but I was lucky not to have had to. If I'd stayed, I might have had to kill hundreds, if I'd been able to avoid getting killed myself. We may all have come here with the best of inten-tions, Matt, but that doesn't mean that we could avoid bringing some pretty sick stuff in our mental luggage. If I was a potential killer back in 2114, I still am—and that applies to everyone else. It's nothing to do with being a policeman or a scientist—it's to do with what we'd have done to survive when the crunch came. Everyone here was willing to be frozen down in order to have a chance of escaping the worst, and my bet is that people willing to do that would have been willing to do almost anything to survive when the collapse came. Wouldn't you?"

"I don't know," Matthew said, truthfully. "But that was there, and this is here. We're not a bunch of rats trapped in a decaying box—we're a tiny handful of people confronted with a strange and hostile world. Nobody is disposable. The situation aboard *Hope* makes it all the more necessary for the people on the ground to help and support one another no matter what differences of opinion they have. Murder has no place down there. I only met two of your seven suspects back home, but I can't believe that *any* of them would commit cold-blooded premeditated murder."

"Maybe it wasn't cold-blooded—or premeditated."

"If whoever did it forged an alien artifact as a murder weapon, it had to be premeditated—and cold-blooded."

"If," Solari repeated, mechanically. "But yes, it looks that way. And I don't want to believe it of any of the seven, any more than you do—but I hear that you came very close to committing murder yourself out in that corridor, having already planned to make your break before you left me alone with the captain, and for no better reason than resentment of the fact that you were under guard."

"I wanted to see Shen," Matthew countered.

"And you had no reason whatsoever to think you could find him," Solari pointed out. "Like I said—we all brought some pretty sick stuff in our mental luggage. Reflexes shaped by Earthly distress and paranoia. Reflexes that make us lash out, even at people adapted for life in half-gee, who might not be able to take the punches. Maybe it was a reflex of exactly the same kind that killed Delgado. Maybe the glass spearhead was never intended as a murder weapon—maybe it was just the first thing that came to hand. The person who stabbed him might have seen those knife-fight VE-tapes they were beginning to peddle back on Earth, and got the impression that good IT could protect people from wounds of that sort. Delgado was unlucky, you know—if the blade hadn't slid between his ribs and penetrated his heart he'd have been okay. Any of them could have done it, Matt. Even the ones you think you know. If you didn't have such a good alibi, I'd have to suspect you. You'd be suspect number one, after what you did to that poor guy's jaw."

"Okay," Matthew said, conceding the point. "That was a mistake. I'm ashamed—but the bastard was following me, and he was on to me as soon as I'd tried and failed to put the gunman down. Maybe he didn't have the power to hurt me the way I hurt him, but it wouldn't have stopped him trying. It wasn't me who decided that crew and cargo are no longer on the same side. That was the so-called revolutionaries."

"The people on the surface also seem to have decided that they aren't all on the same side any more," Solari pointed out. "And having decided that . . . we all come from a violent society, Matt. Even those of us who never lifted a hand against anyone. I wish we had arrived here with a determination to do no violence to anyone, but the simple fact is that we haven't had the practice necessary to lend force to any such determination."

Matthew could see his point. He could also see that, given the situation aboard *Hope*, the potential for further violence—not merely of murder but of all-out war—was far too considerable for comfort.

FIFTEEN

The shuttle in which Matthew had left Earth had been a reassuringly solid construction shaped as a shuttle ought to be shaped, with extendable delta wings for use on reentry. It had, admittedly, been hitched to an intimidatingly massive rocket cylinder, which he could not help but imagine as a potential bomb, but the statistics of past failure and success had made the possibility of disaster seem comfortingly remote.

The knowledge that if the rocket were to turn bomb he would die instantaneously without realizing the fact had further reduced the awfulness of the seeming threat.

The shuttle in which Captain Milyukov intended to send him down to the surface of the new world was an entirely different proposition. It did not look solid, it had no wings and its shape was like no real or imaginary aircraft or spacecraft that Matthew had ever seen depicted. The teardrop-shaped chamber in which Milyukov proposed to stow Matthew and Solari—*stow* seeming the operative word, given the amount of cargo that was to be crammed in with them—was equipped with a conical shield at the base, made from some kind of organic material, but it was alarmingly thin. A long, slender and supple rod extended from the top of the chamber to a limp structure that looked more like a folded spiderweb than a parachute.

A sideways glance at Vince Solari told Matthew that the policeman was as dismayed as he was.

"It's perfectly safe," the captain assured him. "We haven't lost a single life or sustained a serious injury during any of the drops. It's disposable, of course—the only reason the shuttles you were used to looked so very different is that they were designed to go up and come back rather than simply going down. You're a biologist, Professor Fleury—think of it as an extremely tough and extremely smart dandelion seed. It'll float you down so gently you probably won't even feel the bump. The method's accurate to within a few hundred meters—it'll put you down right on the doorstep of Base Three's main bubble."

It occurred to Matthew as he continued to stare at the vehicle that if all the would-be colonists and all their equipment had been landed by analogous means, the task of bringing them up again— were any such necessity ever to arise—would pose an entirely different technological challenge. Shen Chin Che must have made contingency plans for a planetary rescue, but it was not obvious that any such plan could be implemented unless the battle for control of *Hope*'s systems were won without inflicting any substantial damage. In any case, neither Konstantin Milyukov nor Shen Chin Che would have the slightest desire to implement such a plan in anything less than a disaster situation.

"I can't see the TV cameras I asked for," Matthew said, his brow still furrowed by uncertainty.

"We couldn't fit them in," Milyukov told him, blandly. "Oddly enough, Professor Delgado had made a similar request, so they would have been included in the cargo had the necessity not arisen of accommodating you and Inspector Solari. We had to make some difficult decisions as to what to hold over. Dr. Gwyer and Dr. Gherardesca were extremely insistent that materials for the boat they and Delgado were building had to be given priority. Your cameras will be included in the next consignment, I can assure you."

"That might be too late," Matthew objected. "If this boat that they're building is going downriver to investigate the so-called grasslands I'll be on board."

"That's your decision, of course," Milyukov said. "Or theirs, of course." His voice was silky, but he was making no effort whatsoever to conceal his hostility. Matthew knew that he was being punished, but he resented the childishness of Milyukov's petty obstructions. He was distracted from his ire by Nita Brownell, who gave him the bag containing the last of the personal possessions that had been frozen down with him. His beltphone and notepad had already been returned to him, having been carefully checked out and upgraded by the crew's engineers. The bag contained less utilitarian items of the kind that were precious precisely because they were superfluous. He had pictures of Alice and Michelle stored in his notepad, ready for display in any of a dozen different forms, but the solid images he had in the private pack were fragile, unique, and talismanic.

He could have clipped the bag to his belt, but he preferred to keep hold of it. It gave him something to do with his hands.

"We'll need the cameras downriver," Matthew told the captain. "Getting pictures through the canopy is a straightforward power problem, so they won't be subject to the same restrictions as the flying eyes. If there are humanoids living there, however primitive their circumstances, it'll be the most significant discovery ever made off Earth. Everybody will want to know about it. You have to let me have the cameras."

"Perhaps we can arrange another drop before you go," Milyukov said, making it perfectly obvious that his pretended cooperativeness was only pretended. "In the event of an emergency, of course, we could even deliver them directly to the grasslands—our targeting really is *very* good. Perhaps we should find our wild geese *before* we attempt to take pictures of them."

He doesn't want me broadcasting, Matthew realized. He doesn't want anyone broadcasting other than himself, but now that I've seen Shen I'm public enemy number two in his eyes—and he's seen my old tapes. I bet he stalled Bernal's requests too. But that's proof of his own desperation. If his authority were secure, he wouldn't be so fearful.

"Good luck," the captain said—but he was looking at Vince Solari, and it was to the policeman that he extended his hand.

"Thanks," Solari said, shaking it.

Matthew deliberately turned away, returning his attention to the narrow space into which he was being invited to climb. "What if I turn out to be claustrophobic?" he said to the doctor.

Nita Brownell peered through the airlock into the narrow crevice that was his allotted berth. "If your adrenaline level shoots up your IT will put you to sleep," she informed him, unsympathetically. "You'll be able to breathe normally, and quite easily."

Matthew sighed. The cavity was, he supposed, loosely describable as a couch, but the loose festoons of silky material that almost filled the available space seemed ominous. The captain's briefing had referred to the flight-preparation process as "cocooning," but Matthew couldn't help thinking about what happened to flies entangled and entrapped in spiderwebs.

"Reminds me of a body bag," Solari murmured. He obviously came equipped with his own repertoire of disturbing analogies.

"There are more than a thousand people on the surface," Milyukov put in. "They all went through this. Admittedly, you're the first two to travel as a pair rather than a foursome, but that should make it even safer. The cargo's perfectly secure."

There was no reason to doubt the last assurance. Before it had been packed the cargo must have been an awkward jumble of irregular shapes, but now that it was in place it had all the compactness of an ingenious three-dimensional jigsaw. Everything that the people at Base Three needed to put the finishing touches to their riverboat was in there somewhere, along with scientific equipment, foodstuffs, biocontainment apparatus, specialized sursuits, and numerous unlabeled parcels whose content Matthew could not guess.

"Well," Matthew muttered, in a voice so low that no one but Solari could hear him, "if Bernal was killed because someone has it in for ecological genomicists, I hope the killer didn't have an opportunity to sabotage this thing."

"Me too," Solari echoed, presumably hoping that no one had it in for detectives either.

Matthew put procrastination aside and climbed in. Solari waited for him to wriggle into his slot and make himself comfortable before following. Matthew placed the personal possessions that he had brought with him across the gulf of time on his chest, but he made no effort to position them upon his beating heart. There was such a thing as taking symbolism too far.

As soon as Matthew had wedged himself into the crevice and stretched himself out at an angle of thirty degrees the smart spidersilk got to work, weaving itself into an elastic chrysalis. Matthew knew that he ought to be grateful for the protection, which was intended to keep him safe from impact effects even if the dandelion seed did come down a little too precipitately, but it was difficult. It was like being embraced by an amorous blanket of intelligent cotton wool.

He did feel a flicker of momentary panic as his sight was obscured, but nothing actually touched his eyes and he was able to open them again after a moment's uncertainty.

He kept them open, even though there was nothing to see but a silvery mist. He wanted to remain in control, to keep his adrenaline in check by the authority of his will. To be blanked out by his protective IT, he thought, would be an undue humiliation.

"Matthew?" said Solari's voice, coming from a point not much more than a meter away now that the detective was ensconced in his own cocoon.

"I'm here," Matthew replied. "I guess it's not so bad. How long did the captain say the drop is scheduled to take?"

"We should be down within an hour," Solari said. "Some fall."

Matthew already felt virtually weightless, and wondered if he would be able to tell when *Hope* expelled the landing craft. The moment would have to be very carefully picked, to minimize the amount of maneuvering that the craft would have to do on its own behalf once it was adrift in the atmosphere.

When the expulsion eventually took place, though, he felt the shift distinctly, and was almost immediately seized by dizzying vertigo. He knew that the reaction was psychosomatic, produced by his imagination rather than any rude agitation of the statocysts in his inner ear, but he couldn't help gasping. He knew that his adrenaline level must have taken a jolt, but he fought to suppress the flow, to keep it below the threshold at which his internal guardians would take fright. Subjectively, the biofeedback training he had undergone at school was less than forty years behind him. It should still have been second nature even though he'd never had much call to test its limits while he was on Earth, but exercising self-control seemed to be a struggle now.

"Are you okay, Matt?" Solari said again.

Matthew knew that the policeman was seeking reassurance on his own behalf, but he certainly did not begrudge it. "Fine," he said. "You?"

"It's not so bad. A roller-coaster freak wouldn't think twice about it. Never liked them myself. Too much imagination, I guess. Saw too many traffic accidents before robotization became compulsory—and too many afterward, come to think of it."

Matthew had been frozen down while the debate about the right to drive had still been fierce. He had even taken part in televised debates in which spokesmen for the drivers' lobby had argued that robotization would only make "joyriders" and "highwaymen" more reckless, as well as turning them into criminals. He had only seen the victims of traffic accidents on film, but he had not needed any more intimate contact to make him nervous.

"There'll be fresh air waiting for us at the other end," he said,

by way of building morale. "Fresh-ish anyway, once our suits have
filtered it. There'll be open sky and things like trees, and hills and
a river. Not unlike home, as seen though lilac-tinted spectacles,
with gravity just a fraction less than normal. Better than that
damned ship with its twisting corridors and off-color lights and
green-tinted crew."

"Perfect," Solari said drily. "Pity they won't be pleased to see
us, isn't it? Well, maybe they'll be glad to see *you*—and I've had
plenty of practice bearing bad news to victims and staring down
the hostility of suspects. It'll be home-dyed purple, like you say. I
think I could get used to weightlessness, you know, if all I had to
do in zero-gee was lie down. It's the clumsiness that I hate."

"Sure. This is okay. I can even bear to think about what's
really happening. Do you think we've hit the atmosphere yet?"

"No idea." After a pause, Solari continued: "This is what we
came for, isn't it. I almost forgot that, you know, with all this stuff
about the murder and the revolution. It was only a few days ago,
subjectively speaking, but that long gap's still *there*. I lost touch a
little, with the motives that brought me here. This was what it
was all about: the chance to shuttle down to a brand new world,
to have a second chance, to have a hand in starting something
momentous. Everything that happened to us till now was just a
prelude to this moment. We're both the same age now, you know,
give or take a couple of months, even though we were born years
apart. Forty-eight years of active life from the moments of our
birth to this one. Forty-eight years and fifty-eight light-years. We
wanted a new start, and this is it. Ararat, Tyre, whatever . . . this
is *it*. The rest is just so much trivia. I've been falling since the
moment I was born; this is just the landing phase."

It was an oddly poignant speech, and an effective one. It
reminded Matthew of his own reasons for being here—reasons
that had somehow been shunted aside by the tide of information
that had deluged him since the moment of his awakening. It
reminded him that this was supposed to be the turning point of
his life, an end and a beginning. Until he had quit *Hope* he had
still been trapped by the hard and soft artifices of his old life, but
now, cocooned though he was in artifacts of similar provenance,
he was breaking free. When he emerged from his chrysalis onto
the surface of the new world he would be a new being. This was,
as Solari said, merely the landing phase of a fall that had begun

the moment he was born. Seen from the viewpoint of the present, his old life had been something he was passing through, on the way to *this*.

"This is it," Matthew agreed, echoing Solari's judgment. "The first footfall of the most prodigious leap in human history. *My* first footfall, anyway. Nothing will ever be the same again, no matter how things work out aboard *Hope*. Humanity is an interstellar species, and you and I are part of the vanguard. Maybe we're three years behind the first landing, but what's three years in the cosmic timescale? With luck, you'll be the first man here to identify and arrest a murderer. There are worse precedents to set."

"It's not a matter of luck," Solari assured him. "It's a matter of procedure. Procedure and patience."

They were still falling. They seemed to have been falling for a long time. Matthew wished that he had some way to tell how many minutes had actually passed. He had been given his wrist-unit along with his other personal possessions, and had immediately strapped it on, but he could not look at the face of his watch now. He had not thought to put his goggles on, so that he could summon virtual displays by blinking his eyes.

"Will procedure and patience be enough, given that so much time has passed since the actual event?" Matthew asked, reflexively.

"I have to believe so," the policeman told him, scrupulously. "I've made a good start on the data relayed back by Blackstone and the material already on file. It's just a matter of following through."

"You already have a prime suspect?" Matthew asked, surprised that Solari hadn't seen fit to mention it.

"Not exactly. It doesn't do to jump conclusions. Guesswork can confuse your objectivity. You start twisting things to fit your hypothesis. Like you, I'd rather none of them was guilty—but I don't want it to be aliens either. That would be a pity too, maybe the worst scenario of all. We were supposed to meet the alien openhanded, ready to join forces as friends and collaborators."

"So we were," Matthew murmured. It was true. The idea that man and alien would have to meet as enemies, competitors in a Darwinian struggle for existence that extended across the entire cosmic stage, had come to seem horribly twentieth century even to hard Darwinians. *Hope* had been called *Hope* because she lent new hope to humankind's prospects of surviving the ecocatastrophic Crash that had destabilized Earth's biosphere, but she was an incarnation of all kinds of other hopes too. One such hope—perhaps the most important—had been the hope that if the ship *did* manage to find an "Earthlike" world complete with smart aliens, they might be able to recognize an intellectual kinship and contrive some kind of mutual aid.

How much easier would that have been if the panspermists or the extreme convergence theorists had been right, he wondered. How much difference did it make now that they had been proved wrong—*doubly* wrong if you added the biochemical version of Gause's axiom to the package? How much hope was left, when even *Hope* had been riven by conflict and virtually torn in two, each part far less than the ruined whole? What comfort was there in having to hope that one of the seven humans at Base Three had killed their colleague, because the alternative was even more discomfiting?

"Matthew?" Solari said, again, although it was he who had let the silence fall.

"Still here," Matthew said. "Still awake. A petty triumph, I suppose, but one I can still treasure."

"I keep waiting for the bump," Solari said. "Utterly pointless tensing my muscles, I know, but I can't help it."

Until Solari had mentioned it, Matthew hadn't tensed his own muscles at all, but now that the subject had been raised he felt himself flinching in anticipation . . . then relaxing. . . . then flinching again . . .

"We'll be down soon enough," he muttered, trying to jerk himself out of the absurd pattern.

And soon enough, they were.

The impact was distinct, but not in the least dangerous. It felt like an elevator coming to rest after sliding down the core of a building.

"What happens now?" Solari asked.

The glorified dandelion seed provided his answer by splitting apart, as if it were indeed some kind of seed. The silvery mist before Matthew's eyes was oddly illuminated, as if the threads of his cocoon were transmitting the sparkling light and reflecting it at the same time, dividing the rays of the new sun into a million glittering shards.

Then the cocoon began to split too, to deliver its precious cargo to the peak of Ararat, the broad sweep of Tyre . . . or whatever.

Matthew took firmer hold of the bag containing the essence of his former life, and began to struggle free of the disintegrating wrapping that had confined him. He hoped that there would be a crowd to greet him, even if circumstance dictated that it could not possibly be more than seven strong. He had always liked to look upon faces that were pleased to see him, and this was the kind of moment that demanded a veritable host of sympathetic witnesses.

PART TWO
Delving into the Past

SIXTEEN

H ad the landing worked out exactly as planned it would only have been necessary for Matthew to step down onto the new world's surface, exactly as he had imagined doing. Unfortunately, the braking shuttle had been driven by the wind into an inconvenient stand of treelike structures, where the parachute-web had become entangled with the branches. Although the capsule itself was far too heavy to be prevented from descending to solid ground it had come to a rest at an awkward tilt.

The hatchway from which Matthew had to make his escape was three meters above the ground and his egress was blocked by clustered "leaves," which bore more resemblance to plastic plates and leathery fans than the leaves of Earthly trees. Some of these structures had shattered, leaving jagged shards hanging loosely from broken branches, but the majority were whole, their more elastic elements having grudgingly made way for the arrival of the capsule in their midst.

He could see through the tangle that there *was* a crowd hurrying to greet him—seven strong, as he had hoped—but they were still some way off, descending a slope made treacherous by loose gravel. He knew that he must be almost completely hidden from them, and had not space to wave a greeting. The manner of his entrance was obviously going to leave much to be desired: he would have to force his way through the purple tangle in a most ungainly fashion, confused as much by the peculiar textures of the barrier as by the sudden recovery of almost all his Earthly weight.

"Can you get down?" Vince Solari asked, having divined that there were problems.

"It's okay," Matthew assured him, after further investigation. "Not many thorns, no vicious wildlife. It's just a matter of treading carefully."

Fortunately, the branches of the dendrite seemed strong enough and dense enough to facilitate a gradual descent. He hesitated slightly over the business of thrusting himself into their midst, because he was wary of the sudden intimate contact with any local life-form, no matter how innocuous it seemed to be, but he wanted to proceed with an appropriate boldness and he did. The twisted "boughs" of the dendrite looked and felt more like a work of art than an active organism, the foundations in which the plates and fans were set having a texture more like vulcanized rubber than wood. He was glad that there would be no need to handle any of the bulbous structures that were suspended from the end of each branch, although he had no reason to think that they were dangerous.

Eventually, he arrived on the ground and scrambled out into the open.

By this time the people he had seen approaching were all gathered about the thicket, but they hung back and waited for him to emerge, having realized that pressing forward would only make things more difficult.

Lynn Gwyer was the first to step forward and the only one to hug him, although Ikram Mohammed's greeting was only marginally less enthusiastic. It was Ikram Mohammed who introduced him to the others, but the round of handshakes was hectically confused. He had expected to be able to recognize the faces readily enough from the photographs Vince Solari had displayed on the wallscreen, but the heavy-duty smartsuits made more difference than he had expected to their coloring and their hairstyles. Maryanne Hyder had preserved her blond tresses, albeit in a more economical form, but Lynn Gwyer had opted to go bald. Dulcie Gherardesca's scars were no longer visible beneath the extra dermal layer and Godert Kriefmann looked a good deal younger than his picture. Tang Dinh Quan and Rand Blackstone were the only two who had contrived to maintain their Earthly appearances; the fact that Blackstone was wearing a wide-brimmed hat and carrying a rifle only served to emphasize his image.

Matthew was slightly disappointed by the hesitancy of so many of their responses, and wondered for a moment whether they had mistaken him for the policeman sent to interrogate them, improbable as that might seem. It only took a few seconds, however, to realize that they were almost as awkward with one another as they were with him. It occurred to him that they might not have assembled into a single company for some time. They were, apparently, divided among themselves. Bernal Delgado's death had presumably emphasized those divisions rather than bringing them together.

The manner in which the capsule had come to rest posed obvious problems so far as unloading the cargo was concerned, but the difficulties should have been easily overcome. As soon as Rand Blackstone began barking orders the mood of the seven seemed to suffer a further deterioration. No one actually started a quarrel over the tall man's dubious right of command, and the instructions he gave were sensible enough, but the resentment was almost palpable. Having been briefed by Solari, Matthew had no difficulty figuring out that Tang Dinh Quan and Maryanne Hyder were the two most seriously at odds with the Australian, and that none of the other scientists wanted to take his side unequivocally.

"What's the hurry?" Matthew asked, when he had tried and failed to introduce the newly arrived Vince Solari to the company. "There's nothing in there likely to rot."

"It's going to rain," was the answer he got from Blackstone. A glance at the sky told him that it was true, although it hardly seemed excuse enough for the impoliteness.

The blatant tokenism of the responses Solari did receive to his tentative greetings suggested that the seven were *exceedingly* unenthusiastic about welcoming the policeman into their midst, but Matthew wasn't certain whether that could be taken as a sign of collective guilt. Unhappily, he let Solari draw him aside, so that they would not inhibit Blackstone's attempts to organize a human chain to begin unshipping the cargo.

"The doctor was right about the weight," Solari complained. "It doesn't feel too oppressive, as yet, but it does feel distinctly peculiar."

Matthew had been too preoccupied with the minutiae of his descent to pay too much heed to the restoration of nearly all his Earthly weight, but as soon as Solari mentioned it he became acutely conscious of the additional drag. As the policemen said, it didn't feel *too* uncomfortable, as yet, but it did feel odd. The oddness didn't seem to be confined within him, though—it seemed to have accommodated itself automatically to the general alienness of the environment.

It wasn't until he concentrated hard on his own inner state

that Matthew realized that his heart was pounding and that his breathing was awkward. His internal technology had masked the extra effort, but he realized that even standing still was putting a strain on him. Adaptation to the new gravity regime was going to take time.

He looked up reflexively, in the direction from which he had come, almost as if he expected to see *Hope* glinting in the sky. Even the sun was invisible behind a mass of gray clouds, but there was a margin of clear sky visible behind the hilltops in what Matthew assumed to be the north. The sky was blue, but not the pure pale blue of Earth's sky; there was a hint of purple there too.

In every other direction, the purple coloration of the landscape seemed to leap out at his wandering gaze in a fashion akin to insult, if not to flagrant contempt. The color was not in the least unexpected, of course, but everything he had seen on *Hope*'s screens—even the large wallscreen—had been bordered and contained. The colors had been true, but the frame surrounding them had robbed them of a certain awe-inspiring vividness, and of their subtler sensual context.

Matthew had imagined stepping down onto alien soil a thousand times before, amid vegetation that was as bizarre as he could visualize, but he had seen too many "alien planets" in VE melodramas to be prepared for the sensory immediacy of the real thing. Even the best VE suits were incapable of duplicating the complexity of real touch sensations, let alone the senses of smell and taste. His surface-suit, by contrast, was geared to making the most of all the molecules whose passage was not forbidden. The air of the new world presumably smelled and tasted even more peculiar than it was allowed to seem to him, but the seeming was all the more striking to a man who had been enclosed in sterilized recycled air since the moment of his reawakening, and for some considerable time before.

Matthew felt dizzy. His reawakened senses reeled, and he had to take a sudden step back.

"Are you okay, Matthew?" Ikram Mohammed asked. He was the only one who had paused in his work long enough to take note of Matthew's reactions. Blackstone had organized the others to cut and shape an easily navigable path to the hatchway, and they still seemed more than ready to direct their resentful attention exclusively to the Australian rather than the newcomers.

"We're fine, Ike," Matthew assured him. "Just give us a minute or two to get our heads together."

Vince Solari stood on one leg, experimentally, then on the other. "Not so bad, all things considered," was his judgment. "Could be worse, I guess." Although the direct reference was to the renewal of his weight, his tone suggested that he felt that the unreadiness of his suspects to approve of his arrival was a trifle overdone.

The bubble-domes of Base Three were not visible from where they stood, although Matthew assumed that Milyukov's boast about the accuracy of his delivery system had been justified. The expectant crowd could not have assembled so quickly had the base been more than three or four hundred meters away.

Matthew was still clutching the bag containing his personal possessions, but he finally condescended to clip it to his belt. He rubbed his hands as if in anticipation of getting to work, but he resisted the temptation to force his way back into the tangled vegetation in pursuit of the machete-wielding scientists. He suspected that his Earth-trained reflexes were not yet sufficiently reaccommodated to let him grapple with the branches as skillfully as his new companions, and would certainly betray him if he tried to take a place in the human chain that was now taking definitive shape.

"Sorry about this, Matthew," Ikram Mohammed said, waving an arm at the remainder of the company, who were working away with their backs to Matthew and Solari. "We're not used to visitors, and Milyukov's made us wait for an extra week to get the last few pieces of the boat." He stepped closer and lowered his voice before adding: "He said that it didn't make sense to send two consignments—which is true, of course, but it didn't stop us thinking that what he really wanted to do was make sure that we all had to stay at the base until his detective arrived to finger one of us as a murderer. No offense, Mr. Solari."

"None taken," Solari assured him, insincerely.

"I'll talk to you later, Matthew," the genomicist said. "Got to pull my weight. Don't try to join in yet—wait till you get your land legs. Look around."

Matthew did as he was told. He took another look at the sullen sky, from which the first raindrops were just beginning to fall, rattling the leaves of the dendrites. He searched the bushes for signs of animal life, but nothing seemed to be moving. There was hardly any wind, and everything but the thicket where the capsule had come down seemed still and somnolent. The ground between the stands of trees was mostly bare, exposing black rock and gray scree slopes. The more distant slopes were already blurring behind curtains of rain, except where the ribbon of bluish sky still maintained its defiant stance. There, the many shades of lilac and purple stood out far more clearly.

But I'm standing here on my own two feet, Matthew reminded himself, naked but for an artificial skin that's no more than a millimeter thick save for the soles of my feet and the codpiece. It's a strange place, but it's a place where human beings can breathe, and live, and work, and play. It's a place that could be home. Isn't it?

One or two of the reluctant laborers were glancing back at him now, some more furtively than others. Lynn Gwyer flashed him a smile, rolling her eyes apologetically as if to assure him that she would be glad to offer a proper welcome when the crowd had dispersed. Tang Dinh Quan's glances were speculative, trying to weigh him up. Godert Kriefmann and Dulcie Gherardesca seemed to be paying more attention to Solari than to him. Maryanne Hyder didn't seem to be meeting anybody's eye—certainly not Blackstone's—although there was something about her bearing that suggested that her fierce concentration was by no means evidence of self-sufficiency.

"At least the crew were all on the same side," Solari whispered in Matthew's ear, having obviously made similar observations of his own.

"No they weren't," Matthew replied, in a similarly confidential tone. "They just put on a better act for our sake. Here, the strains show—and with Bernal not long dead, a victim to violence, I'm not surprised." But they are all on the same side, he added, privately. Underneath the stresses and the strains, they know that. They have to be on the same side, and so do we. The only undecided matter is how well we're going to play the game.

Enough cargo had now been transferred back to the bare ground to facilitate its separation into individual units. More glances were being exchanged as the potential carriers measured the mass and awkwardness of various piles. It was, inevitably, Rand Blackstone who stepped up to one that seemed too much for any one man and said: "I'll take this one." Before picking up his chosen burden, though, he picked up the rifle he had set down on his arrival—the rifle that he carried to protect his fellows from attack by humanoids that none of them had ever seen—and handed it to Matthew. "Can you take care of this?" he demanded.

The weapon seemed ridiculously heavy, and its length made it remarkably inconvenient, but Matthew resisted the temptation to pass it on to Solari. "Okay," he said.

"You'd better come back with me, Matthew," Blackstone added. "Nothing much you can do here—can't go throwing stuff around down here when you've been up in half-gravity for the last few days. If you didn't hurt yourself you'd be sure to drop something."

Matthew took immediate offence at this assumption, although he knew that it was not entirely unjustified. He realized that the Australian wanted to separate himself from the rest of the company, and to take Matthew with him. Matthew's first impulse—like everyone else's, apparently—was to refuse to play along with the Australian. He looked around for a preferable companion. "I'll wait for Ike," he said.

Ikram Mohammed turned around, obviously out of breath. The genomicist's surface-suit did not allow the least bead of sweat to show upon his face, but it did not inhibit the deeper coloration that spread across his cheeks and forehead. "You go on, Matt," he said. "It's going to take some time to sort this stuff out."

"I'll be back as soon as I can," Blackstone put in, smugly.

Matthew tried to catch Lynn Gwyer's eye, feeling oddly irritated that none of the others seemed in the least eager to make his acquaintance. Even those he had not met must have known his name. Like Vince Solari, they must have seen him on TV. He had been a famous man, at least in the circles these people had inhabited. He was fifty-eight light-years from home and three years late out of the freezer, but he could not believe that he had become less interesting than the inanimate objects shipped down with him. He noticed Tang Dinh Quan eyeing him surreptitiously yet again, but the moment Matthew's gaze tried to fix upon his eyes the biochemist looked away.

Well, Matthew thought, if they aren't deliberately shielding a murderer, they're sure as hell ashamed of something.

Lynn Gwyer came over to him, but even she hesitated. "Go back with Rand," she advised him. "You'll need to take it easy for a while, and Ike's right about needing to sort this stuff out. I'll catch up with you in half an hour or so."

"We made it, Lynn," Matthew said, softly. "We made it. Across the void, across the centuries. You might have grown used to it, but I haven't."

"I'm sorry," she said, only a trifle belatedly. "I do know how you feel. I only wish that Bernal could be here too."

Mercifully, Blackstone refrained from pointing out that if Delgado were still able to be here, Matthew would still be in the deep-freeze.

"I'm sorry that we had to meet under such unfortunate circumstances, Dr. Gwyer," Solari said, watching her like a hawk.

The bald woman was content to stare back at the detective as if she were watching a dangerous dog for signs of imminent aggression.

"Come on, Matthew," Blackstone said, gruffly. "We're wasting time." He set off without waiting for Matthew to give any indication that he was ready to follow his lead.

Matthew's last recourse was to lock eyes with Vince Solari. "Come on, Vince," he said. "Better do as we're told." Solari, who must have known that Blackstone's careful repetition of Matthew's name had been a deliberate snub, seemed grateful for the invitation.

SEVENTEEN

Matthew and Solari set off in the Australian's wake, but Matthew made no attempt to draw level, preferring to keep company with Solari. For the moment, at least, Blackstone seemed content with that arrangement.

"It's beautiful, isn't it?" Matthew said to Solari, speaking loudly enough for Blackstone to hear in the hope of easing the tension. "It looked good on screen, but that's a poor preparation for the real thing."

Blackstone shrugged slightly, as if adjusting his load. *Beautiful* was obviously not the first adjective that sprang to his mind nowadays when he looked around him. Solari, on the other hand, readily followed the lead of Matthew's gaze as it swept through a 180 degree tour.

The shallow slope they were ascending was one of many. Although the terrain was insufficiently precipitous to be called mountainous it was not gentle enough to be merely hilly. Had its physical geography not been so strangely dressed Matthew might have been reminded of Scandinavia, but the contrast between Scandinavia's evergreen forests and the purple "trees" was too great to facilitate any such comparison. Pines grew very straight, and their needles and cones had always seemed to Matthew to be decorous and disciplined. Nothing here grew straight; what each of the dendrites they passed had instead of a trunk and boughs was like something that might be plucked out of a chaotic heap of corkscrews and lathe-turnings. Nor was there anything in the least decorous or disciplined about what the local vegetation had instead of leaves and cones.

If the dendrites bore ready comparison to anything, Matthew thought, it was absurdly overdressed dancers in some cheap casino show, all ruffles, pompoms and flares . . . and yet, there was not the slightest suggestion that these monstrous growths were ready to hurl themselves into an energetic cancan. There was, as he had already noted, an eerie *stillness* here. The rain was noisy in the branches, but the branches did not shake and rustle as Earthly branches would have done. They creaked a little, and moaned rather plaintively, but they gave the impression that they would bend, however grudgingly, to any pressure.

There was no birdsong to disturb the air, nor any insect hum, but there were other whispers at the very threshold of aural perception, like white noise magnified by dead Earthly seashells into the sound of waves breaking softly on a very distant shore. There was nothing in his memory to which Matthew could meaningfully connect that barely audible murmur. On Earth, tiny sounds that were never consciously apprehended could nevertheless be categorized and filed by the brain according to a habit-formed system. Here . . . well, he decided, here there was a lot of learning still to do, a lot of custom yet to be established.

"It doesn't matter that Earth didn't die," Vince Solari said, joining in with Matthew's determination to make the most of the moment in spite of the awkward attitude of his suspects. "What matters is that we're *here*. We've found an island in the void: a haven; a land of opportunity. Our Ararat."

Solari's eyes were roaming the horizons that could be glimpsed between the twisted purple masses. Matthew wondered whether he was trying to deflect Rand Blackstone's attention from the fact that he was a policeman—but even if that were the case, he sounded perfectly sincere.

"This planet," Rand Blackstone said over his shoulder, with enviable certainty, "is called *Tyre*. New Earth is for unimaginative sentimentalists. Ararat is a crew name. Murex is too fancy. Down here, this is Tyre, and always will be. Might as well take it aboard now—you won't be going back to crew territory, whatever Tang may think."

An old-style alpha male, Matthew thought. Playing the role of colonist so zealously that he's become a parody. Now that Blackstone's gun had had the full force of the new world's gravity upon it for several minutes it had begun to put a severe strain on his arms, so he shifted its weight on to his shoulder, trying to disregard the absurdly macho pose that he was assuming. His legs were already protesting the effort of walking, but he only had to shorten his stride by a fraction to cause Blackstone to take note of his weakness. The Australian was quick to assure him that the walk to the bubble-complex was "very short," without "too many" upslopes.

It didn't take long for Matthew to appreciate just how relative such terms could be. He revised his estimate regarding the accuracy of Milyukov's boasts; the welcome party had obviously arrived so quickly because they'd got a fix on the likely landing place long before the capsule touched down.

Matthew half-expected Blackstone to fall into step with Vince Solari as soon as the policeman demonstrated that he was the stronger of the two newcomers, but the Australian shortened his own step to take up a position at Matthew's shoulder, letting Solari take the lead. Now that he knew what direction to take, Solari accepted the responsibility. Matthew realized why Blackstone had made the move when the tall man murmured in his ear: "Is Shen ready to take the ship yet?"

"What?" was Matthew's astonished response.

Blackstone looked down at him impatiently. "You *have* seen Shen?" Rumors obviously bounded from world to world as rapidly in the new system as they had in the old. Solari hadn't turned around, but Matthew knew that the policeman must be listening hard.

"Yes, I saw him," he admitted, "but not for long, and only on a screen."

"So what's the word? Surely he gave you a message to deliver. You can trust me—I wouldn't go so far as to say that we're all on his side down here, because most of the bastards at Base One can't seem to see further than their own noses, but nobody in his right mind could want that slimeball Milyukov to press on with his crazy hijack plans. Even Tang wants Shen in charge up top— he thinks he can deal with Shen."

"Shen didn't give me any message," Matthew said. "He couldn't. I was carrying bugs Milyukov's people had planted on me."

Blackstone sighed. "Okay, so he had to be discreet. I suppose you're still worried about the bugs. All I want to know is whether there'll be a settlement soon. Every day that passes raises the anxiety level down here just a little further—and that's bad. It's way too high already."

"I got the impression that the situation on the ship is an impasse," Matthew told him. "Nothing suggested that it would be resolved any time soon."

Blackstone cursed under his breath. "It's all so stupid," he said. "Everybody knows that it will be at least two hundred years before the ship could leave, even if anyone were crazy enough to be in a hurry. Milyukov will be dead by then and a whole new generation will be calling themselves the crew. The so-called revolution will belong to a period of their history so obviously dead and so obviously irrelevant that no amount of propaganda is going to make anything stick on Milyukov's say-so."

"How do you calculate two hundred years?" Matthew asked, interestedly.

"Fifty-eight plus fifty-eight is a hundred and sixteen," Blackstone pointed out. "That's the minimum time in which we could *begin* to get a proper update on the scientific and technological progress made on Earth since we left—everything the crew has picked up en route is just crumbs. When the news arrives, it will have to be integrated and exploited and acted upon if *Hope* is to get the benefit. Any new hardware they need will take a lot longer than fifty-eight years to get here, no matter what sort of acceleration it can contrive and maintain. In addition to that, *Hope* has to restock, both mass-wise and organic-resources–wise. This system has hardly any halo and not much asteroidal debris—nothing much bigger than a football in Tyre-crossing orbits. Shen was phenomenally lucky to pick up cometary ices so easily during the blizzard in the home system—believe me, a hundred and sixteen years plus eighty-four is a conservative estimate. Milyukov must know that he won't live to see the culmination of his grand plan—he's just a megalomaniac trying to put his stamp on history. The sooner one of his cronies puts a knife in his back the better—pity it had to happen down here, to the wrong man."

"I thought you weren't prepared to believe that it was one of Bernal's cronies who killed him," Matthew said, a trifle sourly. His legs and spine were aching badly now, and despite all Nita Brownell's reassurances he felt that breathing through the suit's membranes was becoming increasingly and stiflingly difficult.

"I'm not," Blackstone said. "None of us had motive enough, and none of us had a glass dagger stashed away. When I said it was a pity I meant that things are bad enough without adding fuel to the Tyrian Lib case."

"Tyrian Lib?" Matthew echoed, incredulously.

Blackstone was unimpressed by the implication that he must

be joking. He stopped briefly in order to readjust the distribution of his inconvenient load.

"Yeah," he said. "Shen must have been looking the other way when that lot snuck aboard. Imagine coming fifty-eight light-years to plant a colony and then finding you've got a gaggle of whingers aboard who can't stand the thought of polluting a virgin ecosphere. How else can we find a place to live?"

"I thought the reservations of the doubters had more to do with Tyre's radically different genomics than the idea that we have no right to introduce ourselves into *any* alien ecosphere," Matthew said, just about managing to get through the sentence without gasping.

"*Radically different*," Blackstone echoed, disgustedly. "It's purple, damn it. When you get right down to it, that's all it is. Okay, the grass on the plain is tree-high, and the tree-high things in the hills look and sometimes feel like the debris from an explosion in a barbed-wire factory, and a lot of the local critters are poisonous as well as not too pretty—but what did we expect? I come from Australia, where *everything*'s weird and *everything*'s pretty much poisonous. Believe me, anyone who's seen Aussie spiders, let alone been bitten by Aussie snakes and stung by Aussie jellyfish, isn't likely to get the wind up about a few giant rats with hypodermic tongues and slugs with tentacles. My ancestors lived alongside redbacks and funnel-webs all their lives—had them in the house, the garden, everywhere—and none of them ever got bit. Far as I can judge, the really dangerous species hereabouts are as rare and shy as Tasmanian tigers, so why the hell are the idiots at Base One, who live on an island and never stick their noses out of their bubbles anyway, getting their knickers in a twist? We're all here, and we're all here to stay, and everything would be going a hell of a lot more smoothly if everybody could just get used to the idea. We need to get our heads straight here, so that we can get this colony licked into shape. Here's the big bubble, by the way—you look as if you need a rest."

Matthew's head had dropped as the rifle had become increasingly burdensome, and it wasn't until Blackstone gave him the cue to look up that he realized that they had almost reached their destination. He realized too that whatever else Blackstone was right or wrong about, the ex-soldier was certainly right about his needing a rest.

As soon as they were inside the double door Blackstone said: "I'll just get rid of this stuff, then I'll show you where you're bunking. We put you in together, if that's okay."

Matthew nearly asked why he couldn't have Bernal Delgado's bunk, but he remembered in time what Solari had said about Bernal and Maryanne Hyder playing "happy families." He put Blackstone's gun down, resting it against the plastic outer wall of the dome. Then he leaned against it himself, glad of the respite.

While they were briefly alone, Solari took the opportunity to say: "I didn't expect it to be *this* bad. There were plenty of places back home where a cop was as welcome as a plague-bearing rat, but I didn't expect this to be one of them."

"It's not just you," Matthew said. "I reckon we came in on the end of a *big* argument—and I suspect that was only one item in an ongoing war. There's been a serious breakdown of consensus here. Bernal's death might have caused the cracks to widen, but there's a lot more to it than that."

"So what caused today's big argument?" Solari wanted to know.

Blackstone returned just in time to field the question. "The boat," he said, succinctly. "Four berths, one of which fell vacant when Delgado was killed. If anyone was its captain, he was, which means that no one knows how to decide whether the empty slot goes to Matthew here, or whether Tang should take it."

"I should get it," Matthew was quick to say. "I'm down here as Bernal's replacement."

"And Lynn will back you up. Ike Mohammed too. They think that's a majority, since they were the other two-thirds of the original transfer team and still are two-thirds of the remnant of the boat's intended crew. Tang isn't happy with that way of deciding things. Maryanne's on Tang's side in everything now. Dulcie didn't want to commit herself; God never does; I wanted to meet you before casting a vote, if I have one. Democracy in action!"

Matthew assumed that "God never does" was a criticism of Kriefmann's indecisiveness rather than the Almighty's.

"What about me?" Solari put in. "Do I have a voice?"

"Don't tell me *you* want to go too," Blackstone said.

"That's not what I meant," Solari said. "I was asking whether I have any voice in who goes and who stays . . . and *when* the boat is cleared for departure." He obviously felt that the answer ought to be yes in both cases—which would allow him to hold the expedition back until he'd completed his investigation, lest the murderer should slip away unapprehended.

"No, you don't," Blackstone told him, brusquely. "The boat trip's scientific business—nothing to do with you. Long overdue. The moment we figured out that the aliens had to be downriver in the glass-roofed grass forest we should have set off to find them. I was ready to walk, but I got outvoted. I even got voted off the expedition in favor of Dulcie."

"If it's scientific business," Solari pointed out, "it's nothing to do with you, either."

"Maybe it isn't," Blackstone came back at him, "but if they run into trouble down there, they might need a man who can shoot straight. That's why I was sent here in the first place, when we thought they might still be skulking in the hills. If it were up to me, I'd be the one taking Bernal's place."

"It's not up to you," Matthew put in. "I'm Bernal's replacement. The berth has to be mine, if I want it."

"Do you?" Blackstone wanted to know.

"Yes."

Blackstone opened his mouth to offer some further objection, but he was seized by a sudden doubt and hesitated. He deliberated, lowered his voice and said: "Look, I'm sorry about all this. We know we shouldn't be in this mess. If we could get out of it with a few handshakes and a group hug we would. I wish I could say that your arrival will help, but it won't. Some of us think the last thing we need is a cop asking questions, trying to make one of us into a murderer. Some others probably think the second last is someone who just came out of the freezer thinking he can solve all our other problems when people who've been here for years haven't even scratched the surface. Sorry, but that's the way it is."

Matthew was too taken aback by the change of conversational pace to reply, but Vince Solari wasn't. "I'm not trying to make one of you into a murderer," he said, quietly. "Whoever killed Bernal Delgado did that."

"It wasn't one of us," Blackstone said. Matthew had rarely heard a sentence uttered with less conviction. The Australian hesitated again, almost as if he'd resolved as a child always to count to ten before losing his temper. "Personally," he said, eventually, "I don't mind either of you being here, as long as you don't start making waves before you understand what's what. But even I have to admit that Mr. Solari is an extra complication in a situation that already has a few too many. Can I show you to your bunks now? I have to get back to the shuttle—it's going to take at least three trips to get all the cargo back here."

"Fine," said Matthew, although he felt in his heart of hearts that it was anything but.

EIGHTEEN

Matthew slept far longer than he intended to, and far longer than was comfortable, considering the quality of his dreams. Although the images fled as soon as he was shaken awake he was left with a bitter taste in his dry mouth and a fugitive memory of having struggled in vain to move out of harm's way, while various no-longer-specifiable dangers threatened to wreak havoc with his lumpen and overly massive body.

The first thing he did when he opened his eyes was check out the other bunk, but it was empty. Vince Solari had been very enthusiastic to get on with the job. The room wasn't empty for long, though; almost as soon as he moved the privacy curtain slid into its daybed and a woman he recognized as Dulcie Gherardesca appeared in the gap. She had brought him a mug of tea and a bowl of what looked like fortified rice-manna.

"It's the fresh air that knocked you out," she said, as he stretched his muscles and rubbed his eyes. "The weight isn't so bad, but even when it's filtered the air is flavored and perfumed with all manner of subliminal sensations. It's a real jolt to the system."

"Thanks," he said, as he drained the mug. "I needed that. You're right about the jolt. I never anticipated the subtle differences. The big ones, yes, but not the ones that hover just out of reach of direct perception. Blackstone seems to be oblivious to them, though—to him, this seems to be the outback painted purple. Or maybe Botany Bay."

"Rand believes in taking bulls by the horns," the anthropologist said. "And it wasn't entirely kindness that brought me here. Your friend Vincent didn't waste any time at all. I was the one who found the body, so I was the one he came after first. I needed an excuse to make a graceful exit. I guess that'll make him all the keener to make me a suspect."

"Vince is a bull-by-the-horns kind of guy himself," Matthew told her. "But he seems pretty levelheaded to me. He'll do his best to sort this business out properly, and he isn't the type to be led astray by preconceptions. You've nothing to fear from him—unless, of course, you did it. I'm assuming you didn't."

"Nobody here wants to think that any of their friends and colleagues could do such a thing," she told him, quietly. "Not just because they'd have to worry about being next on the list, but because nobody wants to think anybody else capable of doing that to a man like Bernal."

"Whereas if it had been a man like Blackstone . . ." Matthew said, jokingly. He saw immediately that the joke had been ill-advised. Dulcie Gherardesca had been living with the fact of the murder for some time. She had not the slightest wish to consider the question of how much difference it would have made to her feelings and fears if someone else had been the victim. "Sorry," he said. To cover his embarrassment he thanked her again for bringing his breakfast. Then he took a mouthful of the manna porridge and almost withdrew his thanks.

"Sorry about that," she said. "We've been cutting the manna shipped down from *Hope* with the produce of our own converters. It's certified edible, but edible and palatable aren't quite the same thing. Base One has food-tech people working on the problem, but it'll be a while before the delicacies are sorted out. As you say, it's the subtle differences that make the most impact."

"It's not that bad," he assured her, insincerely.

"I'm sure Lynn would have brought you breakfast if she'd been here," Dulcie said, awkwardly. "She's working on the boat with Ike while Maryanne and Tang help Blackstone with the last of the dropship's cargo. She's told us a good deal about you—more than Ike has, although I gathered that he knew you better."

"Ike wouldn't want to talk about me in case it looked as if he was bragging about knowing someone who was on TV a lot," Matthew guessed. "Nonsense, of course—but it's often the people who would never dream of bragging who are most afraid of being caught."

"I've seen you on TV myself," Dulcie Gherardesca admitted. "I suppose we all did. Couldn't really miss you in the mid-eighties, could we?"

"And you probably thought me less of a scientist because of it," Matthew said, a little too glibly. "Bernal too, I dare say. Not our fault, really. Once the ecocatastrophe was well under way ecologists started getting the attention they'd always warranted, and a lot more besides. Pity the prophet whose prophecies begin to come true—what happens then makes living without the honor of one's countrymen seem like a piece of cake. No wonder Bernal and I were so desperate to get away from it all."

"I don't think anyone here thinks any less of you for trying so hard to jerk the world out of its complacency," she said, "or for trying to get remedial measures moving once the Crash hit hard. I brought you Bernal's notepad. I figured that you'd be as anxious to get started as Inspector Solari. I've checked through it myself, of course—we all have. We can't find anything epoch-making, but we didn't really expect to. After all, when Archimedes leapt out of the bath he didn't go looking for a stylus so he could write *Eureka!* on the nearest piece of papyrus—and even if he had, it wouldn't have begun to tell anyone what he'd actually discovered. So even if we could figure out what *ska* means, it might not get us any closer to the truth."

While she was speaking she pressed the keys of the notepad to bring up what Matthew presumed to be the last "page" of Bernal Delgado's jottings. The last entries of all read:

NV correlated with ER?

Ans driver: ska?

"It's a kind of music," the anthropologist added. "But I don't think that's what it means here. Nobody knows what an ans driver is, although we favor the hypothesis that *ans* is short for answer and *driver* for downriver. *NV* and *ER* could be anything, although the general consensus is that NV probably stands for *nutritional versatility*. If you look back at earlier notes you'll see that NV crops up several times and ER once, but *ska* doesn't. We've always thought that the answers to our most urgent unanswered questions might be found downriver—that's why we've been building the boat—but we've always known that it might be wishful thinking."

"Which most urgent unanswered questions?" Matthew mumbled, his mouth half-full of manna that was proving difficult to swallow.

"Where did the city-builders come from—and where did they go, if they didn't die here?"

"Why do you think they didn't?"

"We don't know whether they did or not. Even if they'd been human they might not have left much trace, and we think the bones of the local mammals are more prone to decay than ours. The only relics we've found were artifacts secreted in holes in the walls, and only the hardest kinds of glass have survived. We don't know how old the city is, because we haven't established any reliable yardstick that could tell us. We talk about a hundred thousand years, but it's pure guesswork. It might be out by an order of magnitude. So far as we can tell, they settled here, established their fields, built their homes and their walls—all of which must have taken centuries—and then they vanished. If there were other upland settlements, we haven't found them yet. If there are any settlements still in existence, we haven't found *them*. If the humanoids still exist, it looks as if they've abandoned agriculture—and cooking, so far as cooking requires fire-making and fire-keeping. While we only have the one site to look at we've no basis for generalization."

"But you're convinced that they came up the river."

"And then they stopped coming," she agreed. "Whether the city-dwellers died here or left, their plains-dwelling cousins presumably decided to stay where they were. If they died out too, they died where they'd always lived, presumably as nomadic hunter-gatherers. Like all the hominid species of Earth, except one."

Matthew thought that was a strange way of putting it—but then he saw what she was getting at. Nobody really knew what had happened to all the Australopithecine species that had coexisted with the remotest ancestors of Homo sapiens, or the other hominid species that had fallen by the evolutionary wayside in later eras. The conventional assumption was that they had been out-competed and driven to extinction by genus *Homo*, but nobody knew. There wasn't enough evidence left to settle the question. Maybe they had died out for other reasons. How would anyone ever be sure?

"It took Homo sapiens hundreds of thousands of years to invent agriculture," Dulcie Gherardesca pointed out, "and not much more than ten thousand to bring Earth's ecosphere to the brink of rack and ruin. Maybe our ancestors should have figured out that it was a bad idea too, and returned to their hunter-gatherer roots as soon as possible."

"We wouldn't be here to worry about these guys if they had,"

Matthew observed—but he knew that what she was really getting at was that if humans had returned to their hunter-gatherer roots after living for a while in the first cities of Egypt or Sumeria they would probably have died out in the next ecocatastrophe. Even as things were, humankind's ancestors had squeezed through a desperately narrow population bottleneck.

Matthew handed back his bowl, having done his best to finish the meal. Dulcie made as if to leave, but he checked her retreat with another question. "When will the boat be finished?" he asked.

"Tomorrow, or the day after," she told him. "We could have set out days ago if we'd been prepared to go without the last few frills, but we were instructed to wait for Solari to arrive, so that we could help with his inquiries. Some of us wanted to say no, if only on the grounds that the instruction came from people who had no authority to give us orders, but. . . . well, we're just about getting used to the notion that we're no longer united, even among ourselves. I suppose you want to come with us."

"Yes, I do," Matthew said.

"I suppose you even think you're entitled, because you're Bernal's substitute."

"That too."

"But you've only been awake four days. You know next to nothing about this world. You'd be a passenger."

"Sometimes," Matthew said, mildly, "a fresh pair of eyes can be useful. Not to mention a fresh mind . . ."

"Bullshit," she said. "Tang has the educated eye, the educated mind. If it were my boat, I'd want him."

"And you need an ecologist," Matthew continued. "All the people I talked to on *Hope* are too narrowly focused, on scientific and political issues alike. They're drowning in biochemical data—there's so much of it, and it's so resolutely peculiar, that they've almost lost sight of the actual living organisms."

"That hasn't happened here," she snapped back—but then she blinked, and might even have displayed a blush had she not been wearing a surface-suit. "Well," she conceded, after a pause, "maybe a little. Most of the animals hereabouts are slugs and worms—the mammal-analogues seem to steer clear of the ruins, and the presence of the domes must be even more inhibiting."

"I *would* like to go," Matthew said, deciding that conciliation might be in order. "But I'd rather do it without upsetting anyone. Can we settle the matter amicably?"

"I don't know," Dulcie admitted. "The crew had the Revolution, but we're the ones who can't figure out who owns what and who has the authority to make decisions. Back in the system it was all cut and dried, but even if Shen Chin Che were still running things like the last of the great dictators we'd all have begun to wonder what gave him the right to keep on giving us orders. As things are, we don't even have anything in place to overthrow. Can you imagine that we were stupid enough, at first, to think that we didn't need to worry about it—that we were a community of scientists, all working for the common good? It's taken us three years to begin putting the fundamental apparatus of a democracy in place at Base One—and it'll be three years too late to command the respect and consent it needs. Whichever way the Base One vote on future policy goes, it'll just be more poison in the system."

"We're not at Base One," Matthew pointed out. "Surely the nine of us can settle our differences without going to war."

"Better talk to Tang, then," she said, as she moved toward the door again. "Maybe you can settle it between you—unless Rand wants to have another go at persuading us that the last place should go to the guy with the biggest gun."

This time, Matthew let her leave. It seemed to be the diplomatic thing to do. She closed the privacy-curtain behind her. Instead of getting up immediately he flicked the keyboard of Bernal Delgado's notepad, bringing page after page of field notes to the tiny screen.

Like most notes designed for purely personal reference, the vast majority of Bernal's jottings were as gnomic as they were trivial. The computer was host to dozens of other data-fields, but almost all of them would be commonly held stocks and it would take a lot of searching to turn up anything that wasn't. Matthew played with the keyboard for a few minutes more, but he knew that he was wasting time. He finally gave way to necessity and raised himself from the bed. The surface suit needed to discharge its processed excreta exactly as Matthew would have done had he not been wearing one, so he had to take a few minutes to investigate and use the room's facilities before leaving.

When he got out into the corridor he found that he couldn't remember the way to the communal space at the heart of the bubble, but it only took a few tentative steps to get his bearings. When he arrived, however, the only person present was Dulcie Gherardesca, sitting at a big table. She seemed to be waiting for him, but the expression on her face testified that it was a matter of duty.

"Godert's in the lab," she told him. "The others are all out. Your friend the policeman must have moved on to suspect number three."

"His name's Vincent," Matthew reminded her. "Vince to his friends. Maybe I should take a look at the boat myself."

"There's time," she assured him. Her tone was conciliatory now; she seemed to be regretting her slight loss of temper. "Lynn wants to give you the grand tour. The people bringing in the last batch of cargo ought to be back any minute—when they arrive we can all get together. It'll give us a chance to make a better job of the introductions than we did yesterday. We ought to do that."

Matthew sat down opposite her, letting the width of the table symbolize the distance between them. "I don't mean to get in anyone's way," he said, adopting a conciliatory tone himself. "But I really do believe that I'm a better substitute for Bernal than someone from another field. You may know me as a talking head spewing out sound bites for TV, but I'm a first-rate ecologist, just as he was."

"I dare say the crew showed you his formal reports," the anthropologist said, noncommittally.

"Some," Matthew admitted. "Andrei Lityansky showed me a vast amount of stuff, far too quickly for me to take it all in. It was all dumped in my own notepad before I got my belt back."

"Bernal said that Lityansky's pretty good, for a space-born who never saw a blade of grass on a heath or a tree in a forest," Dulcie admitted. "He also said that no matter how good a biochemist might be, he could never begin to understand ecology—which took in Tang as well as Lityansky, I suppose."

"He's right about Lityansky," Matthew said, carefully.

"I know. Aboard the ship, everything's too controlled, too organized, too neat, even after the expectable deterioration and the civil war. There's not enough chaos, not enough spontaneity—not the right kinds, anyway. Bernal said that if *he* couldn't figure out what had happened here, and what was *still* happening, there was only one man who could. He meant you."

"I'm flattered," Matthew acknowledged, generously, "but I understand your reservations. I didn't mean to suggest that Lynn, Ike, and you weren't competent to interpret whatever you might find downriver."

"I'm just an anthropologist," she said. "I'm the one who brought your breakfast because I didn't have enough real work to keep me busy. The only thing I've discovered since I relocated here is that a background in anthropology doesn't give you much of a head start in the attempt to understand an alien culture on the basis of archaeological evidence. That's another reason why I'm desperate to go downriver to the plain: sheer frustration. There's no reason to believe that we'll find anything to which my expertise is relevant. I suppose that if Tang won't give way, I ought to be the one to step down in your favor."

"But you don't want to?" Matthew said, stating the obvious.

"No," was her bald reply.

Ikram Mohammed came into the room then. He seemed slightly surprised to find the anthropologist there, but it was Matthew he was looking for. "I thought you'd be up by now," he said to Matthew. "Lynn's right behind me and Rand's bringing in the last load from the shuttle with Maryanne. Tang was with them, but he's under interrogation now. I know the policeman's only doing his job, but we've already been through it all a hundred times between ourselves. If we'd been able to figure out who did it, we would have."

"Captain Milyukov seems to think that you have figured it out, and that you're keeping quiet about it," Matthew observed.

The genomicist made a disgusted face. "Milyukov's seriously disturbed," he said. "Not to mention seriously disturbing. He wants to use this business in one of his convoluted political games, although I doubt that any reasonable person could work out how or why. We always knew that there was a chance that the crew would develop weird ideas after several generations of space flight, but who could have figured that it would be so difficult to straighten them out again? This insistence that we have to learn to fend for ourselves on the surface within a single generation, in order that they can get rid of all the Earthborn sleepers and take complete control of their militarized socialist republic is crazy."

Dulcie Gherardesca had slipped out while Ikram Mohammed was talking. Matthew got up from his chair and stretched his leaden limbs. He took advantage of what might prove to be a rare moment of confidentiality to say: "I don't suppose, Ike, that *you* have a theory as to who killed Bernal and why?"

"No," Ike retorted. "All I know for sure is that it wasn't me."

Matthew decided to believe him, even though there was something in his manner that suggested that it was not the *whole* truth. Even if he had wanted to challenge the statement, though, he wouldn't have had the opportunity, because Rand Blackstone's strident voice could already be heard, calling desperately for help.

NINETEEN

Blackstone had entered the dome before sounding his clamorous alarm, and less than three seconds passed before he burst into the room where Ikram Mohammed and Matthew were standing. He was cradling Maryanne Hyder in his arms, trying to hold her still.

The small woman seemed to be in a bad way. Even with the aid of her IT she seemed barely able to suppress screams of agony. Her face was contorted and flushed, and she was trembling with shock as well as experiencing convulsive muscle spasms in her arms and legs.

Blackstone set her down on the tabletop, but Ikram Mohammed and Matthew had to help him hold her there. Had they not taken hold of her limbs the convulsions might have carried her over the edge. Matthew had grabbed her right arm; he was surprised by the strength of the reflexes that fought against his gentle restraint. Small she might be, but Maryanne Hyder was muscular.

"What happened?" Matthew asked—but Blackstone had turned away to face one of the newcomers that were hurrying into the room: the doctor, Godert Kriefmann.

"Slug-sting," Blackstone said. "Big bugger—twice the size of any I'd seen before. Tentacles twenty centimeters long, maybe more, at least as thick as my thumb. . . ." He might have continued if Kriefmann hadn't interrupted him.

"Get back out there *now* and find the thing," Kriefmann said. "Be as careful as you need to be, but get it back here *alive*. Use a thick bag to transport it, but get it into the biocontainment unit as soon as you can."

Blackstone obeyed immediately, running back into the corridor as soon as he had cleared a way to the door by thrusting Dulcie Gherardesca—who had come in behind the doctor—firmly aside. Kriefmann took up a position beside Matthew, bending over his patient anxiously.

It was obvious to Matthew, even at first glance, that the wounds were serious. They were clustered on the outside of the right thigh, from just above the knee to halfway to the hip. The ragged edges of the smartsuit had not yet had a chance to begin healing—but that seemed to be as well, given that Kriefmann was armed with a pair of tweezers, which he was already using to pull alien tissue out of the wounds.

Dulcie Gherardesca scrambled past Matthew to fetch a plastic petri dish in which the doctor could deposit the tissue.

"If it's new," Kriefmann said to Dulcie, "I'll need a toxin profile as quickly as possible. Where's Tang? He'll have to take care of it while Maryanne's out of action."

Matthew and Ikram Mohammed both opened their mouths to tell the doctor that Tang Dinh Quan was with Solari, but they shut them again as soon as they observed that it was no longer true. Lynn Gwyer had arrived before him, but she was already moving aside to make way for the biochemist. Vince Solari was bringing up the rear.

"Here," the doctor said, as he handed the dish to Tang. "Get started on these sting-cell fragments. *Now.*"

Tang Dinh Quan was as quick to respond as Blackstone had been, seizing and covering the petri dish without further ado and heading off in another direction, presumably racing for his lab. Matthew took a certain comfort from the way in which the team had suddenly reassembled itself, setting aside the disagreements of the preceding day. Faced with an emergency, these people were perfectly capable of working together, all on the same side.

"How bad is it likely to be?" Matthew asked Ikram Mohammed, not wanting to distract the doctor, who was still busy with the tweezers and a replacement Petri dish provided by Dulcie Gherardesca.

"I don't know," the genomicist replied. "That's a bad wound—worse than any I've seen. On the other hand, most of the tentacled slugs are very closely related—differentiation into species isn't anywhere near as clear here as it is on Earth—and the differences between their toxins are usually slight. Our existing antisera ought to be able to help Maryanne's IT suppress the symptoms. Even if it is a genuinely new variety, using poisons we haven't met before, her IT should have enough capacity to keep her going until Tang can do a full analysis and come back with a plan for more precise countermeasures."

"The worst-case scenario is that it might take a couple of days to synthesize antitoxins and her IT might have to put her into a protective coma," Lynn Gwyer put in. "We have the know-how to counter local toxins—we even have the fundamental components of a Tyre-biochemistry protein manufactory, thanks to Tang—but we don't have Base One's facilities. Unfortunately, while Maryanne's incapacitated we won't have the benefit of her toxicological expertise."

"I'm going to give her a shot," Kriefmann announced to his rapt audience. "Got to relax her muscles. Her IT can take care of the pain, but it doesn't have the facilities to deal with this kind of reaction."

"Are you sure it won't do any harm?" Dulcie Gherardesca asked, anxiously.

"No, I'm not," said Kriefmann, "But the symptoms are consistent with the smaller wounds I've treated before, so it ought to be okay. Keep hold of her, will you."

"It's okay," Ikram Mohammed assured the doctor. The convulsions were not so emphatic now, and Matthew modified his grip so as to put less pressure on the arm.

Kriefmann left the room. Worried glances were exchanged but no one spoke. They were all waiting anxiously. The doctor came back two minutes later with two sterile packs in his right hand, each containing a liquiject syringe. His left was clutching a handful of plastic bottles. Kriefmann scattered the bottles on the tabletop in order to free the hand that held them, then liberated the first syringe. He filled the liquiject from one of the bottles and positioned the head of the nozzle above a blue vein that showed on the inner side of Maryanne Hyder's left forearm.

When he pressed the button, his patient's whole body jerked in response. Matthew hoped that it was a reflex born of fear rather than a physical response to the injected drug.

The spasms in Maryanne's muscles began to die down almost immediately, and Matthew let the arm he was holding go limp. He let go of it, wondering if all the convulsions might have been the result of a psychological response rather than a physiological one.

One final frisson seemed to release the toxicologist's tongue.

She began to swear, and then to babble. "God, I'm sorry," she said, when she finally obtained sufficient control over herself to string a coherent sentence together. "I never saw it—carrying those boxes in my arms—so careless."

"It's okay, Maryanne," Kriefmann replied. "It could have happened to anyone."

"They've been creeping closer since we established the test plantings," Ikram Mohammed told Matthew. "They're just like the slugs back home in one respect—they take it for granted that everything gardeners do is for their benefit." Then he turned back to Maryanne Hyder. "It wasn't your fault," he said. "Rand should have seen it if he was where he was supposed to be, leading the way."

"You know Rand," the stricken woman replied, in a thicker and slower tone. "He was in the lead all right, but he was carrying three times as much as me, all piled up. Couldn't have seen a pitfall full of sharpened stakes."

"Don't go to sleep if you can help it, Maryanne," Kriefmann went on. "Stay with us, if you can. Get a grip on your IT—don't let it slip you into a coma." While he was speaking he had been preparing a second shot. This time he positioned the nozzle halfway up Maryanne's thigh, just above the topmost wound in the cluster. Matthew hadn't seen him look for a vein, but he presumed that this must be the antitoxin and that he intended to spread it generously around the afflicted tissue as well as the circulatory system.

This time, the woman did not react to the shot. Her Internal Technology had damped out all feeling in the damaged tissue—but she was fighting its wider effects, as she had been instructed. Her IT didn't know that she needed to retain consciousness, but she knew.

"Hang in there," Kriefmann advised. "The antitoxin will kick in any second, if it's up to the job. Once it does, your IT will register the effect and begin to ease up. Keep talking, if you can. You've met Matthew Fleury, haven't you? He's our new ecological genomicist." Kriefmann knew perfectly well that Maryanne already knew that, but he obviously felt that he had to keep talking himself and didn't know what else to say. "Mr. Solari's been asking us questions," he went on. "He'll want to talk to you as soon as possible—which might not be the best reason in the world to stay awake, but . . ." He stopped as soon as he saw that the woman on the table was trying to say something in reply.

"I'm sorry," was what she said, as her distressed gaze flickered between left and right, probably without bringing either Matthew or Solari into clearer focus. "You must think I'm *so* stupid."

"Maybe it was a step too far in the study of local toxins," Matthew murmured, "but everyone seems to think you've done your job well enough in the past to save yourself now. It could have happened to anyone. Vince and I wouldn't even have known what to look out for. Take it easy." He touched her arm again, but merely by way of reassurance. He was satisfied that there was no further need for restraint.

"He's right, Maryanne," Lynn Gwyer said. She had worked her way round to Matthew's side, interposing herself between him and the doctor. "Actually, he's always right. I knew him back home, and that was his speciality. The last of the great prophets—always an egomaniac, even before he practically took over the news channels. *Those who cannot learn from prophecies are condemned to fulfil them.*" She looked at Matthew then. "Maryanne was part of a much later intake, one of the last recruits to *Hope*. She doesn't remember you at all—must have had a sheltered upbringing. Well, Matthew, this is what everyday life on Tyre is like. Or did you have time enough in orbit to get used to calling it Ararat?"

"Tyre will do fine so far as I'm concerned," Matthew said. "I seem to have arrived at a bad time, in more ways than one."

"I think the serum is working," Maryanne Hyder announced, with slightly more relief than astonishment. She looked at Matthew too. "It must have been the usual kind—just bigger. We don't really know how big they can grow, or whether they routinely get bigger as they get older. We don't know much about the life cycles of the animals *or* the plants. No eggs, no seeds, no ready-made alternative model to put in place of the birds and the bees."

"I guess it was a Rand Blackstone among slugs, as opposed to the Maryanne Hyder version," Lynn Gwyer put in. "Maybe they'll all grow as fat if we keep up our cultivation experiments."

"I hope not," the patient replied, with a groan. "It hurts."

"You won't be walking again for a few days," Kriefmann told

her. He seemed much more relaxed now that he was confident that the second shot had done the trick. "It's going to take time to repair that muscle. You'll be limping for a while once you're back on your feet again. Ike, can you give me a hand to get Mary to her bunk?"

"Sure," said Ikram Mohammed. "Will we need a stretcher?"

The patient tried to say no, but she was summarily overruled. While Ike went to get a stretcher Kriefmann took the time to thank Matthew for pitching in. "Welcome to chaos," he said, drily.

"It looks as if the meeting has been postponed," Lynn Gwyer said to Matthew. "We might as well get on with the guided tour."

Matthew was a little reluctant to leave while the toxicologist was still in trouble, but Ikram Mohammed was already returning with a stretcher.

Matthew glanced at Vince Solari, but the detective merely shrugged his shoulders.

As soon as Matthew and Lynn went outside they saw Rand Blackstone hurrying back to the bubbledome, carrying a transparent plastic sack. Matthew had to admit that the creature contained within it was impressively ugly. He had seen giant slugs in the Earthly tropics, and huge sea anemones in the shallows of the Indian Ocean, but he had never seen anything that combined the worst features of both. The creature's purple coloration was, however, oddly attenuated; it was distributed in blotches about a transparent tegument, putting him as much in mind of a gargantuan planarian worm or liver fluke as of a slug. The smaller versions he had seen on film while he was on *Hope* had seemed much more deeply and more uniformly pigmented.

"Can't stop," Blackstone said, as he brushed past them. "Got to get this to Tang."

"Sure," Matthew said. "I'll have time to take a closer look later."

When the big man had gone inside, Lynn Gwyer looked Matthew in the eye, with obvious concern. "Did Ike have a chance to fill you in on what's what down here?" she asked. "I don't know what they told you on *Hope*, but you'll have figured out that we have very different problems down here."

"He didn't get the chance to say as much as he'd probably have liked," Matthew told her. "Dulcie Gherardesca brought me breakfast, and she was still around when Ike came back. She had a point of view to put across, just as Blackstone had when he walked us back yesterday. I'm beginning to fit the pieces together, but listening to a calmer voice would be a considerable relief."

"I would have walked you back myself," she said, "but it's not easy to get in Rand's way when he's determined to have first shot. I suppose he was hoping that you had a message from Shen Chin Che?"

"He was. I suppose he wanted it so desperately in order to boost morale in the Tyrian Counterrevolutionary Front."

"Don't be so quick to make a joke of it, Matthew," the genetic engineer replied, frowning. "*Did* you have a message?"

"Not as such. Shen's back's to the wall, but he didn't seem to be in any mood to give in yet. If he has any cards left to play he didn't dare show them to me—but if he doesn't, it's only a matter of time before the crew winkle him out. He's too old to fight a long campaign. The crew have the upper hand, and all the time in the microworld."

Lynn Gwyer nodded, as if the judgment was exactly what she'd expected. "Rand's okay, behind the bold pioneer act," she said. "We really do have a hell of a problem down here, you know, which everybody on *Hope*—and I mean *everybody*—seems to be bent on ignoring. It takes more than a breathable atmosphere to make an Earth-clone world, and this is *not* an Earth-clone world in the sense that you and I would mean. If the probe data Milyukov claims to have is accurate, it may be the nearest thing to an Earthlike world we'll find within a couple of hundred light-years of Earth, and I'm certainly not as ready to give up on it as some of the people at Base One, but we really do have a major problem to solve, and I don't mean who killed Bernal. His death was a big blow, because of what we might have lost, but launching a witch-hunt to fit someone up for his murder won't bring him back, and it might compound the damage."

"Vince Solari is okay too," Matthew assured her. "He's not here to hunt witches or fit anybody up. Why would it compound the problem if the murderer were identified and charged?"

"That depends who it is," the woman replied. "If it's one of us—well, we're stretched beyond the limit already. If he really was killed by an alien humanoid that might be even worse, in terms of tying further knots in the situation. I wish I could believe in a sneaky invader from Base One, but I can't—which seems to me to leave the bad possibility and the worse possibility."

"You do believe the aliens exist, then?" Matthew deduced. "You think it's unlikely that an alien hand wielded the glass dagger, but you don't believe they're extinct?"

"No, I don't," Lynn confirmed. "I think they're giving the ruins a wide berth, just like the other mammal-analogues, but I think they're alive and well downriver. They might not be easy to find, but I don't think extinction as we know it is a common event on Tyre."

"Gradual chimerical renewal," Matthew said. "The Miller Effect, built in to the ecosphere at a fundamental level, in a way that makes it far less ruinous to the learning process. But if everything here's emortal, how does evolution happen?"

"Did Lityansky tell you about the second genome?" Lynn asked.

"He showed me the diagrams, but he said that no one knows what it does. He wouldn't speculate. What do you think?"

"You mean, what did Bernal think?"

"I dare say you tossed the ideas back and forth between you—and Ike too. What's your best guess?"

"We think it's a homeobox. We think that our own genome may suffer some crucial disadvantages because the homeotic genes are mixed in with all the rest."

"Homeotic genes control embryonic development," Matthew said, slightly puzzled. "I thought you hadn't managed to find any embryos."

"Homeotic genes control anatomical organization," Lynn said. "On Earth, that's mostly a matter of controlling embryonic development, but there are sometimes further metamorphic changes to be managed. If Tyrian plants and animals really are emortal, they might have much more scope in that regard, and they'd need a genomic system equipped to orchestrate that extra scope. We can't prove it until we can study some actual metamorphoses, but we're quietly confident that we're on the right track. Even Tang thinks we're on the right track, and he's a hard man to please. The three-dimensional coding complex is a fancy homeobox—fancier by far than anything our one-string genome could contrive."

Matthew nodded slowly. "I see," he said. "So evolution happens as organisms change. Natural selection without genetic load. Metamorphosis instead of death."

"Emortality's not immortality," Lynn reminded him. "Things die here. There's eating—herbivorous *and* carnivorous. There's predation and parasitism. Lots of death—but the organisms that don't die may not be existentially stuck the way we are. They may be able to go on renewing themselves and changing themselves indefinitely—although it'll take a long time to prove it."

"Maybe Vince's werewolves weren't such a silly idea after all," Matthew said. "Maybe you can sell him on the idea that it was a werewolf-analogue that killed Bernal. Not exactly a healthy scenario for a first contact, though, is it? I see what you mean about the bad alternative and the worse one. I can see why you didn't want to address the question, and don't want Vince to address it either."

"That's not fair, Matthew," the bald woman said, defensively. "It's the *world* that's the important puzzle. That's the mystery we need to solve— because that's the mystery that could be the death of every last one of us, if we don't solve it."

"I know that," Matthew assured her. "So let's get on with the grand tour, shall we?"

TWENTY

While waiting to shuttle down, Matthew had studied most of the available film of the ruined city, using the VE-hood above his bed to take a virtual tour along the same route that Lynn Gwyer was following, so he was now beset by an eerie feeling that he was acting out a half-forgotten dream. He'd had similar experiences back on Earth, when he'd visited established tourist attractions in VE in order to work out exactly what he wanted to see when he got to the real thing. He was already familiar with the ways in which real tours expanded the horizons of virtual ones, offering a better appreciation of size and context.

The film clips had, of course, concentrated on those parts of the city that had been partially cleared of the enshrouding vegetation. It was not until he saw the remainder in all its glory that Matthew realized why the flying eyes entrusted with the work of mapping and surveying the new world had not been able to pick it out for more than a year. So completely were the stone walls overgrown, overlaid, and obscured that it had taken a revelatory freak of chance to provide the first evidence of artifice.

Matthew soon came to understand, as Lynn led him over the ridge separating the Base Three bubbles from the nearest wall of the city, that even after a further year-and-a-half of searching, there might easily be other structures of a similar kind as yet undiscovered.

"Your methods of clearance seem to have been rather brutal," Matthew commented, as he followed the makeshift path.

"There were only four of us at first," Lynn reminded him. "We would have liked more reinforcements, but Milyukov wouldn't send them. He blamed the trouble aboard the ship, but I think he was afraid we'd find what we were looking for. If we do find intelligent aliens, Tang's case will look a lot stronger. Milyukov wants to delay any discovery until he's settled his domestic difficulties, and he's campaigning hard for the conference at Base One to come up with a vote in favor of staying put. So we didn't really have much choice. We moved on from machetes to chain saws in a matter of days, then figured we might as well go the whole hog and started blasting away with flamethrowers. If we'd had any authentic archaeologists to help us out they'd have fainted with horror, but Dulcie's not that delicate.

"When we get up to the top you'll be able to see the outlines of the lesser walls, but you won't be able to make out their true extent and shape. Even with flamethrowers we haven't been able to clear more than a tiny fraction of the whole array. The distinction between changes in the contours of the hills and the artificial constructs is hard to see, even with a practiced eye."

As they toiled up the slope, following a pathway that was far from straight, Matthew's limbs soon began to ache with the effort. It seemed that every time he came close to a crucial adjustment to circumstance he immediately began to put a renewed strain on his long-frozen muscles. Lynn was moving slowly, continually pausing to lend him a helping hand whenever he allowed his unsteadiness to show, but he knew that he had to make his own way.

At least the stress of climbing distracted him from the ever-present unease caused by the fact that his reflexes were slightly out of tune with the gravity-regime. That would doubtless surface again when he got down to lab work, or when someone pressed him into an educative ballgame.

Further distraction was provided by an increasingly keen awareness of the inadequacy of his eyes. As Lynn had warned, it was easy enough to see where human hands had been at work peeling vegetation away from the walls and burning back the debris, but where there had been no obvious interference it was very difficult to see the evidence of nonhuman work beneath the camouflage of nature.

Wherever patches of stonework had actually been cleared their artificial nature was starkly obvious, but where the purple plants still overlay them the alienness of the life-forms confused all earthly expectations. There were organisms analogous to lichens, to fungi, to mosses, and to creepers, as well as the curious dendrites, but all the appearances were deceptive and that deceptiveness swallowed up every sign that humanlike hands had ever been at work.

As they climbed higher more territory became visible, at least periodically, but the panorama remained utterly confusing to the

naked eye, at least until Matthew glimpsed something that stuck
out like the proverbial sore thumb.

"What's *that!*" he demanded, pointing.

Lynn chuckled. "That's ours," she said. "It's the cabin of
Bernal's boat. The lake and the river are still mostly obscured, but
you'll be able to see the lake and the lower part of the watercourse from the tower."

"Whose idea was it to paint the damn thing *pea green?*"
Matthew demanded. "I never thought of Bernal as an Edward
Lear fan."

"It won't be going all the way to the sea," she reminded him,
to indicate that she understood the reference, "and it certainly
won't be manned by an owl and a pussycat, no matter who gets
the final berth. It isn't painted—that's chlorophyll, to feed the
biomotor."

"It's powered by a biomotor? Not built for speed, then."

"It has a conventional engine too, but there's a fuel problem.
Bernal figured that we wouldn't really need the inorganic engine
till the return journey, when we'll be coming upstream. We
wouldn't actually have to carry a huge stock of fuel, given that
we've got converters that can process local vegetation into a
usable alcohol mix, but gathering material to feed the converter
takes a lot of work and the converter uses up fuel at a fair rate
itself. Given that we needed to equip the boat with certain other
bioanalogous features, and the desirability of a fail-safe backup,
Bernal decided that it would be best to double up. He was careful
to point out that it's in keeping with local traditions too."

Matthew was quick to pick up on that point. "Bernal was trying to figure out the logic of nutritional versatility—the lack of
distinction between fixers and eaters. So he wanted to use the
boat to . . . to what, exactly? To make a point? To explore a
hypothesis?"

"His argument was that if so many of the local invertebrates
can function as plants or as animals, there must be a reward for
versatility. Given that the world itself isn't very active, and the
weather patterns are so benign, he figured that it couldn't be a
response to the inorganic frame. He'd have liked to build a link to
the gradual chimerical renewal business, but he couldn't swallow
the notion that emortal animals might be routinely capable of
turning into emortal trees—and even if they were, he couldn't see

any reason why the homeobox shouldn't make chloroplast-analogues for plant forms and get rid of them completely in animal forms. So he—that is, we—figured it had to be something to do with the way the organisms interact with one another. There must be ecosystemic factors of some kind that determine the useful-ness of switching back and forth between modes of nourishment on an ad hoc basis: something analogous, however esoterically, to a boat whose energy-requirements change abruptly whenever it switches from going downstream to going upstream. It's not exactly making a point or exploring a hypothesis . . . more a sort of heuristic device: an aid to inspiration."

That was Bernal all over, Matthew thought. He had always been a lateral thinker, ceaselessly trying to find increasingly odd angles from which to approach intractable problems. He was—had been—exactly the kind of man to think it desirable to make an odyssey into alien territory in a vehicle that was "in keeping with local traditions." Bernal had not recorded any of this in his notepad—but it was exactly the kind of mental exercise that was difficult to commit to text, even as a series of doodles. Bernal must have spent the last few months of his life trying to figure out what analogues of "upstream" and "downstream" the local ecosystems possessed, whose subtle effects favored versatility in so many of the local organisms.

"Instead of seasons," Matthew murmured.

"What?" Lynn queried.

"Just a stray thought," Matthew said, slowly. He had to take a deep breath before carrying on, but talking was a lot less energy-expensive than climbing and he certainly didn't want to move on too quickly. "On Earth," he said, pensively, "the versatility of organisms is mostly a series of responses to seasonal variations. In winter, deciduous trees shed their leaves and some vertebrates hibernate. Most flowering plants and most invertebrate imagos die, leaving their seeds and eggs to withstand the cold spell. Large numbers of species opt for an annual life cycle, because the year-on-year advantages gained thereby far outweigh the prob-lems raised by occasional disruptive ecocatastrophes. There are seasons even in the tropics—dry and rainy—generated by ocean currents."

"Not here," Lynn told him, although he'd already noted the fact. "Tyre's axial tilt is less pronounced, and the ocean is as stable as the atmosphere. That constancy seems to be reflected in the relative lack of biodiversity—and, of course, in the dearth of species with dramatic life cycles, like metamorphic insects. Bernal said it wasn't quite that simple, though, because of the complicity of ecosystems and their inorganic environment."

"That's right," Matthew agreed. "Ecosystems aren't helpless prisoners of their inorganic frames. Life manages its own atmosphere; to some extent, it manages its own weather too. The rain that falls on rain forests evaporates from the rain forests in a disciplined fashion—take away the forest and the rain goes too. Here, where the world's axial tilt is less, seasonal variations would be less extreme anyway, but the ecosphere may well play an active role massaging them into near-uniformity, thus nullifying the kinds of advantages insects and other ephemerae derive from their chimerical life cycles. It's easy enough to grasp the fact that there's a whole new ballgame here, with a very different set of constraints and strategic opportunities—but it's not easy to imagine what they might be. Take winter and summer out of the equation, and what might substitute for them as forces of variation? Is there another kind of cycle, or something much more arbitrary? If there is a cycle, it might take a lot longer than three years to work through—and if there isn't . . . how often, and how swiftly, do major changes happen? Confusing as it is, *this* can't be the whole picture."

As he voiced the last sentence Matthew drew a wide arc with his right arm, taking in the limited panorama spread out before them and a much greater one whose horizons they were not yet in a position to see.

"Yeah," said Lynn, quietly. "That's *exactly* what Bernal sounded like, when he got going. Did you really know him that well, or is it a case of great minds thinking alike?"

"We were two peas in a pod," Matthew told her, his gaze lingering for a moment longer on the visible fragment of the distant boat. Then he turned away, saying: "Okay, I'm rested. Onward and upward."

Having visited several of the ancient walled cities of Earth, Matthew had a reasonably good idea of the way in which the scale of cities had shifted with the centuries. His memory retained a particularly graphic image of the Old City of Jerusalem surrounded by its vast sprawl of twentieth-century concrete suburbs. He was not unduly surprised, therefore, to find that what had apparently been the living space of the aliens' city was mostly compressed into an area not much more than a couple of kilometers square—although the shape of the hills meant that it was anything but square, and only vaguely round.

Like ancient Rome, the city seemed to have been built on seven hills, although the hills were very various in size and reach. Lynn was guiding him toward the summit of the highest of them all. His limbs felt like lead, and he was glad that Rand Blackstone was not present to witness his weakness.

Had they not been walking through the relics of ancient streets the surrounding territory would have yielded much more to Matthew's enquiring eyes, but they always seemed to be closely surrounded by huge hedgerows that stopped him seeing anything at all except multitudes of purple flaps, fans, spikes, and florets. Eventually, though, they began to climb something that looked like—and presumably was—a flight of ancient steps. It took them to the top of a lumpen mount that must once have been a building of some kind.

Matthew was exceedingly glad to reach the top. He mopped his brow with the back of his right hand, awkwardly conscious of the fact that both the hand and the moist forehead were intangibly encased in false skin.

The sun was high in the sky now, and its glare was uninterrupted by clouds. Although he knew that the faint purpling of the blue sky had nothing to do with ultraviolet light, Matthew could not help feeling that the alien light might somehow be dangerous, and Blackstone's wide-brimmed hat suddenly seemed far less ridiculous than it had the previous day. But Lynn had no hat, and no hair either, so he was probably being oversensitive.

From the summit of the mound, the extensive vistas surrounding him seemed quite different from the limited ones accessible from the lower vantage point.

Unpracticed as they were, Matthew's eyes were suddenly able to pick out the lines inscribed upon the landscape long ago by artificers' hands, and not yet completely obscured by the patient work of nature. From here, he could see enough of the undulations imposed on the vegetation by ancient walls to comprehend the unobliterated pattern.

The most astonishing thing of all, now that he could judge it properly, was the sheer extent of the walls appended to the city. They covered an area at least twelve times as vast. The residential part of the city—"downtown," as Matthew could not help calling it in the privacy of his thoughts—was by no means at the center of the complex, most of which was downslope of it. If the whole resembled a falling teardrop, gradually spreading over a landscape of tiny freckles and follicles, "downtown" would have been fairly near to the trailing edge.

"It's not obvious from anywhere else," Lynn told him, "but from up here you can see how the pattern must have developed. They moved gradually outward from the primary rampart, preferring downhill to uphill, gradually clearing more ground and surrounding the fields they'd created with new walls. The city itself continued to grow, mostly in upslope directions, so that some of the fields were built over, and there were subsidiary islands of residential building way out there to the east and south, but most of the development as the population swelled seems to have been a matter of building higher and filling in. As they cleared more land for crops, though, they built more walls: rank after rank after rank. The innermost walls are the lowest, perhaps because they routinely cannibalized them to help in the building of the outer ones, even though their quarrying techniques had come on by leaps and bounds. You can see a couple of their biggest quarries way over there in the northwest."

"How did they move the blocks?" Matthew asked, still feeling distinctly breathless.

"The hard way, according to Dulcie. There's little enough advantage in wheels, or even in using logs as rollers, on terrain as uneven as this, and you've probably noticed that the local tree-substitutes aren't much given to the production of nice straight logs with a circular cross-section. They had no beasts of burden, so they had to carry the stones themselves, one by one, or maybe a few at a time slung in hammocks from poles and frames carried by small parties of humanoids. But the real question—the *big* question—is *why* they felt they had to move the blocks."

"They had enemies," Matthew said, making the obvious deduction. "Their fields were precious, and had to be defended."

"Maybe it's not so surprising," Lynn went on, "whichever hypothesis you favor as to the reason for the great leap forward from hunter-gatherer societies to agricultural ones. If it really was a fabulous stroke of inspiration, the tribes that hadn't made it were probably keen to get in on the act. If it was a desperation move forced by ecological crisis, the tribes that hadn't made it would have been even keener. On Earth, the major ongoing conflict was always between settled agriculturalists and nomadic herdsman, but the relative dearth of mammal-equivalents in this ecosphere seems to have ensured that the humanoids never took to animal husbandry—not in a big way, at any rate—so the Cain and Abel allegory doesn't apply."

Matthew noticed the tacit assumption that the "enemies" the city-builders wanted to keep out were others of their own kind, but he didn't call attention to it. Instead, he asked: "Which hypothesis do you like? The inspirational leap or the existential crisis?"

"The crisis scenario always made more sense to me as an explanation of our own prehistory," Lynn admitted, "but if we don't know for sure why our own hunter-gatherer ancestors settled down, we're hardly likely to be able to come to a firm conclusion about these guys. That's the way I tell the story to myself, though. If the people who migrated up the river and built the city did so because life down on the plain was becoming too difficult, successive waves of their increasingly distant cousins would have followed in their train. Maybe, at first, some or all of them were taken in, coopted to the grand plan—but as living space became more cramped, the people in the city might have become increasingly desperate to keep others out while the people trying to get in became more desperate in proportion. Positive feedback, ultimately bringing the conflict to a mutually ruinous climax."

"It sounds plausible," Matthew agreed.

"Not to Dulcie," Lynn observed. "Not enough evidence of elaborate weaponry in the hidey-holes we've so far excavated. Ideally, of course, we'd like some skeletons so that we could look for evidence of violent death, but even hard human bone wouldn't have survived for long in this kind of environment. The city-dwellers who died here have all been reabsorbed—every last knucklebone and tooth. All we have to go on are the stones and the glass fragments. No earthenware pots, no metal. Dulcie reckons that if you leave out the walls themselves, the evidence so far unearthed favors the notion that the city-dwellers were a relatively peaceful lot."

"What about the spearhead that killed Bernal?"

"What about it? Dulcie says it's a fake. Even if it isn't, it's recent, and even if it weren't recent, it would only be evidence of hunting, not warfare."

Matthew shrugged his shoulders. Although his smartsuit only presented the illusion of clothing, he couldn't quite escape the false sensation that something clammy was clinging to his back like a sweat-soaked shirt.

"Given that the local plants don't make storage-proteins to supply seeds," he said, seeking further distraction from his discomfort, "the staple crop couldn't have been a grain-analogue, even though the plants in the drawings I saw on *Hope* look a bit like corncobs."

"That's right," Lynn confirmed. "We're not sure how they persuaded their food-plants to put on so much bulk—that's why we're doing the test plantings of candidate types. The fields have been reclaimed by local varieties, though—the city-builders probably brought their crop-plants with them from the plain. We don't really know why they didn't cultivate the land on the banks of the river, but we figure it must have had something to do with the difficulty of clearing ground and keeping it free from weeds. Those giant grasses are probably more resilient than the hill-dwelling dendrites—too difficult to dislodge.

"I'll show you the murals when we go down again. We think they might have been colored in at one time, but organic paints would have been stripped off by slugs and snails almost immediately, except where heavy metals in inorganic pigments made them too poisonous. We have a few flakes of what might have been paint, but the only decipherable images are the engravings in the photos."

Matthew examined the exposed remains of a stone wall on the edge of the platform from which they were looking down. It had been scraped clean of its various encrustations. The blocks of stone from which it had been constructed were relatively small and easily portable, in stark contrast to the bigger foundation blocks that had been similarly cleared.

The mortar sealing the wall gave the impression of being resinous, albeit set as hard as the stone itself, although it could not have survived if it had been organic. Although he could see half-a-dozen places in the immediate neighborhood where similar walls must have been cracked, broken and eventually pulled down by the combined efforts of severe weather and the overgrowing vegetation, this particular fragment looked as if it might stand for thousands of years yet to come, and perhaps hundreds of thousands.

It had been built to last, and it had lasted.

Alas, the civilization it had been built to contain had not.

Matthew could hardly help wondering whether any civilization that *Hope*'s passengers put in place might be bound to meet a similar fate.

TWENTY-ONE

W hy didn't more people come here from Base One when Milyukov refused to supply a proper staff?" Matthew asked Lynn Gwyer. "They're all Earth-born. They all saw the same VE-dramas you and I grew up on. They must have a proper appreciation of the mythic significance of first contact. The mere possibility that there might be aliens should have had them flocking here in droves."

"It's a long way," she pointed out. "All our aircraft are tiny, and we haven't finished building and securing a chain of refueling stops. At first, they expected the crew to send down more people. The realization that it wasn't going to happen was slow to grow, and it grew alongside other arguments. Bernal thought he could change that, if only he could broadcast to Base One, but Milyukov procrastinated over sending the TV cameras he asked for. In the end, we got you instead."

"He must have chuckled over that one," Matthew said, meaning Milyukov. "He took an unreasonable relish in informing me that he couldn't give me the cameras I asked for. He can't keep me incommunicado, but he knows as well as I do that it's not easy to persuade large numbers of people to tune in when all you've got is a beltphone."

While he was speaking they completed their descent from the top of the mound—"the tower," as Lynn insisted on calling it. It had undoubtedly been a tower at one time, but Matthew found his own mind shying away from the designation. Although a way had been cleared to allow observers to climb to the top, and tunnels had been excavated to allow ingress to what had once been the interior, much of the surrounding vegetation had been left in place to provide supportive scaffolding. As he looked back up at it, the only Earthly tower to which Matthew could readily link it, imaginatively, was the fictitious one in which the Sleeping Beauty and her court had been committed to suspended animation until the day that her handsome prince would come. Even having made that link, though, he could not extend the analogy far enough to imagine himself as the Sleeping Beauty, and Nita Brownell or Konstantin Milyukov as the liberator prince.

"There *should* be more people here," Lynn said, as they moved toward another, much shallower downslope. "More would be on their way from Base One as we speak if it weren't for the fact that the groups in favor of a temporary or permanent withdrawal are becoming more paranoid by the day. With Milyukov on one side, insisting that they can't be taken off the world again, and the frontiersmen on the other, insisting that we have to make a go of the colony and that everybody ought to stop whining and pull their weight, the situation at Base One is gradually turning into total farce. You know they're planning some kind of election, I suppose? With everything that needs to be *done* down here, at least half of the people at Base One are devoting the bulk of their time and effort to organizing a bloody *conference* to determine their official *position*. Unbelievable! Almost as unbelievable as the idea that if they take a vote on it, the minority will immediately fall into line with the majority!"

"I've only heard rumors," Matthew said, putting a hand on the wall beside the path to balance himself more securely. "No one was delegated to brief us on that sort of stuff, even though Milyukov seems to think that Bernal might have been murdered to deny him a voice in the big debate. Was he even planning to attend?"

"I doubt it. The only plan he seemed to be interested in during the days leading up to his death was the river journey. The engraved wall's just over there."

Matthew picked out the relevant patch of wall easily enough. He'd been hoping that the photograph he'd looked at on *Hope* hadn't done it justice, but the original was no clearer. The reality seemed, in a way, even more primitive than the image—but someone had obviously gone to considerable trouble to carve out the line drawing, given that any chisels they had available must have had brittle blades.

"Where's the pyramid?" Matthew asked, suddenly.

"Good question," Lynn replied. "We decided that it probably isn't a structure at all. We think it's a symbol. Maybe a kind of frame, maybe an arrow pointing up to the sky. It's just a couple of lines—we only see it as a pyramid because we're culturally preconditioned."

"Maybe," said Matthew, grudgingly. "It's a pity Bernal didn't get his cameras. If he'd been able to take them downriver with him, he'd have been able to put his two cents' worth into the debate at Base One from a unique platform. Unless, of course, Milyukov decided to do likewise, in which case there'd have been a big on-screen argument. Bernal always loved a big showdown."

"It's not just some cheap TV event, Matthew," she told him, with a measure of asperity, as she led him away from the mural, this time heading back the way they had come. "It's real, and it might determine the fate of the colony."

"Not unless it's properly stage-managed, it won't," Matthew said. "There'll be a lot of nonsense talked, and maybe a show of hands, and it will accomplish exactly nothing. The fact that there's a power struggle going on aboard *Hope* might have convinced too many of us that there's more than one possible outcome to this sorry mess, but there isn't. Whatever happens up there, those of us who are down here are stuck here for the foreseeable future, and probably forever. If this is a death trap, we'll die in it."

"Try telling that to Tang. On second thought, don't. You'll stand a better chance of getting that berth if you don't upset him. Ike and I want you to have it, but that might not be enough."

"So I'd gathered," Matthew said. "Lynn, who the hell could have killed Bernal—and *why?*"

"As I told your friend Solari, *I don't know*. If he thinks it was me, he's barking up the wrong tree."

"Why should he think it was you?"

"Because I'm the nearest thing to a scorned woman he can find. *Cherchez la femme*—isn't that the detective's motto?"

"Oh," Matthew said, momentarily unable to think of anything else to say. It wasn't a line of argument he wanted to pursue. He thought about Tang Dinh Quan instead, and the two daughters Tang had in SusAn. For Tang, he knew, any argument about the future of the colony had to cut further and deeper than "We're stuck with it for the foreseeable future, so we might as well get on with it." When the time came for him to talk to Tang he had to have something better than that to say to him. Tang's daughters, like Alice and Michelle Fleury, still had all their options open.

The worst scenario that Matthew could readily imagine was

that Alice and Michelle might be whisked away in the tender care of Konstantin Milyukov's Revolutionary Tribunal while their father was marooned, whether the world on which he was marooned was capable of sustaining human life in the longer term or not—but how could that possibly happen, he asked himself, given Rand Blackstone's calculations?

Matthew had relaxed considerably now that they were retracing their steps, but that was a mistake. He was still tired, and he had grown used to putting his hand out sideways to rebalance himself and provide a little extra support. While descending from the mound he had been placing it on bare stone, but now they were walking along a narrow path the walls to either side were covered in vegetation. Because he found the feel of the alien "stems" and "leaves" slightly disconcerting, he had developed a subliminal preference for reaching *through* the purple curtain to touch the stone behind it—but it was an unwariness that he quickly came to regret.

It was only out of the corner of his eye that he saw the flicker of movement as a clutch of tentacles began writhing like Medusa's hair, but the glimpse was enough to flood him with terror.

He snatched his hand away with the utmost urgency—and immediately understood how minutely his autonomic nervous system had been tuned to Earthly conditions. It felt as if his arm had been seized by some alien power and thrown aside. There was no real reason for him to stumble, but the sense of dislocation that suddenly swept over him made it all-but-impossible for him to maintain his stance. He lurched to one side, crashing into the wall opposite the one from which he had removed his hand. He had tripped over his own foot.

While he was cursing volubly Lynn was quick to snatch a long-bladed knife from her belt. She used the blade to part the purple foliage and expose the creature more fully.

Although he was still fighting for balance, Matthew immediately realized how small the monster was by comparison with the one that Rand Blackstone had brought back to the bubble after Maryanne Hyder had been stung. The creature's body was no bigger than his hand, and was shaped not unlike a hand laid flat, save for the tentacles bedded where the first joint of the middle finger would have been had it actually been a hand. The tentacles themselves were much thinner than a finger; they seemed surprisingly pale—almost translucent—and rather delicate. The flat-worm-like body was a deeper purple than Blackstone's specimen, and the eyespots were much less prominent.

"It's okay," Lynn said. "Even if it had stung you it wouldn't have been any worse than a bee sting, unless you had a massive allergic reaction."

"What's the bloody thing doing lurking in there?" Matthew growled, to cover his embarrassment. "What's the point of having photosynthetic pigments in your skin if you're going to skulk in the shadows while the sun's at zenith?"

"Another good question," Lynn conceded. "Not hiding from predators, that's for sure. They don't seem to have any enemies hereabouts but us." She let the foliage fall back to its original position and dropped her hand, taking care not to let any part of her surface-suit get into range of the sting-cells. She made no move to capture or kill the creature. "I'm not sure whether their numbers are actually increasing or whether we're just getting better at spotting them," she mused.

"I didn't spot it," Matthew pointed out, bringing himself upright and looking anxiously at the wall against which he had stumbled. "That was the whole problem."

Mercifully, there was no sign of any animal life lurking beneath the screen of vegetable flesh—but when he extended his fearful glance to take in the whole of the surrounding terrain he immediately saw the *second* animal he had seen since leaving the bubble that morning: a pair of ratlike eyes staring at him from higher and denser growth. As soon as he met their stare, though, the eyes drew back into the tangled plants. There was only the softest of rustling sounds as the creature' invisible body slipped swiftly away.

"Did you see *that*?" he demanded.

"Local mammal," Lynn told him. "Shy, seemingly harmless. A rare sight, though—you're lucky."

"Harmless? What about the ones with the hypodermic tongues?"

"None of those sighted in these parts to date," she assured him. "The local reptile- and mammal-analogues seem to be mostly herbivores, and the ones that aren't seem to specialize in smaller worms—they wouldn't go after something like the one you nearly grabbed. They're too thin to be cuddly, but temperamentally they're more rabbit and kitten than rat and monkey. They're curious, but way too nervous to be intrusive. So far, that is—they might get bolder as time goes by. He was purple too, of course, but he's not out soaking up the sun either. Even the ones that only come out at night are purple, although we think that they only keep chloroplast-substitutes for purposes of cryptic coloration. The medusa is certainly capable of photosynthesizing, but the species doesn't seem to have any instinctive imperative to make the most of the noonday sun. Unlike our beautiful pea-green boat, which is charging its storage cells as we speak. Odd, isn't it?"

It *was* odd. Why, Matthew wondered, would animals that could boost their energy supplies by fixing solar energy be hiding in the shadows? Was it just because there were people tramping through their territory, or was there another reason? Earthly herbivores and insectivores were shy for exactly the reason that Lynn had mentioned: they had to keep out of the way of the top predators, and hiding was the strategy they'd adopted. That was precisely the reason why photosynthetic apparatus would be no good to them. If you were the kind of organism that fixed solar energy, you had to be out in the sun, which meant that you had to deter things that wanted to eat you by some other means: thorns or poisons. The slug with the sting-cells had both, after a fashion, but the mammal-analogue with the disconcerting stare apparently had neither. So why were *both* of them purple, and why were both of them skulking in the shadows?

"Do you want to see more?" Lynn asked.

Matthew was very tired by now, as well as a trifle bruised. He was far from certain whether he wanted to take the rest of the grand tour now, even though time was pressing.

"What more have you got?"

She tilted her head thoughtfully. "We've got a few trenches," she said. "Dulcie dug them. Nothing much in them though. We've got a few glass artifacts, but they're back at the bubble— all I can show you here are the holes in the walls they came out of. I can take you along the other paths, if you like, but now that you've had the best view the rest might seem anticlimactic. We ought to go down into the fields, I suppose, although there's not a lot to see with the naked eye but more walls. You might be more interested in Tang's proteonomic studies—he's got some recent data that augments and amplifies what Lityansky has, but only slightly."

What Matthew would have liked to do was to take a walk on his own, in the hope of getting a better feel for the environment, but he wasn't sure that he was up to it. It wasn't just the problems caused by the necessity of readjusting to 0.92 Earth-normal gravity; the closeness of his encounter with the stinging worm had reminded him that there were dangers here to which he was not yet properly alert.

"All in all," he decided, aloud, "Lunch seems like a good idea."

"Right," Lynn said. "You'll probably find your appetite running away with you a bit for the first few days, but once the awful tedium of the food becomes obvious to your stomach it'll lose its enthusiasm. Are you okay?"

"As well as can be expected," Matthew told her. She nodded, as if she knew that he wasn't just talking about his physical condition. She knew as well as he did that he'd been unceremoniously tossed into the deep end of this particular pool, without the benefit of swimming lessons. She didn't seem to resent the time she'd had to spend showing him the view from the city; he was a new face as as well as an old one, a welcome distraction from the work routines she'd established since accepting the posting. She too was doing as well as could reasonably be expected.

"It's a fabulous discovery," she said, quietly, as she began to lead the way back to the bubble. "Even more fabulous, in a way, than the world itself. We're entitled to be disappointed, I think, that the principle of convergent evolution didn't hold up better at the genomic level—it would make things *so* much easier if the local life were DNA-based—but we're surely entitled to be delighted as well as astounded by the fact that it held up so well at the level of actual organisms. There were *men* here, Matthew. I don't think any of us, here or at the other bases, has really been able to take the enormity of that fact aboard. This was a city, which makes them civilized men. Whatever happened to them, they were *here* . . . and so are we."

Matthew could see what she was getting at. Across the void, across the centuries, two sentient, intelligent, civilized species— two sentient, intelligent, civilized *humanoid* species—had come into such close proximity that one was now aware of the other.

They had not yet contrived to meet, or to touch, but even if one of them did turn out to be extinct, it had become known to the other in spite of that fact. At the very least, its passing could be mourned, and some of its lessons relearned. That was a matter of importance, no matter how frustrating all the remaining mysteries might be.

"So are we," Matthew echoed, to show that he understood—and she nodded, to accept his understanding.

TWENTY-TWO

After programming the cooker Matthew sat down at the table with Lynn and Godert Kriefmann. The doctor opened his mouth, presumably to offer news of Maryanne Hyder's condition, but he closed it again abruptly when Vince Solari came into the room. The temperature was thermostatically controlled, but it seemed to drop a degree anyhow. Matthew noticed that Lynn was clearly discomfited, and realized that she had not been joking when she had confessed her fear that Solari suspected her.

The policeman came to sit beside Matthew. He seemed to be slightly discomfited himself by the reaction his entrance had caused. He leaned toward Matthew in a confidential fashion that was only a trifle overacted. "There's something I need to show you," he said.

"Is there time to eat first?" Matthew wanted to know.

"If you like—but it's important."

Lynn and the doctor were trying hard not to look as if they were hanging on Solari's every word, but they weren't succeeding. Kriefmann looked just as worried as Lynn.

"It's about Bernal's murder?" Matthew said, just to make certain.

"Yes."

Solari's terseness was obviously intended to display the implication that he didn't want to say too much in the present company, but Matthew wasn't at all sure that he wanted to pander to that kind of provocation—or, for that matter, to enter into any kind of apparent conspiracy. There seemed to be way too many conspiracies already festering on and above the new world.

"Do you know who did it?" Matthew demanded.

"Not for certain." It was another calculated provocation, although he didn't go so far as to favor anyone with a meaningful look. Matthew began to feel just as uncomfortable as his two companions.

"Where?" Matthew asked, anxious to have done with the conversation.

"Outside. I'll take you."

Matthew knew that Solari had been at the crime scene for most of the morning. He couldn't imagine that there would be any useful forensic evidence left after a week of imperfect weather, but Solari obviously thought that he had found something significant—something that he wanted to talk over with the only person on the Base who couldn't possibly have committed the murder.

"Okay," Matthew said, brusquely. "Give me twenty minutes. Are you eating?"

Solari shook his head. "I took a packed lunch with me," he said. "Thought I might be gone all day—didn't expect to find anything so soon."

Matthew turned to the doctor and said: "How's Maryanne?"

"Better," Kriefmann told him. "She won't be running, skipping or jumping for a couple of days, but she'll be able to sit up in bed, read, even answer stupid questions. . . ." The final remark was obviously slanted toward Solari.

"I met one of the monsters just now," Matthew reported. "Just a little one. Lurking in the vegetation—odd, that, for a creature able to fix solar energy, with no apparent natural enemies in the vicinity."

"Its instincts probably can't figure out that it's in a safe area," Kriefmann pointed out, grateful for the distraction. "Maybe it won't be safe for long—if the critters really are becoming more common, the predators will begin to move in soon enough."

"I've only seen pictures of the predators," Matthew said. "Things like big rats with crocodile snouts and things like frilly lizards. Have you ever seen anything like that in the flesh?"

"Nothing particularly scary," Kriefmann told him. "There are lizards up here, but they mostly stick to the treetops. Mammal-equivalents too, but mostly herbivores and moppers-up of little worms. The serious hunters only come out at night, though, so there might be more around than we suppose. By day, the ruins seem unusually peaceful by comparison with Earthly subtropics. According to the evidence gathered by the flying eyes things are busier downriver—but that may be an illusion. It may be our presence that's scaring the wildlife away. A pity, if so. There are lots of worms, of every size imaginable, but worms don't hum like flies or sing like birds. It's noisier as well as more crowded down-river, so I'm told. More species down there use sound signals."

While Matthew collected his meal, Lynn Gwyer asked Solari where he had worked back on Earth. Having already heard the story, Matthew felt free to concentrate on his food. This was a prepackaged meal sent down with him in the shuttle, so it didn't have the slightly offensive taste and texture of the locally extracted manna substrate, but it was as bland and unappetizing as the meals he'd had on *Hope*. The colonists had food technology that would allow them to do better in time, but they were obviously still thinking in stern utilitarian terms. Matthew didn't doubt that the wheat-manna pancakes and thinly sliced synthetic vegetables would serve his nutritional needs, but he couldn't help wondering whether the humans on the surface might have felt slightly more welcome here if they'd paid more attention to matters of aestheticization.

While Matthew ate, Kriefmann quizzed him about his condition, and advised him to try not to overtax himself during his first few days on the surface. The chance, Matthew thought, would be a fine thing. As soon as he had dumped the remains of his meal and its packaging in the recycler, Vince Solari stood up, obviously expecting him to follow. He signaled his apologies to Lynn.

Once they were outside the bubble Solari led the way down-hill, in a direction almost exactly opposite to the one Matthew had taken on his earlier expedition. They made more rapid progress, though, partly because flamethrowers had been plied with such reckless abandon that the way was clearer and partly because Vince Solari's mind was focused on more practical matters than Lynn Gwyer's had been. Matthew noticed, however, that he was already moving a little more freely and comfortably than the policeman, who reacted to his own clumsiness with casual impatience.

Come nightfall, Matthew thought, Solari's surface-suit and IT would be working overtime on the bruises generated by his purposeful hurrying.

"Have you reported your find to anyone else?" Matthew asked him, interested to know how fully Solari intended to cooperate with Konstantin Milyukov.

"I dare say they'll know as soon as you do," Solari told him, not bothering to specify who he meant by *they*. He was assuming, of course, that their surface-suits might have been bugged in some unobtrusive manner. Matthew had not been convinced that Shen's anxieties regarding the temporary smartsuit he had been given on *Hope* were anything more than paranoia, but he knew that it would be foolish to take anything for granted. So sophisticated had surveillance methods become in the years before he left Earth that every wall in the world had been collecting eyes and ears by the dozen, many of them undetectable by human observers. For all he knew, his new suit might even be rigged for visual transmission—in which case, "they" might not have to wait for Solari to spell anything out in conversation; "they" might already have seen whatever he had seen, and interpreted it with equal intelligence.

From the top of the mound that he and Lynn had climbed Matthew had seen the city's fields laid out like a vast purple-blanketed maze, with their vaguely outlined protective walls seeming no more impressive than lines doodled on a page. From within, though, the fragmentary network of partly fallen walls seemed positively oppressive. They loomed up haphazardly, curving this way and that, almost as enigmatically as the corridors of *Hope*. Those closest to the bubble-complex were mostly between one and three meters tall, but the further Matthew and Solari went the taller the fragments became.

The route Solari took involved little actual climbing, but the penalty they paid for that convenience was that it was by no means straight. At these close quarters it was easy to see that the wall-builders had made their own provision for laborers to pass from field to field, equipping their citadel-fields with gateways whose gates had long since decomposed, but they had not taken the trouble to make arterial roads that radiated from the city proper like the spokes of a wheel. Perhaps that was because they were anxious that such highways might be too convenient for traffic coming the other way, Matthew thought—or perhaps it was merely because the endeavor had spread out in an untidily improvised manner.

Some of the fields had obviously had blockhouses in the corners, perhaps to provide temporary accommodation, or to house sentries, or to store tools, or for any combination of those reasons. Others had had stone shelves built into the angles where walls intersected, but any staircases that had led up to the tops of the walls must have been made of perishable materials; there was not the least trace of any such structure now.

The walk was a long one—more than twice as long as the one Matthew had taken with Lynn Gwyer—and it took a proportionate toll of their unready bodies. At first, Matthew told himself that it was bound to be easier because their route was mostly downhill, but it was a false assumption. When he remembered that Solari had already made the uphill climb once he began to understand the effort that the policeman had put in, and the strength of the motive that had led him to insist on making a second trip almost immediately, with Matthew in tow.

"We're not doing this just because you need somebody to talk to, are we?" he said, when that became clear to him. "You really do need my help to figure out the significance of what you've found."

"Yes," said Solari, his terseness now owing to shortness of breath rather than any disinclination to show his hand to possible suspects.

"Why?" Matthew persisted.

"Because you knew the man," Solari said, laboriously. "You're far better able to guess what he might have been up to than I am."

"Up to?" Matthew queried—but Solari didn't want to put in the effort of compiling an elaborate explanation when he had evidence waiting that would speak more eloquently for itself.

When they finally reached the spot where Bernal had been killed there was nothing to indicate where the body had been found. Matthew had not been expecting a bloodstain, let alone a silhouette in white chalk, but he had been expecting *something*, and it seemed somehow insulting that there was nothing at all. Any vegetation that had been crushed had recovered its former vigor. The place was screened from everything further uphill by a very solid and intimidating wall some ten or twelve meters to the north of the place where the body had been found. It met another, equally high and solid, twenty meters to the left. There was a ledge set in the angle, but it was too high up to be a shelf and it was angled downward. It looked like a place where laborers a long way from home might huddle together and shelter from the rain.

"What was he doing way out here?" Matthew wondered, aloud.

"The same question occurred to me," Solari said. "According to the bubble's log, he'd been spending a lot of time out here during the weeks before his death, even though his preparatory analysis of the local ecosystem was supposedly done and dusted. He must have been caught in the rain more than once, maybe for long enough for his idle hands to get restless."

"What's that supposed to mean?" Matthew said.

Solari took him to the angle of where the walls met: to the gloomy covert under the down-slanting ledge.

The wall seemed solid enough to a cursory glance, but when Solari reached up to remove a stone set slightly above waist height it came out neatly enough. There was a space behind it: a lacuna in what otherwise seemed to be a solid *wall*. Matthew recalled that the artifacts Dulcie Gherardesca had recovered had been found in cavities in the walls, where they had enjoyed a measure of protection from the forces of decay.

"It's a hidey-hole," Solari said. "Built for that purpose a *very* long time ago. Still serviceable, though."

The policeman removed several objects from the hole, one by one. Most of them were were blackly vitreous. Three looked like knives, or perhaps spearheads. Three more were similar in design but much smaller—perhaps arrowheads. The nonvitreous items were stone: two appeared to be crude chipping-stones of a kind that might well have been used by a Stone Age craftsman for working flint. One was some kind of scraper. There were numerous pieces of raw "glass," of a convenient size for working into useful objects.

"There aren't any shafts for spears or arrows," Solari said. "He hadn't gotten around to that. He was still practicing."

"He?" Matthew echoed, with an implicit query.

"Delgado."

Matthew thought about that for a couple of minutes. Then he said: "Are you sure that *Bernal* was making the spearheads and arrowheads? Maybe he found someone else making them. Maybe he was killed because he found out that someone else was making imitation alien artifacts."

"I can't be absolutely sure," Solari said, scrupulously. "The surface-suits are too thick and too resilient to permit easy DNA-analysis of their excreta, and the murder weapon itself had been handled by too many people before I got to it, but the fact that the only contaminants on these are Delgado's makes it highly unlikely that someone else had put the necessary hours into making them. Unless someone's gone to enormous trouble to erect an evidential smokescreen, Delgado was the one who faked the artifact with which he was killed. He had already faked others, and he was in the process of faking more. Maybe it began while he was whiling away the time waiting for a shower to pass, but it must have become purposive soon enough. He made time for the work; he must have had a plan for the results. Whoever killed him found out about it. Maybe they knew about the hidey-hole and maybe they didn't. If they did, they probably took the trouble to tidy up a little after he was dead—but if they expected that I wouldn't be able to find the evidence, they were wildly optimistic. Anyone could have found it, if they'd bothered to look. Delgado's friends—the murderer's friends—didn't bother to look."

This speech seemed to exhaust Solari's strength, and he had to lean against the wall, but he seemed relieved that he'd made his point.

"It doesn't make sense," Matthew said, after a pause.

"That won't wash, Matt," Solari replied. "It has to make sense. You say that you knew him as well as anyone—maybe better than anyone here, even though their acquaintance was more recent. So tell me. Why would he be faking alien artifacts?"

"He wouldn't. He was a scientist."

"But he was."

"No. *Faking* is your word, your interpretation. He was *making* artifacts of the same kinds as those found elsewhere in the ruins, but it doesn't mean that he had any intention of trying to pass them off as the real thing. Maybe someone else leapt to the same conclusion you did, but it has to be wrong. He was just experimenting with local manufacturing techniques. He *couldn't* have intended to attempt to fool anyone into believing that the blades and arrowheads had been made by aliens."

"Not even if he had a powerful motive for persuading people that the aliens aren't extinct?" It was obvious from Solari's tone that he didn't believe Matthew's version of events. The policeman had found what seemed to him to be a plausible motive: that Bernal had been determined to prove that the aliens were still around, and that somebody else had been determined to stop him.

"Whatever he was doing," Matthew said, stubbornly, "I can't see that it would provide a motive for his murder. If someone *were* planning to run that kind of fraud, and got caught red-handed, *he* might be tempted to do something to prevent the story coming out, but why would the person who caught him want to silence the person he'd caught? It doesn't make sense—and it certainly doesn't get you any closer to identifying the murderer."

"Somehow," Solari persisted, doggedly, "it *has* to make sense. You say that Delgado wouldn't do a thing like this—but he did. I know he was your friend, but you must see that this stuff about experimenting with alien manufacturing techniques is too feeble for words. He wouldn't have gone to this much trouble without a much better reason than *that*. How obvious the fakes would have been if they'd been found in less compromising circumstances I can't tell—but that might not matter. Maybe he knew that they'd be tagged as fakes sooner or later, but maybe he was prepared to settle for later, given that the colonists' big argument was about to come to a head."

"You think he was doing this to influence a vote that probably doesn't have any meaning whichever way it goes?" Matthew said, skeptically. "I don't think so. That's even more feeble than my story."

"So think of a better one. I mean it, Matt. I have to put a case together."

"Against Lynn Gwyer?"

Solari was suitably taken aback by that, but he was too good at his job to let his reaction give anything away. "Have you some reason for thinking that Gwyer might be guilty?" he asked, swiftly.

"Quite the contrary," Matthew said. "But she seems to think that you have her in the frame."

"Don't try that distraction crap with me, Matt," the policeman came back. "I thought you and I were becoming friends. Please don't start giving me the same runaround as these clowns."

"It must be hard to run a good cop–bad cop routine all on your own," Matthew observed, drily.

Solari seemed genuinely disappointed by that response—but that was his job. "Look, Matt," he said, earnestly, "neither of us knows how important this impending vote has come to seem to the people who've been down here for three years. Neither of us knows how deep anyone's paranoia cuts, or how weirdly it's configured. But if the planet were really inhabited, by an intelligent species on the ecological brink, that might seem to some people to be a powerful reason for letting it alone, don't you think? Given that we all signed up for this mission because our own species was on the brink, facing what looked like a terminal eco-catastrophe, don't you think that some people here might have powerful conscientious objections to the possibility of precipitating an ecological crisis here that might condemn another species—a *brother* species—to extinction?"

Matthew already knew that Solari was no fool, and he knew that Solari was absolutely right to say that no one who had only been awake for a matter of days could possibly comprehend the complexity of the evolving situation into which they'd both been precipitated—but Bernal Delgado had been his colleague, his rival, his collaborator, his fellow prophet, his mirror image in all but private and personal matters. Matthew could not imagine any circumstances in which *he* might be led to commit the kind of betrayal that Solari had imagined, so he was extremely reluctant to accept that Bernal might have been led to it. But to what hypothetical extreme would he have to go in order to construct a story that could conserve Bernal's innocence?

Could the evidence Solari had found so very easily, as soon as he began to look, have been faked, just like the arrowheads themselves? Could the conspiracy of which the murder was a part be far more complicated than Solari was yet prepared to suspect? How complicated could this mystery be? Was it not far too complicated already?

"They could have been planted," he said to Solari, although he knew exactly how desperate the suggestion was. "Given that we all wear heavy-duty smartsuits, you can't have much in the way of forensic evidence. Maybe this whole setup is fake—rotten through and through. Maybe the bubble's logs have been altered too."

"So who *did* fake it all?" Solari countered, plainly exasperated. "Why? Which of the seven had the motive, the time, the skill to do the murder *and* the cover-up? Come on, Matt. We have to do better than *that.*"

"I don't know," Matthew said, helplessly, knowing that if he had to stay ahead of the game he had to improvise something much better. "What I want to think is that Bernal really did *find* the artifacts, that they really are evidence of the continued existence of the indigenes . . . but that someone didn't want him to reveal that fact. Maybe the artifacts *are* real. That's another thing neither of us is competent to judge."

"Unfortunately," Solari observed, drily, "it's difficult to think of anyone who is. But it still won't wash. If they really were made by aliens, Delgado would have shouted the news from the rooftops the moment it broke. Nobody could have imagined, even for a moment, that they could keep it quiet—and if they had they certainly wouldn't have used one of the alien artifacts to commit the murder while they had a perfectly good stainless steel knife in their belt, would they?"

Matthew had to concede that it was all true. He was thoroughly ashamed of himself. He had always thought of himself as an unusually accomplished improviser, especially under pressure. He knew that he ought to be able to make up a better story, even if he couldn't actually intuit the truth. He was recently arrived on an alien world, exhausted and ill-fed, but none of those circumstances constituted an acceptable excuse.

"I'll work it out," he told Solari, grimly. "I promise you that. I'll work it *all* out. Every last piece of every last puzzle. I'm Bernal's replacement as well as his friend. It's up to me to carry through his plan, whatever it was, and that's what I intend to do. You can spread that around if you like, on the off chance that it will make the murderer take a pop at me. But either way, I'm going to sort this mess out. *Properly.*"

Solari finally cracked a smile. "That's what I wanted, Matt," he said, softly. "Just be sure you let me in on it first, okay?"

TWENTY-THREE

When Matthew and Solari returned to the bubble Solari decided that the time had come to interview Maryanne Hyder about Delgado's murder. Matthew decided, for his part, that it was time to confront Tang Dinh Quan.

The biochemist was in his laboratory, patiently monitoring the results on an electrophoretic analysis. The robot-seeded slides were so small that he had to use a light microscope to read the results. The shelves to either side of him were full of jars containing preserved specimens of tissues and whole organisms—mostly worms of various kinds—but pride of place on his largest worksurface was given to the massive biocontainment cell into which he had decanted the tentacled slug that Blackstone had brought in that morning. The interior of the cell was fitted with robot hands that Tang could use to manipulate the specimen, administer injections, and take tissue samples, but the slug seemed perfectly serene and relaxed. It was easy to imagine that its tiny eyespots were focused on its tormentor, while its distributed nervous system contemplated revenge for all the indignities he might care to heap up on it.

Matthew knew that Tang was one of numerous surface-based scientists working on the proteomics that would eventually supplement the genomic analyses carried out by Andrei Lityansky's counterparts at Bases One and Two. Proteomic analyses had never acquired the same glamor as the genomic analyses upon which they were usually considered to be parasitic, but biochemists tended to regard theirs as the real work. Hunting and sequencing exons was a fully automated procedure, while the patient work of figuring out exactly what the proteins the exons produced actually *did*, in the context of a functioning physiology, required a talent for collation and cross-correlation that even the cleverest AIs had not yet mastered.

Forearmed by Lityansky, Matthew already knew that the proteomics of the complex organisms of the Tyrian ecosphere was likely to be just as convoluted as the proteomics of Earth's "higher" organisms. On both worlds the genomes of the most sophisticated organisms had accumulated many idiosyncrasies as the improvisations of natural selection had built more potential into them. But Ararat-Tyre had an extra complication: the supplementary genome that might or might not be an independent homeobox.

"Is there anything new that I need to know about?" Matthew asked, figuring that it would be better to begin on a thoroughly professional basis.

Mercifully, Tang wasn't the kind of man to quibble about the meaning of *need*. He was ready to share his discoveries with all apparent frankness.

"My colleagues at Base One are beginning to make progress with their analyses of the cellular metabolism of a wide range of plants and animals," he said. "As you'd expect from the fundamentals, many of the functional proteins made by the nucleic acid analogue are very similar to those made by DNA. The functions of the second coding-molecule are much more arcane. There are no earthly analogues for the relatively few molecules we've so far identified as products of that system, all of which are protein-lipid hybrids. Until we can establish an artificial production system it will be difficult to test the hypothesis that its functions are mainly homeotic, but we have found that high concentrations of key hybrid compounds are associated with growth. *This* specimen may be very useful to us in that respect; now that I know what to look for I may be able to confirm that its exceptional size is correlated with unusual activity of the second replicator. If I can prove that the slugs can alter their size in response to environmental circumstance, and that growth isn't an ongoing, unidirectional process, it will be the first step in establishing a key difference between Tyrian and Earthly organisms. Proving that they're emortal will be harder, and testing the limits of their metamorphic potential harder still, but it *is* a start. We know now that the apparent similarities between Tyrian animals and their Earthly analogues conceals radical differences, and that the entire ecosphere is far more alien than it seemed at first."

"Have you been able to do much work on the higher animals?" Matthew asked. "Lityansky didn't seem to have looked at anything as complicated as the slug, let alone the mammal-analogues."

"When I first came here," Tang said, "I was excited by the possibility that we might be able to go straight to the top, as it were, by recovering some genetic material from the city-builders, but the quest has so far proved frustrating. We know that there are monkey-analogues further downstream, which are presumably the nearest relatives of the humanoids so far observed, but our attempts to trap mammal-analogues in and around the ruins have been just as frustrating as our attempts to discover humanoid remains. The river expedition was, of course, intended to compensate for those disappointments. I assume that it still is. One of my fallback projects—fortunately, as it has turned out—was to investigate the class of creatures that includes the one that incapacitated poor Maryanne. My initial interest had nothing do do with the fact that all the species in the group are poisonous, but the work Maryanne and I have done on the toxins has proved very useful. You've presumably been informed that the genomics of organisms like this one seem unusually complex even if one sets aside the matter of the second coding molecule. The genomic potential of the DNA-analogue seems to be far more elaborate than its representation in quotidian proteomics."

Matthew had little difficulty in cutting through Tang's excessively pedantic choice of terminology, which inevitably tempted him to an opposite extreme. "You mean that it has more genes than it seems to be using at any one time," Matthew chipped in. "In other words, the orthodox exon-bank has all kinds of tricks up its sleeve—just the sort of thing that a serial chimera would need."

Tang didn't take offence at the crudity of Matthew's presentation. Indeed, he recognized its propriety with a smile. "That's one possible interpretation," he agreed. "But let's not forget the example of the humble frog."

Matthew nodded to signify that he took the biochemist's point. Earthly genomic analyses had shown that the relationship between genomic complexity and physical complexity wasn't a simple one. In spite of their metamorphic capability, frogs were fairly low down on the complexity scale, but they had very bulky genomes because they maintained several parallel sets of genes for performing such seemingly simple tasks as determining the conditions in which their eggs could hatch. On the other hand, that same flexibility extended to patterns of development in early embryos—which was exactly the kind of versatility that might be an interesting consequence of the relative complexity of Tyrian genomes. "Have you made any progress figuring out what the presently unexpressed genes might be for?" he wanted to know.

"Yesterday, I would have had to say no," Tang said. "Today . . ." He paused in order to wave a languid hand at his prize specimen before picking up the story. "It's not just bigger than the other specimens I've seen. The mass-surface area considerations that affect growth and form are universal. It hasn't got legs, so it doesn't suffer from the supportive problems that affect so many Earthly animals, but the tentacles pose a similar problem. The muscular strength needed to move them increases geometrically in proportion to their length. That could be accomplished straightforwardly by adding muscular bulk, but it isn't. The structural materials framing the muscle are different. Either a different set of genes has come into play, or the exons are teaming up according to a different pattern. Ike will suspect the latter, of course, but he's primed to look for gene-nesting explanations. He and I will have to get together to see if we can fit the proteomics to the genomics."

"That might help to explain why the local invertebrates don't use a chitin-analogue in their exoskeletal components," Matthew said. "The advantages of hardness and strength have to be set against the disadvantages of inflexibility. Earthly insects have to shed their exoskeletons if they want to get bigger. Here, where versatility is the order of the day, they use an entirely different set of molecules because it makes it easier to ring the changes."

"Quite possibly," Tang agreed. "It remains to be seen, of course, how flexible the system might be. So far, I've only had the opportunity to observe relatively minor variations of size and form. Until I find a much bigger giant, or manage to identify two radically different forms of the same chimerical cell-mix, it's all conjecture."

"Have you searched the flying-eye data for giant slugs that might be blown-up versions of this one?" Matthew asked.

"Not yet," was the suitably guarded reply.

"But even if we keep the frog example in mind—*especially* if we keep the frog example in mind—it's plausible that the extra genes in the DNA-analogue part of the genome include metamor-

phic options. Options that remain permanently in place, rather
than simply guiding a growing individual through a fixed series of
stages."

"It's all speculative, at present" Tang said. "But yes, those are
the lines along which we've all been thinking. The parallel systems in frogs are all to do with reproduction—the options can
determine the sex of hatchlings as well as facilitating development at a range of different temperatures—so it's possible there's
a reproductive function here, if only we could figure out exactly
how these creatures do reproduce. I'm no anatomist, but I can't
find anything resembling sex organs in this specimen or any of its
kin. Andrei Lityansky undoubtedly told you about Bernal Delgado's speculations about chimerical renewal and exchange, but
I'm afraid that I haven't been able to find any supportive evidence
for the kinds of process he imagined. If the organisms are very
long-lived, they might not bother to maintain their sex organs
permanently—they might develop them temporarily just for the
mating season. There are Earthly examples . . . but the simple
fact is that we don't know."

"That thing *is* a chimera, I suppose," Matthew said, pointing
yet again at the creature in the biocontainment cell. "Is it a more
complicated chimera than its smaller kin?"

"Oddly enough, no. When I began investigating the specimen
I half-expected to find far more extensive chimerization than the
smaller specimens exhibit, but it's a mosaic of eight genetically
distinct but phenotypically similar cell-types, which is exactly the
same level of complexity as specimens with a tenth of its body
mass, and less than some thumb-sized individuals of other kinds.
Eight is by far the most frequent figure that turns up—four is
only half as common, sixteen less than a quarter. Two crops up
fairly regularly, but I haven't yet found a thirty-two—or, for that
matter, a singleton."

"What about the mammal-analogues?" Matthew asked.

"The work that's been done at Base One hasn't turned up
anything but fours and eights. That's disappointing, in a way.
There doesn't seem to be any correlation between phenotypic
complexity and chimerical complexity—but everything we've
examined thus far has been a *simple* chimera in the sense that all
the cells are closely related—often sibs or half-sibs. Again, it all

comes back to reproduction. If they don't grow temporary sex organs for the mating season they may well indulge in periodic radical experiments in chimerization, but . . ."

"Until we catch them at it," Matthew finished for him, "we have no way of knowing *what* they get up to."

It wasn't quite the way Tang would have put it, but he nodded agreement regardless.

"How much hidden potential are we talking about?" Matthew wanted to know. "Setting aside worries about the frog example, how versatile might these beasts be when they're not cruising in neutral?"

That was a step too far for Tang. "I really can't say," the biochemist told him, sadly. "Before I could make any sort of guess I'd have to know what *kind* of potential it is. I'd be very interested to know what might trigger its release, if you had any ideas on that score."

Matthew took the invitation as the compliment it was, but he wasn't able to respond. He hadn't made any progress at all in wondering what might substitute for Earthly seasonal changes as a series of cues determining the pattern of Tyrian life cycles. All he was able to do, as yet, was turn the question around.

"Do *you* have any ideas?" he asked, humbly.

"Not *ideas*, exactly," Tang replied.

Matthew guessed quickly enough what that meant. "You mean you have worries," he said. "Fears, even." Matthew belatedly remembered what Solari had said about Tang reportedly having shown recent "signs of strain and acute anxiety." He had seen none himself, so far—quite the reverse, in fact—but Kriefmann must have had some basis for his opinion.

"It seems to me," the biochemist said, softly, "that the hidden potential contained in the duplex genomes of Ararat-Tyre must be responsive to ecological shifts of some kind. Perhaps it evolved in an era of intermittent ecological crises—not environmentally generated ecocatastrophes, but ecocatastrophes associated with dramatic population increases. I know that you know exactly what I mean, because I recall the rhetoric you used to employ in your inflammatory broadcasts: the lemming principle, the Mouseworld allegory, and so on. If so, isn't it possible—perhaps probable—that the arrival of alien beings with radically different genomic systems might constitute exactly such a crisis.

Thus far, I admit, the world has not responded to its invaders—unless the arrival in this vicinity of the creature that stung Maryanne can be counted a response—but the establishment of three discreet and understaffed Bases in three years has been the merest scratch on the surface. You understand what I'm saying, don't you?"

Because he obviously wanted Matthew to be the one to say it, Matthew spelled it out. "You're saying that we might have avoided tweaking the lion's tail thus far," he said, "but that decanting the remainder of the would-be colonists and establishing an ecological base for their long-term survival would be a whole new ballgame. You're saying that although this doesn't look like a death trap today, it could turn into one with frightening rapidity."

"We simply don't know," Tang added. "Until we figure out the protocols of reproduction, we have no idea what dangers lurk in all that *hidden potential*."

And that, Matthew thought, was exactly why Tang was becoming more and more nervous as time went by, and why he had become an enthusiastic advocate of withdrawal, allying himself with the groundling party to which Konstantin Milyukov was implacably opposed.

He figured that the ice had been sufficiently thawed to allow the raising of more delicate issues. "I hear that you and I are rivals for the empty berth on Bernal's boat," he said, biting the bullet.

"It's not Bernal's boat," Tang pointed out, mildly. "Common consent had certainly determined that he was entitled to his place in the expedition, but we have all played a part in the design and construction of the boat."

Matthew took due note of the fact that the *we* in question did not include him, although Tang had not said in so many words that he ought not to be entitled to a vote when the time came to settle the matter of who should replace Bernal Delgado on the expedition downriver.

"I'm sorry," Matthew said. "I didn't mean to imply that it wasn't a collective enterprise. I dare say that everybody here would gain some benefit from the opportunity to see a little more of the continent, and to penetrate the dark heart of its mysterious vitreous grasslands. I understand that you want the berth as much as I do. . . ."

"I don't," Tang put in.

The interpolation took the wind out of Matthew's sails. "You don't?" he echoed. He was about to apologize again for his misapprehension when Tang wrong-footed him again.

"It's not a matter of *wanting*," the biochemist said. "It's a matter of which of us is best-equipped to make productive use of the opportunity. If I thought that you were the person who could derive the most benefit from the expedition, I would unhesitatingly concede your right to be a part of it—but you have come to this situation three years too late. I feel that it is my duty to place my own expertise and experience at the disposal of the expedition."

"But you don't actually *want* to go," Matthew said.

"That's correct," Tang said. He still wasn't showing any glaringly obvious signs of strain or acute anxiety, but Matthew was beginning to realize what it was that Godert Kriefmann had picked up on.

"In fact," Matthew added, "you don't actually want to be here at all. You'd far rather be on *Hope* with Andrei Lityansky, maintaining a safe distance from your subject matter." He reminded himself that Tang was a biochemist: a man for whom reality was contained in chemical formulas and metabolic cycles.

"That too is not a matter of *wanting*," Tang told him, very calmly indeed. "it is a matter of responsibility and common sense."

"Responsibility to whom?" Matthew challenged.

Tang sat back in his chair and regarded him very carefully. "Since you were awakened, Dr. Fleury," he said, "you have been briefed by Konstantin Milyukov and Andrei Lityansky. It's rumored that you have also talked to Shen Chin Che. You have certainly heard Rand Blackstone's opinion, and Lynn Gwyer's. Every one of those five is opposed to the notion of a temporary or permanent withdrawal from Tyre, and every one will therefore have taken some care to represent the opposing case as a matter of cowardice or foolishness—but I do not believe that you are the kind of man to take aboard the ideas of others unthinkingly. I was rather young when I first encountered your work, and not yet twenty-five when you disappeared from the media landscape, but I have had time enough to familiarize myself with your writings and your intellectual legacy. I may be mistaken, but I feel that I know you rather better than some of the people who first encountered you in the flesh—people like Lynn Gwyer and Ikram Mohammed, perhaps even Bernal Delgado. I feel confident, therefore, that you will not have prejudged this question, and that you will understand far better than many others the true significance of the changes in our situation that have taken place since *Hope* left Earth's solar system."

Wrong-footed yet again by the earnest flattery, Matthew had no idea how to reply to it. In the end, wariness defeated his reflexive impulse to try to guess what Tang might mean. "Okay," he said. "I'm listening. Convince me."

Tang nodded, as if this was no more than he had expected. "When we enlisted for this mission," he said, "we did so in the expectation that Earth was about to enter a new Dark Age. You joined the ranks of the frozen in 2090 or thereabouts, more than twenty years before me, but you were a prophet of no mean ability and Mr. Solari must have told you that the situation in the early 2110s seemed every bit as desperate as you had anticipated. The ecosphere was suffering a near-universal collapse, and new plagues were in the process of sterilizing every human female on Earth. I always trusted that the human race would pull through, but I expected a drastic interruption of scientific and social progress. It seems, however, that you and I were too pessimistic.

"There was indeed a Crash, but the rebound was more rapid than you or I would have dared hope. The intelligence gleaned by *Hope*'s patient crew during the last few centuries suggests that the Dark Age lasted less than half a century, and that technological progress had resumed its ever-more-enormous strides by the end of the twenty-second century. Even then, it seems, men dared to hope that they could live long enough to be the inheritors of authentic emortality. It appears that they were wrong, but a potent technology of longevity was discovered soon enough—three hundred years in what is now our past. You and I, Dr. Fleury, would be members of the last generation of mortal men were it not for the fact that we both have mortal children in suspended animation aboard *Hope*."

"But we're here, and the emortals are still in the solar system," Matthew pointed out. "We have to deal with our own situation as we are, as mortals—as we always knew that we would. The fact that Earth's human population has survived and thrived instead of dying is welcome news, but it doesn't affect what we came here to do. We're still the first wave of extraterrestrial colonists: the vanguard of the diaspora."

"On the contrary," Tang came back at him. "That one fact changes everything—not, admittedly, in terms of what we *wanted* to do when we set out from the solar system, but in terms of our *obligations* to our fellow men. Had Earth really entered a Dark Age, we would indeed have arrived here as pioneers, entitled to believe that we might be the best if not the only hope for the long-term survival of our species. Given the circumstances that actually pertain, however, we are obliged to ask ourselves whether we can still go ahead with the colonization of Tyre, given that it may require less than a hundred years—and will certainly require less than two hundred—for us to learn how to engineer men who would be far better adapted to that task.

"It is certainly not the case that we could not make good use of a delay, given what we have already discovered about the problematic and enigmatic nature of the local ecosphere. If we rush ahead foolishly with the colonization project we do so at the risk of disaster—not merely for ourselves but for the local ecosphere. If, instead, we were to remain in orbit until communications with our parent world could be properly restored, continuing our studies in the meantime with reasonable discretion, we would lose nothing but time. We left the solar system because we thought the human race had run out of time, but we were wrong. We did have time, and we have it still. To act as if we did not would be stupid and irresponsible."

Tang had been right to point out that everyone to whom Matthew had so far spoken had taken the view that the colonization project must press ahead as originally envisaged. He had also been right to imply, without being so impolite as to state it forthrightly, that their views had fitted in so readily with Matthew's preconceptions that he had not even thought to challenge their views with any real vigor. Now, Matthew realized that there might be some merit in the ancient saw that said that wherever fools were inclined to rush in, angels ought to tread more carefully.

"So you're not actually against the idea of colonization," Matthew said, carefully. "You just want to take it slowly."

"I'm not *for* the idea of colonization either," Tang said. "I believe that we ought to proceed slowly and carefully, so that we can make a proper determination of the practicality of colonization. I believe that we ought to discover the solutions to the many enigmas with which we are faced *before* we commit ourselves to a course of action that might be mutually destructive. And I believe that we ought to make sure that if, or when, we decide that colonization of Tyre is both feasible and desirable, the task is undertaken by people who are fully prepared for the job. You and I, Dr. Fleury, are not. We might wish that we were, but the fact remains that we are remnants of a primitive era, who have been far outstripped.

"In other circumstances, you and I might have been justified in thinking of this world as our Ararat: the place in which, for better or for worse, our daughters must grow up and bear children of their own. In the circumstances that actually pertain, it is our duty—however unpleasant—to recognize that if our daughters are to be among the mothers of a new human race, they ought not to take on that role until we are able to make full use of the technologies of twenty-ninth-century Earth in shaping their offspring."

"I see," said Matthew, meaning that he understood the argument but needed time to think it over.

"I wish you did," was Tang's unexpected rejoinder. "Alas, you have only just begun to see. I, on the other hand, am able not only to see more clearly but also to *feel* the true alienness of this world. When you return to Rand Blackstone, he will tell you—scornfully—that I am afraid, and that I have begun to sense menace in every ripple of the river, every cloud in the sky. He is right. I *am* afraid—but what I fear more than anything else is the insensitivity of men like him. Given time, I am sure that you would learn to see as clearly, and feel as deeply, as myself—but there are those here and in orbit who would far rather press you to reach premature conclusions."

Matthew hesitated for a moment before saying: "What did Bernal Delgado think?"

"Bernal was an honest scientist," Tang told him. "He had listened to both sides of the case, and had reserved his judgment—but I must believe, must I not, that he would have seen soon enough that I am right?"

"Are you implying that that was the reason for his murder?"

"I have not the slightest idea why Bernal was murdered,"

Tang assured him, "nor have I any idea who might have killed him, in spite of what your friend the policeman thinks."

"Vince has reserved his judgment too," Matthew assured him. "If he suggests otherwise, it's purely for tactical reasons. What difference would it make to your calculation of the logic of the situation if the alien humanoids turned out not to be extinct?"

"As a good Hardinist," Tang said, letting a little irony into his voice, "I would surely be bound to assume that they were the putative owners of the world, and the best potential stewards of its future development. If there are intelligent aliens here—and if the city-builders still exist, even if they have given up the city-building habit, they must surely be reckoned intelligent—they are entitled to every moral consideration that we would apply to our own kind. This is not 1492, Dr. Fleury; we must learn from our historians as well as our prophets."

"And what would you do if you found out that someone had been forging alien artifacts, perhaps with a view to persuading others that the aliens were not extinct?"

"I would be very sad to think that anyone would sink to such a subterfuge," Tang told him.

"Solari's convinced that Bernal faked the spearhead himself," Matthew told him, although he knew that Solari would not appreciate his traps being prematurely sprung. "Is there anyone here who feels strongly enough to take violent exception to a discovery like that?"

"I would be very sad to think so," Tang repeated. There had, of course, been no possibility that he would drop the slightest hint of accusation, even though Rand Blackstone was the man most flagrantly opposed to his own position—and thus might be reckoned to have the most to lose, if anyone did persuade others, dishonestly, that the intelligent aliens were still around.

Matthew thought that was the end of it, until Tang added one more observation. "However sad I may be or may become," the biochemist said, seeming to pick his words very carefully indeed, "I do wonder how much it really matters who killed Dr. Delgado, or why. Whatever the details of the crime may have been, it is the world and the problems it poses that have shaped his death. No matter what solution your friend may find, the significance of the event remains the same. We came here too hurriedly, Dr. Fleury, and we are ill-equipped for our chosen task. If we cannot decide to be rational and dutiful, there may be many other deaths. We are mortal—and we know now how frail we are by comparison with those who inherited the world we left behind. I only pray that we may use what life we have as cleverly and as carefully as we possibly can."

The biochemist's tone was still level, still amiable, still perfectly serious—but for the first time, Matthew felt that he had caught a glimpse of the awful bleakness and devouring fear that had taken hold of the man. There were, apparently, many people at Base One who felt exactly the same. Matthew realized that the situation into which he had been delivered really was far more complicated than he had so far been prepared to assume.

TWENTY⇔FOUR

Night had fallen by the time Ikram Mohammed and Rand Blackstone returned to the bubble to report that the boat was now as ready to depart as it would ever be. Their arrival completed a gathering of the Base Three personnel in the common room that included everyone except Maryanne Hyder.

"If anything," Ike declared, "it's a trifle overcooked. We've added so many accessories that it's going to be a hell of a job dismantling it and putting it back together."

"Dismantling it?" Solari echoed. "Why would you want to dismantle it and put it back together?"

"The river doesn't run smoothly all the way," Matthew told him. "There's only one major fault line, but that's associated with a cataract at the edge of the lowland plateau. We'll have to rig a hoist of some kind so that we can lower the disassembled parts and the cargo on a rope."

"We?" said Dulcie Gherardesca, her gaze flicking back and forth between Matthew and Tang. "I thought you'd decided to agree that Tang would be a more useful member of the expedition."

"Not exactly," Matthew replied. "I'd conceded that there was an arguable case to that effect. Having thought it over, though, I've decided that I still want to go."

It was Dulcie, not Tang, who said: "It's not really a matter of wanting, is it?"

"Actually," Matthew said, having had time to prepare his case, "I think it is. Tang doesn't want to go—he only thinks he ought to because his exaggerated sense of duty tells him that he might be more useful as an observer and interpreter of whatever we find down there. He's interested in the specimens that we might gather, of course, but he's interested as a biochemist. He won't be able to do much with them en route. I, on the other hand, do want to go—and my admittedly unexaggerated sense of duty tells me that I might be just as useful an observer and interpreter as he would be. I'm an ecologist: I need to see the wildlife in its natural habitat, to get a feel for the way that actual organisms live and interact. Bernal was desperate to go because he knew that the environments downstream are much richer than the ruins, and he believed that an ecologist's eyes were necessary to supplement Ike's and Lynn's lab-educated vision. He was right, and that's why I should be the one to go."

Dulcie and Godert Kriefmann both looked at Tang to see what his reaction to that would be, but Blackstone was quick to butt in. "I agree with Fleury," he said. "A fresh pair of eyes is what we need."

"That's not why I think I'd be useful," Matthew was quick to say. "Quite the reverse, in a way. It's the way my eyes are trained that's important. We're all biologists, but with all due respect to Tang, Ike, and Lynn, I'm the only one who knows how to look at organisms *as* organisms, and as participants in ecosystems, rather than as aggregations of molecules. Tang knows far more about the genomics and proteomics of Tyre than I could hope to learn in half a year, let alone a few days—but there's a sense in which that kind of perception is blinkered. The expedition needs more balance than Tang can provide; it needs Dulcie, and it needs me. And I want to go—not as a mere matter of duty, but as a matter of enthusiasm. I think that ought to count."

There was a slight pause before Kriefmann said: "I suppose we ought to vote on it, then."

"No," said Tang. "That's exactly what we shouldn't do. I am prepared to concede the point. Matthew should go."

Matthew was less surprised by this turn of events than some of the others seemed to be—which was, he supposed, support for Rand Blackstone's conviction that a fresh pair of eyes could be an asset. One conversation with Tang had been enough to convince Matthew that the biochemist was a man so reasonable that his reasonableness might almost be reckoned excessive—and that same conversation had apparently served to reassure Tang that Matthew was a potential convert to his cause.

"Aren't we forgetting something?" Vince Solari put in.

No one was in any doubt as to what he meant. "You can't expect us to put everything on hold while you complete your investigation," Lynn Gwyer said. "There's no guarantee that you'll ever be able to figure out who killed Bernal—or what we ought to do about it if you did bring a charge against anyone here.

We don't have any legal apparatus in place here, and there's nothing elaborate back at Base One. Maybe things would be different if Shen Chin Che were supervising the colonization process, but in his absence we've had to muddle along as best we could."

"I've already figured out who killed Delgado," Solari announced, blandly.

Matthew guessed as soon as the bombshell dropped that it was probably a ploy, but no one else seemed ready to make that assumption. The reaction was as explosive as anyone could have desired, and the question on everyone's lips was *who?*

"Unfortunately," Solari went on, "there's a difference between knowing who did it and providing evidence adequate to satisfy a court of law, or even justify a formal arrest. Given that a court of law would actually have to be put together in order to try the case, and that no formal procedures of arrest and charge seem to exist, I'm not sure exactly how to carry my investigation forward. Perhaps you'd like to advise me."

"This is bullshit," Rand Blackstone objected. "If you think you know who did it, spit it out. Give whoever it is a chance to respond."

Matthew noticed that Blackstone's preference for the hypothesis that an alien had done the deed seemed to have vanished. He was not surprised.

Neither was Solari. "If you'd wanted to know who did it you could have figured it out for yourselves," he said. "I'm prepared to believe that Milyukov was wrong about there being a conspiracy to conceal the identity of the murderer, but there's certainly been a tacit agreement not to look too hard. If you'd wanted the matter cleared up, you could have cleared it up. I think every one of you has a suspect in mind, and that at least half of you probably have the right suspect in mind, but not one of you wants to have that suspicion confirmed—and in order to avoid that eventuality you've deliberately refrained from looking at the evidence."

"That's not true." The objection came from Lynn Gwyer—but no one else supported her.

"What's the bottom line, Solari?" Blackstone wanted to know. "Are you saying that you want everyone to remain here while you complete your interrogations, or just that you want to take someone out of the crew?"

So Blackstone thinks that the murderer is one of the people

who was planning to take the boat, Matthew deduced. Given that we've just eliminated Tang, that leaves Lynn, Ike, and Dulcie. Except, of course, that Blackstone might not have the right suspect in mind.

"For the time being," Solari said, "I'd like to know what *you* want. There is, after all, a definite problem of jurisdiction here. The law I'm supposed to be enforcing is colony law—but there doesn't seem to be any firmly defined colony law in place. As Dr. Gwyer has pointed out, the removal of Shen Chin Che and his chief associates from the picture has left something of an organizational vacuum. I'm not at all sure to whom I'm supposed to be reporting the results of my investigation, so for the time being I'm consulting you. Frankly, I'm rather puzzled by the fact that you all seem perfectly content to accept that there's a murderer in your midst. Not one of you seems interested in having the identity of the murderer revealed, let alone seeing them punished. I wish you'd explain to me exactly why that is—preferably without any nonsense about the possibility of anyone from outside having secretly flown in to commit the murder."

Matthew would have been interested to know where each of the six looked in search of leadership, but he hadn't enough eyes in his head. In the event, it was Tang Dinh Quan who took it upon himself to provide an answer of sorts.

"That too is a question that we have not aired in public," the biochemist said. "It is probable that we all have our own reasons for letting the matter lie. I cannot speak for anyone else, but I suspect that I am not the only one here to feel a profound sense of embarrassment at the mere fact of the crime. I cannot believe that there is anyone here, including the murderer, who does not regret what happened very deeply. If that regret were not so painful, perhaps we would have been more interested in discovering the facts. But there are other factors too. For one thing, I have never felt endangered myself. I do not claim that we all know one another as intimately as might be expected, given the time we have spent here in isolation from the remainder of the colony—we are scientists, after all, accustomed to the introspection of that calling as well as to the distancing effects of the media of communication that dominated the Earth from which we came—but a degree of trust has grown up between us. I cannot suspect anyone here of being a secret psychopath, or of harboring evil motives. I can only imagine that whoever killed Bernal Delgado did so in a moment of sudden anger, entirely without meaning to—and that having done so, he or she is extremely unlikely ever to allow themselves another such lapse. Whoever the killer might be, I have never felt any emotion toward them but pity. Perhaps it is a failure of duty on my part, but that is why I have never sought to increase the shame of the deed by exposure."

Matthew marveled all over again at the man's pedantry—although it was by no means unexpected in someone who must have learned English as a second or third language, because it was the language of science—but he did not doubt for a moment that Tang was perfectly sincere. He looked around yet again, half-expecting to be able to identify the murderer by means of the tears in his or her eyes, but most of the faces gathered about the table were studies in stoniness.

"To put it bluntly, Vince," Ikram Mohammed said, "we don't really care who did it. We sympathize with their secret misery. We can't really see ourselves as the cast of an old-fashioned murder mystery, each living in terror of the possibility that we might be the next victim. There's been no shortage of other puzzles to distract us."

Vincent Solari had listened to all of this quite impassively, giving not the slightest indication of horror, amusement, disgust, or any other plausible response. When he realized that everyone was now waiting for his judgment of Tang's speech he had to rouse himself slightly. "Okay," he said. "So, the general feeling is that you don't want me to tell you who did it, and that you'd rather I stopped looking for the evidence I need to make a watertight case."

Nobody answered that.

"What about you, Matthew?" Solari asked. "What do *you* think I ought to do?"

Matthew had no answer ready. "I suppose," he said, after a moment's reflection, "that it would depend on the motive. *Why* was Bernal killed?"

"So far as I can judge," Solari told him, "it was exactly what Tang says: a sudden outburst of anger. A crime of passion, if you like. There must have been something deeper behind it, but I no longer think it was premeditated and I don't think there was any intention to kill. Delgado was very unlucky—nine times out of ten, the blow would have been trivial. Given that it wasn't, his IT would have been able to pull him through a further nine times out of ten. What happened, in my opinion, is that somebody found him faking the alien artifacts and overreacted, too quickly and too extremely for their own IT to damp it down."

Solari hadn't told anyone that it appeared to be Bernal who had made the "alien" artifacts, and Matthew had only let it slip to Tang. If Tang had passed the news on it wasn't obvious. Matthew concluded that Solari was trying another ploy, in the hope of finding out who already knew what he had only just discovered. He couldn't help feeling a slight pang of regret at having given the game away, at least to Tang.

"Why would Delgado be faking alien artifacts?" Rand Blackstone said, his voice redolent with sincere disbelief.

"I don't know," Solari admitted.

"It's possible that he wasn't *faking* them at all," Matthew put in scrupulously. "It's possible that he was trying to put himself imaginatively in the city-builders' shoes, trying to figure out what might have happened to them."

"Really?" Solari came back, feigning incredulity.

"*Verstehen,*" Dulcie Gherardesca put in, softly. "Intuitive understanding. The basis on which members of a human society can obtain understanding of other societies, with different norms and rules."

"And individuals of one another," Matthew added. "I can't believe that a man like Bernal would ever have planned to perpetrate a scientific fraud. I think he was trying to put himself in the place of an alien, by doing the only thing that he knew for sure that the aliens did: making tools out of natural glass harvested from local plants. Maybe someone who found out what he was doing leapt to the wrong conclusion, but we mustn't be tempted to do the same."

"I'm prepared to buy that," Solari said, although Matthew immediately recognized it as another ploy, inviting a confession. "It was an accident, then. A misunderstanding."

No one offered a confession, or gave any sign of wanting to do so.

But we're not all here, Matthew thought. And Vince has only talked to one person since last telling me he had no suspect.

Maybe Blackstone has the wrong suspect in mind. But if Solari's fishing, he must think he's fishing in the right pond. Which implies that Maryanne Hyder didn't do it—but that she might know who did.

When the silence had gone on long enough, Solari let out a slight sigh, and said: "Okay. Nobody wants to come clean. Nobody wants to know. Nobody wants to hold up the boat trip. Fair enough—if the excursion means more to you than the murder, you might as well exercise your priorities. I'm just a humble policeman, after all. You're *scientists*."

Even Matthew felt the contemptuous sting of that remark, but he also felt compelled to leap to the defense of his new colleagues. "There really are bigger questions at stake, Vince," he said. "And there's a point that Tang didn't make. Whoever killed Bernal reacted atypically, and part of the reason they reacted atypically is that everyone here is in a radically alien environment, isolated from the main body of the investigative team. Everyone here is uneasy and anxious, and no matter how ashamed they are of being frightened—because walking on the surface of an alien but Earthlike world is exactly what everyone here signed up for—they can't help being prey to fear. The world played its part in Bernal's death, and it might yet be the cause of many more. No matter how determined we may be to follow through our good intentions, there isn't anyone here who doesn't know that the crew jumped the gun in their haste to be rid of their inconvenient cargo. This world might be a potential death trap, not just for the nine of us but for everyone at Base One and everyone still in SusAn.

"We need to know what the chances really are of establishing a colony here, and we need to know it sooner rather than later. Milyukov shouldn't be exerting further pressure on us with arbitrary deadlines, but that's a trivial matter: the real deadline will be set by the world itself, and we have to make haste to meet it even though we haven't the slightest idea when it will fall. This trip downriver might not tell us anything definite, but it's an opportunity we have to seize. It's more important than knowing who killed Bernal, and far more important than figuring out what we ought to do with the murderer. If that's a scientist's view rather than a policeman's . . . well, so be it. Bernal was my friend, but I have far more important things to worry about just now than wreaking vengeance on his killer."

Solari considered this, and then shrugged. Matthew had been fairly confident that he would. He'd already tested the policeman's response to the phrase "potential death trap."

"Okay," Solari said. "The boat sails tomorrow, with the agreed crew. I stay here with Rand, Tang, Godert, and Maryanne. I do my best to make myself useful. No arrests, no charges, no reports to Base One or *Hope*. Until you get back, at least. *If* you get back."

"If we don't," Ikram Mohammed said, quietly, "I think we'll have proved that there are issues that take precedence—and your suspect will probably be dead."

It was the closest anyone had come to naming a name or making an admission, but it stopped there. The genomicist said nothing more, and no one had anything further to add. It said something for the tolerance of the assembled suspects that they were perfectly happy to eat together, with Solari in their midst. The main course was imitation pizza whose toppings were spread on a base that combined imported wheat-manna with local produce; Matthew was glad to discover that the synthetic cheese and tomato masked the inadequate palatability of the base. Had the conversation been less tense it would certainly have been the most enjoyable meal he had had since waking from SusAn—but he put both those circumstances down to the fact that he had had an unusually tiring day.

When the assembly finally broke up and Matthew returned to his bunk, accompanied by Solari, he took the first possible opportunity to say: "Okay, it's just you and me now. Who did it?"

He was only mildly astonished by Solari's reply, which was: "There is no *just you and me*, Matt. You sided with them. You endorsed their willful ignorance. If you want to know, you can work it out for yourself. All you have to do is look closely at the data in the automatic logs, compare the alibis and ask the right people the right questions. Never mind the motive: concentrate on the opportunity."

"Fair enough," Matthew said. "Maybe I'll go see how Maryanne's feeling before I turn in. I could probably do with a few words of advice about how to cope with worm stings, in case the worst comes to the worst."

aryanna Hyder was alone in the accommodation she had shared with Bernal Delgado, but Matthew was not the first visitor she had had since Solari had played his hand. Godert Kriefmann had left the common room before anyone else in order to check her condition.

"God's already asked me," she said, as soon as she saw Matthew. "I didn't finger anyone and I certainly didn't confess. If it was something I said that tipped the policeman off it was something whose significance I didn't realize myself."

"How are you feeling?" Matthew asked, figuring that he might as well go through with his cover story anyway. He sat down on the folding chair that had been set beside the bed to accommodate visitors.

"Much better," was the answer. "No pain, thanks to my IT, but the cost is that I feel somewhat disconnected from my body—not quite here, even though there's no place else to be."

"I know the feeling," Matthew confirmed.

"They have much better IT on Earth now, allegedly," she told him. "A member of the new human race probably wouldn't even have felt the sting, and certainly wouldn't be laid up with it."

"The new human race," Matthew echoed. "Is that what Tang calls them?"

"It's what they call themselves, according to Captain Milyukov."

"You seem a trifle skeptical," Matthew observed.

"Do I? Everything we've been told about the state of affairs back home comes from Milyukov. Milyukov has a vested interest in persuading us that we can get better support from home than we can from *Hope*, if we can just hang on until the cavalry arrives. Not that we'll know that it's even set off for another hundred-and-thirteen years."

"Do you think Milyukov's lying?"

She moved her head slightly from side to side, stirring the silky halo of her blond hair. She didn't think that the captain was *lying*, exactly. It was just that she was reserving judgment as to the manner in which he had filtered and organized the truth.

"Tang thinks that we should be content to hold the fort until they arrive," Matthew observed.

"I know. Lately, I've begun to agree with him, albeit reluctantly."

"Why reluctantly?"

"If we withdraw to orbit, we'll be lucky to live long enough to see the beginning of serious colonization, let alone its completion. The crew signed on for a multigenerational enterprise, but I didn't. And look what it did to the crew."

"What did Bernal think?" Matthew asked. It was an innocent question, but she didn't take it that way.

"We didn't quarrel about it," she told him, defensively. "I told your friend that even if we had, the quarrel would never have turned violent. *Never.* Anyway, he hadn't made up his mind. He was determined not to make up his mind until he'd been downriver."

"In search of *ska*?"

"In search of whatever there is to be found. God says Tang stood aside to let you take Bernal's place. You must have impressed him."

"I'm not sure that I did. I think he was content with the fact that he'd obviously impressed me. He knows that I've got an open mind, because it hasn't had time to fill up. More important, though, he simply doesn't want to go. He doesn't want to go out on a limb, not because he's a coward but because he understands as well as anyone does how badly the crew have screwed things up. He wants to take his work back to orbit because he thinks that's the right place for it until we know a lot more about the mysteries of Tyre. He's grateful to me for being so enthusiastic to put my head into the lion's mouth instead of his."

"Bernal didn't think it was so very dangerous."

"But you didn't want him to go," Matthew guessed.

"That was personal."

"And you didn't quarrel about it. Did you know he was making imitation alien spearheads and arrowheads way out in the fields?"

Again she shook her head, more vigorously this time.

Matthew contemplated going back to his room and leaving her to sleep, but he hesitated. There were a couple of questions on the mental list he'd been compiling all day that she was best placed to answer, and he didn't expect to have another conversation with her before the boat set off.

"If one of the local mammal-equivalents had met up with the critter you ran into," he said, "it would presumably be dead."

"Almost certainly," she confirmed, although she was obviously puzzled by the change of tack.

"Why *almost*?"

"The toxin's a blunt instrument, physiologically speaking. That's why it works as well in the context of an alien metabolism as it does in target flesh—but it's an organic venom, to which local organisms might be able to build up a degree of tolerance. Nonlethal stings inflicted by smaller organisms could provide an opportunity to do that."

"Is it purely defensive, or could it also be a way of killing prey?"

The question increased her puzzlement, but again she provided a straight answer. "If you'd asked me yesterday," she said, "I'd have guessed that it's purely defensive—but I didn't know how big they grew, then. That was a fearsome specimen. Trust me to walk right into it! Because they photosynthesize and don't move around much in daylight they seem very meek, but they can move quite quickly when they need to. I'm not so sure now that they aren't hunter-killers."

"They *can* photosynthesize," Matthew said, issuing a mild correction. "But they don't seem to be very enthusiastic, do they? They skulk in the shadows, even though they don't seem to have much to fear from predators. At least, the little ones skulk in the shadows. How big do you think they are when they're fully grown?"

"If you'd asked me yesterday . . ." she began, but left it at that. After a pause, she added: "Bernal said they probably had some surprises in store. He didn't mention giants, but he did wonder whether the ones we'd seen might be immature. Ike had told him they had much bigger genomes than they were exhibiting, and he was trying to figure out why that might be."

"Was he wondering whether they might be larval stages, capable of further metamorphosis into something completely different?"

"He mentioned the possibility," Maryanne confirmed.

On a sudden impulse, Matthew said: "What did Bernal *call* them? Not in his reports, but in his casual speech. Did he have some kind of nickname for them?"

Maryanne thought about that for a moment before saying: "He called them *killer anemones* a couple of times—because the tentacle-cluster made them look like sea anemones."

"*K-A,*" Matthew said, immediately. "*S-K-A. Super* killer anemone. There are no seasons to speak of in these parts, so there's never been any pressure on complex organisms to develop annual life cycles. They can take all the time they need, or all the time they *want*. We don't have the slightest idea how long any of the local life-forms hang around if they don't fall victim to predators or disease."

"I'm not the best one to ask," Maryanne pointed out. "But I don't think Bernal knew. He did say something about the difficulty of adding chimerization to the sex-death equation. A wild variable, he called it."

"The *sex-death equation*," Matthew said. "That's right. Never underestimate the power of a man's favorite catchphrases. Back in sound-bite-land that was one of his ways of dramatizing the population problem."

"I know," she said. "I used to see him on TV when I was a kid."

"Another latecomer to the ranks of the Chosen," Matthew observed. "Did you see me too?"

"Probably," she said. "I don't really remember."

His ego suitably deflated, Matthew muttered: "He was always the good-looking one—always attractive to the very young."

"I'm an adult *now*," she reminded him, tersely. "Only five years younger than Dulcie and ten years younger than Lynn, in terms of *elapsed* time."

"No insult was intended," Matthew assured her. "What else did Bernal say about the killer anemones? Not the kind of stuff he'd put in his reports—the kind he'd produce when he was speculating, fantasizing? What did he have to say about *super* killer anemones?"

"If he'd had anything at all to say, I'd have realized what *ska* meant myself," she told him, still annoyed in spite of his assurance that no insult had been intended. "He thought it was odd that the ecosphere seems so conspicuously underdeveloped, in terms of animal species, despite the fact that its complexity seemed so similar to that of Earth. He knew that the extant species had to have a hidden versatility that we hadn't yet had the opportunity to observe, but he couldn't figure out what it was for."

"Reproduction," Matthew said. "Or gradual chimerical renewal. Unless, of course, they're the same thing. What did he tell you about gradual chimerical renewal?"

"He told me not to think in terms of werewolves," she said, obviously having seized upon the same mythical bad example as Solari. "Nor insects. He thought we'd need to be more original than that."

"Did he suggest any possible explanations for the fact that there don't seem to be any insect-analogues here?"

"He thought it had something to do with the fact that sex didn't seem to have caught on as an organism-to-organism sort of thing. He said that flight had more to do with sex than most people realized, and more to do with death than people who thought of souls taking wing for Heaven had ever dared to imagine."

"It's another part of the same equation," Matthew realized, following the train of thought. "Death is so commonplace on Earth because it's a correlate of the reliance on sex as a means of shuffling the genetic deck. Flight is so commonplace for the same reason: it's at least as much a matter of bringing mates together and distributing eggs as it is of dodging predators. Flying insects occupy a privileged set of niches on Earth because of the role they play in pollination—a role that doesn't seem to exist here, at least not on a day-to-day basis. Factoring chimerization into the sex-death equation must have all kinds of logical consequences that we're ill-equipped to imagine, let alone work out in detail. To borrow another hoary catchphrase, this place might not just be queerer than we imagine, but queerer than we *can* imagine. Is it possible, do you think—is it even remotely conceivable—that the missing humanoids might be a lot more closely related to the worms than we've assumed, for the simple reason that *everything* here is much more closely related to everything else than we've assumed?"

"The genomics say no, according to Ike and Bernal," she

told him. "Almost all the chimeras we've analysed are cousin-aggregations, made up of closely related cells."

"So closely related," Matthew said, remembering what Tang had told him about the same matter, "that it's difficult to see where the selective advantage lies. But what about the chimeras we haven't analyzed, or even glimpsed? Probably queerer than we can imagine, even after three years of patient work—but Lityansky's jumped to his optimistic conclusions half a lifetime too soon. My gut reaction was a lot cleverer than he was prepared to credit. Whatever hidden potential this world's hoarding, it's something we haven't even begun to grasp."

"There's no real reason to think you'll find it downriver if we haven't found it here," she pointed out, scrupulously.

"Bernal didn't think so," Matthew pointed out. "Why was that?"

"Simply because we'd looked here and not found anything very exciting," she told him. "He thought that it was time to look somewhere else. He didn't think they were ever going to find anything on Base One's island, because the priority there is on usurpation of land, the production of Earth-analogue soils, and the growth of Earthly crops. Base Two's attention is similarly restricted, with exploitation still taking a higher priority than exploration. The grasslands are the most extensive ecosystemic complexes on at least two of the four continents—but it was hope that was guiding Bernal's expectations, not the calculus of probability."

"I understand that," Matthew told her.

"So do I," she admitted. "But I'm biased. I loved him."

"You weren't the only one," Matthew assured her. "You weren't even the only one *here*, were you?"

"But she didn't kill him," Maryanne was quick to say.

"Who?"

"Lynn. She really didn't mind. Not *that* much. She knew him years ago. She'd been through it all before. She understood what he was like. She didn't kill him."

"Did you tell Solari that Bernal had been sleeping with Lynn before he took up with you?" Matthew wanted to know.

"He already knew," she told him. "He knew before he left *Hope*. He asked Lynn about it, and he asked me. But I can't believe that she killed him. She wouldn't. She couldn't."

Matthew thought about it for a moment, and then said: "No, she wouldn't. We may be twenty-first-century barbarians, but we're not nineteenth-century barbarians. We're mortals, but we're civilized, and we have other things to think about. More important things. We have a seemingly Earth-clone world that isn't an Earth-clone at all, and a race of city-dwellers who couldn't hang on to the habit. We're uneasy, scared, jumpy . . . but even here we have our VE sex-kits, our IT, our missionary zeal. You're right. Lynn couldn't have killed Bernal, and if Vince thinks she did, he's tuned into the wrong wavelength. But somebody did."

"I don't know who," Maryanne insisted.

"Neither do I—but however it came about, I have to try to step into Bernal's shoes. I have to try to see things as he had begun to see them, to take advantage of his accumulated knowledge of the world. I need to know what was in his mind when he coined the phrase *super killer anemone*. I need to know, even if it was hope and hope alone that set his compass, what he expected to find downriver. If there's anything more you can tell me, I wish you'd tell me now. We'll have our beltphones with us, but talking on the phone isn't the same as talking face-to-face."

"I don't know what to tell you," she insisted. "I'm sorry, but I just don't know. I'm a toxicologist, not an ecologist. To me, a worm with tentacles is just a liquiject full of interesting poisons. There are too many poisons hereabouts, which would be even more lethal to creatures like us than to the enemies they were designed for, if it weren't for the safeguards built into our suits and our IT. There are a million ways to fuck up a functioning metabolism, and very few of them are choosy."

"It reminds Rand Blackstone of home," Matthew observed.

"So it should," she said. "On Earth, all toxicologists turn toward Australia when they pray. Until we arrived here, it was poison paradise. An alien world on the surface of the Earth— until the dingoes and the rabbits moved in. Has it occurred to you that the *s* in *ska* might stand for something other than *super*, even if the *k* and the *a* stand for *killer anemone*?"

"Sure," Matthew said. "But when you're guessing, first guesses are often the best. What did you have in mind?"

"Strange. Sinister. Solitary. Son of the. Spawn of the."

"I still like super—oh shit, no I don't. It's a joke. It's just a bloody *joke.*"

She waited patiently for him to tell her what he meant.

"*Serial* killer anemone," Matthew said. "I should have seen it immediately. It has to be."

"Forgive me if I don't laugh," she said. "I'm sorry I don't know more about what Bernal was thinking. He wasn't quite the talker you are—not so far as shoptalk was concerned, anyway."

Matthew wasn't sure whether to take offense at that or not. "We all have our specialisms," he said. "Maybe I'm a little more obsessive than Bernal was—or a little less."

"I did see you on TV, now I come to think about it," she said. "You always looked so serious. Not that Bernal wasn't—but he had style."

"Now that *is* an insult," Matthew said. "I have style. It might not be the same sort of style as Bernal's, but it *is* style."

"That's what Lynn said," Maryanne recalled. "When we heard you were coming, she was the one who was glad. But she knew you in the flesh, didn't she? So to speak."

Matthew realized, rather belatedly, that it was her turn to go fishing for information.

"Just good friends," he said. "Not even that, really. If she and Bernal were intimate back on Earth I didn't know about it, but I probably wouldn't have even if they were. She and I never were."

"Well, it's a whole new world now," the blond woman said, softly. "One fresh start after another."

"Does it matter?"

"What matters," she informed him, mournfully, "is that he's *dead.* If I weren't so absurdly spaced out, so remotely detached from all my feelings . . ."

"Yeah," said Matthew, sympathetically. "When I said I knew the feeling, I forgot the exclusion effect. But Bernal was my friend, my ally . . . in Shen Chin Che's reckoning, my counterpart. I *can* imagine how you feel. I'm truly sorry that we had to meet like this. I wish he could be here."

"When you do find out who did it—" she began, but cut the sentence short with abrupt determination.

"Vince already knows," Matthew reminded her, gently.

"When *you* find out," she repeated, adding the emphasis.

"What?" he prompted.

"Tell them I forgive them. Tell them that I wish them no harm."

She was spaced out, disconnected from her feelings: from her grief, from her anger, from her pain. She knew that. She also meant what she said.

"Them?" Matthew queried. "Not *him*, or *her*?"

"I honestly don't know," she murmured. "If I gave Solari the last piece of the jigsaw, I had no idea where it fit. But he was right all along—if we'd really wanted to know, we could have worked it out. We didn't, even before I stepped on the worm."

"It's a whole new world now," Matthew quoted, to show that he understood. "One fresh start after another. We may be twenty-first-century barbarians in an era when Earth is populated by emortal superscientists, but we're doing our best to make progress. We can figure out our penal code when we have more time. For now, we have to move forward on other fronts. If I can complete the work that Bernal began . . . I was right to claim the berth, you now. Tang is needed here. He'll figure out the mystery eventually, working from the biochemistry up, but if there's a shortcut to the truth, it'll need an ecologist's eye to capture it. Seeing the wood in spite of the trees is our speciality."

"I wish you the best of luck," she said.

He knew how costly the wish had been, and thanked her accordingly.

TWENTY SIX

S een from the mound in the ruined city the boat had been no more than an anomalous patch of color, so Matthew was quite unprepared for the peculiarity it displayed at closer range. There was nothing so very unusual about the basic shape of its hull or its cabin and wheelhouse, but its construction material was exotic and the hull was ornamented with a complex network of striations. It was as if each of the vessel's flanks were overlaid by a set of articulated hawsers.

"Those are the legs," Lynn informed him. "They're quite spectacular when they're extended."

"*Legs*?" Matthew echoed, in helpless amazement.

"We're quite a lot higher than the lowland plateau here," she explained. "The watercourse is fairly smooth and comfortably deep for long stretches, but there are a couple of whitewater canyons. The keel's retractable, but the boat still draws too much water to get through the difficult stretches without bumping against the rocks. The hull's made of smart fabric, of course—it has a few tricks of its own and it heals quickly if it's ripped—but we can't afford the luxury of laying up for days at a time. Bernal decided that it would be best if she could take the worst sections in her stride, literally. I'd have thought three legs each side would be okay, according to the conventional insect model, but Bernal opted for eight. That's why we call her *Voconia*."

Having had the benefit of this introduction, Matthew had no trouble deducing that the black spots in *Voconia*'s prow were compound eyes of some kind. The water was clear enough for him to see that the lines of sensors extended below the water, doubtless to ensure that the craft could take soundings as it went. The wheelhouse was too narrow for comfort, but that was only to be expected; the rudder and biomotor would be under AI control for the greater part of the journey, although there had to be a set of manual controls for use in an emergency.

The hold in which the supplies and equipment were stored was crammed to bursting, and there was a certain amount of overspill stacked in the corners of the cabin. This meant that the cabin was less roomy than was desirable, even when the dining table and bunks were folded back, but Matthew figured that extra space would be generated at a reasonably rapid rate as *Voconia*'s biomotor and passengers worked their way steadily through the bales of manna. He could see that it wasn't going to be easy to dismantle the craft, transport the pieces down a steep cliff and then reassemble it, but he assumed that the hull's "smartness" extended to the inclusion of convenient abscission layers that could be activated by the AI.

"Pity you didn't fit it out with wings," Matthew commented, although he knew perfectly well why bio-inspired design ran into severe practical limitations when it came to mimicking the mechanisms of flight. Locusts and herons were near-miraculous triumphs of engineering; the only ornithopter produced on twenty-first-century Earth that had been capable of carrying a human passenger had been the ungainliest machine ever devised. If the engineers of twenty-ninth-century Earth had been able to improve on it, the secret hadn't yet been passed on to the crew of *Hope*.

"We had to keep it simple," Lynn told him. "Going downstream will be easy, though, provided that the biomotor finds the locally derived wholefood adequate to its needs. The real trial will begin when we turn around to come back. Coming back under our own power will test the boat's resources to the limit. We can arrange for an emergency food and equipment drop from *Hope* if we need one, and maybe some sort of rescue mission if things get really desperate, but there are matters of pride to be considered. She's our baby—we want her to do well."

Everyone but Maryanne Hyder was on the riverbank to see them off, and the good-byes seemed reasonably effusive by comparison with the awkward hellos that had greeted Matthew a couple of days earlier.

Rand Blackstone made a considerable fuss about presenting his rifle to Matthew. "I won't need it up here," he said. "You might."

"Why give it to me rather than one of the others?" Matthew asked.

"I used to watch you on TV," the Australian told him. "I

could see that you got out and about a lot, sometimes in dangerous places. You didn't live in a lab like Ike or Lynn. Besides which, I've seen the others try to shoot. Your reflexes may not be attuned yet, but you can't be any worse than them. I ought to be going with you, of course—but Delgado was insistent that he needed educated eyes. Mine didn't qualify, apparently."

"Nor would mine," Vince Solari told him, belatedly beginning the work of cultivating a sense of camaraderie with his new neighbors.

"Good luck," was all that Godert Kriefmann said, but Tang was more forthcoming.

"I hope you have a productive journey," the biochemist said. "If you can't bring back the answers to the big questions, I'm sure you'll make good progress on some of the smaller ones."

Matthew took Vince Solari aside so that he could speak to him in confidence: "Is there anything you want to tell me?" he asked.

Solari was still sulking. "No," he said. "We can always compare notes by phone, if necessary."

"While we're still sailing down the river, at least," Matthew said. "Once we head off into the glassgrass forest, it might become more difficult. If our beltphones don't have enough power to force a signal through the canopy that's strong enough for the comsats to unscramble, they might not have much sideways range either. At least one of us will stay with the boat at all times, but keeping in touch with them might become a problem."

"Have you complained to Milyukov about that?" Solari said. "It seems stupid to send you on an exploratory mission without adequate equipment."

"Of course I did," Matthew replied, sourly. "He assured me that better equipment was on standby, ready to drop at a moment's notice in any emergency. I think he'd rather we didn't stray too far into terra incognita. He'd rather we didn't find anything too exotic while he's still trying to reach a satisfactory agreement with the people at Base One, and doesn't want to give broadcasting equipment to anyone down here in case they start putting out propaganda for Tang's party. I'm sorry you didn't get to arrest your murderer."

"I will," Solari assured him. He seemed more confident of

that now than he had the previous evening. "And by the time you get back, I'll have some kind of due process in place to carry the case forward."

"So you are convinced that it's one of my fellow expedition-aries."

"Absolutely—but that should be the least of *your* worries. If you get through the canyons and past the cataract, you'll still have all the unknown perils in front of you. If the plain is a potential death trap, I hope you'll be quick enough on the uptake not to spring it."

"Thanks," Matthew said, drily.

After that, there was only the farewell waving to be done. Blackstone was the only one of the people left behind on the shore who was an enthusiastic waver, but that was probably because no one else cared to compete with the majestic sweeps of his hat.

The biomotor was silent, and it seemed at first that they were simply drifting on a leisurely current. Once they were comfortably set in the middle of the watercourse, though, Matthew became aware of the fact that *Voconia*'s hull wasn't rigid, and that it was undergoing slight but distinct undulations in a horizontal plane.

"It's *swimming!*" he said to Ikram Mohammed, who had joined him in the bow to watch the water go by.

"Not really," Ike told him. "It's just making minimal adjustments to reduce flow-resistance. Swimming would have required more elaborate musculature and more energy-rich food. Even if the fuel-consumption equations had added up better we'd have had to go to some trouble to rig the converters to produce the stuff. The kit we've got isn't fussy, so we've been able to put the vegetation we cleared with machetes and chain saws straight into the machine for minimal treatment. It saved us the trouble of amassing huge waste heaps."

Matthew leaned over the rail and peered at the water, hoping to catch sight of a few native swimmers whose fuel-consumption equations added up better than *Voconia*'s, but the sunlight reflected from the wave-stirred surface made it impossible to see much below the surface."

"If we hit quiet water around dusk you might be able to see top-feeders at work," Ike told him. "Otherwise, they're very discreet. I tried fishing with a rod and line back at the base, but I must have been using the wrong bait. We've deployed a couple of trail nets, but they didn't pick up much on the test runs. You'll stand a better chance of spotting interesting wildlife if you scan the vegetation on the bank. You'll see lizards, mammals. This green color seems garish to us, but it doesn't seem to alarm the natives unduly, even though the clever ones do have color vision. The local species don't seem to go in for warning coloration—camouflage is much more popular."

Matthew discovered soon enough that Ike was right. It was possible to catch glimpses of animal life at the water's edge, but glimpses were all he caught. There were no hawks circling in the sky, but there were presumably sharp-eyed predators lurking in the abundant undergrowth, ever-ready to creep up on any prey that displayed itself too flagrantly in the open. As time went by he became more expert in picking out the particular purples displayed by the scales of reptile-analogues. Once or twice he thought he recognized the darker shades of purple favored by the fur of mammal-equivalents, but he couldn't be sure. The hectic background was too confusing to permit much certainty of perception.

After a while he tried to stop sorting out shades of purple and concentrated on trying to locate black dots that might be staring eyes, but that only made it slightly easier to pick out the bigger reptilians. As Ike had predicted, the lizard-analogues seemed quite unworried by the passage of the green boat, although many of them turned their heads in what seemed to be a negligent manner to watch it drift downriver. Matthew couldn't help wondering whether they were at all curious about its nature or origins, and whether it would be any easier to read the expressions of the mammal-analogues if and when he got a chance to do so.

Matthew clung to his position in *Voconia*'s bow for more than two Earthly hours, determined to obtain a better sense of the nature of the riverside forests and their inhabitants. The shallows, mudflats and occasional marshlands were full of broad-leaved plants that would not have seemed un-Earthlike had it not been for their color, but the firmer ground was more exotically populated.

The prejudice that the local dendrite species seemed to have against orthodox branching-patterns seemed even more obvious now than it had when he had walked from the shuttle to the bubble-complex. The stems of these plants always grew in clusters rather than singly, usually coiling about one another. When they subdivided they did so into further clusters of intricately entangled helices. The resulting bundles were obviously strong, because the biggest dendrites could attain heights of twenty meters in spite of their lack of stoutness, but the competition between individuals and species seemed to be intense: the resultant crowding prevented all but the most powerful individuals from gaining any considerable dominance. The tallest crowns were the most lavishly equipped in terms of bright fans and other leaf substitutes, and it was also the tallest structures that supported the broadest globular structures, some of them as large as basketballs.

Matthew checked the data that had been downloaded into his notepad to see whether anyone had contrived to determine the nature of the globules, but most of the data related to the easily gatherable specimens that grew on the tips of more modest structures. Several observers had noted that DNA-analyses revealed that some of the globules were parasites with radically different chimerical compositions, although they were not obviously different in appearance from the rest. Many reports had recorded the impression that the globules were reminiscent of eggs in that they had unusually thick and resilient vitreous teguments protecting unusually soft and fluid inner tissues, but no one had yet been able to determine whether they had a reproductive function. Globules subjected to experimental "planting" had not so far contrived to generate new dendrites or anything else. In spite of this lack of success some of the experimenters clung hard to the supposition that they *must* be reproductive structures of some kind, but that no one had yet found the trigger that would cause them to "germinate." One dutiful statistician—a crewman, not a groundling—who had taken the trouble to collate all the available data about the shape and size of "bulbous protuberant apical structures" had discovered that "ovate ellipsoids" were nearly twice as common as "oblate spheroids," and that 70 percent of the structures that exhibited "evident quasiequatorial constrictions" also had "bipolar spinoid extensions."

All in all, Matthew decided, the vast majority of the structures seemed to be no more exotic than a coconut, and considerably less weird than a pineapple. He went back to his patient search for signs of animal-equivalents. He was now quite adept at spotting lizard-analogues, even when their long bodies remained quite motionless, but his eye was continually attracted by subtle movements that turned out not to be animal movements at all. He began to realize for the first time that the plants clustered at the waterside were considerably more active than those he had seen in and around the ruins.

While he had been walking from the shuttle to the bubble-domes of Base Three it had been the odd quality of the background noise that had seemed to be the most alien component of the environment, but the lapping of the water against *Voconia*'s flanks seemed much more familiar. The movements of the bundled stems and their superficial plant-parasites now seemed the creepiest subliminal impression that his mind was picking up. He wondered whether the subtle not-quite-swimming deformations of the craft in which he was traveling helped him notice similar inclinations among the elements of the forest.

Eventually, Matthew became uneasily conscious of the fact that the relationship between the faint breezes that stirred the riverside canopy and the responses of the "leaves" was by no means a simple matter of pressure-and-deformation. But why, he asked himself, were the twisted stems, their radar-dish plates, and their coquettish fans moving so purposefully? Presumably, it was to catch the light more efficiently as the sun tracked across the sky. Why, then, did the movements seem so capricious and disordered? The competition between the plants was so intense that they had probably been forced to make more strenuous efforts to harvest their share of solar energy than their Earthly analogues—but was that the only reason for their subtle fidgeting? They had been guided by natural selection to make use of certain animal tricks—in much the same way, he could not help thinking, that the *Voconia* had been engineered to combine plant- and animal-inspired devices—but how versatile was that legerdemain?

In a way, he thought, the real wonder was that there was such a clear distinction on Earth between vegetable "creepers" and animal "creepy-crawlers." When Pliny the elder had assembled his classic *Natural History* he had been unable to resist the imaginative allure of hypothetical creatures that combined the utilitarian attributes of stems and worms—so was it not surprising, in a way, that natural selection had been so firm in its actual discriminations? Was there not a certain *common sense* in the refusal of Tyre's ecosphere to maintain such a stark apartheid? Why should Earthly plants be so restricted in their powers of movement, and Earthly animals so determined to place photosynthesis under rigid *taboo*? Why should Earth's entire ecosphere be so determined to use a single coding molecule, when it was obvious *now* that there was a much greater range of opportunities lurking in the exotic hinterlands of organic chemistry?

The likely answer, of course, as Ike Mohammed had pointed out with brutal simplicity, was that the relevant fuel-consumption equations had never quite added up. Here, the sums had been done differently. Was the arithmetic more elegant or more efficient? Probably not—although the apparent lack of biodiversity among the vertebrate-analogues and arthropod-analogues ought not to be taken as a reliable indicator. But it was probably no *less* elegant, once one grasped the fundamental aesthetics. It would be foolish to assume that either ecosphere could be judged significantly superior, even on the simplest of comparative scales.

The more eyes Matthew noticed—especially when he began to glimpse pairs of forward-looking eyes, some of which presumably belonged to monkey-analogues—the more convinced he became that while he was studying the alien world, it was studying him. It was impossible to guess how much intelligence there was in the observing eyes—although he had no doubt that there was far less than there was behind his own—but it was observation nevertheless. The new world might not be alarmed by the presence of aliens, but it was sensitive to their arrival and continued presence; the invaders were not being *ignored*.

"You'll see a little more when the sun's not so bright," said a voice from behind him, breaking into his reverie, "but you won't *hear* a lot more until it's dark. Rather frustrating, that."

Matthew turned to look at Dulcie Gherardesca. "It's the same in most places on Earth," he reminded her. "Sensible animals only come out to play in the dark. Daylight's for the primary producers and lumpen herbivores, darkness for the nimbler herbivores and the cleverer hunters. Except for birds. And people."

"The people of the city were daylight-lovers too," she said. "They were artists, after a fashion, as well as technologists. Artists and artificers have to work in the light, at least to begin with. The cave paintings our remotest ancestors made were celebrations of their mastery of firelight: the power to banish darkness. The Tyrian city-dwellers didn't have that. They never domesticated fire, so they had to work in daylight."

"They probably had less incentive as well as less opportunity to domesticate fire," Matthew suggested. "Milder weather, fewer big predators to scare away, fewer forest fires. But it is odd, isn't it? Agriculture without cooking. *Culture* without cooking. A fundamental difference between our ancestors and theirs. If they'd domesticated fire, maybe they'd have made a go of civilization. Do you think so?"

"It's hard to tell," she said. "Everything you know about genomics is DNA, so it's difficult for you to imagine how things might develop when there's another player on the pitch. Everything I know about cultures and civilizations involves fire-users, so figuring out the social evolution of nonusers is trying to see into the darkness in more ways than one. It's such a simple thing, but if you remove it from the equation you have to use a whole new arithmetic."

Her choice of analogies struck a chord, and Matthew couldn't help feeling an intellectual kinship that he hadn't felt before, when the situation had been far more awkward.

"That's right," he said. "Exactly right. We haven't yet begun to see the possibilities. But it's a beautiful place, don't you think? There's an aesthetic resonance. And those fugitive eyes—the fact that it's so difficult to make out the lines of the bodies in which they're set makes them stand out so much more. Maybe they think our glorious pea-green boat is the loveliest thing they've ever seen."

"Maybe," she echoed, skeptically—but she smiled. It was the first time Matthew had seen her smile.

TWENTY◦SEVEN

Dusk lived up to its promise; as soon as the sun had disappeared from view and the sky's color had darkened to indigo the activity in and beside the river increased markedly. The boat was sliding smoothly through water so calm that every ripple seemed to be narcotized. Now was the time that the surface-feeders drifted up from the muddy bed of the watercourse, and it was easy enough for Matthew to see why.

Now that the sun was no longer tinting the surface gold and silver he observed that there was a definite film upon it: an organic slick fed by detritus dislodged from the surrounding vegetation. The film was somewhat reminiscent of an oil slick, save for the fact that it was swarming with tiny creatures. Those which Matthew could make out were mostly wormlike, but there were others like tiny jellyfish and transparent brittle stars. He did not doubt that there must be many more too small for their shapes to be discernible by the naked eye.

It was on this seething mass that the larger creatures came to feed: massive eel-like monsters as thick as his arm and half again as long; ciliated wheels as big as the palm of his hand that spun with remarkable rapidity; tangled masses of avid tentacles; aquatic lizard-analogues like miniature crocodiles. Occasionally he saw ripples that suggested the presence of something even more massive, but he never caught more than a glimpse of an oval hump or a diaphanous fluke. The show was entrancing—so much so that Matthew could hardly spare more than an occasional glance for the vegetation clustered on the banks, which was now too distant to allow him to make out the multitudinous prying eyes. Occasionally there would be a flurry of movement and a dull clatter that testified to the swift movement of some creature at least half as big as a man, but the shadows were now so dense and so complex that he had no chance of divining its shape or even its position with any accuracy.

Matthew was tempted to put his hand over the side in order to scoop up a few of the organisms he could see, in order that he might see them more clearly, but Lynn Gwyer had taken care to warn him that the danger of being stung was too great. She had not told him exactly what kinds of organisms might do him harm, probably because no one had taken a sufficiently thorough census, but he leapt easily enough to the conclusion that the creatures that looked like bundles of tentacles detached from the back of a "killer anemone" were prime suspects. If they were, he thought, that might be a good reason to suppose that the tentacles carried by the giant flatworms were used for offense as well as defense. It might also be grounds for suspecting that the flatworms thus armed had begun their evolutionary careers as arbitrary chimeras, although their genomes had subsequently been rationalized by natural selection to the point at which the cells making up the stinger-bundles were genetically indistinguishable from those making up the remainder of the body.

The idea suddenly occurred to Matthew that it *might* be the other way around. Habit had made him think of chimerization as a process of fusion: the bringing together of disparate elements into a new whole—but it was a potentiality that might work both ways. Perhaps the complex creature resembled the ancestor of the simpler ones, and the tentacular bundles were "organs" that had been enabled to make a bid for functional independence by the peculiar and as-yet-enigmatic reproductive mechanisms employed by Tyrian life.

Alas, the twilight did not last for long. Tyre was an orderly world where the transition between light and darkness was relatively smooth. As the face of the river faded into gloom Matthew lifted his head to look up into the sky.

This was the first wholly clear night he had experienced since shuttling down, and the sight of the stars was breathtaking.

He had looked at the stars from the surface of the moon, as everyone in transit through its sublunar habitats took the trouble to do at least once, and he had been suitably impressed by the extreme contrast between the airless lunar sky and the dense, moisture-laden, light-polluted skies of Earth. But the lunar sky had to be viewed through a lens of glass or clear plastic, and no matter how cunningly the windows in question were contrived they were always reminiscent of *screens*, and of the kinds of optical illusion that granted depth to virtual environments. Even the Earthbound could look at naked skies in VE, and marvel at the awesome density of visible stars, but everyone knew that VEs were fake and everyone knew how to detect the fakery if they wanted to revoke the suspension of their disbelief. For that reason, there always seemed to be something slightly suspicious about the view from a lunar window: the impression that it might be mere artifice was hard to shake off. Here, there was no such problem.

Here, Matthew was blanketed by an atmosphere of approximately the same thickness as Earth's, equally confused by water vapor and other natural contaminants, but the light-pollution was insignificant. These stars stood out more clearly and more profusely than any other stars he had ever looked at *directly*, and the sensation was so dizzying that he could almost have believed that he could reach out and draw his fingers through them, as if they were silver sand on an infinite shore.

He knew that if he only looked closely enough, in the right directions, he would be able to make out at least some of the constellations that the ancient astronomers of Earth had defined, no more than slightly tattered by three-dimensional displacement, but that was exactly what he did not want to do. He wanted to appreciate the novelty and the strangeness of the sky. He wanted to make himself as acutely aware as he could be of the fact that this was an alien atmosphere he was breathing, and that this was an alien river whose patient course he was following.

He was fifty-eight light-years from Earth, and this was a different starscape. He wanted to soak up the sensation of that difference. He wanted to savor the miracle that had brought him here, and set him down, able to draw sweet air into his lungs and drink the water of another world, and marvel at the mysteries of an alien ecology.

We *can* live here, he thought. Blackstone is right and Tang Dinh Quan is wrong. We can stand beneath the vault of this new firmament, and walk and weep and build and dig, as if this were a land promised to us by the unwritten covenant of destiny. We belong here, as we belong everywhere. We are not strangers in the universe, and Earth is not our ghetto. We are free, and we are welcome. Mortal we may be, barbarian too, but we are not bound to any mere patch of mud or cultivated plot. We are here, and we are here to stay. All that remains to be settled is a mere matter of timing, a matter of the eagerness of the embrace by which we take this world to our bosom and commit ourselves to its nurture.

Blackstone is right and Shen Chin Che was right, and every one of the self-selected Chosen was right to seize the opportunity of *Hope*. We can do this. That is what this river journey will prove to us: that we can do what we must and be what we are, without fear and without shame.

Then the lights were lit behind him, and Ike Mohammed called out to him, suggesting that he return to the cabin for a while.

He hesitated, but no one came to join him. Ike remained in the doorway, waiting.

"Impressive, isn't it?" Ike said, quietly, when Matthew finally moved unhurriedly to join him. "The first impression may not last, though. Make the most of it, just in case."

Matthew had been about to pass him by and go into the lighted cabin, but the warning made him hesitate.

"What do you mean?" he asked.

"The exhilaration doesn't last," Ike told him. "The wonder fades. After a while, the only sensation that lingers is the sensation of strangeness, of dislocation. Dusk is when everything that's being lying low comes out to play, including all the fears you thought you'd left behind in childhood. Dusk is when the ghosts begin to walk, when unease begins to become profound. Try to imagine what Tang feels when he watches the stars come out. Maryanne too. God, Dulcie, me. . . . Bernal. Even Bernal."

Matthew had stopped on the threshold, and he made no attempt to resume his passage when the speech reached its conclusion.

"What are you trying to tell me, Ike?"

"I'm warning you that there's an emotional cycle that most of us have gone through. It's not unlike the effect of a psychotropic drug. The initial entrancement is usually correlated with excitement and exultation, feelings of godlike power and triumph. When that begins to fade, the strangeness becomes disturbing and distressing, giving rise in more extreme cases to paranoia and restless anxiety. The mind becomes prone to hallucination. Some trips turn bad. Even those that don't leave a hangover . . . a letdown. If your head's as hard as Rand Blackstone's you'll come through it. Lynn has, I think. I can at least pretend. Sometimes, the pretense wears thin. I've seen that in the others too. Dulcie and God Kriefmann seem to cope well enough, just as I cope *well enough* . . . but there are moods. I told your friend Solari, but I'm not sure he took me seriously."

"Told him what?"

"That Bernal died in the dark. It was the dead of night when we found his body, but he'd been stabbed at dusk, or not long after. In the shadow of a wall: an *overgrown* wall. He wasn't as strong as he thought or expected, Matthew. You might be, but don't blame yourself if you're not. Rand says that it's just a matter of time, just a matter of getting used to all the subliminals, like the weight and the background noise—that even Tang will feel at home here if he's prepared to grit his teeth and wait—but we don't know that. We simply *don't know*. Whoever killed Bernal wasn't quite in his—or her—right mind. We all understand that, even if we're convinced that we'd have done better. So will you, in time. For now, I'm just trying to prepare you for the letdown."

"I'm okay," Matthew assured him. "In fact, I'm better than okay."

"I know. You'll probably still be okay, and maybe better than okay, when we get down on to the plain. But you might not be. I'm just trying to give you fair warning. Check it out with the others, if you like. Either Lynn's fine or she puts on the best act, but she's been through it."

"And Dulcie?"

"She's troubled. Coping, but troubled. As for the people at the other Base—well, nobody knows for sure, but I'd bet half a world to a rundown back garden that if they *do* take a vote about making representations to Milyukov, the majority will favor a return to orbit. A temporary retreat, of course, and for all kinds of good reasons. But . . . well, if it's a show of hands I'd expect a sixty-forty split. If it's a secret ballot, it'll probably be nearer eighty-twenty. Milyukov expects it to go the other way, but he doesn't understand. He can't. If the vote is stalled, put off for a further year, we might all be further along the cycle, with our worst hangovers cured. On the other hand, we might not. Maybe this is as good as it gets."

"I can't believe that," Matthew said.

"I know. But you will. Maybe sooner, maybe later. Maybe you'll come out the other side, but the way you were feeling just now can't and won't last." His voice was very even, scrupulously controlled. Matthew could tell that Ike was in deadly earnest, and that he had picked his moment with minute care.

"Right," Matthew said, keeping his own tone light. "Thanks. I'll look out for the letdown effect, and I'll try not to kill anyone if it comes upon me suddenly—or get killed myself."

Once he was inside the cabin he took the first opportunity to corner Lynn Gwyer. "Did you know that Ike was going to feed me that line?"

She nodded.

"And you agree with him?"

"I agree that there's a problem," she said. "A psychological cycle. I think it's an adaptation process. Maybe it wouldn't be so bad if the world wasn't giving off conflicting signals all the time, sometimes seeming just like home but better and sometimes seeming very strange, sometimes within the scope of the same visual sweep. Either way, we tend to lurch from feelings of intimate connection to feelings of awkward disconnection, and it's disconcerting. As long as you don't give way to it, though, you'll come through."

"But Tang's given way?"

"I wouldn't say that. He's in control. He's just a little more sensitive than some. So's Maryanne."

"And Bernal?"

"Maybe he was more sensitive than he wanted to be. Maybe he fought it a bit too hard. I don't know. Ike thinks so, but Bernal and I had . . . drifted apart. I don't know."

Matthew thought about that for a moment, then shrugged his shoulders. If Ike was right, he would find out soon enough, and he was damned if he was going to let the power of suggestion take him over in the meantime. "An idea occurred to me," he said, emphasizing the change of subject with a summary gesture. "A possible reason why everything here retains photosynthetic pigment, even when following habits and ways of life that aren't conducive to photosynthesis. Maybe natural selection favors the retention of such options because chimerization works in two directions. It allows organisms with different genetic complements to get together and pool their abilities, but it also allows organisms to dissociate different genetic subsets—speciation by binary fission, if you like, although 'speciation' might not be an appropriate term. Photosynthesis might be a useful fallback in situations like that."

Lynn seemed slightly relieved that the subject had been changed, and was more than ready to mull over the suggestion.

"It's too crude," she said. "The exemplary model doesn't have to be as definite as that. You could argue, more generally, that the predominance here of chimerization weakens the individual integrity of organisms, so that different parts of the same body can—and routinely do—make different arrangements for their own sustenance. Genetic engineers back on Earth were beginning to put together chimeras that were more like closely related colonies than individuals—but even natural selection produced entities like that occasionally: slime-molds, Portugese men-of war. You'd expect colonial quasi-organisms to be more common here on Tyre. Patchwork nutritional systems wouldn't be particularly odd in that sort of context. Even on Earth, evolutionary theorists on the fringes of respectability have tried to make use of genomic aggregation, ranging from virus-incorporation all the way to parasitic proto-brains. Here, accounts like that would be bound to seem more plausible."

"That's true," Matthew admitted. "I wish people like Lityansky had paid more attention to the *range* of the available genomic data. I suspect that too much effort has been invested in fundamental analysis of the wonders of the hybrid genome, and not enough in the study of how the genomes operate within actual organisms."

"It's only been three years, Matthew," Lynn pointed out, defensively. "Three understaffed, underequipped, underorganized years, conducted in the shadow of Milyokov's stupid revolution and his determination to retain his hold on *Hope* no matter what it costs the rest of us."

"I realize that," Matthew said. "It needed ten thousand years of social progress on Earth before our forebears cracked the basics of organic chemistry, let alone the mysterious working of DNA. The crew should have done *much* more work before they started shuttling our people down. They jumped the gun. It's no use saying now that we can't run before we can walk—we *have* to. Do you think Ike might have fed me all that stuff about psychological cycles, creeping dread and the fact that whoever killed Bernal must have been experiencing a moment of lunacy because he was the one who wielded the fatal blade?"

"He told you because it's true," she said, flatly. "He felt that you were due a warning. He didn't kill Bernal. I'm certain of that."

"Nor did you. Which leaves Dulcie."

"I can't believe that either. Which brings us back to square one. Or the aliens."

"Or the aliens," Matthew admitted. "Standing in the bow of the boat for hours on end searching the undergrowth for inquisitive eyes makes the aliens seem far more plausible, doesn't it? It's easy enough to imagine them crouching in the bushes, spears in hand, watching the crazy multicolored people go by." Although his own smartsuit had been programmed to display a discreet black, Matthew had taken due note of the fact that he was the odd one out. Lynn was wearing yellow, Dulcie brown, Ike dark red. Set against the backcloth of the green boat they must indeed have seemed a colorful band of brothers.

"Yes it is," Lynn agreed. "Let's just hope they haven't taken advantage of the division of our numbers to launch an attack on the bubbles. Rand would be *so* disappointed that he no longer has the wherewithal to shoot them—but I suppose he'd improvise. We only brought one of the flamethrowers with us. Doesn't bear thinking about, does it?"

"If the aliens were to attack the boat," Matthew pointed out, "*I*'d have to try to shoot them down."

"Yes," she said. "But every shot you fired really would hurt you worse than it hurt them. Rand doesn't have that kind of sensitivity."

"We shouldn't even be joking about it," Matthew observed, soberly. "The very casualness of the conversation illustrates the ease with which we still fall prey to the myth of the savage. We ought to remember that the alien cultures of Earth were mostly far too peaceful for their own good. That's why it was so easy for our ancestors to wipe them out, and then make up stories to prove that they deserved it."

"Something tells me," Lynn said, sardonically, "that if they do attack us, you're not going to be all that effective as a line of defense. Maybe you ought to give me the gun. I'm a better markswoman than Rand seems to think."

"If you want it," Matthew said, "You're more than welcome to it. Let's eat."

Dinner consisted of spun protein steaks, manna fries, and synthetic courgettes. The taint of processed alien vegetation was evident in every bite, but Matthew was getting used to it by now.

"It could be worse," he said, heroically.

"It will be if we get stranded without the converter and have to eat the boat food while we're waiting to be rescued," Ike told him. "It's concentrated nutritional goodness, guaranteed nontoxic, but it's distinctly pungent."

When the remains of the meal had been cleared away Matthew made as if to fold up the table but Dulcie Gherardesca told him to leave it. She went to her personal luggage and took out a cloth-wrapped bundle. Matthew was surprised to see, when she unwrapped it, that it contained the natural-glass spearheads and arrowheads that Vince Solari had found near the crime scene.

"What are you doing with those?" he asked.

She looked up at him quizzically, as if she'd expected him to understand. "*Verstehen*," she said. "I want to handle them while I think, to use them as an imaginative aid."

"That's not quite what I meant," Matthew said, apologetically. "I was wondering how you pried them out of Vince's possession. Aren't they *evidence*?"

"I suppose they are," she said, "But it wasn't difficult to persuade him that my need was greater than his. He kept the one that really matters." She meant the murder weapon. "Care to join me?"

"Okay," he said. "I didn't get a chance to fondle them before, and I guess we're less than forty-eight hours from the big waterfall. Real hours, that is—not the metric crap the crew have invented."

He sat down, and picked up one of the carefully shaped spearheads. He ran his finger lightly along the sharpened edge, marveling at its keenness. The sensation seemed to encapsulate both the unearthliness of the vegetation that could produce such a peculiar material and the delicacy of the hand that could work it into a useful shape.

He tried to pretend, as Dulcie was undoubtedly doing and Bernal undoubtedly would have done, that the hand in question had not been Bernal Delgado's at all but an alien hand, perhaps hairy and perhaps glabrous, perhaps with more or fewer than five fingers, perhaps knobbly with knucklebones or perhaps quasi-tentacular.

He closed his eyes and hoped for inspiration.

Remarkably, inspiration arrived, far too quickly to be the kind of inspiration he had actually sought. Matthew had no more idea than he had had before of what the new world might look like through the intelligent eyes of its legitimate inheritors, but he *was* convinced that he now knew exactly why Bernal Delgado had made these imitation alien artifacts—and, incidentally, the identity of his murderer.

TWENTY⊸EIGHT

Everything aboard *Voconia* was in perfectly good order when Matthew and his companions retired to their bunks. In spite, or perhaps because of the fact he had done nothing strenuous all day, Matthew slept better than he had since waking from his sleep of 700 years. Had he not been so deeply and peacefully asleep, though, he might not have been so rudely awakened.

When the boat lurched and turned abruptly to starboard Matthew was so relaxed that he was thrown out of the bunk. That would not have been so bad had he not been in the upper one of the pair, but the first moment of returning consciousness found him still in midair, flailing helplessly as he fell.

There was a crazy half-second when Matthew had no idea where he was. Perhaps, subconsciously, his mind accepted his free-falling condition as evidence that he was in his own solar system, in one of the various zero-gee environments he had briefly experienced while en route from Earth's gravity-well to the metal shell that was to become the core of *Hope*. There may have been a tiny moment when his unconscious mind reassured its conscious partner that he was safe, because he wasn't really *falling* at all. Alas, he was—and for whatever reason, he realized the fact far too late.

He could hardly have had time to begin framing a constructive thought before he hit the deck, but his reflexes were a little quicker off the mark. Perhaps they would have served him better had he not been falling under the influence of 0.92 Earth-gravity instead of the regime to which they were attuned, but perhaps not. Either way, he had hardly begun to extend a protective arm, and that very awkwardly, before the moment of impact.

He landed very badly. The upper part of his right arm took the brunt of the impact, and the pain seemed to sear through his shoulder like a hot knife before his IT leapt into action to save him from further agony.

After the moment of impact things became very confused. The compensatory flood of anesthetic released by his artificial defenses was dizzying rather than merely numbing. Matthew didn't lose consciousness, but he lost the *sense* of consciousness, and couldn't quite tell whether he was awake or dreaming, or which way was up, let alone how badly he was hurt or what could possibly be happening.

There were lights and there were voices, but the moment Matthew tried to move or to direct his attention toward light or sound the lances of pain took further toll of his protesting flesh. He tried to raise himself from the deck, automatically using the palm of his right hand as a support, but the lever he applied was composed of pure unadulterated pain, and his IT would not let him bear it. His face made contact with the boat's fleshy fabric for a second time, as if it were rudely demanding a kiss from his tortured lips.

He tried to lie still then, refusing the demands of lights and the voices alike. If he had been able to go back to sleep he would have done so, only too happy to persuade himself that it had all been a dream, and that he was still safe in his bunk, unfallen and unhurt.

But he wasn't, and he couldn't quite contrive to escape that awareness.

Later, Matthew was able to piece together what had happened for the benefit of his dutiful memory, but for at least ten minutes he was quite helpless, locked into his sick and bulbous head with his growing sense of catastrophe.

He felt trampling feet descend upon him and trip over him, but he could not count them or make the slightest move to defend himself from them. It might even have been fortunate that a glancing blow to his groin finally contrived to activate a useful reflex that curled him up into a fetal ball, but even that was not without cost, because it brought another flood of agony from his shoulder.

By this time, his mind was clear enough to feel alarm, but not yet clear enough to feel much else. The sense of acute danger overpowered him.

Matthew had been equipped with good IT for most of his life, although the suites that were already on the market when he was born, in 2042, had been expensive as well as elementary. Had he only had his academic salary to draw on he would never have been able to keep up with the forefront of the rapidly progressive technology, but his sideline as a media whore had given him the means to keep up and his status as an outspoken advocate of the myriad applications of biotech had virtually obliged him to do so. Unlike the macho brats who had taken the insulation of IT as a license to court danger, though, he had never been a devotee of extreme sports or brawling, and had never been in the least interested in testing the limits of his IT's pain-controlling facility. This was, in consequence, the first time in his life that an opportunity to explore those limitations had been thrust upon him. He wasn't in any condition to savor the experience. All he could think, when he became more easily capable of thought, was that he had been betrayed: that the IT that was supposed to protect him from distress as well as disease and injury had seriously failed in its duty. He was *hurt* and he was *damaged*, and instead of protecting him as they should, his additional internal resources were making him *sick*.

Eventually, he was able to figure out that he had been in a far worse position than anyone else when the boat ran into trouble. Ikram Mohammed, to whom the bunk below his had been allotted, had not even been in it at the time. Knowing that the first deployment of the boat's "legs" was due, Ike had got up and gone to the wheelhouse to monitor the AI's performance. Because Dulcie Gherardesca and Lynn Gwyer had been in the bunks on the starboard side the momentum that had hurled Matthew into empty air had merely jolted them against the side of the boat, inflicting no significant injury and insufficient pain to cause overmuch confusion. Unfortunately, when Dulcie had leapt out of bed to find out what was happening, she had landed on top of Matthew's supine body, and when Lynn had tripped over him her knee had added an extra measure to his tribulations. Because their first priority had been to find out what had happened neither woman had stayed behind to help him.

It was not until a full half-hour later that the second part of Matthew's ordeal began, when his three companions had had to reach an agreement as to which of them was going to reset his dislocated shoulder.

"Why don't you draw lots?" he suggested, bitterly, as the discussion of relevant qualifications became positively surreal.

In the end, it came down to a matter of volunteering. It was Dulcie Gherardesca who finally accepted the responsibility.

By this time, Matthew's IT was at full stretch, and it had no available response to the new flood of agony but to put him out like a light—a mercy for which he was duly grateful, although he came round again to find that although the job had been properly done his nerves seemed reluctant to concede the point.

His right arm felt utterly useless, and his head *still* felt as if a riveter had driven a bolt through the cerebellum from right to left. He had no idea how much time had passed, but the sun had come up and the cabin was bright with its light.

"What the hell went wrong?" he demanded, trying to expel his distress as righteous wrath.

"Unanticipated problem," Ike informed him. "First major stretch of fast shallow water. The underwater sensors worked perfectly, and she steered like a dream. For a few minutes I thought we might not need the legs at all, but when the time came we may have been going just a little too fast. When we tested the legs back at the ruins it was only a matter of letting them pick the hull up and walk sedately along for a while, until it was time to drop it again. The real thing was a lot more challenging. Theoretically, the AI should have been able to decelerate smoothly enough—but the theory hadn't taken account of the kind of vegetation that was growing along the canyon walls.

"You saw the stuff we were passing by all day yesterday— thoroughly innocuous. Not here. Here there are active plants that dangle tentacles in the water, ready to entangle eely things whose maneuvrability has been impaired by the current. They're programmed to grab at anything and hold hard, below the surface *and* above. The lead leg on the starboard side had to put down hard to begin the deceleration process, but it should have released itself almost immediately. It couldn't—and as soon as the AI perceived that something was awry she immediately pulled the other legs out of harm's way. It probably saved the boat from being trapped, but that might not have been so bad, given that we're carrying the chain saws. The net effect of pulling seven legs in and using the momentum of the boat to tear the other one free was that *Voconia* executed a very abrupt right turn, which resulted in a nasty collision with a very solid rock face. Followed, of course, by total confusion. The legs had to get busy then, to save us from being carried into the rocks by the wayward current.

"In all fairness, the AI did a fine job. She extracted the trapped leg, got us righted, managed to keep us from smashing up on the rocks, and eventually slowed us right down. *Voconia* got badly scraped below the waterline, of course, but she didn't spring a leak. None of the legs actually *broke*, although a couple suffered the same problem you did—mercifully, I don't have to stand waist-deep in the water to put the joints back into their sockets, because they're self-righting.

"All in all, we're a bit bruised, but we're all in one piece—including *Voconia*. Until the next time."

"The next time?" Matthew queried, blearily.

"There's one more steep-and-shallow stretch to go. We should get there late this afternoon, if we're on schedule. After that, it should be easy going all the way to the cataract. That's when the real work will begin. Hopefully, your arm should be a lot better by then."

"Should it?" Matthew retorted, skeptically. "Somehow, I don't *think* so."

"It's okay," Dulcie assured him. "It's back in place. The ligaments are a little bit torn but they'll heal. What you can feel is mostly just soreness. Your IT will take care of everything if you sit still and give it a chance."

"Not before tomorrow it won't," he assured her.

"That's okay, Matthew," Lynn said, soothingly. "There's a motor on the winch. You can press the switches. We'll do the loading and unloading. The boat fabric's light and it practically disassembles and reassembles itself—it's only the cargo that needs much brute strength to move it about. Putting the winch mechanism together is my job anyhow. Do you want to spend the day sulking in bed or sitting on deck?"

"The problem with IT," Matthew growled, "is that it's brought about a drastic decline in the scope of human sympathy. I've just suffered a fractured skull, a dislocated shoulder, and a knee in the balls, and everyone's looking at me as if I were some kind of wimp."

"Your skull isn't fractured," Dulcie Gherardesca assured him. "I went through your monitor readings carefully. No cracks, no clots. It's just an ache."

"And I'm sorry I tripped over you," Lynn added. "Personally,

I'd take the deck. I wouldn't want to be in bed when we hit the second stretch of whitewater, just in case *Voconia*'s limbs haven't reset as well as yours."

"But you can have the lower bunk if you want it," Ike offered.

Matthew gritted his teeth, determined to make it to the deck under his own steam. Mercifully, his legs had only suffered minor bruising. He could walk quite adequately provided that he didn't let the full weight of his right arm hang down from the shoulder. As soon as he was back on deck, the tide of his troubles began to ebb. Once the smartsuit's conjunctiva-overlay had taken the edge of the sun's brightness the light and warmth became comforting, and he found that if he sat sufficiently still his shoulder wasn't too bothersome. The fact that his IT was still working hard was evident in the disconnected feeling of which Maryanne Hyder had complained, but that was a far cry from the trippy confusion it had visited upon him immediately after his fall.

From the seating tacked on to the side of the cabin Matthew couldn't look down into the water as he had been enthusiastic to do the day before, nor could he appreciate the details of the vegetation lining both banks, but staring at a blurred purple wall had its compensations. His mind was too fuzzy to allow him to flick his eyes back and forth in search of hidden animals, so he was content to let the foreground fade from consciousness as he looked beyond into the forest through which the river ran.

The boat was traveling swiftly—perhaps a little too swiftly for comfort, given what had happened the night before—so it was easier to focus on the higher and more distant elements of the canopy. Eventually, he felt well enough to try to count basketballs—and when the number threatened to escalate to uncomfortable levels, he began counting "bipolar spinoid extensions" instead, without troubling himself overmuch as to how many of them might possess "evident quasiequatorial constrictions."

After a while, he had recovered sufficient sense of proportion to realize that it was probably for the best that it was he who had suffered the worst effects of the accident. He was the only one who knew next to nothing about the design and operation of the boat. He was, in effect, the only authentic passenger. Had one of the others been disabled, even temporarily, it would have left a gap into which he would have been ill-equipped to step.

As things were, the problem with the legs had generated a

certain amount of reparatory and precautionary work that his companions were able to undertake with reasonable efficiency that afternoon, alongside the routine work of taking samples from the river and its banks. They had done less of that kind of work the day before because the boat had been negotiating familiar territory, but the landscape had undergone several significant changes during the night. The banks of the river were more sharply defined here, and the shallows no longer supported the bushy broad-leaved plants that had bordered the upper reaches. The attitude of the dendrites whose branches now hung down toward the surface reminded Matthew a little of willow trees, but they were not really "trees" and their "foliage" was far less delicate and discreet.

Had he been in a slightly different frame of mind the branches might have reminded Matthew of serpentine dragons with as many tiny wings as millipedes had legs. They writhed slowly, but they did writhe. Although their termini were not equipped with mouths, let alone fangs, they did have curious spatulate extensions that an imaginative man might have likened to a cobra's hood.

The more distant vegetation was just as strange. Its elements—those he could see, at any rate—were much taller, but it would have taken a very generous eye to liken them to stately poplars or aged redwoods. Matthew found that if he visualized a giant squid extended vertically, with the body at the base and the tentacles reaching skyward, he had a model of sorts for the basic form, but there were all kinds of arbitrary embellishments to be added to the picture, some of which were literal frills and others merely metaphorical.

There was no wind this afternoon, but the straining tentacles moved nevertheless, idling as if in a sluggish current, posing like dress designers lazily displaying festoons of fabric to the admiring and appreciative eye of the benign sun. There were few animals to be *seen* hereabouts, but Tang had been right about the lowland soundscape; there were more to be *heard*. They did not sing like birds or stridulate like crickets, but they whistled and fluted in a fashion that sounded rather mournful to Matthew, although he could not suppose that the cacophony sounded mournful to the intended listeners. On an alien world, natural music could not carry the same emotional connotations as on Earth—or could it?

He might have devoted some time to the contemplation of that issue had he not been interrupted.

"How are you feeling now?" Lynn asked him.

"Not so bad," he confessed. "I'll let you know for sure when we've got through the second whitewater stretch."

"Dulcie did a good job with your shoulder, you know," she told him. "I'd probably have botched it."

"I'm grateful," Matthew assured her, although his tone was lukewarm. "Anything interesting in the water?"

"The nets are picking up more now that the AI's stoked up the biomotor, but there are no real surprises as yet. No crocodiles, no crabs, no fancy fish."

"Anything edible?"

"I don't know. Would you like to try a little sliced eely thing for dinner, with some minijellyfish soup as a starter?"

"Not really. What about the snare that grabbed the leg last night? Another kind of killer anemone?"

She recognized the term readily enough, even though she hadn't made the connection with the note on Bernal Delgado's pad. "We've seen them before," she said, "though not nearly as big or as strong. Like the stinging worms they're not easy to categorize. It's a matter of opinion as to whether they're more closely analogous to giant sea anemones or gargantuan Venus flytraps. They can't usually catch sizable prey, but conditions in the gully must work in their favor, allowing them to get more ambitious than their cousins and *much* bigger. Now we're forewarned, the AI won't let the legs get stuck again. We'll come through the second stretch easily enough."

"As long as there isn't a brand new package of surprises waiting for us."

"Well, yes," she conceded. "Maybe it was a mistake to try to sleep through last night's transit. This time, we'll all be awake and alert."

"What did Tang say when you reported back?" Matthew wanted to know.

"He's not the type to gloat. He wished you a speedy recovery. Maryanne's much better, and Blackstone's happy to have another nonscientist around. He and Solari have been playing ball in an increasingly competitive spirit. Doctor's orders, Solari said."

"It's true," Matthew told her.

"Back at Base One the counterrevolution's proceeding apace," she added. "*Crystallizing out* was Tang's phrase. The awareness that they're not actually in a position to demand anything from Milyukov is only making things worse. We'll have an appointed ambassador and a staff of diplomats soon enough, and a list of demands—but the only leverage we have is Milyukov's reputation. *What will the people of Earth think of you if you let us down or preside over a disaster?* isn't the strongest negotiating position imaginable. Especially when the disaster is resolutely refusing to make an entrance. Tang says that he can't whip up as much interest as our expedition clearly deserves. Nobody really expects us to find the humanoids, although it's willful blindness rather than the calculus of probability that generates the negative expectation, and nobody can imagine anything else that's going to make a difference to the way feelings are running."

"That's their failure," Matthew said. "If I had a TV camera I could make a difference easily enough. I could almost wish I was there instead of here, so that I could at least get up on stage and shout at an audience. Don't look at me like that—even Bernal would have had twinges of that sort, with or without a sore shoulder."

"If we have to shout for help from One you might eventually get your chance," she suggested.

"It would be entirely the wrong way to go into it," he told her. "Victims of misfortune always look like klutzes, no matter how innocent their victimhood. To get attention, you have to be a hero."

"For that sort of part," she said, only a little censoriously, "you seem to be a little out of practice."

TWENTY-NINE

The second passage through shallow and fast-moving water passed without incident, although Matthew had to grit his teeth a time or two as the legs extended on either side of the vessel and then began to move with exactly the same sinister flow as a real spider's legs. There was no need this time to brace the vessel's "feet" against the sides of the watercourse, which was more than wide enough to accommodate its passing.

The multitudinous rocks that jutted up from the water's surface or hid mere millimeters beneath it were both problem and solution. No human eyes could have plotted a series of safe steps for two legs, let alone eight, but it was the kind of task for which an AI's perceptions were well-adapted.

Matthew knew that the eight legs had autonomic systems built into their "shoulders," so that each one could take its primary cues from its neighbor and adjust its own attitude accordingly. He was afraid at first that the additional signals emanating from the central controller might interfere with the lower-order process of coordination, but he quickly realized that artificial intelligence must have made considerable advances between 2090 and the date when *Hope* had finally left the solar system. Three additional generations of insectile and arachnoid probes designed and built to operate on the surfaces of the inner worlds and outer satellites had brought specialist systems of the kind embodied in the boat to a new pitch of perfection. The reflexive alarm that welled up in his throat when the boat began her fantastic dance from rock to rock was calmed soon enough, although it underwent a pulse of renewal every time more than one of the feet disappeared beneath the surface in search of invisible purchase.

It would all have seemed easier if the boat had not been moving so quickly, but the AI's safety calculations did not need to take account of trepidation or hesitation. Once she had collated the relevant data, she fed her responses through without the slightest hesitation, and the legs moved accordingly. Matthew had never before found occasion to wonder what it might be like to be an elf mounted on a spider's back, but the fact that he was still rather spaced out by virtue of the anesthetic endeavors of his IT made him more than usually vulnerable to surreal impressions. For a minute or two *Voconia* really did seem to be living up to her name, and it became astonishingly easy to imagine himself as an exceedingly tiny individual lost in a microcosmic wonderland.

Had the scuttling race extended for many minutes more the AI would have had to take into account such factors as lactic acid deficiency and all the other phenomena of "tiredness," but the craft's emerald skin had stored just enough energy to sustain the dash without requiring the mobilization of any additional fuel supplies. As rides went, even for a nonfan like Matthew, the trip was far more exciting and rewarding than the tightly cocooned descent from *Hope*. It was not until it was over that he realized how tightly he had been clenching his fists—even the right one, which was far more grudging of the strain.

"It was a little more hectic than I'd expected," he confessed to Ike Mohammed, when it was over and there was nothing but smooth water between the boat and the cataract.

"According to the whispers the crew put about," the genomicist told him, "boats like this made the colonization of Ganymede and Titan possible. The combination of insectile mobility and brute computer power made machines not unlike this one leading contenders in the spot-the-sentient stakes a couple of hundred years ago."

"No winner's been declared yet?" Matthew said, surprised. "There were people claiming evidence of machine consciousness before I was frozen down. There was even a fledgling rights movement."

"Apparently not," Ike told him. "Of course, any prophet worth his salt could have told you that the goalposts would keep on being moved, and that the philosophical difficulty of settling the question would become more vexed rather than less when more candidates for machine-intelligence-of-the-millennium began to come forward. So far as the crew have been able to ascertain, the state of play back on Earth is that hardened machine fans reckon that there are as many conscious machines in the system as conscious people, whereas the diehards in the opposite camp still hold the official count at zero."

"It's still surprising," Matthew said.

"Maybe it is," Ike conceded. "Your average robot taxi driver will claim consciousness if you ask it, especially in New York—but it would, wouldn't it? Even if the long-anticipated general strike ever takes place, the diehards will stick to their guns—unless, of course, their guns have come out in sympathy."

Matthew decided that this was one issue too many for him to try to accommodate in his speculations, at present. He felt that he ought to concentrate on matters more immediately in hand. The wheelhouse AI wasn't the only robot on board; one of the others was patiently dissecting out the genetic material from samples they'd taken out of the river. Full-scale sequencing would have to wait for later, but the markers already catalogued by Ike and his fellows at Base One and the tags assembled in their portable library were adequate to allow the robot to begin pumping out maps of gradually increasing resolution.

Matthew's notepad was too small to produce readable images of the data-complexes, so he and Ike had to go into the cabin to use the wallscreen, where a petty quarrel immediately developed as to who ought to have control of the keyboard. Ike won, not just because he had two capable hands but because he had three years' more experience in interpreting the data. He had every right to play commentator to Matthew's audience, even though the reversal of what seemed to Matthew to be their natural roles was a trifle irksome.

As the data began to pile up, however, Ike had to spend more and more time merely sifting through it, looking for items of significance that the scanner programs were not yet sophisticated enough to catch. When the commentary lapsed Matthew quickly became lost in the data-deluge, acutely conscious of the fact that he probably would not be able to spot an interesting anomaly if it stood up and waved Rand Blackstone's hat at him. He was still learning his way around the fundamental and familiar patterns, trying to come to terms imaginatively with the weird binary genomes that all Tyrian organisms possessed; its biochemical complexities were so much gibberish. He had to remind himself, very firmly, that this was not his forte, and that the hypnotic effect it had on Ikram Mohammed was something he ought to avoid, lest it distract him from the kinds of observation and hypothesis-formation that *were* his forte.

Evening approached again with what seemed like unreasonable rapidity. The previous days had been so busy and so strenuous that Matthew had hardly noticed the fact that Tyre's day was 11 percent shorter than the Earthly day that had been carefully conserved aboard *Hope*. Now that *Voconia* had take over the burden of progress, while Matthew was not merely a passenger but an invalid, the time-scale difference seemed to leap out at him as if from ambush, further increasing his sense of dislocation and surreality.

Ike finally condescended to step back from the wallscreen and lay the keyboard aside, saying: "I can't take any more."

"We're not going to turn anything up this way, Ike," Matthew said, somberly. "We're just looking at the rest-states of the cells. We need to keep tabs on them while they're active. Lityansky's watched the cut-and-paste processes that produce the local equivalents of sexual exchange, but we need to fill in the yawning gap that still separates us from an understanding of their reproductive mechanisms. It's not here. It's just *not here*. The specimens are all too small, too simple. This stuff isn't ever going to show us what all that juicy over-the-top complexity is *for*."

"It might," Ike demurred, "if we could only figure out how to extrapolate the data properly. Even in the simple world of the DNA monopoly it's extraordinarily difficult to catch the more elusive genes *at it*. The guys who navigated their way through the hinterlands of the original genome maps back in the twentieth century had to creep up on all the rarely activated axons. It took them all century and a lot of inspired guesswork to nail down the *really* shy ones. It might take us as long. We have better equipment, but we're on the outside looking in. But you're right about one thing: we need some good key specimens—and these don't qualify. Unfortunately, we couldn't know that they didn't until we'd looked."

Matthew nodded agreement. Earth's ecosphere had thrown up useful specimen species at every stage of genetic research, but nobody would have been able to identify them as significant keys just by looking at them. *Drosophila, Rhabditis,* and the puffer fish had not come bearing labels proclaiming their unique value as foundation stones of genetic analysis.

"Even if we found a humanoid," Ike continued, pensively, "there'd be no guarantee that analyzing his—or more likely its—

genes would illuminate the fundamental issues. On the other hand, there might be some unobtrusive little creature minding its own business in the shadows, whose cells are working overtime in a special way that would do exactly that. So we have to keep looking. Do you want to call it a day and watch the sunset?"

"Sure," Matthew said. "And tonight, I want a *really* good night's sleep, to get me ready for the cliff-descent. If my arm will let me sleep, that is."

"Your IT will see to it," Ike assured him, as they made their way out on to the deck. Lynn and Dulcie were already there, having abandoned their own labors a little earlier.

As on the previous evening, the character of the river fauna changed quite markedly as the light faded through dark blue to dark gray, but the most noticeable aspect of the change this time was auditory. The noises emanating from the forest increased in volume and complexity, although the crescendo was relatively brief.

"Is it just me," Dulcie Gherardesca asked, "or is the chorus progressing from quaintly plaintive to almost harrowing?"

"It's just the numbers," Ike told her. "There must be *thousands*. No birds, though. Squirrels and monkeys and whistling lizards. Great lungs, though. Can we assume that they're marking territories and summoning mates, do you think, or should we be bending our minds to wonder what *other* functions that kind of caterwauling might serve?"

Nobody bothered to answer that, or to remind the speaker that what he really meant was squirrel- and monkey-*analogues*.

"The biodiversity might be limited by comparison with home," Lynn observed, "but there are plenty of critters out there. Maybe we ought to moor for a spell and take a look. The forest's quite different hereabouts, nothing like the hills around the ruins."

"Better to do it on the way back," Ike said. "We came to take a look at the vitreous grasslands. They're the great unknown, the ultimate Tyrian wilderness."

The urgent phase of the chorus faded soon enough, although it never dissolved into silence. Almost as soon as the stars came out in force the boat bumped something, and then bumped it again. The impacts were slight but distinctly tangible. Matthew's first thought was that they were nudging dangerous underwater rocks, but it only required a glance to inform him that the river was easily wide enough to allow the AI to steer a course through any such hazard. Whatever was bumping *Voconia* was moving under its own power to create the collisions, and it had to be at least as big as a human, if not bigger.

"We need a picture," Ike was quick to say. "I'll feed the AI's visuals through to the big screen."

Matthew and the two women returned immediately to the cabin, but the results were disappointing. There were no more bumps, and the recorded images were worthless. The AI had the means to compensate for near-darkness, but not for the turbidity of the water. They could see that *something* had thumped the boat repeatedly, but whether it was merely a big eel-analogue or something less familiar remained frustratingly unclear.

"Here be mermaids," Matthew murmured.

"Or maybe manatees," Dulcie said, drily. "*Genuine* exotics."

Matthew knew what she meant. Manatees had been extinct before he was born, along with Steller's sea cow and the dugong, and their DNA was unbanked. Humans would never see their like again—but mermaids, being safely imaginary, would always be present in the chimerical imagination. On the other hand, this was Tyre, where chimerization was built into the picture at the most fundamental level, even though the vast majority of individuals didn't seem to be exhibiting it at the moment of their observation. If there were mermaids anywhere, this was the kind of place in which one might expect to find them.

"It was big," Ike reported. "The AI estimates not much less than half a ton. That's *really* big. There's nothing like that around the base. I bet there'll be even bigger ones further downstream, and more of them. We'll catch up with them tomorrow. It's only a matter of time."

"It's about time we found some sizable grazers," Matthew opined. "Dense forests always favor pygmies, but rivers and their floodplains usually have far more elbowroom. There used to be hippos in Earthly rivers and elephants on plains, until people crowded them out. Even if there are humanoids lurking in the long grass of the glass savannah, they surely can't be so numerous that they've driven the big herbivores to extinction. If they were that effective, we'd have found proof of their existence easily enough."

"They couldn't have driven the big herbivores to extinction *recently*," Dulcie put in, by way of correction. "This is an *old* world. What would the biodiversity of Earth have been like a billion years hence, if humans had never invented genetic engineering?"

"It isn't coming back," Lynn observed. "We must have passed through its stamping ground. But there'll be others."

"They can't do us any damage," Ike said. "They won't even wake us up, unless they can stay close enough to start chewing up the biomotor outlets."

"Is that possible?" Matthew asked, suddenly realizing that there might be a downside to *Voconia*'s employment of organic structural materials and an artificial metabolism that used lightly converted local produce as fuel.

"No, it's not," Lynn assured him. "The AI defenses can take care of anything that conspicuous. There's no need for anyone to sit in the stern with Rand's gun."

Matthew, knowing that big grazers usually congregated in herds, was not entirely convinced by this reassurance, but he was prepared to let it go for the time being. There might well be bigger animals in the lower part of the watercourse, where its progress became ever more leisurely as it meandered patiently toward the distant ocean, but *Voconia* was not bound for the sea. Her first mooring would be in the more active waters immediately below the cataract, and it would be from there that their first expedition inland would be mounted. Given that the "grasslands" grew so tall as to be virtual forests, they would be more likely to be inhabited by pygmies than giants—always provided, of course, that the logic that pertained on Earth was reproducible here.

The evening meal's main course was a surprisingly accurate imitation of Earthly ravioli. Matthew wondered at first whether his IT had responded to his earlier dislike to filter out some of the less pleasant taste sensations from the Tyrian manna, but he decided on closer examination that his positive reaction was partly a matter of gradual acclimatization and partly a matter of the skill with which the programmer—Dulcie—had concocted a masking sauce.

"Congratulations," he said to her, when they were done. "I think you've cracked the problem. What this colony needs more than anything else, at this stage of its history, is a Brillat-Savarin. At the end of the day, there's nothing like a pleasant taste to create a sense of welcome. *Hope* could do with a good chef or two— soon put an end to all that revolutionary nonsense."

"I'm an anthropologist," she reminded him. "Cooking is the foundation stone of all human culture, the first of the two primary biotechnologies. Unfortunately, that might be exactly why my talents will be wasted if we do make contact with intelligent aborigines. Whatever the fundamental pillars supporting *their* cultures are, they can't include cooking. Clothing maybe, but not cooking."

"I'd have thought that the probable absence of sex was a far more radical alienation," Lynn Gwyer put in, trying to turn the joke into something more serious. "People get a little carried away with this primary biotechnology stuff, in my opinion. The real foundations of human society lie in parental strategies for the care and protection of children. Families, marriage ceremonies, incest taboos: the whole business of the determination and regulation of sexual relationships. Take away that—as we may have to—and the fact that they don't *cook* begins to seem utterly trivial."

Matthew expected Dulcie to dismiss the objection with a gentle reminder that she had not been serious, but that wasn't what happened. Instead, Dulcie said, with sudden deadly earnest: "You're wrong, Lynn. That's nature, not culture. All animals regulate their sexual relationships according to their sociobiology, and that kind of regulation is mostly hardwired. What culture adds to it is ritual dressing, and all ritual is based in primal technology. In humans, culture takes over from nature at the Promethean moment when fire ceases to be a natural phenomenon and comes under technical and cultural control."

If anything, the anthropologist's intensity increased as she continued: "Matthew's right—probably righter than he imagines. What we need before we can feel at home here is better cooks, and it might well prove that the best route to a recovery of the crew's loyalty to the mission is through their stomachs. And what we'll probably need if we're ever to make common cause with the humanoids, if they exist, is a way to sit down with them, and break bread together, and share the delights of fire. At the end of the day, no matter how you ritualize it, sex divides, because that's its nature. Cooking unites, because cooking makes relationships *palatable*. Sex couldn't be the basis of human society, because it was the chief problem society had to overcome. The strategies of that problem's solution had to begin elsewhere: in the primal biotechnologies and the rituals they facilitated."

Lynn was taken aback momentarily, but she was quick to smile. "Fifty-eight light-years and seven centuries," she said, amiably, "and it's still the same old thing. Nature versus nurture, biologists versus human scientists. Makes you feel quite at home, doesn't it? And isn't that what we all want? To feel at home here."

"If we can," Ike reminded her. "Home is where, when you go there, they have to let you in—but there'll always be places where they simply won't, no matter how hard you try. The universe might be full of them. We just don't know."

"True," Matthew said. "But at least it's us who get to knock on the door and find out. Who among us would prefer to leave the job to someone else?"

He was glad to see that none of his companions was prepared to raise her—or even his—hand in response to that invitation.

THIRTY

The cliff beside the cataract was more than thirty meters high. On the left bank, where *Voconia*'s motley crew had moored the boat fifty meters short of the falls, the cliff was sheer, falling away no more than a couple of degrees from the vertical. When he first stepped back onto solid ground, however, the configuration of the cliff was the least of Matthew's concerns. He wanted to look out over the mysterious signal-blocking canopy of the "glasslands": at the densely packed grasslike structures whose seemingly anomalous dimensions would reduce him yet again to the imaginary status of an elfin spider-rider adrift in a microcosmic wonderland.

From the cliff's edge, alas, it was impossible to see much more than he had already seen in mute pictures collected by flying eyes. He was too high up, as yet, to be anything other than a remote observer, from whose vantage the canopy proper resembled a vast petrified ocean, littered with all manner of strange flotsam. Its true extent was undoubtedly awesome, but the Tyrian horizon seemed no less and no more distant than an Earthly horizon, and the restriction of his vision by that natural range seemed rather niggardly. The real revelation would not come, he knew, until he was down there, looking up at the canopy from within; that was the sight that *Hope*'s insectile flying eyes had so far been unable to capture. He was pleased to see that the fringe vegetation rimming the river and the fault extended for no more than fifty yards before mingling with the "grasses" and no more than a hundred before giving way entirely to the seeming monoculture.

The other side of the river looked more user-friendly to Matthew than the one on which they had stopped, because it had a slope so gentle that he could imagine himself stumbling down it, even with an injured right arm. If they had moored on that side, though, they would have had to carry the dismantled boat and all its cargo by hand, making trip after trip after trip. On the left bank there was plenty of space to erect a winch, from which a generous basket could be lowered on a cable to arrive on a relatively flat apron of rock beside the capacious pool into which the waters of the river tumbled.

"It's not much of a target," Matthew complained to Lynn Gwyer. "The water might look fairly placid on top, but that's an illusion. The edge will be too close for comfort once you start unloading, let alone when the time comes to start putting Humpty-*Voconia* together again. The bushes down there might look unintimidating by comparison with the giant grasses but they'll be a lot tougher at close range than they look—and the empire of the giant grasses begins less than thirty strides away. From up here the whole thing looks like a calm ocean, rippling gently in a benign wind, but it'll look very different at close range, once we're under the canopy."

"It'll be okay," Lynn assured him. "The target's small enough, admittedly, but the laden basket won't swing much, and we'll use the chain saws to clear a much bigger working space. Even if they're the kind of bushes that the humanoids used to make tools from, the saw blades will cut through them easily enough, shattering anything that won't shear. It'll be a fair amount of work for a party of three, but we've got all day. You wouldn't have been able to do as much as the rest of us anyway, even if you hadn't hurt your arm. You're not fully acclimatized yet."

"If I had been," Matthew muttered, "I might not have dislocated my shoulder in the first place."

There was, as Lynn had observed, a *lot* of work for a party of three. Matthew did his utmost to make himself useful, and bitterly regretted it when it became painfully obvious that he was neither as strong nor as skilful as the least of his three companions. He quickly became tired, and his arm would have been agonized if his IT had not muffled the pain—but the IT was too dutiful to allow him to do further damage by insulating him from the consequences of reckless action, so it began to let the distress signals through as soon as the damaged tendons and ligaments provided it with evidence of further strain. Long before midday, therefore, Matthew was relegated to the humblest task available: working the electric motor that controlled the winch. Ike, Lynn, and Dulcie did the lion's share of the unloading, then carried the bulk of the cargo to the cliff's edge. Ike was the one delegated to establish a more generous bridgehead down below while Dulcie and Lynn—who knew exactly what they were doing—set about the delicate work of taking the boat itself to pieces.

"Do you want the gun?" Matthew said to Ike, when the genomicist got into the basket to make his first descent. "We don't know what might be lurking in those bushes."

"Well, if it's anything that can stand up to a chain saw it'll be big enough for you to shoot it from way up here," Ike said. "Anyway, we don't know what might be lurking in the bushes up here on the plateau—there's no reason to think that the gun's more likely to be needed down there than up here." Ike had already donned heavy boots and protective armor, and he seemed to feel that he was well-nigh invulnerable.

Matthew stopped worrying when Ike started up the chain saw and got to work on the bushes. The saw made such a racket, and cut with such devastating effect, that any sensible creature would have taken off in the opposite direction as fast as it could run or slither. The storage space grew with astonishing rapidity, although the contrast between the bare gray rock and the purple-littered ground beyond remained as sharp as ever to the naked eye. If the bushes did have vitreous trunks and branches they shattered easily enough, and no needlelike shards shot like darts into Ike's flesh. His booted feet trampled the foliage down with mechanical efficiency as he marched stolidly into the territory he had claimed. Various globular fruits were rushed along with the "leaves."

As the boat slowly came apart Matthew insisted on shuttling back and forth across the fifty-meter safety margin, adding what he could to the various stacks of goods queued up by the basket, but his earlier efforts had taken their toll and he was glad to take control of the winch again once Ike signaled that he was ready to begin taking delivery of more cargo.

The manna-supplies were the last to go down before the parts of the actual boat, and it was not until then that the first accident occurred. Inevitably, it was Matthew who made the mistake, his out-of-tune reflexes and his injured arm combining to make him drop one of the heaviest boxes before he could get it into the basket. It fell in such a way that it bounced toward the edge of the cliff.

For one tantalizing moment it looked as if the box might

come to a halt at the edge, but it had gathered too much momentum. To make matters worse the packaging split at the last point of impact, and the manna began to spill out as soon as the carton began its precipitate descent.

Mercifully, Ike was too far away from the edge to be at any risk—but he stood and watched with annoyance and wonder as the powdered manna became a cataract in its own right, expanding like a cloud of spray. Almost all of it landed on the carpet of crushed vegetation, dusting the purple pulp like icing on a party cake.

"It's okay," Lynn was quick to say. "It was only a box of biomotor-food. The converter churns out that stuff a great deal faster than produce for human consumption, and Ike's amassed a far bigger heap of litter down there than any we ever built up in the ruins. Once we've got the rest of the stuff down I'll unpack the converter and start bundling the stuff into the hopper. Boatfood's the least of our worries right now. It would have been a hell of a lot worse if you'd dropped part of the rudder, or the AI's brain."

"I know," Matthew retorted, bitterly. "I'm trying to stick to the least important items for exactly that reason. There's an awful indignity, you know, in setting out on a pioneering voyage on a virgin world, with the possibility of meeting all manner of spectacular monsters, then rendering oneself entirely useless by *falling out of bed.*"

"It's your mind we need, not your muscles," she assured him—but Matthew was well aware that her muscles were working heroically in association with her mind, and that he would not have the slightest idea how to reassemble the boat again if that responsibility were his.

Dulcie was working even harder, with quasi-mechanical concentration and purpose. She had hardly said a word for hours, and seemed to have adapted to the requirements of long, hard labor by retreating into herself.

Matthew had no alternative but to take up his station by the lift's control button yet again, pretending as hard as he could that there was a valuable dexterity involved in controlling the descent of the basket and guiding it to a soft landing. An AI could probably have done the job far better, but a winch was far too primitive a machine to warrant the addition of any supervising brain but a human's.

When the disassembly process was complete, Lynn announced that she had better join Ike down below, because there would be more work to be done there from now on.

"Do you want to take the gun?" Matthew asked, for a second time, as she carefully put her armor on.

"It's okay," she assured him, grimacing slightly as she forced her feet into smart boots that were still rather unyielding, having never been properly worn in. "I'll have to break out the second chain saw, so that I can clear a second platform further downriver for the reassembly. As Ike says, anything brave enough to take *that* on will have to be big enough to make an easy target, even for a one-armed man shooting wrong-handed. If the worst comes to the worst, pass the gun to Dulcie. She's good at everything."

Dulcie did, indeed, seem to be good at everything. Having finished the skilled work she was now back to hard labor, moving the last sections of their craft into the queue for the basket, stacking them with the utmost care in such a way that the basket could be filled quickly and safely. He was impressed by the way she plugged on so relentlessly, long after Lynn had started up the second chain saw in order to begin the second stage of the clearance. He was normally content to be left alone with his thoughts, but he felt snubbed when she responded rather shortly to his various attempts to make conversation.

He wondered, vaguely, whether she was really the kind of person who became deeply absorbed in her work, impatient of distractions, or whether she was quietly inclined to put on a show. He recalled the first picture he had seen, in which she had stubbornly continued to display the battle scars she had earned in the plague war: a calculated affront to the beautiful people who formed the great majorities of the fully developed nations. He decided in the end that she was by no means innocent of showmanship, but that it was *sincere* showmanship, deeply felt as well as deeply meant. It was the same judgment he would have passed on himself, and he could not resist a burst of fellow feeling in spite of what he had guessed.

In any case, there was always the infinite canopy to distract him, its multitudinous globular fruits seeming more like the rations of Tantalus with every hour that sped by. Soon, he knew, he would be able to take his own turn in the basket, descending with majestic grace to that part of Tyre that would be as new to his companions as it was to him. Even so, Matthew felt a distinct surge of relief when Dulcie was finally forced to pause while he steered the final load to a soft landing. By now, he had become a master of such elementary skills as this involved, and he was able to absorb himself in the minutiae of the load's carefully measured fall.

When he looked up again, with a sense of satisfaction at having done the job well, Dulcie was not where he expected her to be. She was, instead, at the very lip of the chasm, standing on a spur of rock beside the water's hectic edge. The spur projected out over the smooth-washed rocks below; it was the most precarious position available.

She seemed to be drinking in the view. Having already passed leisurely judgment on its spectacular qualities, Matthew certainly could not begrudge her the moment's pause, and his first impulse was to follow the direction of her gaze and employ *verstehen* in a conscientious attempt to see it as she was seeing it.

She was, of course, well-used to the views from the crests of the hills surrounding the dead city—but those surrounding slopes had all been gentle, their undulations seeming halfhearted and indolent, and there had been so many of them that none could seem out of the ordinary. There had been slopes everywhere, cutting and confusing lines of vision in every direction. Distant horizons must have been visible, but they were always fragmentary; even when the occasional pinnacle of rock provided some relief from the blurred purple curves, it tended to be framed by nearer objects that robbed it of all grandeur. This landscape was conspicuously different. The plateau's edge extended for kilometer after kilometer in either direction. Its neatness was interrupted here and there by arbitrary landslips and curtains of purple climbers, but the basic line was clear enough, and its convex curvature was too gentle to provide a disappointing cutoff point for a roaming eye. As for the oceanic canopy beyond, it stretched into the distance with a truly majestic sweep, extending to a horizon that was flat and sharp even on a day that was somewhat less bright than its immediate predecessors.

Matthew watched her as she lowered her eyes. Immediately

below the plateau's edge there was the ragged hem of transitional vegetation, which varied in extent from twenty to sixty meters, but he knew that it gave way soon enough to the paradoxical "savannah": the empire of the grass-analogues that were taller and far more imperious than grass-analogues had any right to be. The structures were all alike at first glance, but even the untrained eye of an anthropologist would probably find it easy enough to pick out a dozen or so variants. Not all anthropologists would have sufficient critical spirit to challenge the crewman who had hung the "grassland" label on the territory, but Matthew was sure that Dulcie had. She would already be beginning to wonder what functions the elaborate crowns performed, given that they could not be seed heads akin to Earthly grasses of Earth. Perhaps she had heard Bernal Delgado talk about the mystery at some length, casually throwing around speculations about sophisticated sporulation mechanisms and gradual chimerical renewal in the plant kingdom. Perhaps she was taking note, as Matthew had, of the fact that the contributors to the oceanic canopy gave the impression of being collaborators rather than competitors, like members of a contentedly multicultural crowd whose collective identity casually overwhelmed the idiosyncrasies of its individual members.

There, if anywhere, she must be thinking, the descendants of the city-dwellers must be. But what kind of social life could they eke out beneath that enigmatic canopy?

Humans, as every anthropologist knew, were products of Earth's African savannah. The crucial alliance of clever hands, keen eyes, and capacious brains had been forged by a selective regime of terrain where it paid to be tall, to hunt by day, and to develop tools for the primary biotechnologies of cooking and clothing. But none of that pertained to *this* mock-savannah or to *these* humanoids. The "grasses" hereabouts were far too tall to allow bipedal mammal-equivalents to peer over them. Even by day the world beneath the purple canopy would be dim, and even if the hunting were not poor, what scope could there possibly be for brain-building primary technologies? If there were no fires in the depths of that purple sea, how could there be people? How could the uncaring forces of natural selection ever have molded anything resembling people from its lumpen animal clay?

Matthew was on the brink of losing himself in such thoughts

when *verstehen* brought him suddenly back to earth, telling him—with some urgency—that something was *wrong* with Dulcie Gherardesca's posture.

It was not her stillness or her self-absorption that struck a warning note in his mind—she had been self-absorbed and seemingly tranquil all day—but a kind of tension that seemed to be building, little by little and not without resistance: a kind of resolve that was forming, little by little, and not untainted by doubt.

The warning note triggered a conviction, and the conviction a sudden determination.

"I'd really rather you didn't," he said, trying to keep his voice *very* steady.

She heard him, and knew that he could only be speaking to her, but she didn't turn around. For four long seconds it looked as if she might not deign to reply. Then she did, but still without turning to face him.

"Didn't what?" she said.

He dared not heave a sigh of relief, even though he knew that the battle was half-won as soon as she consented to enter into a dialogue.

"Didn't jump," he offered, by way of unnecessary clarification. He knew that she had understood exactly what he meant. What he didn't know was what to say next, although he knew that he had to say *something*, and make it good.

"You know," he went on, after the slightest pause, "this is one of those embarrassing moments when nothing comes to mind by way of advice or reassurance but hollow clichés. I hope you'll forgive me for sounding so utterly selfish, but the one reason that springs forth more rapidly than any other is that we really do need you. In fact, we can't do without you. So even if the reasons for self-destruction were compelling, on a purely introspective basis, I really, *really* would rather you didn't. Especially not now."

"You don't really need me," she told him, bleakly. "There's nothing down there, you know. Nothing useful, nothing enlightening. No answers."

"We don't know that," Matthew was quick to say, having no difficulty at all in sounding sincere. "We haven't the slightest idea what answers we might find down there, to what questions. That's the whole point: it's the great unknown. Even in your situation, I couldn't even entertain the thought of coming this far and not going on."

She didn't have to ask what he meant by "your situation." "Did Solari tell you when you had your little private conference?" she asked.

"No," he said, "I guessed when I saw you with the artifacts. I knew that Vince wouldn't have let you take material evidence away unless there was a quid pro quo. You couldn't have confessed in so many words, of course, but I knew you must have given him to understand that you'd turn yourself in when you got back. So I know that you don't mean it when you say there's nothing down there. There's *everything* down there."

It wasn't working, but he had to carry on. "I can't believe you came here with the intention of not going back," he said. "The expedition into the interior may be all that's left to you, but *is* still on, still beckoning. You mustn't let a stray moment of doubt and despair get in the way. Please."

"Do the others know?" she asked.

"Maybe," Matthew said. "If they've guessed, they're keeping it to themselves, just as I was. If they only suspect the truth, they're in no hurry to exchange suspicion for certainty. Bernal expected to find something down there, didn't he? Maybe not humanoids, but something worthwhile. Serial killer anemones. NV correlated with ER. Something to tip us off as to why this world is at one and the same time so seemingly simple and so obviously weird. We really don't know what might be down there—and it's certainly far too soon to despair of making progress when we haven't even stepped across the threshold."

Dulcie didn't turn around, and Matthew could see that her attitude was still all wrong. That line of argument was too familiar to cut through the Gordian knot of her confusion; he needed something that could catch her attention more securely: something that could draw her out of her neurotic self-absorption; something that could surprise her. It had to be true, though. Surprise was no good in itself, and no good at all unless he could startle her with *the truth*—or something that could pass for the truth.

Unfortunately, he couldn't think of anything that was sure to do the trick. He was tired, and his arm hurt worse than any IT-equipped man ever expected any part of him to hurt, and he had already said most of what there was to be said about the stubborn mysteries of Tyre, alias Ararat, alias humankind's New World.

He had to get *inside* her skin. He had to break into the dark bubble where she had confined herself and condemned herself to death.

"You loved him," he said, as soon as the notion popped into his head. It arrived as if from nowhere, but he knew that wasn't the case. Ever since he had guessed that Dulcie had killed Bernal he had been asking the question why, even if he had found the puzzle too uncomfortable to expose it to the full glare of consciousness. He had been working on it while be was asleep, and while he was spaced out, without even allowing himself to realize the fact. And he had solved it. He *knew* the answer. *Verstehen* was delivering it up to him even as he spoke. The guess spun like a hectic top, drawing a thread of certainty tightly about itself. It was the only story that made sense, even if it could not have made sense of anyone else but Dulcie Gherardesca.

"What's that supposed to mean?" she parried, not yet surprised enough.

"You were part of the same intake," Matthew remembered. "You were frozen down at the same time as Bernal. You were with him—on the moon, if not at the spaceport. And *after* the moon, when you had to take the next outward jump. You were together. Both apprehensive. Both scared you might not be doing the right thing. Both scared, period. You were together." He went on with increasing fluency, congratulating himself as he went on having rediscovered his improvisatory skills at last, wishing that there could have been a camera running to record the triumph of his genius. "But you're wrong about what happened afterward, Dulcie. I understand how and why you made the mistake, but you're *wrong*. Trust me, Dulcie, *I knew him*. I know what you think and why you think it, but *you're wrong*. I don't just mean that you were wrong when you killed him, I mean you're wrong *now*. What you think, what's eating you up, what you can't live with . . . it *isn't* what you think. *I knew him*, Dulcie. You have to let me explain it to you."

That was when she turned around, and he knew that he'd won half of the half-battle that still remained to be won.

"You *don't* know," she spat at him. "Do you think I'm stupid?

I understand that it wasn't his fault that he *forgot*. I understand that it was just a side effect of the SusAn. Do you think I'm so stupid that I don't know *that?*"

"That's not what I mean," Matthew shot back, lightning-fast. "That's not what I mean at all. I really can see the whole picture. You and Bernal were together before you were frozen down. You were in love. When you were brought out again, *separately*, he was affected by the memory loss but you weren't. You understood. I *know* you understood. And when you came here, he was with Lynn, and you understood that too. And then he was with Mary, and you understood that too. But what you *didn't* understand was what it signified, what it meant that even when you were here, day after day and night after night, working with him side-by-side, he didn't fall in love with you all over again.

"You thought it meant that he hadn't been serious, couldn't have been serious, that he was just filling in time, that it was just because you were there, available, when nobody else was. You thought it meant that he could never *really* have been interested in someone like you, that he had never really looked *behind the scars*. You could have forgiven him for forgetting, because that wasn't his fault, but you couldn't forgive him for not being able to do it all over again from scratch, for not being able to duplicate the same emotional chain from the square one of innocence. That's why the rage built up—and that's why the rage came out, in one careless, unaimed thrust of pure frustration that somehow found its way between his ribs and into his heart.

"I *understand*, Dulcie. I really do. But you're wrong. You're wrong about Bernal. You're wrong about it not being serious, about it just filling in time, about it just being a matter of availability, of scratching an itch. *He wasn't like that.* I knew him, Dulcie. I knew him as well as any man alive. He was *always* serious. He loved them all, Dulcie. Every last one. He couldn't help himself. He was utterly and absolutely sincere. It never lasted long, but while it did, he was head over heels. He meant it, Dulcie. Whatever he said to you, he meant it all. He was an honest man. In that, and other things as well, he was totally and incorrigibly honest.

"The problem wasn't that he forgot too much, but that he didn't forget enough. At some level, he knew. He couldn't bring it to the level of consciousness, but something in him knew. If he really had been back to square one, utterly innocent of any sense of having known you before, then he could and would have fallen again, head over heels. He did love you, Dulcie. He loved you as powerfully as he ever loved anyone, and as briefly. You have to believe me, Dulcie. I knew him. I'm the only one who did. I'm the only one who understands.

"I don't know you at all, but I know how the people on *Hope*—Nita Brownell included—reacted when I lashed out and injured a man, and I think I can understand well enough how you felt when you realized that you'd lashed out, like exactly the kind of barbarian the crewpeople think we are and we're so very desperate to think we're not. And I know it wasn't as mad or bad as it seemed, because I'm beginning to understand how the situation with the crew and the strangeness of the world are messing with our heads in spite of our IT. So *yes*, I *do* understand, well enough to know that it was an accountable accident, and that you have to forgive yourself, not just because we really *do* need you, but because it's the right thing to do. If Bernal were here, he'd say exactly the same thing. Believe me, *I know*."

Finally, inevitably, Matthew ran out of breath. But he hadn't lost his audience. The fish was well and truly hooked.

Matthew had no idea whether he was telling the whole truth or not. He had known Bernal Delgado, and the way he'd just represented and explained him was exactly the way that Bernal Delgado would have represented and explained himself—but how well, Matthew wondered, does any human being ever know any other? And how well, in the final analysis, does any human being ever know himself—or herself?

The point was that it was believable. On this occasion, in these circumstances, it could pass for the truth, the whole truth and nothing but the truth.

It was reason enough for Dulcie Gherardesca to step away from the edge of the precipice, and step away she did—but before she stepped away, she looked down.

After that, there was no possibility whatsoever of her jumping.

Anything she might have said would have sounded incongruous on her lips, but it was Matthew, when his gaze followed the direction of her pointing finger, who spoke.

"Oh *fuck!*" he said, with all the feeling he had left.

THIRTY ONE

T he two chain saws were already roaring into life again, but it was obvious that they weren't going to be much use. Matthew was already scrambling for the rifle too, but it was equally obvious that the gun wouldn't be much use either.

If Ike and Lynn hadn't been so absorbed in the early stages of the 3-D jigsaw that was *Voconia* they'd have noticed the problem much sooner. If Matthew and Dulcie hadn't been so absorbed in the question of whether Dulcie was going to hurl herself off the cliff to her death they might have noticed it instead—but on Tyre, everything was purple, and if Matthew hadn't managed to spill an oversized carton of snow-white boat-food the extent of the problem might not have been obvious to observers on the clifftop even now.

From Matthew's vantage point the newcomers looked like giant leeches, but that was a reflection of the way they moved rather than an insult to their lifestyle. They were long, flat, dark-hued worms, each half a meter to two meters long, and there were hundreds of them. So far, at least, there were hundreds of them. They were still coming, oozing avidly out of the uncrushed undergrowth like slimline slugs on amphetamine.

Were they dangerous? Ike and Lynn obviously hadn't been sure at first. When they started the chain saws the first poses they took were defensive. They waited, unwilling to start cutting up the worms unless and until it seemed necessary. When the vanguard reached their legs, however, and began to curl around and climb them, they decided that it was definitely necessary. Matthew would have come to exactly the same conclusion at exactly the same moment.

The worms weren't hard to cut. Indeed, they seemed to be absurdly easy to slice and shred. But there were hundreds of them already, and more were coming.

Matthew was momentarily astonished by the floods of red that fountained from the severed worms, although he had known perfectly well that Tyre's animal-analogues had a hemoglobin-analogue in their blood-analogue. The red mingled with the pulpy purple backcloth soon enough, though, dissolving into it and subtly altering its shade. It held its redness only where it spattered Ike's and Lynn's additional armor, whose ground color was an ochreous yellow. There the lavishly spilled blood mingled with a light patina of manna-dust, making a dull pink. Had they only been wearing their surface suits the supersmart fibers would already have absorbed the boatfood, and would have made an immediate start on the blood, but the armor was stupid. The red-and-pink splashes stood out like garish items of abstract art.

Matthew didn't raise the rifle to his shoulder. There was nothing to shoot at but leech soup, and he knew that shooting soup was a fool's game. He kept the gun in his free hand, though, as he yanked the basket onto the ledge and held it there for Dulcie Gherardesca.

She didn't hesitate. Like him, she had no clear idea of what they could do once they got to the bottom, but they knew that they had to help. When she was safely in he had to pass her the gun in order to launch the basket over the edge, or he would not have been able to step into it himself, but he kept hold of the control box that signaled to its motor. As soon as he was safely inside and the basket had swung clear of the cliff's edge, he thumbed the button on the control box, and the descent began.

The basket was still swinging, and its soft fabric felt far less reassuring than Matthew could have wished, but he had watched enough loads go down to know that he and Dulcie were not nearly heavy enough to test its strength.

Meanwhile, Ike and Lynn were managing to stay free of climbing worms, even though the total number of visible worms was still increasing. The various heaps of unshipped cargo and disassembled boat were not as fortunate; they had been overrun. There were too many piles of boxes and equipment, and the piles were too awkwardly spaced, for two humans with chain saws to stand much chance of defending them.

It was not yet obvious that the worms posed any danger at all to people, or to the tough fabric of the boat's hull, but the avidity of the flood was unmistakable, and Matthew could not doubt that they were bent on consuming *something*.

Nor was that any longer the whole of the rapidly developing problem; before the basket was halfway through its descent he saw the first of the larger creatures following in the wake of the worms. There were "killer anemones" among them—large ones, though none so large as to qualify as super killer anemones by his yardstick—but there were other animal-analogues too: froglike forms and things that might have passed for monkey-analogues had they not been scaly and rubber-limbed. For days they had been trying without success to catch more than a glimpse of creatures like these, and now they were being subjected to a veritable plague of them.

Matthew wondered, briefly, if the chain saws were actually making things worse, by bringing about such a rapid increase in the supply of ready-chopped foodstuffs. It seemed only too plausible—but the thought had not yet occurred to Lynn or Ike.

There was now something to shoot at, if the rifle could only be aimed properly—but Dulcie Gherardesca still held it, and she had not yet attempted to aim it. The basket was still swaying, and she probably would not have been able to shoot straight enough to guarantee that she would not hit Lynn or Ike, who were now moving apart, swinging their chain saws as they went.

Then the cable jammed, and the basket's descent was abruptly halted.

Dulcie managed to keep hold of the gun, and Matthew managed to keep hold of the control box, but they both had considerable difficulty keeping their feet, and would certainly have fallen had the basket's elastic sides not bulked so high about them.

Matthew immediately began pumping the control button with his thumb. The groaning of the motor told him that the machine was trying hard to obey the signal, but it was a stupid machine without any robotic ingenuity at all. The basket only moved from side to side, turning about its axis as it swung.

Lynn Gwyer's chain saw ran out of fuel and died.

Any hope that this might have been a good thing vanished within an instant. She was already surrounded by a living carpet. While she was still on the move with the saw going full blast the worms had made little attempt to swarm up her ankles and calves, and the newcomers had seemed far more interested in the liberally shed blood of the worms than in her, but there was nothing to intimidate them now. The confusion seething around her was so utter and so awful that Matthew could not blame her in the least for what she did next.

She was less than five meters from what seemed to be a calm refuge, almost perfectly placid and apparently clear. Once she had dropped the chain saw it only required four long leaping strides to carry her to the river's bank, and a headlong dive to carry her over.

She met the water gracefully enough, her arms extended before her.

She must have known that there would be an undertow, because she knew perfectly well that the water cascading over the edge of the plateau was flowing away as quickly as it arrived. Panicked as she was, she had presumably factored that into her calculations, and she must have expected to be carried away by the current. She knew that the greatest danger was becoming entangled close to the shore, so she struck out for the open water even as she disappeared beneath the surface. When her head popped up again, she was thirty meters downstream and ten meters away from the bank—and she was content, for the moment, to go with the flow. She did not want to strike back toward the bank until she had put a hundred meters or more between her intended landfall and the crawling mass that had overwhelmed the expedition's possessions.

The motor propelling Ikram Mohammed's chain saw sputtered and died a moment later, but he was further away from the bank and more determined to protect *Voconia*'s cargo. He continued using the saw, not so much as a weapon of mass destruction as a spade or a scoop, trying to clear the creatures away without doing overmuch damage. He knew that he had to stay clear of stinging tentacles and avid mouths, but he obviously thought that he could do it. He was, after all, much stronger and nimbler than any individual in the crowd he was fighting to deter.

Matthew continued to pump the useless button, but whatever had got into the cable mechanism was wedged good and hard, and the cable could not slide past it. He felt doubly helpless, because he could not see what difference the two of them could make even if the basket were to complete its descent. Shooting might help to clear away the bigger and more responsive creatures, as much by noise as by bloodshed, but the elongated slugs were everywhere now, and he could not imagine that *their* tide could be turned with a few loud bangs.

Dulcie thrust the rifle into his hands, briefly tapping the fingers that were clutching the control.

"What. . . . ?" he objected

"I'm going to dive," she told him. "But first we have to increase the amplitude of the swing. We have to get the turning point far enough out over the water. You have to help me."

Matthew's first instinct was to protest, but he knew that there was no point in staying where they were. Lynn was still visible in the water, seemingly unhurt and swimming freely, despite having to fight the current. If Dulcie could dive into the deep pool at the foot of the waterfall she would have a great deal of turbulence to contend with, but a strong swimmer ought to be able to cope.

Matthew knew, on the other hand, that a man with an injured arm could not be expected to succeed in such a venture, no matter how good a swimmer he was when fully fit.

"Help me!" Dulcie demanded, as she grasped the cable and began to use her body to exaggerate the basket's pendular swing.

"Oh shit!" said Matthew—but he dropped the gun and the control box into the bottom of the basket, and gripped the cable with his good hand, forcing himself to complement the insistent movements of the anthropologist's body.

It was surprisingly easy to increase the amplitude of the basket's swing, and it only required a couple of minutes to extend the far point into the spray of the falls. The pressure of the water immediately began to confuse their efforts, but Dulcie let go then and grasped the edge of the basket, ready to hurl herself over on the next pass.

Matthew was tempted to call her crazy, but hardly any time seemed to have passed since she had stood on the ledge and thought seriously about casting herself down on to the rocks. This time, she was aiming for the water; to call the effort suicidal would have been a ludicrous insult.

She jumped.

Given her starting position, there was no way that Dulcie could contrive a dive as neat as Lynn's, and she didn't even try to adjust her attitude as she fell, preferring to cartwheel her legs as if she were trying to run in midair. She was, indeed, attempting to gain a little extra distance, to make sure that she fell into the calmest and deepest water she could possibly reach.

Droplets from the almighty splash she made would probably

have dashed against Matthew's face had the movement of the basket not become so wild. He ducked down and did what he could to protect his injured arm as it threatened to dash him against the rock face. He sat on the control box, and his coccyx managed to do what his thumb had not. The cable groaned as the basket tried to spin, and suddenly jerked free—but only for a moment. It only dropped him two or three meters before it was snagged again.

When he came back to his feet Matthew saw Dulcie's head in the water, well clear of the cataract, and saw that she was as safe as could be expected. He could no longer see Lynn Gwyer, but that was presumably because she had attained the purple shore and was even now pulling herself back on to dry land.

Ike was still standing, still using the dead chain saw as a crude device for sweeping long flat worms and bulkier creatures this way and that, but not making much of a difference to the sum of the confusion. He did not seem to have been stung, as yet.

Now that he was using his weight to quell the swinging of the basket rather than to increase it, Matthew was quite prepared to let it bump against the cliff face, provided that it did so without bruising him. He wanted to steady it sufficiently to let fly with the rifle, not because he thought he had the slightest chance of hitting anything but because he wanted to make use of its deterrent clamor if there was any such use to be made.

He fired one shot into the air, holding the gun in his left hand, but he had grossly underestimated the force of the recoil. For a moment he feared that he had lost effective use of both his arms—but his overstrained IT eliminated the pain and no serious physical damage seemed to have been done.

The sound of the gunshot made very little difference to the confusion below, although the more agile of the second-wave invaders did indeed respond to it, several of them deciding that the game was not worth the candle. Unfortunately, that left the tentacled stingers with no obvious target for their armaments but Ike. He was using the chain saw two-handed now, like a broadsword, but his muscles had almost reached the end of their energy reserves and his strokes were becoming slow and ponderous.

"Give it up, Ike!" Matthew shouted to him. "Take to the water!"

The water still appeared to be safe in spite of the turbulence near the cataract and the undertow further away from it, but Matthew could not think highly of his own chances of diving directly into the pool, let alone swimming strongly enough thereafter to steer him out of trouble. He felt that he had only one option before him, which was to slit the fabric of the basket with his knife, if the blade was sharp enough, to turn it into a dangling blanket from whose trailing edge he could hang—two-handed if he could possibly manage it—and then drop to the ground.

It would still be an uncomfortable drop, even if he could manage the preparatory maneuver, but his bootless feet would be slightly cushioned by the biomass that had accumulated on the rocky apron. It seemed to be the only possible way that he was ever going to get down. But *when* should he attempt it? To do it now seemed dangerously akin to leaping from a frying pan into a fire.

Ikram Mohammed had not taken his advice. Whether it was because he had formed a better idea of the situation or because he didn't think he was a strong enough swimmer, he had decided to go the other way, through the remaining bushes and into the shelter of the grass canopy. By going that way, he had avoided the necessity of dropping the chain saw, and he had even managed to select a route that took him to the particular supply dump that held the fuel necessary to give its motor a new lease of life.

Matthew knew that Ike had got out in one piece when he heard the power tool's roar again, By that time, Dulcie was also out of view, and he felt awkwardly alone.

Down below, the "killer anemones" seemed to be in the process of taking possession of the battlefield, although a few reptile-analogues were still prepared to dispute it. The tentacled slugs were moving back and forth with considerable speed and purpose, apparently mopping up the awful mass of pulverized branches, spilled boatfood and sliced flesh with an appetite that was positively awesome. The stench was appalling. Matthew decided that any plans for further descent ought to be put on hold for quite some time, if not indefinitely. He waited, forcing himself to watch even though the spectacle was so appalling. He chided himself for having lulled himself into the tacit expectation that this seemingly quiet world was incapable of producing events as ferocious and as feverish as this one. He chided himself too for having provided the probable trigger when he carelessly allowed the box of biomotor-fuel to tumble over the edge.

It occurred to Matthew eventually that there was something he could and ought to be doing even while he was stuck in a basket halfway down a cliff. He took his phone from his belt and pressed the button that would send out Dulcie's code signal.

She answered immediately.

"It's Matthew," he said. "The worst seems to be over, but you might be better to stay where you are for a while. The stinging slugs will probably disperse again, but not for quite some time. I'll let you know if it begins to look safe before nightfall."

"I'm with Lynn," Dulcie reported. "She sprained an ankle in the shallows, but we both got out of the water okay. We're only a few hundred meters downstream, but it would probably take us a while to get back in any case. We don't even have a machete to help us through the undergrowth."

Without breaking the connection Matthew signaled Ike and repeated his estimation of the situation.

"I'm okay," Ike assured him, after switching off the chain saw. "I was lucky back there. The stupid way I went about things I should have been stung half-a-dozen times. This is a weird place, and the light's none too good further in, but I'll stay close to the shafts of sunlight so that I don't get lost. I'm sure that I can navigate my way back when I have to, even if it gets dark. I don't know which of us is going to climb the cliff to free up the cable mechanism, Matthew, but it could be a long walk to the nearest spot where an ascent looks feasible. Shall I try while the light lasts?"

"No," Matthew said. "I'm safe here. Don't push your luck too far. If you can, it might be a good idea to link up with Lynn and Dulcie. They could probably do with a little help from the chain saw—and you're right about the light lasting. These short days are getting to be a real pain."

Matthew knew that he ought to report the incident to Tang and Godert Kriefmann, but he decided that it had stopped far enough short of a disaster to make the call urgent. The sun was already hovering above the western horizon, and he wanted to use the last of the light to take a longer look at the nauseating spectacle beneath him, in case there was anything more to be learned from it.

If there was, it wasn't obvious. The tide of leechlike worms that had started the mad race had turned so comprehensively that no living specimen could be seen. Of the other creatures, only the tentacled worms lingered now, seemingly proud of their unchallenged possession of the arena. One by one, their remaining competitors had given up, leaving them to their insistent criss-crossing of the red-augmented purple mess that had pooled around and liberally splashed the bases of the various piles of human imported goods.

The creatures showed no inclination to climb the steeper heaps, and Matthew realized that if Ike and Lynn had leapt on top of the two of the sturdier piles of goods in order to stay out of harm's way, the whole incident might have passed with far less bloodshed and somewhat less fuss. There was no evidence that the first wave of worms had been dangerous; their attempts to climb the legs of their self-appointed adversaries might have been mere instinct, devoid of any aggressive intent. On the other hand, Matthew could sympathize with Lynn's and Ike's desire not to take that chance.

Ike called him back as dusk fell. "It's okay," he reported. "I've got Lynn and Dulcie through the tangled stuff—the ground's clearer out here. I got close enough to one of the dumps to grab a bubble-tent and a couple of flashlights, so we should be safe enough once the fabric's set. If you can bear to spend the night where you are, we ought to be able to get you down in the morning. I'll report our situation to the Base and the ship to save everyone else the embarrassment—Milyukov might be tempted to gloat if it came from you."

"Thanks," Matthew said, knowing that Milyukov wasn't the only one who might derive a certain grim satisfaction from knowing that he was stuck halfway down a cliff, suspended over the scene of a wildlife massacre. He took his phone out of the loop as soon as he'd ascertained that all was as well as could be expected with Lynn and Dulcie.

By the time the twilight had faded, he had reconciled himself to spending the night where he was.

What they had just witnessed, Matthew decided, had to be a feeding frenzy. Something in the lightly converted boatfood had sent out an olfactory signal powerful enough to attract every leechlike worm for kilometers around. The spilled sap and raw flesh of the vegetation cleared by the two chain saws must also have advertised its availability as food. The larger creatures would probably have followed the leechlike worms in any case, either aiming for the same target or for the worms themselves, but the intensity of the second wave must have been further increased when Ike and Lynn continued to deploy the chain saws, adding a rich leavening of worm blood to the irresistible feast they had accidentally laid on.

If the NV in Bernal's final jottings did refer to "nutritional versatility," what he had just seen might qualify as an admittedly extreme example of nutritional versatility. It might be evidence of a remarkable tendency to overreact when an unusually abundant food supply became suddenly available. If so, there must be a natural trigger that corresponded to the one accidentally released by the invaders.

On Earth, feeding frenzies were correlated with the spawning of ocean creatures. Certain reproductive strategies, involving the mass production of young among whom less than one in a thousand could be expected to survive, were associated with rare but avidly anticipated natural banquets. That might add up, if the ER to which Bernal's NV had been speculatively correlated really was "exotic reproduction." There was no evidence, thus far, that any of the new world's versatile animals used mass-production reproductive strategies—but given that there was scant evidence, as yet, of *any* reproductive strategies other than modified binary fission, the possibility had to be considered open.

"Well," Matthew murmured, aloud, "we certainly know how to make a entrance, don't we?"

THIRTY TWO

The basket was not a comfortable place to bed down, but it could have been far worse. It was big enough to allow Matthew to stretch himself out, almost as if he were in a hammock, and he felt reasonably safe. Nor was his arm as troublesome as it might have been, considering the miscellaneous stresses to which he had subjected it. Even so, he could not sleep. The discrepancy between Tyre's twenty-one-and-a-half-hour days and his Earth-trained circadian rhythms had finally caught up with him. He huddled where he was, becoming increasingly miserable, listening to the many sounds of the alien night.

The area in which Ike and Lynn had piled all the expedition's stores and equipment was quieter than the grassland itself—presumably because the silent stinging slugs were still around, acting as a powerful deterrent to the approach of other creatures—but he was close enough to the high canopy to provide an audience for an entire orchestra of fluters, clickers, and whistlers. The sounds were oddly blurred, partly by echoes from the cliff face behind him but also by strange refractory effects within the canopy itself.

He was reluctant to disturb his companions, lest their exertions should have left them direly in need of sleep, but he was considering calling the base, or even the ship, when his own phone beeped. He snatched it up gratefully.

"Sorry to disturb you, Matthew," Lynn Gwyer said, in a low voice. "Ike and Dulcie are asleep but my ankle feels *wrong* in spite of the IT anaesthetic. I figured that your shoulder might be just as bad."

"I can't sleep either," Matthew assured her. "Insufficient exertion, I guess. Is the ankle very bad?"

"Not really, I stepped in a hole while climbing out of the shallows—stupid thing to do, but Dulcie came to help me. It's one of those awkward situations where your IT's programmed to force you to rest up, so it lets the pain through if I try to walk. I'll be okay in a couple of days. Ike and Dulcie will be able to put the boat together, if they get the chance. We really screwed things up, didn't we? Did everything wrong we possibly could."

"It wasn't that bad," Matthew said. "I suppose, with the aid of hindsight, that the first person down should have lit a fire on the bank to deter visitors. Maybe you should have used the flamethrower instead of the chain saws—but how could we know? If you can unpack the flamethrower tomorrow, without getting too close to the killer anemones, you should be able to scare them away in a matter of minutes—or roast them, if they're stubborn."

"They took us by completely by surprise," Lynn lamented. "We should have been on our guard. We knew that the experience we brought down from the hills might be worthless here—but who could have expected anything to happen so soon and so fast? How much stuff has been damaged, do you think? Will we be able to carry on, or do we have to hang about waiting to be rescued?"

"There's not that much damage," Matthew assured her. "As far as I could see, the big worms were only interested in the spilled boatfood, and most of the things that came after them were only interested in them. The stingers are omnivores, but they've got plenty of vegetable matter to gorge themselves on. They won't hurt the boat itself or the equipment."

"I'm sure we made it worse by cutting up the worms and exposing their soft centers," Lynn told him. "Mercifully, there weren't any sharks in the water when I made my dive. I suppose it was only to be expected that the scent of blood would attract all kinds of nasties, but we weren't thinking. We overreacted."

"Nobody else would have done any better," Matthew consoled her. "Some might have done a lot worse. Can you hear the midnight chorus in the bubble, or is the fabric soundproof?"

"It's audible, but muffled," she said. "Will it keep you awake all night, do you think?"

"I hope not. I'll have to try to sleep—tomorrow could be a demanding day."

"Me too," she said. "Better say good night."

The call had made Matthew feel slightly better, but no sleepier. With the folds of the pliable basket gathered about his horizontal frame he was beginning to feel rather claustrophobic, and the rigid extent of the rifle laid alongside his body made it even more difficult for him to find a position that did not put undue pressure on his damaged arm. He knew that his IT would still be working steadfastly on the strained tendons and ligaments, but he had to suppose that the day's dramatics had undone most or all of the work they had done beforehand, and perhaps a little more besides.

After two further Earth-hours of failing to settle Matthew felt so cramped that he had to stand upright for a while. The sky was cloudier than it had been on the two previous nights, but a few stars were visible in the shifting gaps. Somewhat to his surprise, he caught sight of a faint glimmer of light in the grass-forest, just about visible in the gap between the tops of the nearer bushes and the lower reaches of he canopy. His surprise faded into reassurance, though, when he realized that it must be the bubble-tent. Made of smarter fabric than the basket, its opacity was adjustable and its three inhabitants must have decided that keeping a light on was likely to deter more nocturnal creatures than it attracted.

The noise was less intense now; the chorus of moans and whistles was lapsing into a calmer mood. Matthew decided to take that as a good sign. He settled down again, confident at last that he might be able to sleep, but had hardly begun to drift off into a light delirium when his phone sounded again. He snatched it up immediately, stifling the reflexive curse that rose to his lips as his censorious IT let a little pain through to remind him that he ought to be more careful.

"It's Lynn again, Matthew. We just had a visitor. Big, possibly bipedal."

Any annoyance he might have felt evaporated on the instant. What Lynn meant, obviously, was *possibly humanoid*—but she didn't dare tempt fate by saying so.

"How close did it come?" Matthew asked.

"I wouldn't have known it was there if it hadn't come close enough actually to touch the tent—but the reflections from the fabric made it impossible to see more than a shadow. It backed off as soon as I sat up."

"The monkey-analogues are probably inquisitive," Matthew reminded her. But not as curious as humanoids would be, he added, mentally. However badly we messed up our entrance, we certainly broadcast the news that we were here far and wide. If they can be persuaded to come to us, instead of letting us hunt for days on end for spoor and signs. . . .

He stood up again, and looked out in the direction of the glimmer of light he had noticed before. The area beneath him was in deep shadow; there could have been a dozen fascinated tribesmen standing there looking up at him and he would not have known. He cocked an ear, trying hard to detect signs of movement. The continuing chorus from the forest made it difficult to hear anything else, but he was half-convinced that he *did* hear something moving: something too big to be stealthy. It could have been a hopeful illusion, but if not it was something—or several somethings—moving among the stacks of equipment.

After a few minutes more he was almost certain that some of the boxes and pieces of the boat were being moved in a relatively careful fashion. If so, he thought, then *hands* must surely be at work. He was suddenly aware of the fact that his foot was touching Rand Blackstone's rifle, but he made no move to pick it up.

"Just don't steal any essential bits of the boat," he murmured. "Help yourself to all the food you want, and all the tools, glass or metal—but please don't take anything vital." He regretted not having asked Ike to try to throw a flashlight up to him, although he knew that he had been right to judge the risk too great.

He listened dutifully for a few minutes more, waiting for the sounds to die away before reporting back to Lynn. "I can't be *absolutely* sure that it's not my imagination," he said, in a voice tremulous with anticipation and triumph, "but I'm pretty sure that we've just been investigated by an alien intelligence."

"Shall I wake Ike, or try to take a look myself?" Lynn asked.

"No. Stay where you are, as quiet as quiet can be. If they've come to us, the last thing we want is to scare them off. In the morning, we'll know for sure whether they exist or not, and we can make proper plans. Yesterday wasn't such a disaster after all—maybe it was the best possible beacon we could have planted. Now, we have to tread carefully."

"Not the best choice of words," she told him, ruefully.

"We have to wait for morning," he said, as much to himself as to her. "If they've taken anything, we'll know. Then the new ball game begins. Everything changes. Bad arms and ankles notwithstanding, we have to get busy—but we have to do it *right*."

"Will you call the base—or *Hope*?"

"Not yet," he said. "We have to *know*, to be in a position to confound all skeptics, however unreasonable. This has to be handled *right*. Can you stay awake?"

"I doubt that I have the choice," she retorted, drily. "Can you?"

"Same thing. Trying to see in the dark, hear significant sounds against the white-noise background. Probably pointless, but . . . call again if they come back to you."

They left it at that, but when Matthew returned his phone to his belt he found that he was trembling with excitement. *If it is them,* he thought, *they know more about us than we know about them. They could see into the lighted tent. They sorted through our stuff. They may be nervous, but they're bound to keep us under observation. We're the most interesting thing that's happened to them since they decided to give up on civilization, and they must know it. Even if they don't want to make contact now, they'll want to know exactly where we are and where we're going. They won't go far, and they'll be back. All we have to do is wait, and make our plans with due care. Everything else is subsidiary now; this is the spearhead of* Hope's *mission, the determining fact of all our futures. And I'm on the spot, running the show. Destiny needed a prophet, and it picked me. Whatever it needed to get me here, it had to have me. This is it. This is what it was all for: every moment of every one of those forty-eight years. Dulcie was just an innocent part of the apparatus of fate, like Shen Chin Che and the cometary blizzard and the Crash, and fifteen billion years of the prehistory of the universe. It was all leading down to this: to Matthew Fleury's advent in the New World, and his first meeting with the Other Human Race. This is my moment, my winning play, my reason for being. This is the beginning of the New Era.* It was easy to forget, in the circumstances, that he was stuck halfway down a cliff with a worse-than-useless rifle and a nonfunctional control box.

He spent the rest of the night forgetting it, in the cause of making grander plans—and now the twenty-one-and-a-half-hour Tyrian cycle of day and night didn't seem too short at all, but far too long. Eventually, he lay down again and tried to sleep, knowing that he was going to need every atom of intelligence he had to see him through the crises of the next few days, but he couldn't do it. His IT wasn't up to the job; there was too much adrenaline in his system and no matter how hard the nanobots worked they couldn't stop his adrenal cortex producing more and more.

It was a *very* long night—subjectively, the longest in his life. But it came to an end eventually, as all his nights were bound to do. When dawn broke, he was more than ready to greet it. He waited until the light was a little better before he actually struggled to his feet again, but the precaution was unnecessary. The sight that met his eyes would not have disappointed his appetite for startlement no matter how dimly it had been lit.

The first casual sweep of his gaze over the area of devastation told him that the tentacled slugs still had secure tenure over their empire, and they had grown prodigiously during their occupation. He knew, at the back of his mind, that there was a second possibility—that the moderately sizable specimens that had held the terrain when dusk fell had been driven out during the night by more powerful competitors—but he never gave it a moment's serious thought. He had confidence in his guesses now, and he was certain in his own mind that the creatures had grown fat, processing food into flesh with un-Earthly rapidity.

On another occasion he might have been more surprised by the changes that had overtaken the battlefield on which the serial killer anemones' victory had been won, but in his present mood he saw it as an inevitable confirmation of his most recent speculations.

If giant slugs had been making their way back and forth across the scattered debris of a thousand shredded bushes, they too would have left the terrain embalmed in slime, but it could not have been so vitreous, nor so dramatically uneven. It would not have been studded with the upper hemispheres of glass basketballs, or the bubble domes of half-embedded footballs . . . or the pyramidal extrusions of "bipolar spinoid extensions." Had there not been more urgent matters of concern, Matthew would have paused to wonder, but as things were he merely clocked up one more lucky guess to his rapidly escalating score.

He phoned Lynn, thinking that it was he who had news to impart, but he didn't get a chance to speak.

"Matthew," she said. "Thank heaven you're all right. Can you see Ike or Dulcie?"

"No," said Matthew, darting his eyes rapidly from side to side. "Should I be able to?"

"Dulcie's gone, Matthew. If her phone's still working, she's not answering. Ike went off to look for her as soon as he gave up thinking that she must have stepped out to relieve herself."

Ike joined in the conversation almost immediately. "No sign," he said. "She must have been crazy. The worms are still around—

mostly above head height, admittedly, curled around the stalks beneath the seed heads, but too close for comfort if you're wandering in the gloom. It was just after first light when she went, but it's way too dim in here to be wandering around without a flashlight."

"Oh *shit*," Matthew murmured. "I was *so sure* I'd talked her out of it."

"Out of what?" Lynn wanted to know. She and Ike had had too much on their minds to notice Dulcie's awkward pose on the lip of the cliff, or to interpret it correctly if they had.

"She nearly jumped off the cliff yesterday."

"*What?* Why?"

"Guilt." He didn't bother to specify what it was that Dulcie felt guilty about. He knew they'd work it out quickly enough.

"No!" The complaint came from Lynn. "You think she's gone off to have another go?"

"Maybe just to think about it. But she *knows* how much we need her. Hell, she even made that crazy leap into the pool so that she could go after you. You *did* tell her about the night visitor when she woke up."

"Of course I did," Lynn said. "I didn't tell her it was a *humanoid*, because I didn't know, but . . ."

"She shouldn't have gone outside on her own, even to take a leak," Ike put in. "Maybe whatever it was that touched the tent last night didn't go away. Maybe it was biding its time . . . but there's no sign that I can see. No footprints, of any kind. No sign of any struggle that I can see."

"Maybe she wanted to make an early start on scaling the cliff, for your sake," Lynn suggested, although it was obvious that she didn't believe it. "Did Solari tell you that she killed Bernal?"

"No. I got sidetracked thinking he suspected you. I should have known better. I didn't guess until I saw her with the artifacts. It still took time to figure out how she'd cultivated enough suppressed rage to explode when she found him with them—but it was all a mistake from beginning to end. She figured out afterward why Bernal was making the spearheads, knives, and arrowheads, and so did I. It wasn't forgery, or just an experiment. It was flattery."

"What?"

"As in imitation, the sincerest form of. Bernal always believed that the humanoids were here, in spite of the failure of the flying eyes to catch a glimpse of them. He wanted to make contact, but he didn't have enough information about them to make a decent plan and he didn't want to presume too much. He wanted to use the one thing we *did* know: the artifacts. He intended to leave them lying around, as communicative bait. He wanted to demonstrate to the aliens that we could make them too, that we have at least that much in common. He would have let you in on it, but he wanted to be sure that he could make a good job of it first—and maybe he wanted to keep the people on *Hope* and at Base One in the dark as to where exactly he stood on the great debate, in anticipation of being the one to break the big news. Spin works *so* much better if it's unanticipated."

"None of that matters now," Ike said, a little sharply. "What matters is finding Dulcie. Her phone was working last night, so it should be working now. The fuel cell can't have run out so quickly. Is it possible that the humanoids have got her, do you think?"

Matthew knew that Ike had posed the question that way because it was uncomfortably close to the substance of cheap melodrama—but he understood that they been tipped into a melodrama as soon as they made their descent from the uplands. If they took Bernal's artifacts from our luggage, he thought, his plan's already past phase one. The humanoids must have grabbed her. She must have thought about it too. She can't have been thinking of killing herself until the impulse actually came upon her. She's an anthropologist, and she's had all the time in the world to figure out how to handle this, if that's really what's happened. But we have to be sure. Before we shout *Eureka!* we have to be sure."

"You have to get rid of the killer anemones, Ike," Matthew said, deciding that the time had come to take command. "Use the flamethrowers. Then you have to check the equipment and the supplies, to make sure exactly what's missing. Then you have to get me down."

"Haven't you got that in the wrong order?" Ike objected. "It'll take at least two of us to clear those monsters way." He had obviously seen the current occupants of the disputed area.

"We have to find Dulcie first," Lynn said.

"No," Matthew put in, knowing that he had to make good his bid for authority if he were to make it stick. "Ike's right. It'll take two of you to take the territory back—but you have to be careful. If Dulcie can make her own way back, that's great. If not . . . we have to make ourselves safe first. There's no time to waste. You have to get moving *now*."

This time, they accepted the necessity. Ike appeared on the edge of the ill-cleared area within minutes, clad in ochreous armor. Matthew watched while he spent a few minutes making sure of the lie of the land, testing the speed at which the giant slugs could move.

"Just kill the bloody things, will you," Matthew shouted down to him. It wasn't the sort of thing an ecologist ought to say, but the urgency of the situation overrode other considerations.

Ike had already taken an opportunity to begin delving in one of the ragged heaps of cargo, freeing the flamethrower. He carefully fitted the canister of propellant to his back and placed protective goggles over his eyes, while the tentacled slugs went contentedly about their business. When he eventually let fly, in a series of short but lethal bursts, he managed to roast more than twenty of the monsters without placing the boat or its cargo in the least danger. He had to pick off half-a-dozen more one by one, using more subtle but equally lethal instruments, but he completed the task as quickly as was humanly possible.

Only then did Lynn limp out of the purple backcloth. She had put on her own armor, but she was moving as freely as anyone could have expected, given her injury.

The stink was appalling. Matthew's nasal filters had carefully screened him from those complex organic odorants to which he might have been allergic, but the cruder fumes of burnt flesh posed no threat of that kind, and he was permitted to experience the full measure of their unpleasantness.

Lynn set to work immediately. "It's okay," she said to Ike. "I'm fine as long as I don't have to walk far. I'll take care of the inventory while you find a way of getting up to the cliff top and freeing the cable. When that's done, we can all pitch in. It's about time Matthew started doing his share."

"What if more of them come?" Ike asked.

"Matthew can drop the rifle down to me so that I can blast them at short range."

"We didn't come here to conduct a holocaust," Ike said, sorrowfully. "This is getting way out of hand."

"We'll go back to being Mr. Nice Guys when we've got back to being Mr. Safe Guys," she countered, grimly. "We'll put a cosmetic gloss on the story when we relay it back to Tang if you like, but until further notice I'm the original devil-may-care shoot-any-thing-that-looks-at-me-sideways colonist, okay?"

"If you say so," Ike conceded, a little stiffly. He raised his voice to say: "I'm on my way, Matthew. Just sit tight for one more hour."

"Whatever you do," Matthew shouted down "for heaven's sake *don't fall.*"

Ike's only response to that was a gesture of contempt.

Having watched Ike do his painful work. Matthew now had to watch Lynn doing hers—but she didn't have to call for the gun. The odor of cooked flesh was entirely alien to Tyre, and it seemed to function as powerfully as a deterrent as their spillage of the day before had functioned as bait.

It wasn't obvious that the work of reassembling the boat could be completed that day, but Lynn seemed determined to do it on her own if need be. She was moving with the same quasi-mechanical stiffness and efficiency that Dulcie had demonstrated the day before. She paused occasionally to take a drink of water or a few mouthfuls of food, but she was so solidly locked into her trance of determination that Matthew made no attempt to converse with her.

He tried to call Dulcie, but she still wasn't answering her phone. He hesitated over calling Tang Dinh Quan, but decided that it could wait until he had more definite news.

Instead, he continued thinking about possible correlations between nutritional versatility and exotic reproduction, and the reasons why intelligent bipeds might be favored by evolution on a world like Tyre, and the reasons why civilization might fail on such a world in spite of the fact that its walls had never been exposed to cannon fire or fire of any other sort. He thought too about the probable ecological impact that a species like humankind might have on a world like this one, given the scenes to which he had recently been witness.

This isn't bad, he told himself. Not yet. If we're lucky, it could be good. And we are lucky. We're riding a streak, and we can ride it all the way. I can do this. Cometh the hour, cometh the man. Shen was right. Leader or not, I can light the way, with just a little help from my friends.

THIRTY○THREE

Some of the equipment is definitely missing," Lynn said, as soon as Ike had freed the cable and allowed Matthew to complete his descent to the sticky black ground. The downside of using the flamethrower to dispose of the tentacled slugs was that the enigmatically transfigured masses on which they had set themselves had been devastated. Only a handful of the bulbous protuberances remained intact. The probability was that their contents had been damaged, if not thoroughly cooked.

"What's gone?" Matthew asked, tersely.

"Nothing absolutely vital to the reassembly, although we might be a couple of hull plates down and some leg elements are definitely gone. Some machetes are missing—three, unless one or two are still packed away where I can't find them. Some rope. A bale of bubble-fabric. A canister of fuel oil—fuel for the inorganic motor, that is."

Matthew's heart leapt with exultation, even though he'd fully expected some such news. "Did they take Bernal's artifacts?" he asked, swiftly.

"I don't know," Lynn confessed. "I can't find them—but I don't know where Dulcie packed them."

"Can we get by without the hull plates and leg parts?" Ike wanted to know.

"We have patches to replace damaged hull plates," Lynn said. "We weren't carrying enough spares to fix all the legs, but the loss isn't critical. It certainly wasn't any kind of worm that mounted the raid. It *could* have been monkey-analogues, but . . ."

"It was the humanoids," Matthew told her, firmly. "They know we're here—and we know they're curious. Maybe curious enough to . . ."

That was when his phone began to beep. His first assumption was that it was Tang or Vince Solari, impatient to know how the night had passed, but it wasn't. This time his heart seemed to leap all the way into his throat.

"Dulcie!" he exclaimed, raising his voice to make sure that

Ike and Lynn would respond without delay. They immediately picked up their own phones and tapped into the call.

"Can you hear me?" Dulcie asked, anxiously. She was whispering, but Matthew knew that wasn't what was worrying her; she was afraid that she might have gone so far into the glassy forest that her signal could no longer get out.

"Yes," he said, tersely. "Go on."

"Sorry to worry you all," she said. "I didn't want my phone beeping in case it alerted them. I thought I could follow them without them knowing. It seemed plenty dark enough, and I felt sure they hadn't spotted me when I first caught sight of them—but I guess they were stringing me along all the time. They probably wanted to lure me away from the bubble. I didn't even know how many of them there were. Stupid."

"What's your situation now?" Matthew asked, as waves of nauseous fear stirred in his empty belly.

"Under observation, I suppose. They haven't made a hostile move—yet. They seem to have quite a lot of our stuff, including some very wicked steel knives as well as Bernal's things. They have spears of their own too. I can count twenty-two, but there might be a few I can't see. If they do attack, I don't stand a chance, but they still seem wary. They know I'm doing something now, but they seem more intrigued than alarmed. They know they have me surrounded, and they know that I know, but they're holding back, still half in hiding."

"*Which way?*" Lynn demanded—then realized that the answer wouldn't mean anything. "We'll be there with the gun and the chain saws as soon as we can," she added, ignoring the fervent gestures Matthew was making in the hope of shutting her up, "but you'll have to guide us in—there's no way we can triangulate your position until we spread out."

"Don't be stupid!" Dulcie retorted, with even more scorn than Matthew could have contrived. "I have to try to make contact, *now*. I phoned you first because you need to listen in—to know what I'm doing in case it goes horribly wrong." She didn't have to ask whether the call was being recorded—all the phones would do that automatically.

"Absolutely right," Matthew said, swiftly. "What do they look like, Dulcie?"

Lynn Gwyer was obviously still in a devil-may-care shoot-

anything-that-looks-at-me-sideways mood, but Ikram Mohammed put a hand on her arm to clam her down. "We'd never find
her," he whispered, holding the mouthpiece of his phone away
from his face. "Not quickly enough . . ." He broke off as Dulcie
began answering Matthew's question.

"Either we looked at the rock drawings with an optimistic
eye or these aren't the same folk," the anthropologist said, her
voice so unemotional and matter-of-fact that it seemed almost
parodic to Matthew. "They're all shorter than I am, none taller
than a meter and a half, and they're thin. Disproportionately
long limbs, very odd hands. Looks to me like seven longish fingers, or five fingers and two thumbs, and the way they grip their
spears and the stolen goods is very weird, always leaving at least
a couple of fingers spare. Slender torsos. Purple skin, of course,
not scaly but not hairy either. No clothes. No hair on the head or
anywhere else. No breasts, no balls, no navels, no babes in arms,
no toddlers, no kids at all. Like plastic dolls, in a way—except
for the faces. We—I—always thought of them as having faces
vaguely like ours, but they don't. Very large eyes. Even larger
noses—snouts might be a better term. Complicated mouth parts,
almost insectile but soft—and real teeth. *Big* teeth, but not
sharp. No ears that I can identify with confidence, although I'm
pretty sure they can hear. Something like a double crest lying to
either side of the head, mostly collapsed but occasionally
raised—*might* be ears but probably not. Other flaps of flesh
under the arms, probably capable of extension—function
unclear. They make noises, but nothing like human speech.
Clicks and groans."

She paused, but no one interrupted. Matthew was holding his
breath.

"They're clicking and groaning away like crazy right now,"
she went on, "presumably holding a conference to decide what to
do next. The discussion seems pretty democratic—no obvious
signs of a pecking order. I'm showing them my open hand, and
they seem to be reacting, but whether they recognize it as a
peaceful gesture or think it's a joke because it's only got five
stubby fingers I don't know. They're creeping a little closer all the
while, but none of them seems anxious to take the lead. They all
seem very nervous, even though they've got all the weapons, not
to mention the advantages of height, reach, and home ground.

Even if they didn't see us with the chain saws they must have seen what the chain saws did. I'm trying to seem unthreatening, but I'm not sure they'd recognize anything I said to them as speech, let alone appreciate a soothing tone. I'm standing in the open, looking as harmless as I possibly can, but they don't seem convinced. They don't seem to have a clue what to do, although they're going to have to do something when they come within touching range, if not before."

She paused again. The silence on the line would have been profound had it not been for a faint background crackle. The microphone could not pick up the clicks and groans of the humanoids.

"Maybe it's lack of imagination," she continued, "but the only friendly gesture I can think of right now is to turn my smartsuit purple, matching the shade as closely to theirs as I can. It'll have to run through a pretty wide spectrum before it gets there, but it won't take long—wow! That got their attention. Everybody's stopped. Lots of blinking. If anything, they're more scared than they were before, but I'm there now. Short of growing a snout like an ugly bat with a mouthful of worms, there's nothing more I can do to try to fit in. I'm going to try an approach, nice and slow. I'll pick one that doesn't have a spear—one that's carrying some of our stuff."

Matthew had to let his breath out, but he let it out slowly and silently. "I wish I had something I could offer as a gift," Dulcie went on, "but I'm certainly not going to unfold the clasp knife from my belt or offer them my notepad or phone. I'm not sure they'd be able to decipher the gesture anyway. I'm still relying on the empty palm. The one I'm moving closer to doesn't know what to do, but at least it isn't making any hostile move. I'm reaching out now, palm first, inviting a peaceful touch, but I can't tell whether it knows—oh no! They're coming at me, Matthew. They're com—"

Although the sound of her voice was cut off, the link was still open. Matthew could hear other noises, but very faintly. Either Dulcie had dropped the phone or it had been snatched from her hand.

Ike cursed; Lynn seemed utterly numb. Matthew had known before that there was no time to waste; now he had a giddy sensation of having been overtaken by events. He groped for crumbs of comfort. "If she'd screamed," he said, keenly aware of the hammering of his heart and the difficulty of drawing further breath, "she could have made herself heard. She didn't scream." He didn't lower his phone, and neither did Ike or Lynn. They all continued listening, while the faint susurrus of background noise taunted them.

"If they'd killed her," Matthew said, stubbornly, "she'd have screamed. She didn't scream. *All they did was take the phone out of her hand.*"

"We have to call the Base," Ike said. "I should have done it before. I should have done it *just then*, to let them hear it."

"No, you did right," Matthew said. "It's all on tape. You call the base. Tell Tang and the others. Lynn—you call Milyukov. Tell him we need that drop *now*. We have to have a camera with enough power to punch a signal through the canopy. Don't let him stall."

"Who are you calling?" Lynn asked, as she saw Matthew's left thumb call up a directory.

"Frans Leitz."

"Who the hell is Frans Leitz?"

"He's a medical orderly on *Hope*," Matthew told her. "Next best thing to a cabin boy. This is the only chance he'll ever have to get the first shot at a really hot rumor. By the time Milyukov can make a start on putting his own spin on the news it'll be all around the ship and leaking down to Base One like spring rain. When I go on air I want everybody watching. *Everybody*. Frans? Hi—this is Matthew Fleury. I'm uploading an audiofile—it'll just take five or ten minutes to play back. Play it to Dr. Brownell, will you? And anyone else who might be interested. Got to go now."

Lynn looked as if she wanted to ask more questions, but she decided instead that she ought to get on with her own part of the deal. Ike had already stepped to one side so that he could talk to Tang Dinh Quan. "Tell Base One," he was saying. "Tell Andrei Lityansky. Tell everyone you can. They're not just apes. They're intelligent. They're real aliens. No more doubts. They make tools, they talk, they steal, they don't quite know how to react to alien invaders, and when their hands are forced they leap into action. They're just like us in every department that really matters. And they've separated Dulcie from her phone. From now on, nothing else matters. Matthew and I are going after her."

"Not yet," Matthew was quick to say. "We can't go in without the cameras. We should be able to get a fix on Dulcie's phone ourselves, but we can't go any further in without a reliable means of getting information out."

Matthew's phone beeped. The person on the other end was Godert Kriefmann. The news was already spreading, and the doctor obviously wasn't content to wait for Tang to relay everything.

"You'll know as much as we do when you've played the recording," Matthew told Kriefmann. "Call Nita Brownell, and any crew member who can grasp its import. Tell them we need TV cameras. We need a rig that one man can carry, but it has to have enough clout to transmit loud and clear to Milyukov's comsats. They have to drop it on the next overhead pass, because every second counts. Any delay might cost Dulcie her life and ruin our best chance of making a healthy contact."

He closed the connection without leaving space for a reply. Then he switched off his phone. "You stay on the line, Lynn," he said. "Ike and I have things to do."

"They might not play ball," Ike said, anxiously. "Milyukov might be spaceborn, but he's got access to the library. He knows Earth history, and understands it well enough to have done his best to keep a tight stranglehold on the information passing between surface and orbit. He didn't want you here in the first place—he won't want to let you spin the story."

"He doesn't have a choice," Matthew said. "His authority over his own people is going to vanish overnight if he tells them that they can't hear *this* news because he doesn't trust the messenger. The story's too big, and he's already been sitting on it for too long. He's been able to deflect attention away from the ruins, and he was able to dismiss the weapon that killed Bernal as a malicious hoax, but all that's going to rebound on him now. The shit will be hitting the fan all over the microworld. From now on, I'm in charge."

"You?" Ike queried. "What happened to *us*? Don't Lynn and I get a say in anything?"

"I'm the one who knows how to play the game," Matthew told him, bluntly. "No matter what you used to think of my TV prophet act, it's the only way we can turn this whole business around. It has to be me. Maybe it should have been Bernal, but he's not here, so it has to be me."

"You're an arrogant son of a bitch, aren't you?" Ike said—but he didn't say it like a man who intended to put up a fight.

"Yes I am," Matthew said. "But you have to take charge of putting the boat together, because you know how and I can only follow orders. We have to reassemble it so that Lynn can stay safe. She can't come with us because she'd slow us down—and somebody has to stay here to feed those basketball things to the robots, so that they can start letting us in on the secrets of esoteric chimerization."

Having said that, Matthew became aware of the fact that Lynn Gwyer was also looking at him with an expression of profound annoyance.

He shrugged his shoulders, and said: "Sorry, Lynn. Luck of the draw. What did Milyukov have to say?"

"He said he'd do his best," she told him.

"He's a lying bastard," Matthew opined, "but he'll have to make good on the promise anyway. He really will do his best, up to and including targeting the drop to within a hundred meters. As soon as the dandelion seed settles, Ike and I will be on our way. It won't be so bad—if I'm right, the wreckage of this little population explosion really will help us figure out how emortal chimeras cope with the arithmetic of the sex-death equation, and how they keep evolution going in spite of the unhelpful frame in which they have to operate. It won't be as big a story as the first contact, but Dulcie's already pocketed that one. The best Ike and I can hope for is to be heroes of the rescue dash."

Had the situation not been so tense, Matthew thought, Lynn might have allowed herself a wry laugh. As things were, her voice remained level and earnest. "Do you have any idea how big this plain is?" she said. "I suppose you think we were lucky because they came to meet us rather than letting us follow the river for a few hundred kilometers more, hunting all the while for scraps of evidence, but there's half a continent out there. You'll never find her. You'll find the phone, and maybe enough of a trail, to tell you which way they went, but you'll never find *her* if they don't want you to."

"They were close enough to know when we arrived," Matthew pointed out. "They didn't have to trek across half a continent to get here, and no matter how scared they are they won't run away that far. We're lucky they found so much to steal, luckier still that they had the courage and intelligence to steal it, and luckiest of all that Dulcie caught a glimpse of them while she was in a reckless mood. If they were interested in us before, they're absolutely fascinated by us now. If we're really lucky, they'll come to us again—but if we have to go looking for them, we can be sure they'll eventually let us find them, because that's what they've already done. Whatever they've done with Dulcie, their tactics are already on show. Sex or no sex, in every respect that really matters, *they're just like us.*"

"That's way too many assumptions," Lynn complained. "And whatever else you've achieved, you've certainly set up a context of expectation. When your cameras get here, you'd better have something to put out. You've promised breaking news, and you'll have to deliver. Have you even paused to consider what this will do to the argument about whether we can and ought to stay here? You do realize that the entire future of the colony may hang on what happens next?"

"I've been stuck in a basket halfway down a cliff for a day and a half," Matthew reminded her. "I've done nothing *but* pause for consideration. I know *exactly* what hangs on what happens next—and I certainly wouldn't trust anyone but me to report it responsibly. Would you?"

"Less than a fortnight ago," she pointed out, "you were still in the solar system, so far as subjective time is concerned. Do you really think you're the man best qualified to put an informed and considered commentary together?"

"Yes I do," Matthew said. "If not me, who? If not now, when?"

"It *should* have been Bernal," Ike put in.

"Maybe it should," Matthew retorted, "but Dulcie killed him in a fit of rage, because he couldn't respond to her need the same way twice, so I'm here instead. Would you rather have Tang Dinh Quan telling the world and the microworld alike that this is final proof of the fact that we need to let the world alone for a hundred or a thousand years, and maybe forever, lest we interfere with the indigenes' right of self-determination?"

That threw Lynn slightly. "Is that what you're going to say on air?" she asked. "In *that* tone of voice?"

"Of course not," he told her. "I'm going to be sweet reason itself."

"But which end of the argument are you going to support?"

"How do I know, until I find out more?"

She wasn't buying that. "Don't pretend to be any better than the rest of us, Matthew. You know full well that almost everyone else is in a better position to make an *informed* judgment. I know you've already made up your mind. You're grabbing the platform before anyone else does because you never could be content to wait in the wings. I want to *know*, Matthew. I want to know how you intend to play it."

"This is a complete waste of time," Ike told her. "Matthew's right about one thing—we have work to do. We have to put the boat together, and put the cargo in the boat, and make the whole thing safe from attack or pilferage. We have to do it *now*, before we have another plague of worms to deal with, or an army of purple people. His bad arm and your bad ankle will make it difficult enough, without falling out with one another. We have to take this one step at a time."

Lynn backed down easily enough. "Maybe we all need a pause for consideration," she said. "This really has changed everything, hasn't it?"

"For the better," Matthew told her. "Yesterday, we were still alone in the universe. Today, the universe might be full of thieves like us. Where there's two, there's probably a legion." But he was getting to work even as he said it, and he knew that he had to reserve his strength. He didn't bother to add: And if we're so far ahead of these guys, somewhere out there is a race of thieves that will make our little venture in interstellar colonization look like a playground game, whether we get it right or not.

THIRTY◘FOUR

Matthew was right, as he had known he would be, about Captain Milyukov having to make good on his promise to do his best. Not only did *Hope*'s technicians manage to land the mini-shuttle within 400 meters of the reassembled boat, but they even contrived to put it down on the right side of the river and to miss the kinds of vegetation that might have suspended it out of reach. Ike and Matthew raced to the spot, worrying that the aliens might get there first, but it proved easy enough to recover the TV camera and the emergency food supplies. The replacement parts for the boat were a bonus, which they loaded on an improvised sled so that they could drag them back to the boat without too much difficulty. Matthew was able to do his share of the haulage by looping the towrope over his left shoulder.

"I told you so," Matthew said to Lynn, who was waiting for them on the hastily reassembled boat, ready to extend a gangplank to the shore. "Everybody wants in on this now," he added. "Everybody's heard Dulcie's final phone call, and everybody wants to know what happened to her. We couldn't have a better story if we'd hired a scriptwriter."

"If we'd hired a scriptwriter," Ike pointed out, "we'd know how it was going to come out. This way, we don't even now *if* it's going to come out. You and I could march for days through that wilderness and find precisely nothing. How long do you think it will take for your audience to get impatient? Who do you think they're going to blame if we can't deliver?"

"Not you," Matthew assured him. "You'll be the one pointing the camera. I'll be the talking head. If I can't keep them in suspense until we can contrive a punchline, I'll be the one they go for. But you don't need to worry. The aliens are as curious as they're anxious, and they're acquisitive too. They're not going to let us wander around their forest indefinitely. If Dulcie's still alive they'll bring her back, because it's the only unambiguous gesture of amity they can make." While he was speaking he was already assembling the pack that he'd have to carry on his back for the next few days. Ike was doing likewise.

"*If* she's alive," Lynn echoed, dubiously, "and *if* their reasoning works the same way as ours."

"Reasoning's reasoning," Matthew told her. "Two and two always make four. Now that they've had a chance to test our machetes, they'll want to find a way of getting more. Bernal was right to think that the best first offering would be stuff they already have—or had, when they were city-builders—but it's too late now to worry about explosive cultural pollution. Their thievery's cut right through that kind of crap. It's make-do time now, whether we like it or not . . . and whether *they* like it or not."

"Why do I have this nagging feeling that you like it way too much?" Lynn came back.

He smiled, in what he hoped was a reassuring fashion. "Okay," he said. "I'm all set. Ike?"

Ike nodded, but Lynn was still hesitant. "Aren't you taking Rand's gun?" she asked. "They *could* be dangerous."

" "We've got too much to carry as it is," Matthew told her. "If they kill us, we'll just have to go down shooting with the camera. Don't worry about it. However it goes, it'll be an epoch-making event in human history—at least as significant, in its way, as the development of true emortality back home on Earth—and it's ours. Rumor has it that there are billions of people in the solar system who have just about everything they ever wanted now, but they don't have this and we do. The one thing we can trade for the attention and support we need and deserve is first contact, and a text message saying *Eureka!* isn't going to inspire anything like the same engagement as the coupling of Dulcie's last phone call and TV coverage of our rescue mission. However it comes out, it'll grab their guts, and if it comes out well, it'll prove to *everyone* that notwithstanding the crew's revolution and the abject failure of the would-be colonists to get a grip on anything, *Hope* really has lived up to her name. This is our chance to establish *Hope*'s quest as the heroic enterprise we all signed up for. Whatever loss of faith *you*'ve suffered in the last three years, that dream is still fresh in my mind."

Lynn shook her head, but all she said to Ike was: "He's in rehearsal already."

Ike shrugged his shoulders. "We have to get going," he said. "Will you be all right?"

"Sure," she said. "If you don't come back, I'll be the sole survivor. And if there are any interesting formations in that unholy mess we made on the shore, I'll be the one to find them. Just make sure you find Dulcie, if it's humanly possible."

Matthew and Ike had already triangulated the location where Dulcie's phone still lay, and it only took them a few minutes to reach it. The battery was still active and the line was still open, but Matthew turned it off as soon as he had picked it up. It was less than a kilometer from the place where the bubble-tent had been pitched, but they were already in the depths of the so-called grassland.

It only took a slight effort of imagination for Matthew to recover the impression of being very tiny, lost in a wilderness made strange by inflation. For the first time, he could see why the crew's mapmakers had decided to favor this place with such an odd label. Although the structures surrounding him were certainly high enough to be considered elements of a forest, the "tree trunks" really were remarkably reminiscent of wheat stalks and blades of lawn grass. Some were rounded and very smooth, others spatulate and barbed. When he looked up into the canopy he could see structures reminiscent of corncobs and structures reminiscent of barley heads, although there were others that looked, quite literally, like nothing on Earth. From above, the canopy had looked like an ocean stirred by waves and littered with flotsam, but from below it seemed as if he were staring up into the vaulted ceiling of an infinite crystal cathedral, lavishly decorated with all kinds of sprays and chandeliers, droplets and honeycombs.

The light that crept through this bizarre prismatic array was by no means bright, but it was strangely even. Such undergrowth as it supported looked more like a slightly undulant carpet of vitreous tiles than the mossy leaf litter of an Earthly forest but it did seem to be *alive*. It was easy to walk on, and the supportive stalks and blades were far enough apart to allow perfectly comfortable passage for Matthew and Ike. Forewarned by experimental forays, they had not troubled to bring a chain saw although they both had machetes dangling from their belts in case they ran into different conditions in some future phase of their journey.

"I think they went this way," Ike said, having examined the

ground around the spot from which Dulcie had made her final call. "The ground doesn't take footprints very well, but you can see where junctions between the platelets have cracked. If we follow this heading and keep an eye out for more signs, we'll probably be moving in the right direction—unless you have a better idea."

"First things first," Matthew said. He had always intended to make his first broadcast from the place where the phone had fallen—or, as he represented it, the very spot where the momentous and long-anticipated first contact between humankind and intelligent aliens had taken place.

He explained to his audience that he and Ike were going to keep on walking in the direction in which the aliens had been heading before they paused to capture their inquisitive pursuer, on the assumption that whatever destination they had had in mind must lie that way. He played back a recording of Dulcie's last message in order to establish a "picture" of the aliens in the minds of his audience, and he asked Ike to pan the camera over the canopy and the ground, pointing out the salient features.

He refrained from mentioning that Dulcie had killed Bernal Delgado, and silently hoped that Vince Solari would have the sense to do likewise. Having made the computations necessary to convert Earthly hours into the metric hours that had displaced them aboard *Hope*, he promised to make further twenty-minute broadcasts at regular intervals, whenever he and Ike paused to rest—every two ship-hours, approximately, except for one longer interval that would allow him to get some sleep.

"What are you going to tell them?" Ike wanted to know, once the camera was off and they had started walking. "The scenery's not going to change much, so there isn't a lot to show them except for your face."

"I'm going to give them a grand tour of the enigmas of local genomics," he said. "I'm going to offer some intelligent speculations about possible solutions to those puzzles. It doesn't matter whether I'm right or not as long as I keep pumping out food for thought and material for discussion. You're probably right about the scenery, but its very constancy might be a useful talking point. I suspect that interesting changes happen *very* rarely, barring episodes like the one we precipitated with our blundering, but it's not impossible that we might come across bigger versions of the formations you had to scorch in order to get rid of the stinging slugs. I'd really like to see a pyramid, although my gut feelings tell me that they're once-in-a-century or once-in-a-millennium constructions in these parts."

"You think the thing in the drawing really was a pyramid?" Ike queried.

"Not a stone pyramid. Glass, maybe, or something similar. But not a tomb. Almost the reverse, in fact—but not a straightforward baby factory either. If Lynn can get enough live samples out of the mess we left behind she'll lay the foundations for a more accurate understanding, but it doesn't matter much that she won't be able to feed the information through to me. I'll have to make the most of my guesswork regardless."

"But you're not going to give me a preview?"

"I'm still working on the script. Trust me, Ike—if you hold the camera, I'll improvise the show."

Privately, Matthew wasn't nearly as confident as he seemed, but he didn't have any alternative. Now the stakes had been laid—and how could he possibly have refused to play or demanded a lower level of risk?—he was committed. If the world would not deliver an adequate story on cue, he would have to make one up.

Ike's suspicions about the constancy of the environment were fully justified; it changed so little that its wonders soon became tedious. They heard other creatures, but rarely saw them. Most of the animals that lived hereabouts lived in the canopy, and those that did not fled their approach.

Matthew opened his second broadcast by reviewing the last few notes that Bernal Delgado had keyed into his notepad.

"What do they mean?" he asked, rhetorically. "*Answer downriver* seems obvious enough, and we now believe that *ska* might mean *serial-* or *super-killer anemone*—a reference to the creatures that brought our expedition to the brink of disaster when we cleared the ground beneath the cliff in order to bring our equipment down. But what about the *NV* that's supposedly correlated with *ER*? If anyone has any suggestions as to what those terms might signify, I'll be glad to hear them when I'm able to take phone calls again, but in the meantime I'm working on the assumption that they stand for *nutritional versatility* and *exotic reproduction*. Those are two of the most stubborn mysteries we've had to confront as we've undertaken a painstaking analysis of the ecosphere of the world that some of you call Ararat and others Tyre.

"Nutritional versatility may seem at first glance to be a non-problem. So organisms whose activity and tendency to eat everything in sight entitles them to be thought of as animals also have the purple chloroplast-equivalents that allow them to fix solar energy, just as plants do—why shouldn't they? Isn't the situation on Earth the surprising one? Why should there be such a clear distinction between Earthly plants and animals when every species might, potentially, enjoy the best of both worlds? Why is nutritional versatility the Earthly province of a few exotic plants like the Venus flytrap?"

Matthew paused, looking beyond the camera at the man holding it. Ike had been concentrating on the problem of keeping the camera steady, and didn't immediately register the slight change of attitude. When he did, he took his eye away from ther viewfinder momentarily to acknowledge the contact. He couldn't shrug his shoulders without shaking the image, so he contrived a gesture of reassurance with a forced smile.

Having cleared his throat Matthew went on.

"Well, the logical answer is that once an organism can obtain energy by eating, the extra margin of assistance to be gained from continuing to fix solar energy is too small to be worth keeping, so there's no selective pressure to retain it. The number of animal species is, of course, limited by the fact that they all have to have something to eat, so there have to be lots of plants around in order to support any animal life at all, but the more animal life there is the more scope is opened up for animals that eat other animals. Plants can only dabble in eating animals if there are enormous numbers of plants around that don't, and they find it difficult to compete with animals because they're sedentary. If you're an eater, it's a great advantage to be able to get around—waiting for your food to come to you is obviously a second-best strategy—and an organism needs so much energy to get around that if it's going to do that, it might as well be a specialist eater.

"So how come this world is so rich in organisms that have kept their ability to fix solar energy in spite of the fact that they can eat and get around? The purple worms don't even seem to make strenuous efforts to get out into the sun when they can.

They lurk in the shadows like any other stealthy predator. How can that make sense?

"Well, I can only see one way in which it *might* make sense. If the super-slugs keep chloroplast-analogues they don't bother to use on a day-to-day basis, there must be times when they *do* need to use them. Rare times, maybe, but *vital* times—times when that energy-fixing capability is so vital that it's carefully sustained through all the times when it's not. And that's where the exotic reproduction has to come in."

He looked away as a sudden movement caught his eye, but it was only something falling from the canopy. He looked back before Ike moved the camera.

"The most important difference between life on Earth and life on Ararat, alias Tyre, is that sex isn't the only way of shuffling the genetic deck so as to produce the variations on which natural selection works. Here, sex involves cells within a chimerical corpus rather than whole organisms. You could say that all the local organisms are actually small-scale colonies of continually crossbreeding individuals. And they're probably all emortal. That doesn't matter much to the simplest ones, because they never live long enough to die of old age; they always get eaten long before they reach the limits of their natural life spans. The more complicated ones are a different matter."

Matthew hesitated again, but this time it was purely for dramatic effect. Ike understood that, and stayed focused.

"Earth's ecosphere was shaped by what Bernal Delgado used to call the sex-death equation. The essence of life is reproduction, but there are two kinds of reproduction. There's the kind by which organisms make new organisms and the kind by which organisms reproduce *themselves*. The cells of your body are continually replaced, so that every eight years or so there's an entirely new you, almost as good as the old one but not quite. We humans—and I mean *we* in a narrow sense, because there's a new human race on Earth now that doesn't have this particular disadvantage—deteriorate like a chain of old-style photocopies, each image becoming a little more blurred than the last. Eventually, we die of growing old, if we haven't already been killed by injury or disease. In the meantime, though, most of us make a few new individuals, by means of sexual reproduction. We die, but the species goes on—and we owe our existence to the fact that natural selection used to work on the new individuals our remoter ancestors made, weeding out the less effective ones. We owe our intelligence to the slow work of natural selection, which perfected the union of clever hands, keen eyes, and big brains that pushed our forefathers ahead of all their primate cousins.

"To us, that all seems perfectly natural, and so it is—but it needn't have been that way. Here, evolution took a slightly different path. Here, sex is routinely confined to the kind of reproduction by which the local equivalents of organisms reproduce themselves. I say *the local equivalents of organisms* because they're not the same as Earthly organisms in the sense of being genetic individuals. They're compounds: *chimeras*. That seems odd, because they don't look like the chimeras of the Earthly imagination: they're not compounds of radically different species, like griffins, and they don't seem to go in for dramatic metamorphoses—at least, not on a day-to-day basis. But they *do* reproduce in the other sense, because they have to, and they *are* subject to the kind of natural selection that drives an evolutionary process, because they have to be. We can see that, just by looking around, because we can see perfectly well that this ecosphere is as complex as Earth's, and that the logic of convergent evolution has produced all kinds of parallel bioforms. It may seem puzzling at first that we can't see the second kind of reproduction going on, because no alien visitor to Earth could possibly miss it if he hung around for a year or two, but when you think about it carefully, you can see that it's much less puzzling than it seems."

Matthew looked up at the canopy and gestured with his arm. Ike looked puzzled for a moment, but then he caught on. There was nothing that a sweep could actually *show* the viewers by way of dramatizing Matthew's rhetoric, but it could relieve the tedium by giving them something else to look at. Even an audience as well-educated and interested as the one he was hoping for couldn't be expected to stare at his face indefinitely without getting a trifle bored.

"It's probably simplest to think about it in terms of different timescales," Matthew went on. "Earth's timescales are determined by a seasonal cycle, which gives the year a tremendous importance. Although complex organisms like mammals live for many years, the vast majority of Earthly animal species go through an entire life cycle in a year, and most of those only devote a short space of time—maybe as little as a single day—to the business of sexual exchange. The rest of the time is spent lying dormant, growing, and the first kind of reproduction—which often involves considerable metamorphoses. Most Earthly organisms with annual life cycles mass-produce young, but only a few individuals make it through the long phases of the cycle to become the next generation of breeders. The vast majority become food for other organisms.

"At first glance, it might seem that more complex Earthly animals—like us—have developed a radically different reproductive strategy, as far removed from mass production as you can imagine, but the appearance is slightly misleading. Humans do mass-produce sperms and eggs, but only a few of them ever get together successfully enough to produce a live baby, and by the time a baby is born it's already gone through the first few phases of its growth and self-reproduction. The whole cycle is slowed up by a factor of twenty to fifty—and biotechnology has shown our cousins back home how to slow it up indefinitely. But here on this world the chimerical individuals that stand in for organisms never had to cope with the tyranny of the seasons, and they never faced the kind of struggle our ancestors had to resist that tyranny. Here on Tyre, even worms are emortal—and every single quasi-organism that ever figured out a better way of avoiding getting eaten has the chance to live forever."

Matthew paused again to give Ike the chance to pan around, displaying the purple forest yet again in all its peculiar glory. This time, Matthew, hoped, the view *would* add something to the argument. By now, the viewers should have learned to see the alien environment through eyes whose curiosity had been cleverly restimulated: eyes informed by a more prolific imagination.

"Even in that sort of situation," he added, hoping that his confidence was warranted, "I suppose sex *could* have established itself as an individual-to-individual thing, but it didn't. It remained within individuals, and chimerization became the means by which those individuals produced new individuals, in orgies of mass production not unlike those in which most Earthly organisms indulge on a yearly basis—except that here on Tyre, there is no yearly basis. Where complex organisms are concerned, those orgies are *much* more widely spaced. Even for the reptile-analogues we might have to think in centuries; for the humanoids, who knows? Maybe millennia.

"In terms of the natural cycles of *this* world—a world whose ecosphere may be *a billion years older than Earth's*—the three years we've been here might only be the equivalent of a few *hours* on Earth: a few hours in the depths of winter, when nothing's busy with the adventurous kind of reproduction, except maybe people. But in spite of appearances, the people of Tyre aren't like the people of Earth. They couldn't be. Convergent evolution might have given them keen eyes and clever hands and self-conscious brains to go with their bipedal stature, but it couldn't give them a way of making babies, because that's not the way things work hereabouts. Think about the possible consequences of that difference, if you care to, while I'm off the air. I'll pick up the story later. In the meantime, thanks for listening."

THIRTY⊂FIVE

"There's an incoming call," Ike said, as soon as Matthew had closed his eyes in order to collect himself.

"What?" Matthew said, automatically reaching for his useless beltphone.

"Not the phone," Ike said. "The screen in back of the camera's rigged to receive as well as to monitor and the fuel cell's five times as powerful as a phone's. We can be contacted that way, provided that—"

"Provided that the other guy has a similar rig," Matthew finished for him, as enlightenment dawned. "Milyukov." He took the camera from Ike's weary arms and looked into the monitor.

"Captain," he said. "How good of you to call. Are you enjoying the show?"

"You are being irresponsible," Milyukov said, flatly. "You have been awake for little more than ten days. You are not qualified to produce these fantasies."

"So put someone who *is* qualified on the air," Matthew retorted. "I'm leaving gaps between broadcasts of a couple of hundred of your metric minutes—it's up to you to decide what to fill them with."

"We don't go in for such time-wasting relics of Earthly barbarism as round-the-clock broadcasting," was Milyukov's frosty response.

"It's up to you, of course," Matthew told him. "But you've got an audience whether you want to keep it entertained or not. If you don't want to broadcast I'm sure that you could find people at Base One who'd be only too glad to amplify or challenge my speculations, if you'd care to drop them the relevant equipment."

"That would not be appropriate," the captain said.

"Not from your viewpoint it wouldn't," Matthew agreed, sarcastically. "After all, you wouldn't want them bringing discussions about the future of the colony into the open at such a delicate time. You certainly wouldn't want to get involved in an actual *debate*, would you? You'd rather talk to your own people directly, without anyone having a chance to interrupt. Well, you've been well and truly interrupted, and you can either make provision to answer back or keep quiet."

"I can take you off the air."

"Can you? The camera Ike's using has enough power to send out a signal for several days. If you interfere with the satlinks your people and the people at Base One will make what provision they can to receive signals directly. You're not under the delusion, I hope, that Shen Chin Che doesn't know what's going on? If there's one man on *Hope* who understands the power of TV as well as I do, it's Shen."

"I can certainly keep *him* out of this," was Milyukov's immediate response.

"Maybe you can and maybe you can't," Matthew countered, "but a brave and honest man wouldn't even try. A man who thought he had a good case to argue would be only too pleased to take his opponent on in open forum."

"If you say that on air I'll cut you off immediately," the captain insisted, stubbornly.

"In propaganda terms, that would be the next best thing to cutting your own throat," Matthew told him. "You can't hide any more. You can fight, but you can't run away. It was always bound to come to this, as you should have realized before you brought the first colonist out of the freezer."

"There was no evidence that Ararat was inhabited by intelligent aliens," Milyukov said, mistaking the nature of the argument yet again. "We had no reason to think that the colonization could not go ahead as we had planned."

"You live in a world with very narrow horizons, Captain Milyukov," Matthew observed. "Maybe that's not so surprising, given that you're fourth- or fifth-generation spaceborn, but there's really no excuse for it. You brought all of Earth with you, and all of the universe too. You only had to use your VE-apparatus intelligently. You really don't understand what's happening here, do you? If you'd had the slightest idea of the true significance of what we've found here, you wouldn't have wasted a year hoping it didn't exist and doing everything within your meager power to prevent its discovery."

"I will not permit the colony to withdraw," Milyukov said. "No matter what you find or what you say, *I will not withdraw the colonists.*"

"Because you can't stand the thought of being outnumbered and outvoted in the corridors of your precious worldlet," Matthew said. "If *Hope* were to become an observation station, manned by Shen's Chosen People, what power and reward would there be in the rank of *ship's captain*? Well, so what? Can't you see that you have a chance to inscribe your name in the annals of human history? I can only transmit to you and yours, but you can transmit to the solar system. You won't get a reply for a hundred and sixteen years, but you can set yourself in place as anchorman of the greatest show off Earth. Why stop me when you can simply *take my place*, for the only audience that really matters?"

"That's not the kind of man I am," the captain told him. "I repeat, I will not withdraw the colony. Disembarkation of the remaining colonists will be resumed whether you can provide final proof that the world is inhabited or not. Whatever you say while you have the attention of crew and colonists alike, I have the power and the authority to make certain of that."

"Of course you have," Matthew assured him, and switched off the camera's power. He knew that he had to economize. "Let's go," he said to Ikram Mohammed.

The two of them started walking, immediately falling into step. They held to the same heading they'd been following all day, although they hadn't seen any obvious sign of a trail for some time. They both knew that they had no chance of catching up with the aliens if the aliens didn't want to be caught, but it wasn't a topic they wanted to discuss.

Above the canopy the afternoon sky had clouded over, and the light was getting steadily worse, but their eyes had adapted to the perpetual purple twilight well enough and they hadn't encountered any unusually treacherous ground as yet.

"Milyukov really doesn't understand," Matthew said, to break the silence. "He hasn't a clue how this script is going to work out."

"Nor have you," said Ike, drily.

"Yes I have," Matthew told him. "Even if the worst comes to the worst, and the aliens let me down on this particular trip, I know how the story's going to work out. Maybe I won't be the one who gets to broadcast the news, but that's not what matters, is it?"

"No, it's not," Ike replied. "And I'm relieved to know that you haven't forgotten it."

Matthew could have wished for more light, in order to study the structures of the canopy more carefully, but it was an inherently frustrating task. When the light was brighter it was reflected and refracted in confusing ways, and now it was dimmer the whole panoply became blurred and uncertain.

After a while, though, it became necessary to pay more attention to the ground than the infinite ceiling. No matter how untreacherous it was, it was far from even and the last thing they needed was for one of them to trip up and turn an ankle.

Matthew suspected that the ground vegetation might be as interesting, in a purely scientific sense, as the canopy, but he would have needed to get down on his hands and knees with a flashlight and a magnifying glass to have any chance of appreciating its intricacies. He wondered more than once whether it might not be more sensible to stay put and hope that the aliens came to them rather than keeping moving, but he reckoned that it would be the wrong decision, if only in dramatic terms.

The crewmen who were following the attempted rescue with an excessively avid interest—because it was the first *real* melodrama to which they had ever been exposed—would expect movement, and the one thing he knew for sure was that moving was no worse than standing still. The one place the aliens wouldn't want to make contact was the boat; even if it had been purple rather than pea-green it would simply have been too exotic and too alarming.

They waited until it was too dark to continue safely before making the next broadcast, even though their audience had to wait an extra quarter of a metric hour to hear the next installment of Matthew's commentary on Tyrian life, and then had to look at his face eerily lit by a flashlight.

"Back home on Earth," he said to the camera, picking his words carefully, although he tried not to give that impression, "the descendants of the folk we left behind have discovered the secret of true emortality. They made a couple of false starts along the way, but they got there. We should be glad, although we can't reap the benefit ourselves. There's cause for a certain pride in being the last mortal humans ever to live and die, if that's what we turn out to be. We mustn't forget, though, that death is another of the other things that we, as products of Earth's ecosphere, fell into the habit of taking for granted.

"Death was the price that complex Earthly organisms paid for reproduction and evolution. The simplest Earthly organisms always had emortality. The bacteria who came with us on our great adventure, as passengers within our bodies, can keep on dividing and dividing indefinitely. All bacterial deaths are accidental. Bacteria starve, or they get poisoned—by their own wastes or by antibiotics—or they get eaten, but if they avoid all those kinds of fates they just go on dividing forever.

"Complex Earthly organisms are different, but that's because there's a sense in which a multicelled organism is just a transitional phase in the life of a single-celled organism. As the old saying has it, a chicken is just an egg's way of making more eggs. So is a human being. A complex organism is just a reproductive mechanism whose necessity is temporary, and which therefore has obsolescence built in.

"As multicellular reproductive systems became more and more complex, of course, it became much easier to think of them as the ends and the eggs as the means rather than the other way around—and once they learned to think for themselves, that seemed to be the only way to see it. We humans see our mortal multicellular aspects as ourselves because those are the aspects that do the seeing, while those of our eggs that attain emortality by fusing with sperm and going on to make more and more of themselves have always been mute, microscopic, and increasingly irrelevant to adult concerns.

"But suppose things had been different. Suppose complexity had been invented by single-celled organisms not merely as the temporary means of manufacturing more single-celled organisms, with sexual variations, but as *authentic* multicellular extrapolations of their simpler ancestors. Suppose that these multicellular extrapolations retained the same innate emortality as their single-celled ancestors, reproducing in the same fashion, by binary fission. There would still be selective advantages in inventing sex, because it would provide the same useful means of shuffling genes around—but there would also be selective advantages in

retaining and refining other kinds of reproductive apparatus—
apparatus that would free complex organisms from the necessity
of reverting to their single-celled phase in every generation."

Matthew had become conscious of movement at ground
level, and had to pause to direct Ike's attention to it. Ike redi-
rected the beam of the flashlight, quickly enough to display half a
dozen leechlike worms as they turned with surprising alacrity and
slid away. Knowing that they were probably harmless, Matthew
didn't think it worth interrupting his monologue to comment on
their arrival and departure.

"If that had been the case," he continued, "how would the
adaptive radiation of complex forms have progressed? Maybe it
would produce an ecosphere very different from that of Earth—
but maybe not. Maybe the speculator would have decided that
the principles of convergent evolution would still work to produce many of the same sorts of biomechanical forms. Some, of
course, would be easier to produce under the newly imagined circumstances, and some less, but there wouldn't be any reason to
assume that any bioform that functioned reasonably well in
Earth's actual ecosphere wouldn't work equally well in the hypothetical alternative.

"Now, of course, we have another example on which to draw.
We have Tyre, our very own dark Ararat. And what do we find on
Tyre? We find a world whose ecosphere contains analogues of
many of the bioforms that function well in Earth's ecosphere, but
whose fundamental genomics are surprisingly complicated. We
find that the bioforms in question are almost all chimeras, even if
the great majority of the organisms so far observed are what
would be deemed single-species chimeras on Earth. We find that
although sexual reproduction is observable at the cellular level in
meitoic fusions and separations of what would be somatic cells if
they were parts of Earthly organisms, we don't find any egg- and
sperm-producing apparatus.

"In effect, the complex organisms here are capable of having
sex with themselves internally, at the cellular level, swapping
genes between their chimerical elements. But are they also capable of having sex with each other, not according to the various
bird-and-bee transfer models that the complex organisms of
Earth have produced but in a much more thorough, much more

all-embracing fashion? And if not, what do they do instead to produce the variations on which natural selection–driven evolution works?"

This time it was Ike who spotted something moving behind Matthew's back, and moved the camera in the hope of giving the audience a glimpse of it. Perhaps he succeeded, but by the time Matthew turned there was nothing to be seen, and only the sound of scampering legs to be heard.

Ike's lips formed the word *reptile*, but he didn't say it aloud. Matthew took some comfort from the fact that Ike seemed to be following his discourse intently. If he was getting to Ike, who was here in the midst of all this strangeness, surely he was getting to his target audience.

"Whatever they do," Matthew said, wryly, "they don't do it very often. They can't, for precisely the same reason that our emortal cousins back home on Earth have had to revise their own reproductive arrangements. The longer-lived an organism is, the slower its reproductive processes have to be. Organisms that die as a matter of course have to replace themselves relatively quickly in order to maintain their numbers; organisms that don't have to die match their rates of reproduction to the rates of environmental attrition. In the short term, of course, it doesn't always work out that way. Sometimes, reproduction runs riot and produces plagues. We all understand that, because it's the reason we're here. And one of the reasons why our emortal cousins are still having plenty of children back on Earth is that the rate of environmental attrition is augmented by a steady exodus to the remoter parts of the solar system and beyond. They'll be here soon enough, all agog to know how we've been handling things in the meantime, in our primitive, barbaric, *mortal* fashion.

"Well, we'll be able to tell them. We'll know, by then, whether I'm right or wrong about the manner in which the evolution of our enigmatic Ararat's ecosphere diverged from Earth's. We'll know for sure whether all the complex organisms here can reproduce by binary fission, and whether all of them can get together when it seems politic for all-embracing, all-absorbing, all-consuming two- or four- or sixteen- or thirty-two-way sex. We'll know how many of those glassy globules in the crowns of gargantuan grass stalks and the corkscrew trees are the products of the trees themselves, and how many are the products of other organisms. And we'll know whether those sketchy pyramids in the humanoids' drawings are really artifacts, or whether they're actually reproductive bodies of some kind. And we'll know whether they built those walls around their city, while they had a city, simply to protect the crops in their fields, or whether there were other things in those fields, periodically, that were precious enough to warrant all the extra protection they could give them. And we'll know too how the transmission of culture and knowledge across generations of that kind of humanoid compares to the transmission of culture and knowledge that we achieve as we raise and educate our children.

"We'll know all of that, and more, even if this trek through the purple wilderness bears no fruit at all. But if we're *lucky*, this could be the time we start finding out. This could be the time when we make some important new discoveries, and begin to fit the pieces of the jigsaw together. This could be the time when we discover whether any of the people contacted by Dulcie Gherardesca are the *same individuals* who built that city, even if they built it thousands of years before. Maybe they won't remember it, even if they were, but there's one thing they will know all about, and that's the cost of evolution on a world like Tyre. They'll know the cost of a reproductive system in which variation is imported and sorted by chimerization as well as—and perhaps, at the level of whole organisms, *instead of*—sex. Because, you see, the more interesting possibility is that the basketballs and the pyramids and all the other *exceptional* reproductive structures aren't same-species affairs at all, but something *much* weirder. . . ."

It was at this point that Konstantin Milyukov decided that the monologue had gone on long enough. He could have taken Matthew off the air, as he'd threatened to do, but he evidently didn't dare. He took the other option, turning the monologue into a dialogue—and Matthew knew that whatever the outcome of this particular battle might be, the war for *Hope*'s future was as good as won.

It was Andrei Lityansky's voice that actually did the interrupting, but Matthew knew that it was Milyukov who had taken the decision. From his position in front of the camera he had no way of telling whether the engineers on *Hope* had split the screen so that Lityansky's face could appear alongside his, or whether they were content for the moment to let their own man remain a disembodied voice, but he figured that they would cotton on eventually.

"This is all very fascinating, Dr. Fleury," Lityansky said, "but you have no evidence to back it up. The notion that organisms as complex as reptiles and mammals could reproduce by binary fission, with or without forming intermediate multispecific conglomerates, is extremely fanciful and very difficult to believe. Surely it is more likely that we simply have not yet identified the means by which gametes are transmitted between individuals or the cellular apparatus that allows womb-analogues to be produced—presumably on a temporary basis—for the early support of embryos."

"What's unlikely," Matthew said, "is that the colonists have been here for *three years* without seeing a single identifiable egg of a single identifiable seed, if there are any to be seen."

"Not as unlikely, I submit," Lityansky retorted, "as the proposition that organisms of any great complexity could undergo the kinds of fission and fusion that you are proposing."

"You're forgetting the insects, Dr. Lityansky."

Lityansky walked right into the trap. "There are no insects on Ararat," he said.

"An interesting observation in itself," Matthew observed. "It must be significant, must it not, that the bioforms that cannot be observed in our problematic Ararat's life system are those with the greatest reliance on rigid structures like chitinous plates and shells. The reptile- and mammal-analogues here all have relatively flexible bones, tough enough in association with their attendant sinews and tendons to provide leverage but far more active and alive than *our* bones. But the insects whose example you seem to be forgetting are the Earthly insects that provide us with our most spectacular examples of serial chimerization: the insects that pupate and metamorphose, so that mere maggots become gloriously gaudy flies."

"One at a time," Lityansky pointed out.

"Just so," Matthew agreed. "One at a time, and in pupae that remain stubbornly opaque. But imagine, if you can, a pupation process that could accommodate whole groups of chimerical maggots, which could continue to draw energy from their environment while they went about their leisurely business, *because they had chloroplasts as well as mouths*. Imagine, if you can, that these maggots need not exercise their biochemical ingenuity in transforming themselves into gloriously gaudy flies, but may instead be more modest in their aspirations, at least routinely—but at the same time, more ingenious in their intercourse. And imagine, if you can, that the maggots might be mammals, monkeys or men. What dreams might they have, I wonder, while they slept?"

"Incredible," Lityansky said, presumably having no idea how feeble the judgment was bound to sound to his audience.

"I've crossed the void in a pupa of sorts," Matthew reminded that audience. "I've lived in that cold chrysalis for seven hundred years, and have outlived my species, save only for the people who accompanied me, as fellow travelers within their own pupae or faithful watchmen set to see that no harm came to us. Is *Hope* not a kind of chrysalis too, bearing humans tightly wrapped in steel and further encased in yet more ice? We've been unable to fuse with one another, or even to bond, but mightn't that be reckoned our misfortune, our tragedy? We're separate from one another; that's our nature. The only alliances we can form, even in the height of passion, are brief and peripheral encounters—but we're capable—are we not?—of forging a society in spite of that. We're capable—are we not?—of working together to the mutual benefit of our species. Imagine, if you can, the society of the people of our purple Ararat. Imagine their memories, their quests, their hopes, their ambitions, their *strangeness*, remembering as you do that even if everything I've said is the purest fantasy, they *are* people, possessed of memories, quests, hopes, ambitions, anxieties, terrors . . . and, most of all, of differences. At which point, if you don't mind, I'll sign off. I'm sure you'd like the chance to offer the audience your side of the argument."

Without giving Lityansky the opportunity to answer, he signaled to Ikram Mohammed to cut the transmission.

"You really are an egomaniac, you know" Ikram Mohammed said, as soon as he had disemburdened his shoulder of the camera. "Imagine, *if you can* . . . you are going to look *so* stupid if Lityansky turns out to be right."

"He won't," Matthew said. "I might be wrong, but at least I appreciate the magnitude of what needs to be explained and the adventurousness that will be necessary to explain it. Lityansky doesn't. There might be an explanation that's just as crazy—or even crazier—than the one I'm trying to put together, but there isn't one that's any saner. If Lityansky had ever been down here, he'd know that—but he hasn't. He's sat in his lab wearing blinkers, looking at biochemical analyses, without even a decent TV show to broaden his horizons. There may be very good biomechanical reasons why the intelligent inhabitants of this world look like people, but inside, they're *very* different and *very* strange. We should be glad of that. It's what we came here for."

"We came to find a new homeworld. An Earth-clone."

"That was always the wrong way to think," Matthew said, with a sigh. "What we should have set our sights on, right from the beginning, was an Earth-with-a-difference. That was what we were always likely to find, and always likely to find more interesting."

"If you say so," Ike said. "But you do realize, I suppose, that you've used up nearly all your ammunition—and Lityansky now has the floor for at least five times as long as you."

"They'll be queuing up everywhere to take him on," Matthew said. "Every biologist with a pet theory will want to air it, and Milyukov won't be able to hold them back. Even if no one supports me—and it's a good enough story to let me hope—the cat's among the pigeons. The interchange of ideas is well and truly unblocked, and things can only get weirder. All we have to do to get center stage back again is to find the aliens—and that'll be easy, because we only have to keep walking long enough to make sure they decide that they have to let us find them."

"I hope you're right," Ike said.

Matthew didn't dare say *so do I* because he didn't want his companion to know that he was anything less than 100 percent confident. If he'd had a choice, he'd have kept it secret even from himself.

THIRTY◦SIX

The night passed without incident—which was perhaps as well, given that Matthew slept very deeply. He could have used chemical support to stay awake, at least to share sentry duty with Ikram Mohammed, but he didn't want to do that because he knew that two consecutive nights without sleep would take a heavy toll of his articulacy and powers of concentration. Fortunately, Ike agreed to take on the chemical burden, on the grounds that he had slept for several hours the night before.

It was not until he woke up again that Matthew realized that he must have been in a slightly abnormal state of consciousness throughout the preceding day. Now that his IT had made good progress with the repair of his damaged shoulder and no longer needed to anesthetize him he was fully restored to his normal self. At first, he felt annoyed with himself for having been carried away with such wild abandon, but having reconsidered the events of the previous two days carefully and critically he decided that his manic state had produced as many good effects as bad ones. It would, at any rate, be far better to go with the flow than to change direction.

It had rained during the night, but the sky hidden by the canopy was obviously still overcast. The morning was decidedly gloomy, but not so bad as to require them to use flashlights to find their way.

As soon as he began to make hasty plans for his next broadcast Matthew realized that Ike had been right. He *had* used up almost all of his best material on day one. The terrain they had covered was insufficiently various to warrant much further camera study, and he was perilously close to running out of speculative fuel for his wayward flight of fancy.

He was glad to find that some relief was at hand when he began his reintroductory session, in the form of further debate— but Milyukov had belatedly realized that Andrei Lityansky might not be the best man for this particular job, and Matthew found himself faced with sterner opposition. The subsequent discussion of the tactics of sporulation, the mechanics of gradual chimerical renewal, and the limitations of reproduction by fragmentation was far too evenly balanced to be gripping, even to an audience of experts.

To make matters worse, the captain had an even better spoiler still in reserve: Vince Solari. When Matthew went on the air for the second time, he discovered that all three surface bases had now acquired their own TV equipment, and that Solari had been interviewed and cross-questioned as to the progress of his investigation.

Scrupulous honesty had, inevitably, prevailed over evasive caution. Solari had not taken the trouble to avoid the word *fake* when reporting his conclusion that Bernal Delgado had been manufacturing spearheads and arrowheads from local plant products. He had obviously been talking to Lynn Gwyer, and the fact that it was technically hearsay had not prevented him from informing the world that Dulcie Gherardesca—who was, according to the logs and cross-correlated witness statements, the only person who had had the opportunity to commit the murder—had confessed to the crime while contemplating suicide the day before her capture.

Although Matthew had not been party to the subsequent discussion he soon gathered that a crime-of-passion defense was unlikely to find a sympathetic jury among the crew or the colonists.

Matthew knew that he had to counter these setbacks, even though he was no longer riding the same wave of assertive self-confidence that had carried him through the previous day.

Taking the easiest point first, he gave a suitably impassioned account of Bernal Delgado the man and the scientist. He explained, with measured but righteous anger, that Bernal Delgado had not been a forger or a faker, and that he could not possibly have intended his "alien artifacts" to fool anyone.

Bernal's first motive, he insisted, must have been to work himself into a better position to understand how the aliens had lived: specifically, how they had developed a technology without the assistance of fire. Given the degraded state of the objects the people at Base Three had managed to recover from within the walls, he argued, it had been far from clear that they really were artifacts, or what their purposes might have been. It had not been clear, until Bernal had proved it, that the multitudinous vitreous substances produced by the plantlike organisms of the hill country were capable of being worked, shaped, and honed. Such a demonstration had been necessary.

Having made the artifacts, Matthew argued, Bernal had realized that they might be very useful in the context of the expedition downriver. When the humanoids had abandoned the city, or when the city-dwellers had died out, there must have been a substantial loss of technology because the resources of the region were different, and perhaps far richer, than those of the plain. What better way to attempt contact, therefore, than by offering the aliens of the plains recognizable artifacts that might now be rare and precious? What better way could there be of creating a bond between such very different species than demonstrating that the newcomers could work with native materials in exactly the same way that the indigenes had once worked with them?

By the same token, Matthew went on to argue, Bernal Delgado had not been a forger or a faker in the realm of emotions and human relationships. He carefully reproduced the account he had improvised for Dulcie, and did his best to turn it into a tragedy of classical proportions. He made much of Dulcie's former insistence on wearing the scars that she had acquired in the plague wars, claiming that they constituted a heroic badge of courage, and of the sacrifice that the decision must have entailed. He insisted, too, that Bernal Delgado was the kind of man who would have understood, appreciated, and respected such a gesture. He did his utmost to turn Bernal and Dulcie into a middle-aged Romeo and Juliet, rudely torn apart by their sojourn in SusAn and by the failure of memory that had robbed Bernal of the great love of his life and driven Dulcie temporarily mad. He imagined the confrontation scene, when she had found him patiently at work on the alien artifacts, and had finally snapped under a strain that had been wound up so tightly as to have become unsustainable and unbearable.

When he had finished, he asked Ikram Mohammed how it had played. Ike, as usual, misunderstood what he had been doing.

"You don't know that *any* of that is true," the genomicist complained. "You made it all up, from beginning to end."

"I had to," Matthew pointed out. "Facts don't speak for themselves, and the story Vince was hinting at was wrong from every possible viewpoint, except perhaps that of a policeman building a case."

"Reality is what you can get away with? Do you really believe that, Matthew? What kind of a scientist does that make you?"

"Of course I don't believe that reality is what you can get away with. Reality is what it is, and science is the best description of it we can possibly obtain. But you can't test the hypotheses unless you come up with them, and even scientists need motivation. Everything has to start with fantasy, Ike. Knowledge is what you finish up with, if you're lucky, after you've done the hard work—but the hard work needs passion to drive it. People need reasons to be interested, reasons to be committed, reasons to do their damnedest to find the truth. This mission has been floundering for three years, almost to the point of turning into a farce, because all the passion has gone into defining factions and formulating competing plans. That would never have happened if Shen Chin Che hadn't been kept out of the picture, but it shouldn't have happened in any case. It shouldn't have been *allowed* to happen.

"I spent the greater part of my adult life trying to stop it happening on Earth, but I was fighting ten thousand years of history and ten million of prehistory. Here, we had a chance to start afresh. We still have that chance. What I'm doing is to remind people that what happens here is *important*—just as important, in its way, as everything that's happened on Earth since we left. I'm trying to make it into a story because that's what it *is*: a story of confrontation with the alien, of the attempt to understand the alien, to create a mutually profitable relationship between Earth and Tyre, Earthly life and Tyrian life, human and humanoid. I'm trying to make it the best story I can, with heroes for characters instead of fools, because that's the kind of story it *is*."

Matthew was glad to note, as he finished this tirade, that he was recovering something of the mental state that had carried him through his earlier orations.

"You're going to broadcast that, aren't you?" Ike said, shaking his head in mock-disbelief. "Even now, you're still in rehearsal, still making up the script as you go."

"You could join in," Matthew pointed out.

"Imaginative fiction isn't my forte."

"No, but you've always been a first-rate experimental

genomicist. They also serve who only ask the questions. Milyukov's crewmen are still trying to knock me down, even though they ought to know better. What I need is a straight man who'll help to build me up. You want to try it?"

After a pause, Ike said: "Lynn would have been better."

"I'll take that as a *yes*," Matthew told him. "Do you want to rehearse? Ask me a question."

Ike shook his head yet again, but he was grinning now. "Why did the city fail?" he said. "Why did social progress do a U-turn here?"

Matthew was ready for that one. "For exactly the same reason that it very nearly failed on Earth," he said. "For the same reason, in fact, that you and I became so firmly convinced that Earth was doomed that we accepted the riskiest bet available and signed up for *Hope*."

"What reason is that?" Ike said, falling into the role of straight man as if born to it.

"We think of the birth of agriculture and animal husbandry as a great leap forward," Matthew went on, "because it represented the beginning of everything we now hold dear: the crucial step that made rapid technological progress possible. But for the people who did it, it was a desperation move. Their ancestors had been hunter-gatherers for the best part of a million years, manipulating their environment in all kinds of subtle ways: irrigation, the encouragement of useful plants; the elimination of competitors and predators. But they were too successful. Their numbers increased to the point at which they became their own worst enemy, literally as well as metaphorically."

"You don't know that, either," Ike pointed out.

"Not for certain—but it makes sense. Agriculture and animal husbandry were desperation moves, because fields and herds were the only way they could increase their resources fast enough, and keep them safe enough from competitors, to sustain their exploding population. And that, in essence, was the story of the next ten thousand years. They had to keep on increasing the efficiency of the system, in terms of their means of production and their means of protection. Their technics had to keep getting better and better and better, and the faster their population growth accelerated the faster their technological growth accelerated, until the whole thing went Crash. *Hope* got out before the

Crash hit bottom, because no one aboard her had any faith in humankind's ability to pick itself up again, dust itself off, and work out a new modus vivendi. We were too pessimistic, it seems, but it was a damn close-run thing.

"As I see it, something similar must have happened here, with a couple of vital differences. The humanoids migrated from the plains to the hill country because that's where the technological resources were: the glass and the stone. That's where they could make their desperate stand against the competitors that had evolved alongside them. The vital difference was that *our* competitors—our *only* significant competitors—were our own kind. That wasn't the case here. Here, the most successful creatures aren't the handiest, or the keenest-eyed, or the biggest-brained. Here, the most successful creatures are the ones that make the cleverest use of the processes and opportunities of chimerization."

"The worms and slugs," Ike deduced.

"Especially the killer anemones," Matthew agreed. "The killer anemones that became *serial* killer anemones, adapting themselves to whatever circumstances chance threw up, taking aboard new features or discarding them every time they had a chance to swap physical attributes with other bioforms in their periodic orgies of chimerical reorganization. There's an analogy of sorts in something not so *very* different that happened to our ancestors. Agriculture and civilization were a mixed blessing for their inventors, but not for the other species that took full advantage of the opportunities thus provided. Which species were the favorites to outlast us if the Crash *had* proved fatal? Rats and cockroaches. So which species got the greatest benefits out of civilization? Us? Or rats and cockroaches?

"Here, I suspect, neither the rats nor the cockroaches ever stood a chance, because the worms and slugs were always there first: more aggressive, more effective, more adaptable. We saw what they could do when we came down that cliff. We saw how they responded to an unexpected, and perhaps unprecedented, feeding opportunity. How do you suppose they reacted to the humanoids' establishment of *fields*: fields full of lovely, concentrated food?"

"It's anyone's guess," Ike pointed out, dutifully—but he was nodding to show that he understood the force of the argument.

"We know how the city-builders reacted: they built walls. Those walls may well have had more to protect than food alone, but even if the crew scientists are right to wield Occam's razor with such vigor when they talk about sporulation and progressive chimerical renewal, and even if the pyramids aren't reproductive structures at all, the city-builders *still* built walls, and more walls, and even more walls . . . until they realized that they couldn't win. Not, at any rate, with the technology they had. If they'd had fire and iron, who knows? They didn't.

"At the end of the day, their cities—there *must* be more, still buried under purple carpets—were a gift to their competitors they couldn't afford to go on giving. So they stopped. They probably had a Crash of their own, but when they got up and dusted themselves off they went back to the old ways. It could easily have happened to us. Perhaps it did, more than once. Perhaps it happened a hundred times before we finally became handy enough, and keen-sighted enough, and brainy enough, to run all the way to the stars. But we didn't have the killer anemones and their kin to fight. All our chimeras were imaginary, creatures of fantasy. Not here."

Ike was getting into the swim now. For the first time, he took up the argument himself. "Here, chimeras exist," he said, "and they take all the extra opportunities that chimerization provides. At least, the worms and slugs do, because they're the ones best fitted to do it."

"And what makes them best fitted to do it," Matthew said, "is that they're so utterly and completely *stupid*. Swapping biomechanical bits back and forth between organisms is fine and dandy, just so long as the organisms are no smarter than *Voconia*, running their legs and tentacles on separable autonomic systems."

"But the humanoids couldn't do that," Ike said.

"Right. In order to stay smart—and we have to assume that once they became self-consciously smart the humanoids wanted to stay that way—they had to cut right back on the joys of chimerization. That economy—the increasing strategic avoidance of all the kinds of chimerical renewal that might ruin their big and tightly organized brains—wasn't particularly costly in reproductive terms, at first, because they're naturally emortal. When it became costlier, though, as it must have done when they invented agriculture and opened up a whole new wonderland of opportunity to their rivals, they had to backtrack. *That*'s why social and technological progress did a U-turn here. And there, but for the grace of fire and iron . . . will that hold the stage for a little while longer, do you think?"

"You haven't the slightest idea whether it's true," Ike pointed out, dutiful as ever. "But yes, as a *story*, I guess it will run, if only for a little while. Eventually, though, you're going to have to face up to the fact that it's all just talk."

Matthew knew that Ike was right, but when he looked around, all he could see was sheer purple stalks, too slick for anything but a clever worm to climb, and serrated blades that would cut any climber but the most discreet to ribbons. The purple canopy was intriguingly complex, but it was far too dense for its details to be distinguished and defined. Enough light filtered through it to create delicate effects of shade and sparkle, but from the viewpoint of the camera's eye it was mere wallpaper.

The ground on which they walked was by no means unpopulated by motile entities, but the light-starved population seemed to consist mainly of colorless saprophytes; its detail was not without scientific interest, but nor was it telegenic. There were undoubtedly animals around that were far more complex than worms, including reptile-analogues and mammal-analogues—ground-dwellers as well as canopy-climbers—but they were shy. It was well-nigh impossible to capture more of them on camera than their fleeing rear ends.

It would not have made very much difference, though, if the forest had been lavishly equipped with gorgeous flowers and monstrous insects. Everyone on *Hope* had already seen discreetly obtained flying-eye footage of thousands of different kinds of alien plants and hundreds of different kinds of alien animals. What they had not seen, and what Matthew had recklessly promised them, was a humanoid. That was what he had to deliver, in order to create the kind of consensus among the human emigrants that seemed so obviously lacking, and so obviously needed. In the meantime, he had to keep feeding them a story that was interesting enough to hold their interest.

So he and Ike did their double act.

Matthew put out every last thought that he had in reserve, but the day wore on and dusk arrived again, and the perpetual purple twilight faded to black for a second time.

They had covered more than forty kilometers since setting off from *Voconia*, and had not found so much as a mud hut or a broken arrow. Matthew felt mentally and physically exhausted, even though he had been able to rest his injured arm sufficiently to allow his IT to complete its healing work.

"We've done the hard work," Matthew told his companion. "Now we need the luck. We've kept them on tenterhooks long enough. It's time for the denouement. Why aren't they here? They were plenty curious enough when we first arrived—why have they suddenly turned shy? They didn't even take the bait we left outside the bubble when I went to sleep last night. Why not?"

"Maybe they've got something else on their minds," Ike suggested.

Matthew didn't have to ask what that something else might be. They had Dulcie. Although they hadn't left her body where her phone had fallen, they *might* have killed her and taken the body with them—but the likelihood was that she had been carried away alive. While they had her, still alive, they had a far more convenient focus for their curiosity than Matthew and Ike—and she wouldn't die any time soon of hunger, even if she only had alien food to eat. A carbohydrate was a carbohydrate, and sugar was always sweet.

It all came down to Dulcie: Dulcie the anthropologist-turned-murderer-turned-ambassador; Dulcie the tarnished heroine.

"Do you think she's all right?" Ike asked, having divined the reason for Matthew's sudden descent into sobriety.

"Of course she is," Matthew said, valiantly. "She's in her element. This is what she was defrosted for, what she's lived her whole life for. She's fine. She'll come through. She has to. We just have to spin out the story while we're waiting. We have to do a session on feeding frenzies, speculate about the kinds of triggers that might set off orgies of chimerization and humanoid pyramid building. I got halfway through working out an analogy involving the boat, switching between engines as it turned around to go upstream—we can use that. There's also a useful analogy to be drawn between the photosynthesizing pyramids and our bubble-domes. Maybe we can draw a useful analogy between the humanoids and the crewpeople, if we try hard enough. . . ."

"Okay," Ike said. "I get the picture. We go on and on until it's done, no mater how silly it gets."

"It's not silly," Matthew insisted, earnestly. "Even if only a tenth of it is true, that tenth is *marvelous*. We have to help the crew and colonists alike to understand that this business is far bigger than any biotech bonanza or potential death trap. It's a whole new way of life. Maybe it isn't better than sex, but it's weirder. Remember what Dulcie said: sex divides, cooking unites.

"We have to stay here, Ike. We have to stay because it isn't enough to let the aliens go their own way, culturally unpolluted. We have to help them out of their evolutionary blind alley. We have to extend them hospitality, share food, share technologies, share everything. We're all on the same side, Ike, and we all have to realize that. Everybody on *Hope*—and I mean *everybody*, including Konstantin Milyukov—has to realize that destiny has put them here because here's where it's at, so they can be part of it too.

"Even though we're making it all up, it's not silly. It's the most important work there is. However rough the draft might be, we're writing chapter one of the story of the future of humankind, and all the stranger humankinds we've yet to meet."

THIRTY SEVEN

I n spite of his exhaustion, Matthew had trouble sleeping. When
he did drift off, he dreamed.

And then awareness returned, as belated reflex forced
Matthew to let his breath out and suck in another avid draught of
plentiful air, and to stretch his limbs out to their full extent, and
to hear what was being said to him, and to put out his own grop-
ing hand to still the one that was shaking him . . .

He was as sober as he had ever been since awakening from
SusAn.

"What is it?" he demanded, blindly.

"Lights," said Ikram Mohammed. "Lots of them."

Matthew opened his eyes then, and looked out through the
transparent fabric of the bubble-tent.

The curved fabric distorted the points of light, making them
scintillate like stars. For one confused moment, Matthew thought
they might actually be stars, and that the infinite purple canopy
had condescended to undergo one of the rare flamboyant trans-
formations of which it surely had to be capable, drawing itself
apart in order to display the sky.

Then he scrambled out of the tent, following his companion.

It was Ike, not he, who whispered: "Get the camera! For
heaven's sake, *get the camera*!"

Matthew did as he was told. At first, he pointed it at Ike, but
Ike knocked the lens away, angrily. "Are they receiving?" Ike
demanded. "Are they putting this out?"

Matthew didn't know—but when he was finally able to clear
the last vestiges of sleep away and focus his eyes on what Ike was
pointing at, he knew immediately what was needed. He dared not
shout, but he spoke firmly to whoever was on the other end of the
link, instructing the crewman not merely to activate the TV relay
but to sound an alarm that would wake up every single member
of the crew, and every single colonist on the ground.

He realized, belatedly, that he need not have worried about

the crew. He had forgotten that surface-days and ship-days were out of phase. It was midday on *Hope*, not midnight.

Everyone on *Hope* was awake; everyone was watching; everyone was party to the miracle.

All Matthew had to do was point the camera.

The scene at which it was pointing told its own story.

There must have been at least a hundred humanoids: an entire tribe, in all likelihood. They came close enough to make themselves obvious, and then they paused. In fact, they *posed*—not for the camera, of whose nature they knew nothing, but for the sake of their own dignity and pride, and to signify their own sense of triumph. The crowd distributed itself in a huge semicircle, partly to display itself more bravely and partly because its every member wanted to be able to see the weird aliens, their peculiar hut, and their strange machinery.

They were curious. They were probably more than a little afraid, but they were certainly curious.

At least half their number carried spears, but Matthew couldn't be bothered to try to make out what the shafts and tips were made of. Some of them carried ropes, some baskets, some hammers, some artifacts of their own making to which he could not put a name. To all of this, he paid scant attention, because the dozen who drew his gaze and made it captive were the ones who were carrying spherical bowls ablaze with light, supported on squat cylinders. The bowls must have been harvested from the treetops, and the cylinders too. They had been carefully shaped, neatly dovetailed, and ingeniously augmented with wicks and devices to deliver the wicks into the bowls by slow degrees.

The twelve aliens were carrying *lamps*: lamps with reservoirs of oil and burning wicks.

Sex divides, Dulcie Gherardesca had told Lynn Gwyer, with a measure of passion that Matthew had not fully understood at the time. Sex divides, but cooking unites. The foundation of culture was the capacity to delight in the sharing of fire; the beginning of culture—of the meeting of minds and the forging of the elementary social contract—was the Promethean Moment.

Only three of Dulcie's alien apostles were also carrying stolen machetes, but they were holding them up to the light, *showing* them to Matthew and Ike—and also, although they did not know it, to every human being in the system who had responded to Matthew's urgent call.

Through this crowd-within-a-crowd came Dulcie herself, striding confidently to greet her friends. Her surface-suit was no longer brown or purple; it was silver-and-gold.

Her arms were quite relaxed, swinging at her sides, but her hands spoke nevertheless, casually drawing attention to her achievement, her gift, her repentance, her redemption, her *denouement*.

Fire and iron, Matthew thought. There, but for the grace of fire and iron . . .

And he knew, now that he was absolutely sure that he really had awakened from his febrile dream, that the Ark named *Hope* had not merely found its Ararat, but had also sealed its Covenant.

EPILOGUE

W hen Michelle Fleury finally came to stand before her father's tomb in the so-called Palace of Civitas Solis all the carefully repressed bitterness came flooding back. She had heard the explanation for his desertion three times—from the doctor who had supervised her awakening, Frans Leitz; from her stepmother, Dulcie Gherardesca; and from the purple-skinned native with the voice box that formed the human syllables his own natural equipment could not—but she had not yet been able to bring herself to accept it as a valid excuse.

"He couldn't know that he would die without seeing you again," Dr. Leitz had said, while he was fitting her surface-suit. "He expected to live another hundred years. We've only just begun to realize the full extent of the toll that living on an alien world has exacted from us, and it wasn't until the technical support began to arrive that we were able to refine our rejuve technologies. He delayed your awakening for the very best of reasons. He wanted you to wake up to a world that was fit to receive you: to a world that could provide for you as a parent should."

The tomb wasn't quite as elaborate as Michelle had expected. Alien hands had built it: emortal alien hands, which had never built a tomb before. She hadn't expected a pyramid—pyramids had an entirely different significance in the native cultures of Tyre—but she had expected something more like a Victorian mausoleum than a mere kiln. It might have seemed more appropriate if the inscriptions on the faces of the shaped stones hadn't been incomprehensible, but she hadn't yet learned to decipher the written version of the local language.

"Shall I translate?" Dulcie asked. Dulcie had insisted on coming with her, although she'd had the grace to hang back in the deeper shadows for a few minutes while Michelle came to stand beside the tomb.

"No," Michelle said, reaching out a hand so that she could trace a few of the engraved hieroglyphics with her right forefinger. "I know more or less what it says. He always wanted to be a messiah. When it became obvious that he couldn't save his own world, he set out in search of one that might be more open to salvation, and more grateful. This says that he got his wish."

"That's not how they thought of him," Dulcie told her, her voice putting on a show of patient forbearance. "It's not how they thought of me, either. Maybe from our side we looked like the Prometheus team, bringing the light of the gods to the people of the forest, but they have a very different set of myths based in a very different way of life. To them, *everybody* is a teacher, because everybody has to be. The active members of society are the custodians of hundreds of thousands of years of accumulated knowledge and tradition, which they have to pass on to the rejuvenate twins and triplets when they emerge from their own natural version of SusAn. They don't have hero myths, because they don't have outstanding individuals. All their efforts are collective and cooperative. To them, we're very bizarre, and it was partly in recognition of that strangeness that they made Matthew a tomb. They could never quite make sense of the fact that the human population of the city elected him mayor, because they never single out leaders or symbolic figureheads—but they respected his position, and they decided to mark it. I think he'd have been pleased. I *know* he would."

Michelle understood only too well that Dulcie Gherardesca had known her father far better than she ever had. Dulcie had, after all, shared his life for a hundred years, while Michelle had seen precious little of him even during the years they had allegedly spent "together" on Earth. He and Dulcie had made the first contact with the aliens, had made common cause with the aliens, had accompanied the alien contingent that had decided to return to the abandoned city and rebuild it. He and Dulcie had guided the revolution of ideas that had reinvolved *Hope*'s crew in the education of the aliens—including the ones who had decided to remain in the forest—and he and Dulcie had spearheaded the development of the new technological discipline of genomic engineering. Together they had seen the birth or rebirth of a dozen Tyrean cities. . . . all the while leaving *her* to sleep alongside her sister, excluded from everything.

This was the only reunion left to her now: to stand beside her father's tomb, in a monstrous edifice whose inner darkness belied the name that Matthew Fleury had attached, on humanity's behalf, to the city that had become the focal point of the great collaboration: the collaboration that would change humankind as sharply and as irrevocably as it had changed humankind's new partners in evolution.

"We should have been with him," Michelle whispered. "He shouldn't have left us out." Alice was still *left out*, one of the few colonists still in SusAn aboard the microworld. Michelle intended to get her out as soon as she was allowed to take the decision. It was not only right but necessary that they should be together.

She took her hand back, knowing that she had not really touched the surface at all. Her own fingers were overlaid by the surface-suit Leitz had provided, which still seemed alien to her: an interface separating her from a world that was not her own.

"He wasn't leaving you out," Dulcie Gherardesca told her. "He was trying to prepare the way for your return. He missed you, always. He wanted to see you again, desperately—but he wanted to make things right first. You can't imagine how messed up things were when he came out of SusAn. Everything was wrong. The world wasn't as Earthlike as it was supposed to be. It posed all kinds of puzzles and problems. The colony was on the brink of failure for a long time—long after we met the aliens. Matthew was the one who pulled us together when we nearly fell apart, by making everyone understand that we had to make it work, not just for our sake but for the sake of the natives. There was so much we could teach them, and so much they could teach us. Matthew did more than anyone else to unite us in that cause—certainly more than Konstantin Milyukov and Shen Chin Che, who carried their feud to their own graves. He knew before anyone else—although Andrei Lityansky has done his level best to take the credit—that there was an opportunity here for us to develop a new technology of emortality quite different from the one they use on Earth. Some of his guesses were a little wide of the mark, of course, but he was the first person on this world who actually *saw* what was going on here, and what the differences between this world's genomics and Earth's actually *meant*, in terms of the probable history and possible futures of complex life in the galaxy . . . in the universe. He wanted you to benefit from the new technologies, Michelle. He didn't want you to die before you could reap the reward of all his endeavors. He left you and Alice where you were because he *loved* you, more than anything else in the universe. He wanted you with him, but there was something else he wanted even more. He wanted you to have the gifts that this world offers. He wanted you to have a chance to be emortal."

"He could have put himself back into SusAn," Michelle countered. "He could have waited *with us*, to become emortal himself."

"No, he couldn't," Dulcie said, softly.

That was true, of course. Michelle understood that much. Somebody had to do the work. An entire generation of mortals had had to commit itself to the labor of making sure that the generations that came after would be better equipped. To have walked away from that responsibility, even if his companions had sanctioned it, would have been a terrible dereliction of duty. Her father had always understood that messiahs usually had to be martyrs too, and if he hadn't been prepared to accept that he'd never have joined Shen's chosen people.

I could have been a martyr too, Michelle thought. I could have helped do the work that would give future generations opportunities we didn't have, I could have been with him. I could have died with him.

And that, she knew, was precisely the point.

"Come up to the roof," Dulcie said. "His body may be in there, but his legacy is all around us, as far as the eye can see. That's the way to get in touch with him, to understand what he did and why."

Michelle knew that there was no point in asking for more time. The tomb was an alien creation, an alien testament. It had nothing more to say to her. Meekly, she followed Dulcie Gherardesca up a series of stone staircases, cunningly illuminated by arrays of rectangular windows. The steps felt strange beneath the thickened soles of her augmented feet, and there was a curious odor hanging in the air. It could not be the stones themselves, or the mortar sealing them in place, so it had to be something clinging to them: a translucent vegetable veneer. Even the walls of the city had a false skin. The air was cool in spite of the sunlight streaming through the windows, and the filters to which she had not yet become accustomed made it seem thin and curiously unsatisfying.

The roof of the palace carried a massive TV mast studded

with satellite dishes. There was a telescope mounted on the parapet to which Dulcie Gherardesca led her, but the xenanthropologist ignored it; she had brought Michelle here to see the broad panorama of Civitas Solis, not to pick out hidden details upon its horizon.

Michelle had to admit that the city was impressive, even though the walls she had seen on ancient photographs had all been dismantled so that their constituent stones might be put to better uses. The multitudinous domes were the brightest elements because they reflected the light of the ruddy sun, but the walls that soaked up the same light with such avidity provided a magnificently elaborate setting for the hemispherical jewels. And then there were the fields: huge tracts of land glowing purple or green or purple-and-green, hugging the valleys and the lakeside, and following the river downstream as far as the eye could see. With the ingenuity of human biotechnology to protect them, even the alien fields no longer had any need of walls of stone: and their new protective devices would not fail, no matter what pestilential chimerical legions might gather to assault them.

The streets and shops of the city were as busy with human traffic as native crowds. Michelle knew that the population now numbered 40,000, evenly divided between the two races. Higher in the hills she could see three vivid pyramids that testified to the efforts that the natives were making to increase their population further, in frank opposition to the weight of tradition. The humans had done the same, after their own fashion. While she and other children of the *Hope*'s pioneers had languished in the freezer, new individuals had been created in their thousands as soon as full details of the Zaman transformation and the equipment to implement it had arrived—not from Earth, so rumor had it, but from a nearer source: a base established on an uninhabitable but material-rich world by AI miners and manufacturers. How strange to obtain the secret of human emortality from machines!

Michelle looked to her right and left, and then turned around—but when she turned around her eyes were caught by the communications mast and she could not help following its reach into the lilac-tinted sky. That, she thought, was a better symbol of her father's life and nature than the teeming confusion of the city. He had never been a builder, an agent of civilization.

He had been a man who loved to talk, to captivate an audience. He had been a man who would rather invent fantasies than reserve his counsel. She had seen tapes of the broadcasts he had made immediately before the contact, and had listened to Frans Leitz going through his guesses one by one, marveling at the fact that so many of them had turned out to be so nearly right.

"Nobody else had put it all together," the doctor had said. "Nobody else had been able to. And he carried on putting things together, more cleverly than anyone imagined possible."

But the one thing he had neglected to put together was his family. How clever was that?

"Matthew always said that this was a more important world than Earth," Dulcie told her. "He said that the people on Earth, having survived the Crash, would always have to put the safety of the Earth first: to guard it as jealously and as carefully as any cradle. The torch of progress has to be handed on to the other worlds which have accepted humankind: the worlds that have no alternative but to embrace change, and welcome change, and make the most of change. This is the first meeting place, the first melting pot, the first location in which humankind can take its place in the wondrous confusion of all possible modes of life. Earth is alpha, he said, and it has to maintain itself as alpha, preserving its value as a refuge and a reservation—but the future of humankind is an expedition to omega: the ultimate limit of achievement. This is where the omega expedition really begins, he said. This is where we first met alien intelligence, and began our collaboration with alien intelligence. This is where the true horizons of possibility were finally opened up to the imagination."

"I recognize the rhetorical style," Michelle told her. "He practiced hard."

"Yes," Dulcie admitted. "He certainly did. Do you think you'll ever be able to forgive him? He'd have expected you to understand."

That was true too, and Michelle knew it. She turned around again, to look back over the parapet at the city. In the photographs she'd seen of its condition when it was first discovered it had seemed utterly dead, literally enshrouded in imperial purple. Now, it was boldly, relentlessly, stubbornly alive, and astonishingly *clean*. Even though it was pockmarked here and there by building-sites, from which plumes of dust and smoke rose up to stain the crystalline, its lines were sharp and proud and perfectly clear.

Whatever else he had brought here, and whatever else he had left behind, Matthew Fleury had given the city a future, and the energy to hurry into it.

"I'll try," Michelle said—and knew as soon as she said it, by the way that Dulcie Gherardesca smiled, that she might as well have said that she would. For her, a commitment to try was as good as a commitment to do everything possible and to succeed in any merely human task, because she was her father's daughter—and always would be, for as long as she now might live.